UNTIL IT WAS LOVE

PIPPA GRANT

Editing by Jessica Snyder, HEA Author Services
Proofreading by Emily Laughridge & Jodi Duggan
Cover Design by Qamber Designs

This book is dedicated to mustaches everywhere.

If you love them, I apologize. The book demanded this treatment for the 'stache. If you hate them, you're welcome, but again, I can't take credit.

It's all Fletcher and Goldie.

And really, this book is dedicated to them. Thank you for all of the hours of utter joy (and cackles) that you brought me while letting me tell your story. I'll never forget our time together.

1

Goldie Collins, aka a life coach not currently regretting any of her decisions...which is about to change drastically

IS THERE anything more satisfying than watching someone you don't like make a serious mistake with their facial hair?

Yes, yes, I know. In the grand scheme of life, there are probably worse decisions than neglecting to take a razor to your upper lip for ten years.

But Fletcher Huxley's absolutely horrific mustache is giving me the kind of glee that probably can't be balanced with a simple donation to a food bank or volunteer stint at a blood drive.

And considering he showed up to this blood drive with a cameraperson in tow, and that he's recording himself looking like that apparently with the thought that it'll help advance his social media side hustle—yep.

My petty glee meter overfloweth.

"Oooh, Evelyn, look at that," Odette, my seventy-two-year-old

PIPPA GRANT

neighbor and one of my pro bono clients, says. "Goldie's making eyes at one of the rugby players."

"*Ew.*" I wrinkle my nose at the Black woman in the bright pink *Outlive Our Ex-Boyfriends Club* T-shirt. "No. *Never.*"

"Mm-hmm." Her smug grin and dancing brown eyes say she doesn't believe me.

"Which one?" Evelyn replies. She's a sixty-nine-year-old white woman in a matching T-shirt, though both her jeans and her dyed brown hair are the height of stylish. She's also three inches taller than Odette and the VP to Odette's president in their seasoned ladies' club.

"The one that looks like MacGyver," Odette tells her.

Now all three of us are staring at the large tattooed white man sitting in the blood-draw chair. We're at a senior center near the hockey arena, and my companions are tracking how many donors we get today. They want to beat the number that their rival club, *Old Man Bikers*, got last week.

"If I were forty years younger, I'd make a pass at him, but not before I told him to shave," Evelyn says.

I grab a warehouse-size box of single-serving Goldfish cracker packets from beneath the refreshments table along the wall. "The 'stache isn't all that's wrong with him," I mutter to myself.

"I couldn't date him," she continues thoughtfully. "I'd kick the bucket before him, and what fun would that be?"

"None at all," I assure her, louder so that she can hear me. "Even if he kicked the bucket before you, I'm sure it would be awful to date him."

"We could murder the mustache though," Odette says.

Evelyn cackles. "And we could write its obituary."

"*The facial hair of the scowly tattooed giant died an untimely death when runaway kitchen shears—*"

"No, when there was an accident with a weed eater," Evelyn interrupts.

2

"*When a runaway weed eater older than color television picked the wrong time to malfunction,*" Odette intones.

The visual makes me smile.

For the record, there are very few people in this world that I genuinely dislike. Three, to be specific.

My ex-boyfriend.

My former best friend.

And Fletcher Huxley.

Trust me when I say they all earned my dislike.

I rarely spend time dwelling on any of them, but there's Fletcher, *right there*, impossible to ignore with that mustache. The sight of him is making my chest suck in on itself a little at the memory of what he did the last time I saw him.

Which was supposed to be the *last* time in my entire life.

And unfortunately wasn't.

"I'm not sure about the weed eater," Evelyn says. "That might do damage to more than just the 'stache."

"Depends on the skill of the handler."

I'm actively working on calming my rising pulse and enjoying my friends' conversation instead as a young white woman who's finished giving blood approaches our table. I quickly shift my attention to her.

"Hi! Thank you for your donation today. Rock star! How're you feeling? Apple juice and Goldfish?"

She takes both from me, but looks over her shoulder at the four chairs currently occupied by very large men who came in while she was in her own chair. "Who *are* those guys?"

She's a little younger than me with bright blue hair, a nose ring, and clothes that say *work-from-home professional of some kind.*

"Copper Valley Pounders players," I reply.

"Is that college hockey or something?"

"Professional rugby. Relatively new here in the States. The Pounders are one of the original teams in the league though.

Tickets are on sale now for their next season. You should check it out. It's similar to football, but with different rules and no pads." The words taste a little like trash, but I do have good reason to support the team.

Even if I don't have happy thoughts about their newest player, who should still be overseas and *not here*.

"Huh." She takes her snacks and moves the seven steps necessary to reach the *sit here and eat your snack while we make sure you don't pass out* tables under the fluorescent lighting of the cafeteria-like room.

"You meet him yet?" Odette asks me.

"Who?"

"Bad Mustache guy."

Once.

A long, long time ago, when his facial hair wasn't as thick.

Not that that's what I remember most about him.

And I'm sure he doesn't remember much about me either. Or if he does, the memory is stuck somewhere in that awful 'stache.

Which is about where it belongs, considering what he said that day.

"Nope," I tell Odette while I pretend I'm adjusting my bra but am actually rubbing at my chest to try, once again, to calm my heart. The man did serious damage. "Haven't spoken to him at all."

"If you block out the mustache, he's not bad-looking," Evelyn says. "Here. Hold up a finger like this and squint, and you can see his face without the mustache in the way."

"Quit staring," Odette tells her. "He'll think you're interested."

"Or he'll think I have a cute granddaughter. I *did* pass these sexy genes down a couple generations. Oooh, he's looking our way." She winks and wiggles her fingers at him.

He slides his arrogant gaze back to his cameraperson.

And I suppress a shiver.

I've healed from a lot of things in the past six years.

4

What he said is not one of them.

"What if he's a loud chewer?" Odette says. "Or what if he tosses his underwear next to the laundry basket? When *we* date, it's one thing. We're too old to be in it for anything other than a good time. When we help our granddaughters date, we need to have higher standards for them. They don't have to get married, but if they want to, we don't want them with loud chewers who don't pull their weight around the house."

"Hey, cafeteria lady," one of the players yells directly at me, "I feel weak. Bring me some Goldfish. The graham cracker kind. In the blue and pink bag."

That player?

He's the reason the rest of them are here.

And he's here because I threatened to tell all of his teammates about the time he confused his own snot for brain matter when he was sixteen if he didn't help me get half the city here today.

I wouldn't have—I truly wouldn't—but my brother has been a big enough ass himself in the past two years that I know he sometimes thinks I would.

And I'm all in on using whatever means I have at my disposal to help Odette and Evelyn and Sheila, the third member of their little club, beat the Old Man Bikers Club.

Yes, they really call it that. And no, *bikes* isn't code for *motorcycles*.

The club is a bunch of old guys from our neighborhood who get together to ride their bicycles around Copper Valley when the weather's nice enough.

Between Odette, Evelyn, and Sheila, they've dated half the club.

At least, they did before the massive betrayal. Now, they don't date any of the old bikers.

I'll miss these women *so much* when I leave next month.

But we'll stay in touch through text and socials. They've promised to send me all of the obituaries they write with *the real juicy stuff* the next time one of their exes dies. And I've promised to send them real British tea and pictures from everywhere around London.

They might come visit too.

"You have to finish your donation before you get the prize," I call back to Silas.

Two of his teammates snortle. The third—Fletcher with the Bad 'Stache—shoots Silas a dirty look and then says something to the cameraperson capturing his every move.

Probably *start over on a new take since Silas ruined this one.*

Dude has no idea his facial hair is already ruining it for him.

It's thick and growing over his lips and has a part in the middle. The edges are even thicker, and it looks like he tried styling gel to get the 'stache to do…something.

Fletcher Huxley's upper lip is where Wyatt Earp's mustache went to die.

And the petty thought does more to lower my pulse than anything else has since I spotted him twenty minutes ago.

I oblige my baby brother and take him a package of Goldfish and a bottle of apple juice.

Much as I love to razz him, and much as he's completely screwed up my dating life the past two years, I don't want him passing out.

"See?" Silas says to the guy closest to him. "They like it when you ask nicely and give them nicknames."

Porter winces. He's new to the team for the upcoming season, one of the smaller and younger guys, with red hair and a full beard that he, too, claims he's considering trimming so that his mustache is the prominent feature of his face.

"You're an ass, Silas," I tell him.

He grins at me, blue eyes as full of trouble as ever. "I *have* a nice ass."

I grin back. "Oh, donkey farming is your backup plan when this rugby thing doesn't work out?"

His teammates hoot.

Two of them, anyway.

The fourth scowls across the other two at my brother once again.

That, I remember from Silas's update when we had dinner together last weekend.

This old fucker who got cut from the Premiere League in the UK joined on. Fletcher Huckleberry or something. Dude thinks he invented rugby. Walks around like a god. Has this cameraperson following his every move like he's some kind of influencer. His game isn't shit anymore and he's only here because no other English team would take him after Nottingshire released him. He's gonna ruin our game and management is too stupid to see it.

This season should be fun for Silas.

But considering what Silas did the last time I had a date, and the time before that, and the time before that, and—you get the picture. Point is, I'd be lying if I said I wasn't exuberant at the idea of my brother's pending suffering at the hands of Fletcher Huxley too.

When I'm not here to watch.

I love my brother, but our overall relationship can best be described as complicated.

Thanks, Mom and Dad.

"You and your brother are proof positive that gene distribution is fucked up," Odette murmurs to me when I rejoin her at the refreshments table. Evelyn's moved to help Sheila at the check-in desk at the other side of the tent.

"I keep waiting for my mom to admit he actually arrived on a spaceship and is some kind of aliens-on-earth experiment they can't talk about."

She cocks a look at me, then cracks up.

And that's when I make the worst mistake of my life.

I glance over at Fletcher Huxley.

His cameraperson has left him, and apparently so has the nurse who removed the needle in his arm. He's holding two fingers to the white gauze on his elbow, but he drops it to reach behind himself and pull his shirt over his head, leaving him bare-chested there in the seat.

Tattoos on his biceps and shoulders? Check.

Chest hair? Also check.

The straining neck and forearm tendons that guys get when they spend too much time at the gym?

Yep.

It disgusts me that he'll probably be walking around town with a girlfriend from the upper echelons of Copper Valley society within the next two weeks.

But that's not my problem.

And unfortunately, I do have a problem when it comes to Fletcher Huxley in this exact moment.

That problem?

He's gone sheet-white.

His face. His abdomen. His arms.

He's a ghost, and when it comes to blood drives, I know exactly what that means.

"Flag the nurse," I tell Odette while I spring into action. "Any nurse."

"It's always the big buff men, isn't it?" she murmurs while I grab Goldfish and an apple juice and she heads around the table in the opposite direction.

I tuck the snacks into my hoodie pocket. "This'll make six since you all started volunteering here last year."

No idea if she heard me. I'm already halfway across the room to the chair at the end of the row.

Fletcher's rising from the donation chair.

8

His skin is so pale that the dark hairs on the non-tattooed half of his chest look black as night in comparison.

"Fletcher. Sit down," I order.

Lie down is probably better.

Definitely where we're going.

I hear laughter and vaguely realize my brother's flirting with both of the nurses working on this side of the tent.

Causing a distraction.

Getting phone numbers.

My brother annoys the crap out of me.

"Fletcher," I repeat as I reach him. "*Sit down.*"

Bright green eyes land on me. Bright green eyes with dilated pupils. "I'm fine."

I grab his arm. "Don't think so. *Sit.*"

He takes one more step toward me. "Hummingbird," he mutters.

What?

What *what?*

My jaw flaps open, and I half stumble myself.

Hummingbird.

I haven't been called that in years.

Why is Fletcher Huxley saying Hummingbird?

I shake myself and grip his other arm too.

As much as I can, anyway.

Dude has *thick* forearms. "Fletcher. *Sit.*"

His eyes roll back in his head, but the stubborn ass of a man takes one more step toward me.

Like he thinks he can walk this off.

Or like he thinks I'm going to catch him.

All two hundred and thirty or so pounds of him.

"Fletcher—" I shove into his chest, hoping to force him back into the chair, but it's too late.

Because Fletcher and his grotesque mustache and all of the

9

weight in his over-muscled arms, neck, and thighs, are collapsing on top of me.

He smells like a summer sunrise hike in a pine forest.

That's what goes through my head as we both crash to the floor, me twisting to avoid landing on my bad hip, him completely unconscious, the mustache from hell inches from my face.

I grunt under the bulk of him squishing my lungs while the nurses come running.

And his tall, skinny, emo camera guy appears overhead, snapping away. "Oh, this is good. Can you smile a little? Maybe slap his cheek while you're smiling? This will blow up his socials. He'll love it."

It's official.

Even when he's passed out cold after giving blood, I still actively dislike Fletcher Huxley.

2

Fletcher Huxley, aka a guy who doesn't need to catch a break, because he's making his own fate, dammit

GOLDIE COLLINS IS A BADASS.

Good thing. I need a badass.

"She has more followers than I do," I mutter to my dog. The two of us are in the driver's seat of my Range Rover, stalking Goldie's Instagram page for any last tidbits of information about her before we get out and accidentally run into her as she's finishing up the soccer practice she's coaching this morning.

I flip over to the tab where people have tagged her in posts.

Unlike *my* Instagram page, she doesn't have a hundred tags with the four pictures random people took of me passing out on her at the blood drive the other day.

Plus the photos we're pretending my own photographer didn't take.

They're all bloody awful. I'm sprawled across her midsection, shirtless, my mouth hanging open, my eyes half open too like I'm dead, in almost every last one of them.

Goldie, though?

In one photo, she's gaping down at me, her dark hair splayed across the tile floor, one arm trapped. In another, she's squeezing her eyes shut while she tries to shove my shoulder. The third, she's grim-faced as she makes a *this wasn't how I saw this going down when I came over to help him* face at a nurse who's showed up. And in the last, she's smiling at an older Black lady while sitting on the floor beside me as a nurse touches my face.

Probably tapping it and trying to wake me up.

Would've been more effective if she'd slapped me though.

Fucking needles.

Fucking blood draws.

But the publicity from me passing out is selling tickets and getting attention for the team.

Worth it.

As for Goldie—her Instagram page has satisfied clients tagging her in pictures of them graduating college or opening their dream bakery or lifting weights or posing with her while she signs one of her books for them.

The picture of Goldie cheering on the lady lifting weights is hella impressive.

The older woman must be three hundred if she's a day, with arms about the width of a pencil, and she's curling thirty pounds.

I can curl a little more, but my arms are also thicker than a pencil. Plus, I'm not even a half-century old yet, much less three.

Sweet Pea licks my phone screen.

I stroke her short dark fur with my thumb, the rest of my hand tucked around her tiny body. "Knock it off, you little beast. That's not breakfast."

She grins up at me, pink tongue lolling out, big black eyes shining happily. She's five pounds of fearless in a short-legged, long-bodied, overactive waggy-tailed miniature dachshund body. If she could speak, she'd be like that tree guy in those Marvel movies, except instead of saying her name, she'd yelp *everybody loves me* all day long.

As they should.

While I tell people I got her because I knew it would look good on my socials, the little creature owns my cold, black heart, and we both know it.

"Time to do this," I tell her.

The pipsqueaks have been out on the soccer field for half an hour now. Not likely they'll go much longer.

Not at their heights and not in this weather.

It's not cold. For winter, I mean. My research says the team should've been playing inside the big dome next to the fields, but they apparently took advantage of the unseasonably warm January temperatures instead.

Unseasonably warm January is still cold though.

Especially for my dog.

I strap Sweet Pea on her pink leash, but I carry her until I'm off the gravel parking lot and on the grass surrounding the soccer fields. Thought about putting her in the baby sling I sometimes use with her, but that's overkill.

For today.

If Goldie says no today, I'll try again in a few days with Sweet Pea in the sling.

No one can resist a big burly dude with a tiny dog in a pink sling.

On the chance Goldie is the persuadable type, I pause to snap a few selfies of Sweet Pea and me with Goldie in the background. Can't see any of the kids' faces. Not clearly, anyway.

Perfect.

The grass is wet with dew, so I end up carrying Sweet Pea

anyway. Make it about three feet toward Goldie's field before a woman stops me with an *awwww, your dog is so cute!*

She's pushing a kid covered with a blanket in a stroller, clearly here for soccer practice for another kid not much older, but there's no ring.

Damn right I flex the pecs and biceps as she's petting Sweet Pea. And yeah, damn right I'm not wearing a coat.

If I'm recognized and more people take pictures, I need to look good. Not that it's likely, but there's always a possibility.

The fate of the American Rugby League could depend on my pictures.

Also, I'm Fletcher bloody Huxley.

I don't get cold.

"Are one of these rugrats yours?" the woman petting Sweet Pea asks me with a friendly smile.

"Here for a friend," I reply.

"Nice morning for it."

I make a noncommittal noise.

"Need to enjoy it while it lasts, considering the snow in the forecast," she adds.

"Yep."

Her kid fusses in the stroller, so she flaps her hands in its direction and gets out of my way.

My marketing coach would be banging his head against a wall. *Be nice, Huxley. Say something flirty but not too flirty, show off the Pounders shirt, and tell her she should get tickets to a match.*

I look back at the woman opening one of those compartmentalized containers with cut-up grapes and little cheese cubes and browning banana pieces to hand to her kid, and I grimace.

Pretty sure she's not the rugby type.

I reach Goldie's field before her practice is over and stay far enough back that I could be a simple guy trying to convince his dog to take a piss while the dog prances in the cold wet grass and telegraphs *pick me up, you wanker, it's cold down here.*

But I'm not so far away from practice that I can't observe the whole thing.

Goldie's in tight black leggings and an oversize gray sweatshirt with *Reynolds Park Soccer Club* stamped in large letters on it. Her pink baseball cap has a logo I can't read from this distance, and her eyes are hidden behind her own sunglasses.

No telling if she's seen me or not.

Recognized me or not.

Cares or not.

But the bigger question I have at the moment?

Why is someone with jet-black hair named *Goldie*?

"Great job, Campbell," she says to a little boy with red hair who's maybe eight inches taller than the ball. Or possibly a little taller. They're so *small*. "Kick it again! Oh, Sienna, look at you go! You got it all the way to the cones! And Hallie! High five, girl! You've been practicing at home, haven't you?"

These kids suck at soccer. They're probably still ten years away from understanding what *offsides* means, and when they trip over the ball, they roll on top of it about like Sweet Pea would if she could jump as high as a soccer ball.

It might be cute.

If you're into little kids.

And if you have the misfortune to like soccer more than you like rugby.

Not that it's the kids' faults their parents have poor taste in sports.

At the end of practice, the kids maul Goldie in a group hug while she tells them they're all the best little soccer players in training she's ever seen.

And not for the first time since leaving the only country I've called home as an adult to return to the States, I get an unwelcome knot between my shoulder blades while my own previous coach's face flashes in my brain.

They can both go to hell.

The knot and the memory.

And Coach.

All three.

The parents swarm Goldie next. She takes the longest time with a blonde who's weirdly familiar in a way that I can't place. Her kid—one of the little girls—demands to be picked up, which the blonde obliges.

And then the kid lunges for Goldie, who catches her as if they do this all the time and peppers kisses all over the little girl's face.

"More, Aunt Goldie!" the kid shrieks.

Aunt Goldie.

Fuck me.

That's why the blonde is familiar. She was in the parking lot at the arena.

Because she and Silas Collins have a kid? That would explain *Aunt Goldie.*

Exactly what the world needs.

Finally, the next round of soccer practice people start arriving, and Goldie's players' parents take the hint and leave. I approach while she's shoving soccer balls into a giant black mesh bag.

"Nice job," I say.

She glances up at me, eyes still hidden behind the sunglasses, but the rest of her face says *dammit, he didn't leave.* She doesn't reply until she's head down over the balls again.

"Good morning, Fletcher. What brings you to the soccer fields this morning?"

"I don't pass out on women without making it up to them by taking them out to dinner."

Her head lifts again.

I don't smile, but I don't scowl either. Apparently my marketing and PR guru is doing *something* good for me.

"That was remarkably straightforward," she finally says.

"I don't like bushes enough to beat around them."

"So ironic, considering your face," she mutters.

I blink. "What the fuck's wrong with my face?"

She heaves one of those sighs that transports me back to high school, answering another easy question wrong. Not because I couldn't get it right, but because I didn't care.

School wasn't my future.

Rugby was.

End of story, no matter how my old man felt about that.

She pulls her sunglasses off and sets them on the brim of her hat so she can look me dead in the eye. "I had to assure at least three parents that there wasn't *retro adult entertainment* being filmed here later after they spotted you and the thing growing under your nose."

Sweet Pea barks in glee.

Or possibly agreement.

I eye my dog.

She grins back at me.

Goldie doesn't fawn over her. Instead, she turns her back to me, bends over, and starts stacking cones.

While putting that curvy ass on display.

Speaking of adult entertainment…

I clear my throat and order my dick to not look at her ass. "I didn't get a chance to say thank you for your assistance the other day. Can I please take you to dinner?"

"Not necessary, but thank you."

I stroke my mustache. "Lunch?"

"No, thank you."

"Breakfast, then. Coffee. Pastries. An omelet."

"While I appreciate your very kind offer, it's truly unnecessary.

17

I let people—even people with mustaches like that—pass out on me all the time."

"You do?"

She straightens, cones tucked under her arm. "No, actually, you're the first. Usually when big burly dudes pass out at the blood drives, someone's able to convince them to get on the ground themselves before the unconscious part happens. Or they sit in the chair and do it. But rest assured, the next time I volunteer at a blood drive and another overdeveloped dude with a needle allergy needs a little propping up, I'll be there for him too if necessary."

"It's the mustache then." Ouch.

I like my mustache.

It's a statement piece. And I'd keep it even if mustaches weren't having a moment.

You could say I started the mustache trend, considering how long I've been wearing one. And I *was* famous in Europe. Me being a trendsetter is a logical leap.

"Lovely to see you, Fletcher. Good luck this season." She swings the bag of balls up over her shoulder and starts around me.

"It would be a great PR piece for the team if a community leader like you agreed to go on a thank-you date with me for saving my life."

Her golden-brown eyes swing toward me, but she doesn't say a word.

Not out loud.

Her eyes are saying plenty.

Most of it boils down to *you truly are a jackass, aren't you?*

"Coach Goldie?" a guy calls behind us. "This guy bothering you?"

We both turn and look at the tall, dark-haired, lanky white guy who also looks weirdly familiar. He has a dark-haired little rugrat hanging onto his long leg, and there's a curvy woman with a double stroller not far behind him.

18

"Yes, but I'm fine," Goldie says. "Thanks, Coach Beck."

"You sure?"

"He's one of my brother's teammates."

The guy's eyebrows silently ask Goldie if that's actually an answer.

"I'm harmless." I hold up Sweet Pea. "See? Cute dog. I'm a good guy."

I am not a good guy.

But I'm not *that* kind of a bad guy.

"He's asking my opinion on what he should do with his mustache," Goldie says. "And he didn't like it when I said he can't grow another dog on his upper lip."

Coach Beck snickers.

So do two women approaching with their kids.

"Can you say that again on camera?" I ask her. "That'll be gold on my socials."

"Absolutely not. That was incredibly unkind of me, and I shouldn't have said it."

"It was bloody funny."

Her face scrunches up like she's wondering what the hell's wrong with me.

And then she shakes her head. "Have a good practice, Coach Beck," she calls.

He nods to her, apparently deciding she has me well in hand. "You here through the end of the season?"

"Yep."

"Sarah and I have to have you over for dinner before you leave. The girls are gonna miss you."

"I'd love that. Thank you." She waves, bends over to wiggle her fingers specifically at the tiny human clinging to the man's leg, then heads back toward the parking lot.

I tag along. "Old boyfriend?"

"Former underwear model, actually. I taught him to coach three-year-olds last spring. Lovely wife. Cute kids."

I can't tell if she's serious. "Where are you going at the end of the season?"

"New job."

"When's rugrats-with-soccer-balls season over?"

"That's not actually any of your business."

"You don't like me at all, do you?"

She glances at me, still marching toward the parking lot. "Why did you say *hummingbird* right before you passed out on me?"

"What?"

"Right before you passed out at the blood drive, you looked at me and said *hummingbird*. Why?"

"I didn't say a thing."

"You did. You said *hummingbird*. Do you honestly not know why you said that? Because I have half a clue why you'd say it."

Last time my ears went this hot, I was staring down my old coach while my heart hammered in time to the speed at which my career was spiraling out of my control.

"Is that your astrology sign or something?"

Sweet Pea snorts.

My dog.

My dog *snorts* at me.

She, too, knows that I know exactly what *hummingbird* means.

"It was my nickname." Goldie's speaking slowly, enunciating every word. "In college. When I played soccer. When I broke my hip."

Confession: I've known Goldie Collins was a badass for a long time.

I've followed her on socials for several years, one of her hundreds of thousands of followers who tune in to watch her videos and feel like she's speaking straight to my soul when she says *today might be hard, but so was yesterday, and you did it. You can do it again today. I believe in you, and I want you to believe in yourself.*

I own both of her books on *being a better you*. Even read one of them.

I know her nickname on the soccer field was *Hummingbird*. I've known it for years, and I'd prefer she didn't know I know it.

What I didn't know that makes me even more uncomfortable though?

What I didn't know until three days ago, when I dropped at that dumb *team building* event that I went to for the publicity, was that Goldie Collins and Silas Collins have the same parents.

I swallow and pretend I'm not a Goldie Collins fanboy. "You played soccer in college?"

She rolls her eyes. "Yes, Fletcher. I played soccer for UCLA. Went to the college showcase in London my senior year and didn't play because I had a broken hip. So I was in the VIP box. *With you.*"

I'm in a T-shirt in fifty-degree weather and I'm sweating.

I remember that VIP box. I will *always* remember that VIP box. "I'm a big deal in London. Spent a lot of time in VIP boxes. You'll have to be more specific."

"It was the one where you told your buddy *Collins is such a whiny-ass baby*. Does *that* ring a bell?"

My entire body jolts like I've been tackled by a fullback made of lightning, and I squeeze Sweet Pea hard enough that she yelps.

I loosen my grip on my dog, shaking my head. "No."

"Shocking."

"I didn't say that."

"You don't remember saying it because you didn't care that you said it. I will forever remember that you said it because it was rude, unnecessary, and frankly, pretty fucking demoralizing. I was twenty-one years old and coming to terms with the fact that the life I'd planned for myself on the soccer field was over."

I shake my head again but she holds eye contact and keeps talking. "You, on the other hand, were a professional athlete at the top of his game with two championships to your name. You weren't some rando ignorant rich guy who'd bought his way into that suite. You were someone who could have—who *should have* understood how devastating a career-ending injury is. So thank you for offering to take me on a date that would benefit you far more than it would benefit me. I'm always grateful when my nemeses straight-up tell me they haven't changed."

This time, when she walks away, I don't follow. I stand there, my shoes getting soaked with the morning dew, my dog glaring at me as if I'm not the man she thought I was.

"I wouldn't have said that about you," I call after Goldie as soon as I'm able to find my voice again.

She doesn't answer.

She doesn't have to.

The fact that she's calmly shutting the hatch on her silver Audi SUV without so much as looking in my direction says it all.

Goldie Collins has said all she intends to ever say to me for the rest of her life, and I am a complete and total wanker.

3

Goldie

I SHOULDN'T STILL BE FUMING over Fletcher Huxley when I arrive at Give Two Sips Sunday night, but I *cannot* scrub the man out of my head.

It was so bad this afternoon that I blanked out on a client and had to ask her to repeat her last three sentences during a coaching call. It was so bad that I realized I forgot to drink my coffee when I found it sitting on my counter six hours after I brewed it. It was so bad that I didn't hear a word of the audiobook I listened to on my walk from my apartment to dinner.

I cannot get the man out of my mind.

"Moving or men?" Odette says to me as I scoot onto the red velvet curved booth seat beside Sheila. About once a week, the ladies invite me to join them here as an honorary member of their club. It's always at Give Two Sips, their favorite wine bar, which is a couple blocks down from the apartment building where we all live.

We're having dinner far more often the closer my move gets.

I think about lying—moving *is* stressful—but they'd see right through me. "Fletcher Huxley asked me to go on a date with him basically as a PR stunt to get attention on the Pounders. I'm fine. I'm leaving the country. But he's stuck in my brain. *Why?* I don't have to see him again ever, at all, for any reason, and he's still there."

Not because I'd consider indulging him in that date.

Because he hurt me. He was an athlete I'd watched and admired, and he said a shitty thing about my decision to leave sports that hadn't truly been my decision at all, but a decision life forced on me.

Odette passes me a wine glass full to the brim.

Rosé spritzer.

These women love me.

And now I'm getting teary-eyed.

I leave Copper Valley for London in three weeks and six days with no idea when or if I'll be back. But a life-coach-on-staff residency with the Worldwide Coaching Association in London will be amazing, and I'm as excited to go as I am sad to leave the people I love.

I'm also eager to prove all the doubters wrong.

She's too young. She's too inexperienced. She must have a good consultant telling her what to say.

You're never too young to support other people.

And since my soccer career ended, I've found so much joy, validation, and purpose in coaching. I'm incredibly honored on top of all of my excitement, and I've been studying and expanding my coaching offerings for the past two years to get ready for this.

"Did he shave the mustache?" Odette asks.

"No. It's as massive as ever. I think he might've had extensions added."

Evelyn *tsks*. "Honey, that'll do it. If a mustache like that asked me out, I'd have to take to my bed for days no matter how hot the rest of him was. And I say that as a woman who's had a massive crush on Burt Reynolds for as long as I can remember."

I almost choke on my spritzer.

"What's wrong with his mustache?" Sheila asks, completely seriously, as if she didn't check him in at the blood drive. At sixty-five, she's the youngest of their trio. Her white hair is almost long enough to lay flat again after a round of chemo for breast cancer last fall, and she's stronger every time I see her now that she's also finished radiation.

"It's the pinnacle of examples of why very few men should ever attempt a mustache," Odette replies.

Evelyn hums in agreement.

"And he's the pinnacle of examples of why men shouldn't exist at all," I mutter.

Which I don't mean.

Mostly.

Odette sips her chardonnay and studies me like she knows exactly where my brain is, and probably also like she knows I don't want to talk about it.

Evelyn starts to ask me to explain, but Odette taps her glass twice on the table. "Ignore him. Problem solved. And, unfortunately, we need to move on to business. I have an announcement. Steve died."

I take a swig of my spritzer to keep the automatic *I'm so sorry* from slipping out of my mouth.

Even after two years of learning better with this group—they prefer facing death with irreverent humor—I still sometimes almost slip.

"Funeral home Steve?" Sheila asks.

"Mailman Steve?" Evelyn says at the same time.

"Drugstore Steve," Odette replies. "Heart attack in the condom aisle. Do *not* question me, Evelyn. That *is* what happened, and if you don't believe me, you can walk your little tush down there yourself and ask the pharmacist."

"Oh, that's a terrible way to go," Sheila says. While I love all three of these women, Sheila is easily the kindest-hearted. She's the one who'd leap in front of a bus to save a baby. The one who'd canvas a neighborhood looking for a missing cat. The one who'd kindly chide strangers on the internet who leave trollish comments on basically any post that's ever existed on the internet.

"We're going to need to see the security cameras," Evelyn says dryly.

Odette smirks.

I know that smirk.

She has the security camera footage.

"Was he shopping for the condoms?" Evelyn asks. "Or restocking them?"

Odette shakes her head over her chardonnay. "He was showing a customer where they were located."

Sheila gasps. "Imagine being that customer and thinking your sex life caused a man to die. They should get flowers too."

Evelyn pats her hand. "I'm sure the pharmacy gave them a few good coupons for their trauma." She looks back at Odette. "Was it someone he knew?"

Odette shakes her head. "No, and they didn't even ask any strange questions. At least, not according to my sources."

"Was he dating anyone?" Sheila asks. "Do we need to send her flowers?"

"Recently remarried," Odette reports. "Sometime in the last year or so."

"*No*," Evelyn says. "Didn't you call him *Gets Around Steve* when you broke up with him?"

"Apparently he found some vag worthy of the shackles."

"The poor woman." Sheila plops her obituary notebook on the table. The cover is a soft blue fur, and it comes with a dangling pen in the same color with a blue powder puff on top. "I hope she married him for his money. I can't imagine heartbreak is any easier in your later years."

"Well, she certainly didn't marry him for the D," Odette murmurs.

Evelyn produces her obituary notebook too. It's a soft leather journal with a leather cord wrapping it shut and thick, torn-edge linen paper inside. If I weren't selling or giving away everything I own before embarking on the next phase of my life as a life coach in residence in London for three months followed by at least two years of life as a digital nomad touring the States, I'd have severe journal envy.

Especially when she pulls out the fountain pen that she uses with it. "What are the odds he was cheating on her?" she asks Odette.

Odette sighs. "Let's focus on the pre-final-wedding time of Steve's life, shall we?"

"When did you and Steve date?" I ask Odette while she, too, digs into her bag for her obituary notebook.

"About three years ago," she tells me as she pulls out the familiar hardback featuring a cat riding a unicorn with rainbows coming out of both of their eyeballs. "I went into the drugstore—the one by the park about four blocks over with the questionable window displays. I was looking for hand cream, and I left with his phone number."

"He was in the Old Man Bikers Club," Sheila tells me.

"He's the reason we *hate* the Old Man Bikers Club," Evelyn corrects.

"And he passed on before he could see that we won the blood drive donor bet," Odette muses.

"You think they'll pay up?" Evelyn asks.

Sheila squints at her. "Why wouldn't they?"

"Because they're dicks," Odette replies.

"But fair is fair," Sheila insists.

Evelyn pats her hand. "Never change, my friend. Odette, you and I will handle collecting our winnings."

Odette nods. "After dinner. Five minutes ladies, and…go."

All three of them go head-down over their notebooks, their pens scratching, while I lean back in the plush booth with my spritzer, pop an earbud in, and attempt to relisten to the chapter I missed while my brain was wandering on my walk here.

I love this place. It's two stories high with walls of windows, so even though we're in the heart of a major city, there's a good bit of light. Every table has leafy green plants. More vines and leafy plants hang between the copper light fixtures dangling from the beam ceilings. We don't always get one of the plush velvet corner booths, but we're in here regularly enough that the staff will sometimes save one for us.

Everything in our part of Copper Valley was once warehouses and factories that eventually closed down as the city changed from a manufacturing hub to the environmental engineering heart of the East Coast, but now, it's a neighborhood with wine bars and the cutest bookstore and a cookie shop that I will miss almost as much as I'll miss my friends.

Especially these friends.

We met when Odette hired me to be her life coach after one of her best friends passed away. She'd decided she wanted to live the rest of her years to the fullest instead of waiting around for her turn to be next. We'd been working together for maybe eight or nine months when she and her friends adopted me as one of their own after I went through a bad breakup.

And now I get to hang with them regularly and watch them create alternate obituaries for ex-boyfriends, and sometimes close friends, as their own way of mourning. Or they'll invite me along when they volunteer at blood drives and other neighborhood events. Sometimes I call bingo numbers at the community center in the basement of our apartment building, and sometimes they come and cheer on my niece for dance recitals and soccer practices.

Not that Hallie's old enough to be exceptional at either yet, but she's old enough to be freaking adorable when she tries.

And I'm getting teary-eyed again at leaving them to pursue my dreams and amazing opportunities, so I sip my spritzer, kill my audiobook, and slip over to the bar to order apps to share instead of waiting for our server to circle back to us.

I was supposed to be touring the world playing soccer. Doing in my own sport what my brother does in his. But when a freak injury on the field left me with a broken hip and broken dreams, I had to piece together a new life.

And now?

Now I don't miss what I don't have and I don't regret the direction my life took. I love what I do. I love my job. I love my clients. I love speaking engagements and giving seminars on finding your passion. I love that I get paid to write books about my philosophies and experiences. I love teaching classes online and in person to help people find the courage to explore new opportunities in their careers, their love lives, and their *life* in that time when they're not working or caring for everyone else. I love using social media to spread messages of belief in ourselves and trust in the world that when one opportunity slips away into the wind, another will appear.

I'm so excited to go to London. Excited for who I'll meet and what I'll learn and what I'll give back. And it's okay that I'm sad at what I'm leaving behind at the same time.

I get to be both. And in the meantime, I'm seizing every opportunity I can find here too.

Going to one last wedding with Odette as my plus-one. Taking Hallie on a pre-birthday date, since I'll miss the actual day. Seeing friends for lunches and dinners. There's still a cooking class I want to take. I want to see the Thrusters, our local professional hockey team, play one more time, and I want to have a cheesy eighties movie night with my friends and apartment neighbors one last time too.

That's what I'm thinking as I finish ordering apps at the bar to be delivered to our table and turn back to my friends.

What's supposed to happen now is that I'll go back to the table where Odette, Sheila, and Evelyn will each read the obituaries they've written for Drugstore Steve based on their knowledge of his life. Specifically, the juicier parts or the weirder parts or sometimes the *very* personal parts. We'll laugh. We'll gasp. One of them might actually shed a tear, because a man *did* die.

And then they'll vote on which obituary will get posted on their *Mission: Outlive Our Ex-Boyfriends* group blog.

That's what's supposed to happen.

What actually happens is that I turn around and discover that someone is sitting in my seat at the table with my friends.

Not only have they been interrupted in their timed five minutes to write the best obituary for Drugstore Steve that they can possibly write, but they've been interrupted by someone who's at least half a foot taller than me, at least eighty pounds heavier, who possibly can't put his arms all the way down to his sides because he's overdone the weight lifting and has oversized biceps and triceps, who has messy dark brown hair, and who, I suspect, is still sporting a mustache that could be a stunt double for Stuart Little.

Worse, though?

As if this *can* get worse?

Worse is that Sheila's face is telegraphing *I have seen a cute dog and I want to pet it soooooo badly*.

He brought his dog.

And as I approach the table, I realize he not only brought the dog, but he's *carrying it in a baby sling*.

A pink baby sling.

And Evelyn—cynical, thrice-divorced but man-loving Evelyn—appears to be struggling hard to resist the allure of big man with tiny dog in a sling too.

Only Odette is still straight-faced.

Probably because I sometimes tell clients personal stories when I'm coaching them if they're veering down the *you can't possibly understand how hard it is to start over in my circumstances* path. And Odette has a memory and attention to detail and a way of putting puzzle pieces together that would've been useful to the CIA if she hadn't loved teaching so much.

I wonder if she's pieced together that my issue with Fletcher Huxley is more than just his mustache.

"Goldie, look at this," Sheila gushes as I reach the table. "This man who tried to suffocate you while he was unconscious at the blood drive came by to apologize to *us* for worrying us over you."

Fletcher looks up at me, all sincere-faced choir boy *I am here doing good deeds*, and smiles sheepishly.

Fletcher Huxley.

Former rugby god of England. Jaw chiseled by an Italian sculptor. Hooded green eyes straight out of a Brontë novel. A thick neck that's the envy of social media gym rat influencers everywhere. The pornstache. And the ego that would put the entire Copper Valley Thrusters championship-winning hockey team *and* the Copper Valley Fireballs championship-winning baseball team, combined, to shame.

And he's smiling *sheepishly*.

"Goldie," he says with a nod while he scratches his dog's head. "Always nice to see you."

Sheila squeals like he's asked me to marry him and I've fallen all over him sobbing in joy.

Ew.

"I'd say the same, but I can't see you past the pornstache," I

31

reply, matching his sheepish smile with an overdone *haha, I'm so funny* smile.

Like I'm joking.

But I'm not.

I got over rugby players the day my brother became one, and I've never once regretted that life choice. Not to lump them all together, but in this case, yes, I'm lumping them all together.

"*Goldie,*" Sheila hisses.

Evelyn makes a strangled noise.

Odette hums softly, which you only notice if you know Odette well enough to listen for it. It's her *please pass the popcorn* hum.

Fletcher unfolds his body from my seat with the grace of a cat stretching after an afternoon nap in the sun. "Don't need to interrupt you ladies any longer," he says. "Noticed you were here on my way past and didn't want to miss the opportunity to apologize for scaring you all the other day. You ever want tickets to a match, I'll hook you up."

He slides a card onto the table, nods to me once more, passes by *entirely* too closely—close enough that I can smell something subtly woodsy and tobacco-ish along with something that smells like dog shampoo, close enough that I can feel heat radiating off of him, close enough that I can see the thick veins in his forearms—and then walks away.

Just walks away.

Doesn't repeat his request for me to be a publicity stunt.

Doesn't tell me that my memory is wrong about our last interaction. Or that he does or doesn't care about that.

Simply walks away.

Everyone around us watches his ass as he goes.

And I don't think it's because he's in sweatpants, or because said sweatpants have POUNDERS written across the ass.

I think they're watching him and his ass because even though he'll never be known here in America the way Silas tells me he was known in the UK—rugby isn't that popular here—his presence says *you should know me.*

"I don't trust him," Odette says as I slide back into the booth, which is still warm where his ass was.

I sip my spritzer and pretend I can't tell warm from cold on my butt. "Lucky all of us, we'll never have to see him again. Did you all get your obituaries written?"

Evelyn and Sheila share a look, then both look at me.

Evelyn slides Fletcher's card off the table and into her purse.

The rest of us stare at her.

"Oh, let an old lady get a thrill at telling the world a big hot rugby player personally invited her to a match. I'm demanding a backstage pass too. Or whatever it is in the sports world. I don't have to like his mustache to take advantage of this situation."

Even I smile at that. "I'm related to one of the other players. I can get you into the locker room before a match. Probably into the announcer booth too. Without you having to call the devil."

"The devil?" Sheila asks. "Why would you call him the devil?"

I drain the rest of my spritzer. "Obituary time! Let's have them, ladies. I can't wait to learn more about Drugstore Steve."

4

Fletcher

I'M SQUEEZING peaches in Crunchy, the organic supermarket down the street from my flat—my *condo*, I mean—when a tingling sensation tells me I'm being watched.

I keep squeezing peaches while I do a slow perusal of the produce section without being obvious about doing the slow perusal. It's a trick you learn when you're on display often enough.

I don't catch anyone watching me, but I see something that catches *my* eye.

A tall-ish white woman with a great rack, long legs, and black-brown hair tied back in a ponytail under a pink baseball cap leaving the produce section to head deeper into the store.

Hello, Goldie Collins.

And thank you, rugby gods.

And also my good hearing and Silas Collins's big mouth.

My sister's moving to London so she's cooking me dinner tonight because it's an asshole move for her to leave and say she's never coming back to watch me play ever again.

I was walking Sweet Pea when I saw Goldie leave a residential building about four blocks from my flat—my *condo*—the other day.

So I followed her to the wine bar.

I was basically going the same direction anyway.

Don't ever let it be said that I can't read a room. After I made my move to impress her friends—and mostly failed—and then she hit me with that over-happy smile, I knew I was fucked with her.

I can find other ways to get attention on the team and the league and fulfill that promise I made to myself after Rafferty cut me from the club in Nottingshire.

But having the good fortune of guessing when she'd be in the grocery store in the neighborhood we apparently share, getting last-minute things to make poor Siley-wiley his din-din?

This is a sign.

I randomly toss three peaches in a bag and follow her.

Not too surprised to find her frowning over chicken breasts.

When you cook for a pro athlete, you frown over chicken breasts a lot.

"I suggest the strips instead of the whole breast," I say as I stop next to her.

She doesn't seem startled, but she does slide an eyeball my way under her ballcap.

"Makes it finger food so he doesn't have to figure out how to use a knife," I clarify.

She grabs the package of whole breasts and puts it in the cloth basket hanging off her arm.

I grab a random package of raw chicken strips and follow her as she heads toward the dairy section.

"I don't remember saying—saying what I'm sure you remember correctly that I said. It does sound like something I'd say." I'm speaking low and quick. This is my only chance. Could've said it on Sunday, but I didn't want an audience. Not when that meant four people wouldn't believe me instead of one.

"I watch a lot of sports. Don't catch a lot of names, and I watch a lot on mute. But I remember your nickname. The Hummingbird. Number nineteen. UCLA. Broken hip ended your career and hurt all of women's soccer for you not being in it anymore. It made the news. I remember. Number thirty-four from your team plays for WNSL now. The Scorned. Here in Copper Valley. No idea what her name is. She didn't have a cool nickname."

Goldie slides me another unreadable look, but she hasn't told me to fuck all the way off yet, so I keep talking. "I was talking about a different Collins in the VIP box. Had to be. Probably your brother, actually. I met him that summer. Camp for spoiled rich American kids to buy one-on-one time with real players. He *was* a whiny-ass baby there. They all were, but he was the worst. It's why I remember him. That was the same summer you were supposed to play in the showcase. I looked it up. Also, he's still a whiny-ass baby. You should hear him in the training room."

For someone whose social media presence is all *you can do it!*, she has a seriously strong straight face.

"And I'm sorry," I add.

It's an afterthought.

I know it.

She knows it.

She stops in front of the first dairy case and studies the cottage cheese and sour cream. "Thank you."

"You're still a badass," I tell her.

"I know."

That actually makes me smile. "And your brother is...not...that bad."

She turns to face me at that. "My brother is absolutely that bad."

I open my mouth.

36

She holds up a finger. "And he's still my brother and you can shut up now."

I stand still next to her while she grabs a carton of cottage cheese. Don't eat the stuff myself. Don't eat a lot of dairy, actually.

Miss clotted cream though. Which I will *not* be confessing out loud here.

Reputation to uphold and all that.

I trail along while she moves to the yogurt section two cases down. "You know, the team succeeding would help...all...of the players," I say slowly.

I get an eye roll of *this again?*

"And if you're doing this move across the pond right, cooking will get harder and harder the closer you get to leaving," I add. "Who wants to buy another full carton of salt for two last meals? You might even need to eat out more the closer your move date gets."

She grabs a tub of plain Greek yogurt and moves on toward the cheese.

Likes dairy. Noted.

"I guess your mates have you covered though, don't they? Nice ladies."

"They would eat you alive, spit you back out, and then take pictures while the raccoons finish off your remains," she murmurs.

Fuck. I'm smiling again. "Good kind of mates to have."

"The best."

"Bet they're always trying to set you up with their grandsons."

"Nope."

"They don't have grandsons?"

"Life isn't all about who you date." She reaches for a package of aged white cheddar—the highest-end stuff—but stops and looks at me again.

Fully *looks* at me.

There is something going on in her head. Something big. Something with wheels and levers and gears.

If it were me, I know what I'd be thinking.

Temporary fuck buddy.

She's leaving.

I'm staying.

Moving is stressful.

And fucking is the best part of dating, so why not do the fucking part and skip the dating?

But I've been on this earth for thirty-four trips around the sun, two divorces, at least three drinks in my face for voicing my opinion, and enough lectures from my father about how to treat a woman that I don't say it out loud.

Anymore. I don't say it out loud anymore.

If she says it, though, I'm in.

I like badasses.

She's hot.

Funny too. Don't always find that in a fuck buddy.

But I won't be the one to suggest it first.

She's going to.

I can feel it.

I can *see* it in the way her face is moving like she's plotting out every step that will make this palatable for her.

I wonder if she wants me for my dick but will make me wear a bag over my head so she doesn't have to remember it's me.

She honestly looks as if she's contemplating exactly that while she stares at me. And then also contemplating if I'd be in for it.

It's hell to stand here and let her watch me while she's thinking all of this, but I do it. I stand there. I take the scrutiny. I play dumb.

I pretend I have no idea what she might be thinking right now.

"Ohh, Margot, *look* at that ass," someone whispers loudly behind me. Someone who sounds elderly. And horny.

38

"What's a *pounder?*" an equally elderly-sounding, though far more confused, voice replies. "Is that what each cheek weighs?"

Goldie squeezes her eyes shut and pinches her lips together, and I can't tell if she's trying not to cringe or trying not to smile.

Possibly both.

"I don't know, but he could pound me," Margot's friend says.

"*Greta.* Steve's barely been in his grave for a week."

"So add about forty years, and that's how long it's been since I had a good pounding. I didn't marry him for his penis."

Goldie makes a noise and turns her back fully on me, fully on the women too.

I look over my shoulder at them.

One's white. One's Black. Neither are over five feet two inches. Both are wrinkled from forehead to gnarled fingers.

The white lady's using a cane. The Black lady's holding onto the shopping cart.

And when their gazes reach my face, I smile and wink.

"*Ack!*" The white lady falls back into a soup display on an endcap.

"*Kill it!*" the Black lady shrieks. She lifts her umbrella and waves it at me. "*It's eating your face!*"

"It's only a bad mustache," Goldie chokes out. She's dropped her basket and is already helping the white lady out of the cans. "Are you okay, ma'am? Can I get you a chair? Does anything hurt?"

"Just my eyeballs," the white lady gasps. "Lord have mercy, *why* do men do that to their faces? They all think they're Tom Selleck, and they are *not.*"

Goldie makes another choking noise that sounds half like a whimper.

"Margot, I think we're not supposed to shop today," the Black lady says. Apparently Greta.

"Or ogle men's asses when your husband's just been buried," Margot snaps back.

"In my defense, we were only married for six months."

A manager rushes over and offers to finish shopping for the two women.

Goldie makes a face at me. "Could you *turn back around?*"

"Do you know him?" Margot asks her.

"He works with my brother," Goldie answers.

"What's a *pounder?*" Greta asks.

"I believe that's the name of the professional rugby team in town."

"What's rugby?"

"It's a sport where men wear short shorts and no protective equipment, and they try to get a ball that's like a bloated football down the field, which they call the pitch, to score while never throwing it forward but sometimes kicking it."

"That sounds dumb."

"Women should've invented sports."

Margot suddenly gasps. "Oh my gosh. Oh my gosh. *I know you.* Greta! Greta, this is *Goldie.* From the Instagrams. Goldie who believes in us!"

Ah, hell.

I know where this goes.

But Goldie doesn't seem to need a bouncer. She smiles—and it's a pretty fucking brilliant smile, blinding almost—and easily shifts into her public persona.

Which doesn't seem all that different from when I've seen her and watched her every time she doesn't know I'm around.

Like it's *her.* The her that I'm not allowed to know.

And this is where she shines.

Got a lot of respect for that.

The manager recognizes her too. Asks for an autograph.

The women want to know if she's excited for her move to London.

And I'm the problem. Me and my mustache—it's not *that* big or that ugly—are the problem.

I snag Goldie's basket off the floor, grab that brick of cheese she dropped and add that too, and head to the front of the store, where I pay for both of our groceries, and then sit and wait.

Without flashing the 'Stache of Glory at anyone else who might think it's a live animal growing on my upper lip.

After about ten minutes, Goldie appears near the register, looking around and frowning. I lift up her canvas basket and jerk my head toward the exit when she spots me.

"You didn't have to buy my groceries," she tells me when we meet up at the sliding glass doors.

Points to her for not asking what she owes me.

It's like she knows I'll tell her nothing.

Partially so that I know that I've won a game Silas doesn't even know we're playing where I get a point because I basically bought his dinner, and he'll probably whine about it.

Yes, it's a dumb game.

Shut up. I like it.

"Seemed more useful than playing bouncer," I tell her.

"I'm my own bouncer."

"Figured. You're a badass. And that's a compliment."

"Thank you."

I tuck one hand into my pocket and slide a glance at her while I let my own grocery bag swing from my other hand. "You get recognized a lot?"

"More often than I expect, but then, I don't expect to get recognized at all." She sucks in a big breath and pauses at the entrance to the parking garage that I suspect neither of us is heading into. "*If* I agree to be your date for *one public event*, with the word *public* to be defined more clearly before I fully agree, I want you to know that I'm doing it for my own personal reasons that have nothing to do with you."

Yes. She totally wants to get with the Fletch-meister. "Fair enough."

"I assume you have other reasons you'd ask me specifically."

"Mostly because you're hot." It's true enough. And it's an easy way to tell her I'm up for that no-strings fling anytime she says go.

She rolls her eyes again.

"You don't think you're hot?" I ask.

"I wouldn't get recognized in public and have as big of a social media following as I do if I didn't fit the description of *classically attractive.*"

"That was a lot of words to say *yes, I know I'm hot.*"

"If you wanted *any* hot woman on your arm, you could basically walk out your door, cover up your mustache, and shake your ass a little, and you'd have more options."

"The 'stache is my brand."

"Maybe you need a brand makeover."

It's a good thing I have a lot of experience being the one to walk away from arguments. "I also think it adds a dimension to my visibility if I take out the woman I passed out on after giving blood instead of a random woman who wants to get pounded by my ass."

"If you shaved, I think Greta would be interested. And dating a woman old enough to be your grandma is also very newsworthy."

"Studly Rugby Player Falls in Love with Grandma Who Tried to Save Him from His Own Facial Hair."

She laughs.

She actually laughs.

And then she seems to realize she's laughing at me, stops herself, and goes full-on straight-faced again.

Something in my chest hiccups.

Something in my pants moves in a much bigger way.

"You might be an ass in a lot of ways, but it's lovely that you have a nice sense of humor about the part of your face that I will actively be ignoring if you propose a date that I agree to."

She knows her worth. I like that. "I'll find a date you'll agree to."

"Best of luck to you." She holds out a hand to shake on it.

Fine by me.

My hand swallows hers. Her skin is every bit as soft as I'd hoped—*expected* it to be, her grip warm and firm without starting a handshake battle that would probably prove she *can* be her own bouncer.

Yeah, I'd definitely fling with her.

"So…your number?" I say, turning up the rizz as high as it can go.

"I don't believe you need my number to get in touch." She extracts her hand from mine and steps back. "Thank you again for the groceries. Have a lovely evening."

Watching her walk away is a good start to the evening.

But the better part?

She's given me a challenge.

Find a date I'll accept.

Game. Fucking. On.

5

From the Instagram direct messages of Goldie Collins

RugbyFletch: It's not every day I slide into the DMs of a woman I've been following for a few years.

CoachGoldie: Have you ever followed a woman for a few years?

RugbyFletch: That's classified.

CoachGoldie: Much like your mustache should be...

RugbyFletch: I've been doing research on mustaches. Did you know the first mustache to change the world was worn by a serf who led a labor uprising against the nobles in Europe in the fourteen hundreds? It also protected him from getting the black plague and having bad dates. The 'Stache That Changed The World.

CoachGoldie: Fascinating. And so very real-sounding. Almost as fascinating and real-sounding as Steve's obituary...

RugbyFletch: Who's Steve?

CoachGoldie: Never mind. I assume you have a proposal?

RugbyFletch: I have it on good authority that you like flash mobs.

CoachGoldie: Hey, look at that. You can block people on this app. There's this button, and if I click it, it gives me the option to never have to hear from you again.

RugbyFletch: Fine. I'll cancel the flash mob. But I make no promises about the singing telegrams.

CoachGoldie: Are you delivering it yourself?

RugbyFletch: That would require the singing part to happen, which is not happening.

CoachGoldie: Good point. Silas annoyed me at dinner, so I pulled up that karaoke video you were tagged in and played it until he cried for mercy.

RugbyFletch: That was my evil twin. And if you think he's bad, I'm worse. Which is why I don't karaoke.

CoachGoldie: Do you have siblings?

RugbyFletch: None that claim me.

CoachGoldie: Understandable.

RugbyFletch: We could hit the ballpark. Or a hockey game.

CoachGoldie: And hide in mascot costumes so I'm not seen in public with you.

RugbyFletch: The whole POINT is for you to be seen in public with me.

CoachGoldie: Fine. You win. Since it's what you want anyway, you can come to soccer practice with the little kickers Saturday morning and I'll show you how to kick a soccer ball. If you do well with that, I might even teach you how to aim it too.

RugbyFletch: *video of himself kicking a rugby ball a very long distance to score a drop goal*

CoachGoldie: *video of herself kicking a soccer ball from the corner of the field and it hooking into the net*

RugbyFletch: My PR person would likely say that the two of us having a public date where we eviscerate each other in our respective sports isn't the good kind of photo op that I personally think it would be.

CoachGoldie: You have a PR person?

RugbyFletch: Don't you?

CoachGoldie: Why do you need a PR person? Does this have to do with why you were kicked off the Leopards?

RugbyFletch: Check your sources, Hummingbird.

CoachGoldie: Speaking of my sources, what's your version of why you and my brother hate each other?

RugbyFletch: He's a whiny-ass baby.

CoachGoldie: And you're a paragon of maturity...

RugbyFletch: My ego gets left in the changing room when I step out onto the pitch. SOME PEOPLE have yet to learn how to do that.

CoachGoldie: *video of Fletcher having a hissy fit on the pitch in the middle of a match*

RugbyFletch: Not ego. Appropriate reaction to a shitty illegal tackle that hurt one of my mates and ultimately cost us the match.

CoachGoldie: So your ego has nothing to do with wanting to win?

RugbyFletch: Everybody wants to win. Basic human nature. Ego is thinking I'm the best at what I do.

CoachGoldie: I'm going to sit here a minute and let you read that back to yourself. Possibly several times.

RugbyFletch: I AM the best at what I do. But I also BELIEVE that my teammates are the best at what THEY do, and we're better when we all do our best TOGETHER. Except your brother. He's a spoiled ass who's wasting his potential thinking being a rugby god is the same thing here as being a hockey or football god. And don't get me started on the number of illegal tackles he had called on him last year. Which has no reflection or bearing on you, as you are two separate people who did not choose to share a gene pool.

CoachGoldie: Huh.

RugbyFletch: What?

CoachGoldie: Am I talking to Fletcher Huxley or his PR person?

RugbyFletch: *selfie of himself lifting a middle finger sideways to cover some of his mustache*

CoachGoldie: Thank you. I appreciate the clarification.

RugbyFletch: How do you feel about carousels? There's that big one at Reynolds Park. And it's next to an ice cream stand. We could eat and then ride and puke.

CoachGoldie: That would be on-brand with how we met.

RugbyFletch: I appreciate your openness to continuing to include bodily fluids and functions in our arrangement.

CoachGoldie: Okay. I get it now. I see why the PR person is necessary. Kudos to you for recognizing your shortcomings.

RugbyFletch: Mock all you want, but you'll know who brought the fans to the stadium when I'm done with my plans.

CoachGoldie: Did your PR person recommend the mustache and the sweatpants too?

RugbyFletch: This mustache has done more to pad my bank account than three years' worth of my UK rugby salary.

CoachGoldie: That German car company paid you that much?

RugbyFletch: You watched my car commercial?

CoachGoldie: Silas kept annoying me, so I kept googling you.

RugbyFletch: Your relationship with your brother might need a PR person.

CoachGoldie: He's my toughest client and I love a challenge.

RugbyFletch: He doesn't strike me as the type to hire a life coach and mean it. No offense. You're clearly good at your job.

CoachGoldie: Oh, he doesn't KNOW he's hired me. It's pro bono volunteer work. Plus, his kid is stinking cute as hell, and I can't see her if I'm a dick to him.

RugbyFletch: Rather than comment on the horror that is your brother procreating, I'm going to suggest we take over one of the big red tour buses that run through downtown Copper Valley and give our own commentary.

CoachGoldie: Already did that with a client whose dream was to drive a bus. Try again.

RugbyFletch: There's a weird-ass pirate town an hour or so away. Good photo ops.

CoachGoldie: You'd have to shave first, because I'd insist we go to the bakery, and the owner has the cutest little kid who'd cry in terror at the sight of you. In my weaker moments of wanting to write my niece's future for her, I secretly ship the two of them. Don't tell anyone or else you'll find out the lengths I'll go to in order to protect my secrets.

RugbyFletch: You are not giving the 'Stache the credit it deserves. One day, you'll realize how wrong you are.

CoachGoldie: I'm okay with being wrong. Also, I think we should do this. *link to a local restaurant's special events page*

RugbyFletch: Hold on. I have to go wipe the drool off my phone. Why are there still dates available for private classes?

CoachGoldie: It's brand new and they haven't started advertising yet. ALSO, it should be a team event. Since you're doing this for team publicity.

RugbyFletch: You've been sitting on this since before I slid into your DMs, haven't you?

CoachGoldie: I have a little over three weeks left to enjoy my time here. I'm booking this for myself one way or another. If you want to join me for your own purposes, you can, provided you invite teammates. But also, you have to include Silas.

RugbyFletch: Are you Coach Goldie-ing me?

CoachGoldie: Sure. Let's go with that.

RugbyFletch: That wasn't a yes.

CoachGoldie: I have a client call in fifteen minutes and I need to prep. So you can either agree my idea is the best idea and set it up, or maybe I'll see you around sometime, but probably not.

RugbyFletch: You're not just a badass. You're also a hardass.

CoachGoldie: Seize the day, Fletcher. I want to do this before I leave, and you have way more at stake than I do if you want to join me.

RugbyFletch: Which day should I seize?

CoachGoldie: Tuesday's best for me.

RugbyFletch: Consider it done.

CoachGoldie: Great. See you then.

6

Goldie

I'M LATE. I'm late, and I hate being late, but when a client is having a breakthrough about exploring a career track that they'd never thought possible, and their dreams are blossoming before their eyes, I stay on the video call to see it through.

My life is a series of *I can't have it all so I'll deal with the complicated feelings that come with hating being late but loving why I sometimes am.*

I told Fletcher I'd meet him at All Clucked Up, a local farm-to-table restaurant that recently started offering cooking classes, so when I tumble out of my apartment building and find him leaning against the wall, I stop so fast I almost trip.

It tweaks my hip, and I grimace before I can catch myself.

"Okay there?" He clutches my elbow, steadying me, his grip sending a very unwelcome jolt through my arm.

"I told you there was no reason for you to pick me up." I pull my arm back. I'm in a coat, and this is Fletcher Huxley. There is zero reason for my body to react like an attractive man touched me.

A slow smile spreads over his face. His mustache is outrageously styled tonight so that the part under the center of his nose is even more prominent, with his 'stache hairs smoothed and oiled so they point to the sides like an old cartoon villain's pencil 'stache, but way thicker. And yet, he still falls into that box of *classically handsome*.

His jawline and the Roman nose and the hooded green eyes might overcome even the most awful of awful facial hair.

Especially when he smiles.

There aren't a lot of shots of him smiling on his Instagram page. Or in official team photos anywhere.

But *handsome* doesn't equal *attractive* by default. *Attractive* is far more nuanced.

"You were thinking of standing me up," he says.

Worst part?

He sounds happy about it.

Like we're in a game and he's winning by virtue of the fact that he sideswiped my plans to stand him up.

No, that's not the worst part.

The very worst part is the thrill that I get from being the one winning this round, no matter what he thinks.

Competitive? Me?

Guilty. "Incorrect. I am very much looking forward to this tonight."

"You appear to be telling the truth, and yet..."

I am one hundred percent telling the truth. And I have zero interest in letting him in on my little secret of why.

Not yet.

"You didn't bring your dog. I thought you took her everywhere."

"She's having a spa night."

I subtly test my hip. Little creaky, but not unbearable by any means, which suggests a weather front might be moving in. With all good on the mobility front, I turn down the street to head toward All Clucked Up. Good distraction in case my face is doing what I suspect it would do at the idea of a mini dachshund getting a blow-out, having her toenails done, and lying on a massage table.

I wonder if she's in a little pink robe that matches her pink leash.

How freaking adorable would that be?

And then I decide he's lying purely to see my reaction, and I get control of the *aww* that's likely all over me right now. "Too bad she'll miss all of the good food."

"I'll take her home a doggy bag."

Score another one for Fletcher.

Not that I mind as much as I thought I would. Chatting with him on Instagram the other night was fun. Unexpectedly so.

Fun enough that I'd be going with him tonight without an ulterior motive? No.

But fun enough that I don't regret it? Yes.

I don't like grudges, and there was something earnest enough in his apology at the grocery store that I'm choosing to believe him.

I'm still wary, but I believe him.

"And your personal paparazzo?" I ask. "Are you seriously here for a publicity date without evidence?"

He's apparently been waiting for the question. He has his phone out, one arm around me, posing for a selfie before I catch on to what he's doing. And he has his phone pocketed again and is nudging me down the street before I can eke out a demand to see the photo.

"They'll meet us there. You usually late?"

I'm not flustered because he touched me again. I'm startled that I put my guard down so soon into our "date." That's my story, and

I'm sticking to it. "I'm punctual ninety-eight percent of the time, and I have a very good reason to not be the other two percent. Does a lack of punctuality bother you?"

"Unnecessary rules bother me. What constitutes a good enough reason to be late?"

"People."

"And here I thought you were going to say a bad hair day."

"Your face would know those…"

He smirks.

All he needs is a trench coat and a top hat and he truly could be a cartoon villain. Though cartoon villains aren't usually so thick in the neck and arms. Or straining their black *Copper Valley Pounders* T-shirts. Or walking around in forty-degree weather in only T-shirts and tattoos to keep their upper bodies warm.

He's in jeans tonight. I pause and slowly peer behind him.

No letters on his ass.

He dressed up for this.

He flexes one ass cheek, then the other.

Yep.

Still Fletcher.

I start walking again. "Are you contractually obligated to always wear Pounders merch? Or did you use your mustache's profits to invest in the team?"

Every time I poke at his mustache, he smirks or grins or preens. "My mustache isn't the only body part that's made me more money than my rugby salary."

"*Ew.*"

He swipes a hand over the 'stache, and this time, I'm pretty sure it's because my reaction made him smile so big he might've flashed all of his pearly whites.

"First my ass, now my dick. I see where your mind is, Goldie Collins."

"I've known rugby players Silas's entire life. I know where *all* of your minds always are, even when I don't want to."

"You still checked out my ass. Not that I mind. I'm game for you liking my ass."

"I was making sure you didn't have any messages written on it tonight."

He slides a look my way as we walk. It's only about three blocks. Not far. And we pass my favorite bookstore on the way. Penny For Your Thoughts is closed for the night, but I hear guitar sounds coming from inside as we walk past the window display of romance novels and travel books.

The owners must be hanging out inside.

"Do you always look so happy when you're rapid-firing zingers at your dates?" Fletcher asks.

"Do you always look so happy to be the recipient of the world's best zingers?" I counter.

"Are you getting them all out now before we have to behave ourselves in class?"

"Why would we behave in class?"

"Your brother's going to be there."

I smile. It's too big, but *oooh*, the way I'm looking forward to this… "Oh, did he agree? Who else?"

Fletcher doesn't answer. He's watching me again.

I purse my lips together to try to squelch the smile, but it doesn't work.

"What are you planning, Hummingbird?"

"To learn how to cook myself a farm-to-table feast before I leave for London."

"Huh."

My hip twinges again. Has to be weather coming in.

Or else Fletcher *is* the weather.

But given the way a swift winter breeze kicks up, it's likely a normal weather system.

We reach our destination, and Fletcher leaps the last two strides to beat me to the door and hold it open for me.

"For your awareness," I murmur to him as I pass through the entrance, "when I put my mind to being someone, I'm *all in*. And for tonight, I'm your publicity stunt."

I don't know if he's smiling or scared now, or possibly both, but he puts his hand to my lower back as we walk up the newly opened stairwell to the side of the entryway to my favorite restaurant in the neighborhood.

Rosalia, the owner, waves at us from across the kitchen space as we reach the top. "Goldie! You made it. Please, come, come. We're ready to begin."

She's always had a small market attached to All Clucked Up where she sells extra produce and local delicacies, but she's expanded into the former office space above the restaurant and installed a U-shaped counter with barstools around it to host cooking classes.

Tonight is one of the first of her classes. I'm glad Fletcher agreed to this because I love the idea that she'll get as much of a boost in visibility from this as the Pounders will.

Fletcher leaps into action to help me out of my coat as I stop next to the line of hooks at the top of the stairs, and then we continue into the bright cooking school space.

There's an industrial-size stovetop behind the middle stretch of gleaming white countertops and professional-grade ovens stacked on top of each other along the back wall. Paintings of olive branches and tomato vines and fresh herbs are on the walls above the counters and cubbyholes for supplies.

Each of the seats tonight—there are apparently ten of us, including Fletcher and me—have cutting boards, knives, and bowls of colorful bell peppers in front of them, along with bowls of chips and salsa for snacking while we cook.

Fletcher puts his hand to my lower back as we head toward the two open seats. Honestly, the amount he's touching me would make me squirm if I wasn't constantly reminding myself of my bigger goal.

Oh, look. There's Silas. And this is my moment.

The moment that my plan comes together.

I watch as my brother puts two and two together and realizes that I'm here as Fletcher's date.

Silas's usually arrogant smirk fades behind saucer eyes and a slack jaw for a split second before he snaps his mouth shut, his lips thinning and his eyes narrowing.

And lucky all of us—the last set of open seats are right next to Silas and his date.

"Nina!" I say, hugging my brother's nanny. "I didn't know you were coming."

Yes, his *nanny*.

My brother brought his freaking *nanny* as his date tonight.

His baby mama's gonna kill him if they lose another nanny because of his antics.

"Oh my god, I didn't know *you* were coming," Nina replies. She's a little shorter than me with bright purple hair, white skin, and whatever shirt she's wearing under her apron is probably hilarious. Her entire collection has cartoon animals with funny sayings on them.

Softer, she whispers, "He got stood up by someone he met at a bar last night and didn't want to look like a solo loser, and I *love* Rosalia's desserts. Don't worry. Brittany won't have to kill him."

"You will forever be my favorite of all of his nannies." I pull back from hugging her and finger wave at my brother. "Silas. Hope you brought your safety knife."

He glowers.

Flat-out *glowers*.

Good.

Serves him right for what he's done to chase away the four guys who were fabulous long-term, casual-relationship material for me over the past two years.

I'm well aware that Silas's heart is in what he thinks is the right place. My breakup with my last serious boyfriend wasn't pretty, and more, my life wasn't pretty for a while afterward. Miller Boynton shredded my heart and took more of my confidence—and friends—with him than he should've.

So Silas chasing away every guy I've dated since—I get it.

And that ends.

Now.

Do a publicity stunt with Fletcher to help the team?

No, thank you. He's the kind of guy who could find any number of other publicity stunts to achieve his goals.

Show up to a team publicity event on the arm of my brother's least-favorite teammate to make a statement about the opinions he gets to have in my dating life?

Yes, please.

We pass Nina and Silas to get to the two empty seats, and because I'm a total giver, I walk one step farther and take the seat next to Crew.

Which leaves Fletcher sitting next to Silas.

Oh. *Whoops.* However could I have overlooked *that* detail?

Silly, silly Goldie.

Where *is* my brain?

Crew eyeballs me. He's a six-foot-two Black man with kind eyes off the pitch, but don't piss him off on the pitch. Yes, yes, I know more about my brother's team than I need to. Despite the parts of our relationship that are complicated, we do see each other frequently enough that I'm aware of the people in his life.

"You understand we're *in a kitchen* with all of the dangerous *kitchen things?*" Crew mutters to me with a jerk of his head toward my date and my brother.

"We're all adults here," I reply happily. I lean around him and smile at his date, a stunning woman with brown skin and black hair swept back in a low ponytail. "Hi. I'm Goldie. I'm here with Fletcher. Funny story—we met when he passed out on me after giving blood. So cute, right? What's your name and how do you know Crew?"

While Triya introduces herself, I hear rumblings behind me and murmurs all around the whole table.

We haven't even started, and already, I'm calling tonight a success.

7

Fletcher

THERE'S something going on between Goldie and whiny-ass Silas that she hasn't told me about.

Not my problem though.

Not when my camera person isn't the only one here. The team sent the official photographer too.

Best behavior, Fletcher.

Easier said than done when I hear the reminder to myself in my old man's voice every time.

"Keep your fucking hands off my fucking sister," Silas mutters to me while the chef claps her hands and starts telling us about what we're making tonight. Two cheese courses and flan.

At my request.

"Your sister's a grown-up and can decide who she does and doesn't want to spend time with," I mutter back.

"She doesn't know about *you.*"

"You're being rude. Listen to the instructor."

He starts to say something else, so I grab a chip, fill it with salsa, and shove it in my mouth.

I get a satisfying crunch in my ears instead of Silas's voice, and holy hell.

That's good salsa.

Sweet, but with a kick.

I like it.

Gonna have to run an extra mile to make up for the chips tomorrow though.

Bloody old body that doesn't burn calories anymore the way it did when I was fifteen.

"Oh, I *love* the cheese dip here." Goldie leans into me, her hand on my thigh. "I didn't see that on the menu. Did you ask her to change it?"

"Yep."

"*Fletcher*. That was so sweet of you."

She's talking too loudly. Not so loudly that the whole class can hear, but loudly enough that Silas can hear.

There's definitely something going on there.

We're all ordered to go wash our hands at various sinks around the space, so we do.

Goldie beats me back to her seat. Silas's date beats him back too.

I'm still stuck next to the wanker.

But worse—I want to know what he did.

I want to know what he did to Goldie that she's antagonizing him with me.

And there is *zero* doubt in my mind that that's what's going on.

I shouldn't care why. I should care about shredding this cheese that we're being told to shred into these bowls.

Which I'm doing with enough concentration that I almost miss Porter's snicker across the way.

"Get your mind out of the gutter," his date says loudly enough for all of us to hear.

"He's not wrong," Silas says, bumping into me. "You really can tell who's got the cheese grating stroke down."

"Jerking off is healthy," Crew says.

Loudly.

Isabella, the team photographer, rolls her eyes and shuts her camera off. Shade, my personal paparazzo, as Goldie says, keeps snapping pictures.

"You want to sell out the stadium this year or not?" I say to the room. "Quit thinking like wankers and get back to cooking so Isabella can do her job. And say sorry to her too."

A small chorus of *sorry, Isabellas* go up around the counter while I get a round of eye rolls and dirty looks.

I lift my brows.

Not looking for apologies for Shade. He's used to me. Plus, I pay him double what any of his other jobs were offering.

"Sorry, Rosalia," the guys add. With more eye rolls in my direction.

I pretend I don't notice. The same way I pretend I don't notice the tension underlying the team whenever more than three of us are together. "Better. Shred your cheese."

"Very nicely done, Coach Fletcher," Goldie murmurs. Her cheese is grated and in a perfect fluffy pile inside the baking dish.

"Thank you." I don't want to be a coach.

I want to own the whole fucking league and make it as popular here as American football is.

And then I want to send Rafferty a screenshot of my bank account and my awards and my old-ass body still playing too.

You're washed up, Huxley. Over. Done. Can't bloody well keep up anymore. Do you fancy being remembered as the bloke who couldn't run the length of the pitch anymore, or shall you make a dignified exit while you still have fans? Someday you'll realize I'm doing you quite the favor.

Fuck him.

That wasn't his call to make.

I got right in his face, told him I was heading back to my homeland to make American rugby even bigger than British rugby, and that the next time I set foot in the UK, it would be for him to kiss my ass while eating his words.

Got my work cut out for me, but I can do it.

I *will* do it.

No matter who doubts me. No matter the uphill battle. No matter what gets said about me in the press here or across the pond in the meantime.

We get the rest of the shit mixed in with the grated cheese, and then all of the dishes go in the oven while we're told to pick up our knives.

"*Please* switch spots with him," Crew mutters to Goldie.

"Our best opportunities for growth come when facing our own deaths," she replies pertly, which makes both Crew's date and Silas's date crack up.

I dislike how much I like her right now.

"Keep your knife away from me," Silas mutters.

"There are cameras, dumbass. If I was going to cut you, I'd do it without witnesses."

"Oh, here," Goldie says to me. "If you're comfortable holding the knife that way, that's fine, but you *look* uncomfortable. Try holding it this way."

She slips half behind me and covers my hands with hers, repositioning my grip on the chef's knife.

Goosebumps break out on my forearms and my dick lifts a sleepy head. She smells like a cupcake. Like a vanilla cupcake fresh out of the oven.

"You've handled knives before," Rosalia says to Goldie.

"I watched a lot of cooking shows a few years ago." Goldie looks at me. "How's that feel?"

"Quit fucking touching him," Silas says.

He's not muttering now.

Goldie smiles back at him as if his growling and grumbling don't faze her in the least. "Do you know that after Fletcher passed out on me, he tracked me down to apologize and offer to take me to dinner? I thought that was *so sweet*. First, he tries to save someone's life by giving blood, then he tries to power through not feeling great so they won't have to throw away his donation, and then he apologizes to *me* for what was clearly not his fault. It says a lot about a person, doesn't it? Silas, sweetie, let Nina do your cutting. We don't want you back in the emergency room for stitches."

Yep.

He pissed her off *bad*.

But worse?

Now *I* feel like a complete and total ass because she's painting me like a saint when I am *not*.

Not even close.

And I know she knows it.

"Oh, look at you," Goldie exclaims to me. "Rosalia, look at how uniform Fletcher's peppers are."

"Good knife grip," I grunt.

She pats my ass.

She pats.

My ass.

Silas growls.

My dick is at full mast.

Crew, Porter, Tatum, and their dates are all watching us with varying degrees of amusement mixed with horror. They're all at least eight years younger than me.

Every last one of them.

They're all still suspicious of the European rugby god in their

63

locker room. There's no *oh, he's good—we're winning this year* that came with my entry to their team.

It's pure suspicion.

Like there aren't at least three other guys from the highest echelons of international rugby who could've retired but came here to Copper Valley to play for the Pounders instead in the past few years.

But they're not me.

Apparently I have a reputation.

And bloody Rafferty gave an interview live on the telly about my exit from Nottingshire that wasn't complimentary.

We mix the cheese dips and get them in the oven, then chop more peppers and some onions.

I cry.

Not ashamed.

Fucking onions.

But the kitchen's starting to smell like cheese, and Rosalia turns her attention to frying fresh tortilla chips while we get a break to sit on our stools and have some wine.

I don't touch mine.

Goldie sips hers delicately.

Silas slurps his.

I slide him a look.

He stares right back at me and slurps again, then chokes on it.

"Whoa, whoa, whoa, hold up," Tatum suddenly says.

He's a rookie. Same as me, he grew up traveling the world. Father was a diplomat. Learned rugby in South Africa. And he's pointing at Goldie.

"You're *that* Goldie. Coach Goldie. *You can do it* Goldie."

She inclines her head with a smile. "Guilty."

"And you're related to *Silas*?"

"We're pretty sure at least one of us was adopted. Probably me, since I remember when he was born."

"And you're dating the old guy?"

"The *veteran*," I correct.

"It's a first date," Goldie says. "A second is up to him."

She beams at me, and *fuck me*.

I've fallen into a cave full of cupcakes and rugby balls except with the sun shining and sand at my feet and someone on the way with a strawberry daiquiri. My favorite things.

It's a fake beam.

Zero doubt it's a fake beam. She's clearly chuffed with herself for how well this is going for her own intentions.

All of this warm squishy bullshit in my chest is an optical illusion. A *chesticle* illusion.

"You got some…" I clear my throat.

Brush a drop of wine off her upper lip with my thumb.

Don't smile back.

Can't.

Not when my heart is hammering and my dick is straining my jeans and she's blinking at me, her pupils dilating as her smile drops away too.

This is *not* part of the plan.

I don't do this rubbish.

"Aww, they're so cute," Silas's date says.

"Thank you," Goldie says softly.

Fuck me fuck me fuck me fuck me.

I don't know if she's pretending or not.

But I know I'm sending that loud beeping oven timer on an all-expenses-paid vacation to the Caribbean for having such fucking awesome timing to go off exactly now.

Goldie whips her head toward the sound, her nostrils quivering. "*Oooh*, is the cheese dip done?"

I grab my wine with a shaky hand and take a gulp.

Then look at Goldie's profile. The slender neck. Dimple in one round cheek. Arched brows. Dark hair pulled up in a high ponytail and waterfalling down her back.

She's shed her coat and cardigan and is in a black tank top and a long skirt with little hummingbirds sipping off flowers all over the fabric. A random person passing her on the street would think she was a kindergarten teacher.

But she's not.

No, she's walking, talking, breathing temptation.

So very far from the easy publicity stunt she's supposed to be. That she *agreed* to be.

Clearly for her own purposes.

"If you fuck my sister, I will fuck you up so hard you won't know where your mouth ends and your asshole starts," Silas says to me.

I turn and face him.

And stare.

And stare.

And stare some more.

I don't blink. I don't break eye contact. And I don't say a single fucking word.

Whiny-ass baby has good stare stamina. I'll give him that.

He's not blinking either.

I crack one knuckle. Then a second. Then a third.

All without breaking eye contact.

Kinda nice that the onions already lubed my eyeballs.

Makes this easier.

"Silas." His date pokes him. "Go get our cheese."

"One minute, babe."

"Call me babe again, and you'll be looking for a new nanny again."

He breaks the staring contest with a muttered *fuck*, but points his fingers at his eyeballs, then mine. "We're not done."

"Your sister's a grown-ass adult," I reply. "Let her do the threatening herself."

"Aww, you're so sweet." Goldie pecks me on the cheek. "I think we can have that second date after all."

Silas is red as a stoplight.

I'm hard as a steel plate.

And I'm slowly realizing that I'm not in charge here.

Goldie is.

She's playing *both* of us.

And fuck me one last time, it makes me like her *even more*.

8

Goldie

WELL.

This is going even better than I could've imagined.

Even the part where my face got close to Fletcher's mustache when I leveled up the game to kiss him wasn't as bad as I thought it would be.

His cologne is nice. It's smooth with a hint of spice. Sandalwood and patchouli. It fits him.

"He's been divorced twice," Silas mutters to me while we pull our cheese dishes out of the oven.

"And you have a kid, a nanny you're in danger of losing, and the world's best baby mama who tolerates your bullshit. Maybe don't throw ridiculous standards at my dates when your life's even more complicated."

"He's also a grade-A asshole."

"Aw, I love it when you love your teammates."

"He'll fuck you and leave you, Goldie."

"Maybe I want to get fucked before I go to London. Maybe I'm using him for his big, thick, long—"

"*Fine.* Fine. Okay? Fine. Just—stop talking."

"Rude, Silas," Porter says. "Get out of the way. The rest of us want our cheese dip."

I smile at my brother.

He glowers back.

I don't say *stay the fuck out of my love life*.

He doesn't reply *when hell freezes over*.

It's all understood.

I circle the counter back to my seat next to Fletcher, whose wine is nearly gone.

"Don't these look amazing?" I say as I set the two dishes in front of us and leave the hot pads on the counter beside them.

"Delicious," he grunts.

Aww. He's humoring me.

Such a good date.

Surprisingly so, actually. Tonight has weirdly surpassed my expectations.

"How many dates has he fucked up for you?" he asks.

See? More surprises. Who knew Fletcher Huxley could be so intuitive?

I smile darkly over my glass. "Every last one in the past two years."

He keeps staring, a silent demand for more information.

And with Silas sitting down on his other side, well within earshot, and me with absolutely nothing to lose tonight, I oblige the demand. "There was the first date at my favorite wine bar where he plopped right down at the table with us, pulled out a private investigator's report, and proceeded to demand answers for why the man ran a stoplight once when he was seventeen."

Fletcher's mustache quivers but his eyes give nothing away. "Go on."

"The guy after that started getting spam text messages about everything from erectile dysfunction to porn sites from a slew of unknown numbers, one on top of the other, to the point that he tried to shut his phone off, and instead, it started screaming *I send dick pics* and he had to ask the chef to drop it in boiling oil to get it to shut up."

"Like that old virus that bricked half the phones in the world a few years ago?"

"Exactly. Like someone with a trust fund and ridiculous standards paid a hacker to make it happen for my date."

More poker face.

I wonder if he's taking notes.

Silas is ignoring us, but Nina's leaning around him to listen in.

Also—it was undeniably Silas.

His nanny at the time called me the day after she quit and started asking questions about my date that were too specific.

Way too specific.

I thought he was making it up, but also, it's Silas, so I wanted to warn you, she'd said.

"The pinnacle of douchiness, though, was when he insisted on a double date at the fair, bullied my date who was afraid of heights into getting on the Ferris wheel, and then paid the operator to stop the ride for twenty minutes while we were at the top."

Nina gasps.

Crew makes a noise behind me.

I smile brightly at Fletcher. "But now I have you! It's so awesome that you're teammates. He has to get along with you."

The 'stache twitches again. I think it might have saluted me.

As it should.

"He whines most on leg day," Fletcher says. "I'll have Coach double his squats and presses."

"My hero."

"No, no, don't eat yet," Rosalia chides as Crew starts to dig into the batch of freshly fried tortillas she sets in front of him. "One last step."

No.

Is she serious?

She grins at my face. "One last step," she repeats.

"Do *not* eat yet," I agree. "It's not done."

This might be my best date in even more than two years.

I've gone from Gleeful Revenge Goldie to full-up Giddy Goldie in ten seconds.

Sometimes, I'm still a little kid.

Eating the cheese dip here is one of those times.

But not because cheese dip is a special indulgence I don't let myself have. It's more because of how it's served.

And Rosalia is pulling out the Everclear—don't judge—which is a massive indication of what's coming next, and which I seriously hadn't expected in this class.

Too much room for something to go wrong, you know?

But she's circling the counter on her side, splashing the alcohol on everyone's individual cheese dip.

You can tell who's been here before because they're grinning as big as I am.

When she's doused all of our dips, she disappears under the countertop for a second, then emerges with a handheld kitchen torch.

"This was worth being your date for the evening," I hear Nina say to Silas.

I can tell by the way Fletcher's mustache twitches again that he heard it too.

"Samesies," I murmur.

He gets as close to grinning at me as he's ever come.

I'm almost getting used to the 'stache.

Or possibly I'm developing coping skills that block it out of my vision.

Rosalia circles the group again, touching the Everclear with the flaming torch to light our individual cheese dips on fire.

I'm ready with my camera when she gets to ours. This is absolutely going up on my socials. And I don't seem to be the only one.

There are phones recording videos and taking snapshots all over the kitchen. Isabella, the team photographer, and Shade, Fletcher's personal paparazzo, are both ready.

I get a five-second video of the flames, then snap a picture, and then I hear my name.

"*Goldie*. C'mon. Pose before the flame goes out," Fletcher says.

I spin on my stool. Shade is there waiting while Fletcher holds his flaming cheese dip with his hands in the oven mitts that are a tad too small for him.

"Can you do your magic to erase the mustache before you post this?" I ask Shade.

He smirks.

Fletcher wraps an arm around me and holds the flaming cheese closer to both of our faces.

We both smile, and Shade snaps a photo with a murmured, "Good, good. Goldie, laugh at something, you're on video... Good. Thank you. Now, shift closer to him. Huxley, that mustache is an abomination. Goldie, hold still, and—"

And before they can say *all done*, or whatever they were going to say next, Fletcher jostles into me, the flaming cheese tilting precariously in his hand.

"Sorry not sorry," Silas mutters as the dip tips, and I suck in a breath and Fletcher juggles the dish, flames wobbling side to side while I leap away.

The flames aren't high, but *they're still flames*, and you know what's about to happen.

Fletcher's going to drop it down his front and set his shirt on fire and *where is the fire extinguisher?*

Except that's not what happens.

What happens is that Fletcher recovers his balance and grip on the flaming cheese, blows it out, and then...

Blows it out again.

Except the cheese is already out.

Not out?

His mustache.

His mustache *is on fire.*

He blows the cheese one last time, and my initial freeze reflex thaws, and I leap into motion.

Stop, drop, and roll.

I can't stop, drop, and roll him.

But I can smother.

With—with—I grab the salsa at my spot and fling it onto his upper lip with one hand—*I don't know, it looks wet*—and then grab a towel with my other hand and smother his face with it.

"What the bloody fucking *fuck?*" he chokes behind my hand.

He's fighting me, and *dammit*, he's strong, but I have adrenaline on my side, and I'm gripping him by the back of the neck and smothering his mustache with all of my might.

"You're on fire! Hold still!"

"Oh my god, the 'stache," Crew says reverently behind me.

"Do you think it survived?" Tatum whispers.

Fletcher's eyes flare wide. He rips my hand off his mouth and stares at me in absolute horror while the rest of the room falls silent.

It's not a comfortable silence either.

This is the kind of silence that I'd assume comes with stumbling upon a cave full of moldy cheddar cheese. Or the kind of silence that comes when you get the phone call that your childhood home was eaten by a sharknado.

I can hear my own heart beating.

I might even hear Fletcher's heart beating.

I haven't had the courage to drop my gaze from his deep, *you did not set this up to light my mustache on fire*, outraged glare to the carnage that may or may not be waiting beneath.

Salsa.

I threw *mango salsa* on him to try to put out the little smoky flames eating the ends of his mustache.

Legit, I don't think anyone in the room is breathing right now.

Except possibly Silas.

Who will be getting the very, very worst Thanksgiving present I can dream up to give him this year.

It's a Collins thing.

Don't ask.

Fletcher lifts his hand to his face.

I don't so much see it as I feel him moving, and I know that's what he has to be doing.

And that's when I let myself look.

My gaze drops from his flashing green eyes to his nose, and then lower.

And *ohhhhhhh fffuuuuuuucccccckkkkkk.*

The right side of his mustache is singed halfway off. The hairs that are left are extra curly, and they crumble into ash under his fingers as he gingerly touches the area between his upper lip and his nose with two fingers.

He's still staring at me.

This is my fault.

I asked to come here. I told him to make it a team activity. I knew there was zero chance Silas would see this opportunity come through his email—which he monitors as if the fate of the free world depends on it—and *not* jump at the chance to have dinner here tonight, even if he had to use a knife and cook some of it himself.

And then I made the two of them sit next to each other.

Silas might be the one who bumped him—and I'd bet it was on

purpose—but I was the one who put everything else in motion to make this exact moment possible.

Stop it, Goldie, I order myself. *You are not responsible for the world.*

Fletcher looks away from me, and you could legitimately hear a mouse drop a flake of cheese in the silence that descends even heavier as he turns to look at Silas.

I gulp.

Pretty sure everyone else in the room does too.

My friends will be writing my brother's obituary at our next dinner.

And the way I have zero doubt about the validity of that statement is what hurtles me into motion.

I grab Fletcher's arm and tug him toward me, but he is a steel-plated boulder and I can't move him.

Which means leaping between the two of them is my only option to prevent a murder tonight.

And so that's what I do.

9

Fletcher

THE WANKER. Burned. My mustache. Off.

I don't know what Goldie says to make him run away before his face can meet my fist. I don't know what else we're supposed to cook the rest of the night. I don't know what my baby teammates are saying without saying it out loud.

I just know I'm *done* here tonight.

"You get that?" I ask Shade, my voice unrecognizable in my own ears.

He nods, and even he—my gay emo personal paparazzo—looks like he just personally visited the River Styx and will never be the same.

Impressive.

And that fucking noise in the back of my head—*at least it'll lead to ticket sales*—can shut the fuck up for the night.

What will Sweet Pea think?

Will she recognize me?

Forget this bullshit.

I'm going home.

"Fletcher, I am *so sorry*," Goldie says as I step around her.

I pull off my apron and drop it on the counter, then head for the stairs.

She follows. "I shouldn't have made you two sit together. Can I —can I do anything to help?"

"That'll get great press," I mutter. "Good job."

"I'm so sorry," she says again.

Sure she is.

She hates—*hated*—*fuck*—my mustache. "It'll grow back," I hear my ego reply, "and it'll be bigger and better than ever."

I'm not looking at her while I head for the door, but she's following me and I can practically feel the way she's wincing.

I've spent maybe two hours with her over my entire life, and I can feel her wincing.

Awesome.

"It will," she says hesitantly as I shove out of the door and onto the street.

Two fit men walking their dog both gasp and give me a wide berth.

"He's not a serial killer," Goldie calls after them. "He plays rugby. He can't help his resting serial killer face."

One of them—the one in a wool coat with a perfectly-tied plaid scarf—looks back at us. "Do you need help, ma'am?"

I roll my eyes and head in the direction of my flat—my *condo*.

She says something else to the couple and then I hear her feet pounding on the pavement as she chases after me.

"Go away," I say through clenched teeth.

I need to get home, survey the carnage, mourn, and then pick myself back up, and I need to do it *without* witnesses.

"I don't think you should be alone right now."

"I'm *fine*."

"You look like you're three seconds away from turning into the Incredible Hulk."

"Resting serial killer face is like that."

She whimpers.

It might be covering a laugh.

She, too, can fuck right off.

The entire Collins family can.

"Is your skin burnt?" she asks softly. "If your skin is burnt under the mustache—"

"I'm *fine*."

I didn't realize I was on fire.

I thought the *cheese* was still on fire.

But the worst part of this?

I don't eat a lot of dairy, and *I still wanted the bloody cheese.*

And the cheese and veggie quesadillas. And the flan.

We were going to have flan.

I have a few more days before preseason training starts in earnest. A few more days for my bloody old man body to recover from a cheat night before I have to be ready every damn day.

And now all that's left of my mustache is the *ash* part, and I had enough chips that my body will think we had our cheat night and *I didn't get my fucking flan.*

I cross a street without waiting for a crosswalk sign.

Goldie keeps up, and where I flip off a car that honks at me, she must make a much more polite gesture, because once again—

"Ma'am? Are you okay?"

"His grandmother died in a freak accident involving a forklift and a baby grand piano," she calls back. "It's not you. He's having a bad day. We're so sorry."

"You're a little fucked up," I mutter.

"You *cannot* keep walking into streets without looking both ways first. What are you, *two*?"

"People who throw salsa at me to put out my flaming facial hair don't get to accuse me of being a toddler."

"It was the first thing I saw. And nobody else was coming to your rescue. Probably because you can be a serious asshole when you want to be. Sorry, ma'am. Sorry. I don't usually talk like this. He fired me from a job because it's bad optics for us to slee—to go to dinner together when he's the boss and I'm his assistant. But he's worth it. Most of the time."

"I doubt that," the young woman pushing a stroller sniffs. "None of them are worth it."

"I'm cheating on him with his best friend," Goldie calls behind us.

I don't have a best friend.

I have my dog.

I have rugby.

I have a backstabbing former mentor.

I have a bunch of teammates who were my family but who are still across the pond and whom I haven't seen in two months.

I have a personal paparazzo.

But I don't have a best friend.

Jesus.

I *am* an asshole.

I hit the door to my building, turn, and glare down at Goldie. "I'm home. You're dismissed."

"Is this really your building, or are you telling me that so I'll leave you alone?"

I punch in the code, blocking it from her view, and the door clicks open. "Follow me and I'll call the police."

Her gaze wavers and goes shiny.

Fuck.

Fuck fuck fuck.

"I was having a nice time. A surprisingly nice time. Thank you for—for everything. If you need—"

I don't wait to hear what else she's about to offer.

I don't want to know.

Not when that face and those eyes and everything else about her say she's about to offer to be my friend.

I have Sweet Pea.

I have rugby.

I have a mission.

I have new teammates to win over, which—fuck me again—has never been what I'm good at, but I'll bloody well try until I'm dead.

That's all I need.

10

Goldie

LEAVING the country is looking better and better by the day.

Why?

Because after a long day of selling a few more things out of my apartment, three client meetings, a welcome video call from the association hosting me in London for the next few months, confirmation that my work visa came through, and paying a very large deposit on the apartment I'm renting in London, all I wanted to do was chill for a few minutes in the wine bar and read part of a book before Odette, Evelyn, and Sheila got here.

Instead, I'm glued to the social media commentary about Fletcher Huxley's mustache accident.

The TikTokers are calling it the *mustache-ident.*

Also, *what is rugby and where do I see Fletcher Huxley play?*

No one's seen him the past two days. He walked into his swanky condo building after our cooking class and hasn't left.

The team's training is unofficial until next week. Can't do

anything official as a team until preseason training starts. Half the guys have other jobs to supplement their income in the off-season because rugby doesn't pay much here.

In the US, it's a *do it for the love* sport, not a *this is how you get rich enough to drive a sports car* sport.

Yet.

I have an inside source in management on the team, and she tells me ticket sales have exploded since Fletcher posted the video himself of his mustache catching on fire and me putting it out with salsa and a towel. They're not selling out the stadium yet, but they've surpassed last year's total ticket sales already.

"Oooh, if it isn't our viral girl!" Evelyn says as she slides into the booth with me. "How's life for Fletcher Huxley's 'Stache Savior?"

I pocket my phone with a sigh. "All three of my clients today asked me some variation of *does he smell nice* and *are you dating him?*"

"And?" Sheila says, sliding into the other side of the booth with Evelyn right on her heels.

"We are *not* dating. That was supposed to be a thank-you-for-letting-me-collapse-on-you dinner that would also piss off Silas enough for him to get out of my love life."

With a side of a fraction of the publicity Fletcher's *actually* getting for the Pounders.

I have overdone my job.

Also, yes, my brother would one thousand percent fly across the Atlantic Ocean to scare away anyone he thought I was dating when I get to London. Even if it meant fines from the team for missing training or even a match.

Me moving overseas for most of his rugby season isn't enough to stop Silas.

"Have you seen Fletcher?" Sheila asks.

I shake my head.

Do I *want* to see him?

A week ago, *gosh, I miss Fletcher Huxley* would not have been a thought I had. It still isn't, but *I should make sure Fletcher's okay* is something that's been swirling.

I could slide into his DMs, but I wouldn't believe a thing he told me.

If he told me anything at all.

He'll show up for training next week.

He wouldn't miss it.

But him showing up for training and acting fine no matter what his face looks like and him *being* fine are not the same. And who knows? By next week, he could've grown a bunch of the 'stache back.

Which should not be my concern. I am not his keeper. I'm not even his friend. And I certainly didn't like the 'stache.

So I've been putting my move first and my clients at a very close second, and pretending for the moment that I have no other cares in the world.

The server stops at our table. "Afternoon, ladies. Just three of you?"

I shake my head, but Evelyn and Sheila nod. "Just the three of us."

"Where's Odette?" I ask.

They share a look.

It's not *guilty*, exactly, but it's not *good* either. This one falls somewhere between *she's holding a bedside vigil for an ex-boyfriend* and *one of her kids had an emergency and she had to fly to Milwaukee to babysit for a couple days.*

Both of which leave a sinking feeling in my stomach, and I hope today's long day is making me misinterpret this.

"We need a few minutes," Evelyn tells the server.

"But let's get started with some of those vegetable rolls," Sheila adds.

"Do I want to know what Odette's up to?" I ask my friends. More importantly, *when will she be back?*

"She's a little under the weather," Evelyn says.

My pulse kicks up. "Like we should be taking her soup under the weather, or we need to go see her in the hospital under the weather?"

"She pulled a muscle in Zumba," Sheila says.

"And re-tweaked her knee getting out of her car at the doctor's office when she pulled in to get the other muscle checked out," Evelyn adds.

"The doctor told her to rest it for a few days. All of it."

"And she knows what happened the last time she didn't listen, so she's following doctor's orders this time."

Evelyn's obsessed with staring at something outside the window. Sheila's concentrating very hard on sipping from her water glass.

Neither one of them is making eye contact.

"She can't come with me to the wedding on Saturday," I say flatly.

"She thinks she can," Sheila says. "She's planning on it. That's why she hasn't told you anything yet."

Evelyn sighs. "But we think you might want to make other plans."

Dammit.

"Are either of you free to—" I start, but they both shake their heads.

"I'm heading up to DC to watch my grandbabies so Oliver and Mika can go to a fancy gala," Sheila says.

"My high school class is having a memorial for our favorite student teacher, and a few of my old friends aren't doing so well." Evelyn frowns at her silverware. "Might be the last time I see them."

"Odette might still be up for it," Sheila adds.

"But we're a little concerned about what might happen if she gets out on the dance floor."

Understandable.

Odette doesn't let anything hold her back.

Which means I might have to go to this wedding alone.

"Is there anything I can do to help her?" I ask.

"She should only be down a few days, and the senior center's filled up a small meal train sign-up already," Sheila says.

"Mostly we wanted to tell you since we don't think she should be on a dance floor," Evelyn says.

A *meal train*?

They're underplaying this, and my heart gives a lurch as I wonder how badly Odette's hurt.

"You *want* me to tell her I've found another date."

Evelyn shrugs. "Even if it's a lie…"

I'm not going to lie to Odette. I'll go check on her myself tomorrow and level with her.

If she's not at club night at the wine bar, and if Evelyn and Sheila are this concerned, she absolutely should not go with me as a pity date to a wedding that I mostly want to go to, but not entirely.

Which means I might have to do this alone.

I've done worse in the past few years.

Like setting a guy's mustache on fire with flaming cheese.

Of the issues facing our group right now, me going to a wedding solo is taking a very distant back seat to making sure that Odette's recovering okay.

"When does she go back to the doctor?" I ask. "If she needs a ride—"

"Don't you worry about a thing," Evelyn says. "Sheila and I have her. You need to worry about your move first."

"And that nice young man's mustache next," Sheila whispers.

London will be amazing.

But the closer it gets, the more I realize how much I'll worry about these three when I'm gone.

"Don't make that face," Evelyn orders me. "We'll be a phone call away, and we'll call often."

"And we'll come join you for parts of your road trip once you're back in the States," Sheila adds.

"You're going to have the best time in London." Evelyn wiggles her painted-on brows. "And you might even meet a proper British hottie to bring home with you."

"But where am I going to find three seasoned ladies to have wine with while they write alternate obituaries for their ex-boyfriends?"

"It's just three months," Sheila says.

"Just three months," Evelyn agrees.

"And it's so good for your career."

"And we are *so proud* of you."

"You've earned this, Goldie."

"No regrets. We forbid it."

The server comes back—which is quite a relief since all of us are getting misty-eyed—and we order our usuals since we still haven't looked at the menu.

I ask what's new with my two friends, both because it's normal and because I don't want to think about how much I'll miss these ladies when I'm in London.

None of their ex-boyfriends have passed since we last had dinner together, so instead, they tell me the various places they've visited in Europe that I should check out during the weekends while I'm doing my residency.

They're so excited for me that I forget I'll miss them, and I start to realize how quickly my three months in London will fly by.

After dinner, I should go home.

Make a few more hard decisions about what I'm keeping and what's going of what's left in my apartment.

When I get back from London, I'm not coming back here.

Not permanently, I mean. Silas is still here. My ladies are still here. I'll visit.

But when I return to the States, I'm embarking on a lifelong dream to see all of North America. I haven't decided where I'll start, but it'll be a fabulous adventure regardless of where the road takes me.

My job is mobile. I can do it from anywhere. My clientele is already mostly scattered around the country, so there won't be much change for them when I'm across the pond. I'll just have to monitor time zones.

I rented a storage unit for my books and a few sentimental keepsakes. My car is going in storage since I'll use it when I get back. I'll keep the basics for a bare-bones kitchen and bedroom, but otherwise, if I can't wear it or eat it, everything is going.

And then I'll write my next book about the experience.

My agent already sold it on spec to the publisher who bought my first two books.

And the other big thing this road trip will do—it'll tell me where I'm supposed to live next.

I love my brother, complicated relationship and all. I love Sheila and Odette and Evelyn. I have a lot of acquaintances and connections around Copper Valley whom I see regularly, but it hasn't been *home* since my breakup with Miller.

London isn't only about my job.

It's about a hard break from being in a community where I haven't totally fit for the past two years.

It's a fresh start.

It's a return to optimism after a couple years of healing.

And it's what I should head home to prepare for.

But instead of doing the responsible thing when Evelyn and Sheila depart, I stay at our table long enough to call Odette and check in on her.

And I hear exactly what Sheila and Evelyn implied.

There's a hint of pain in Odette's voice that suggests she should not be getting out on a dance floor two nights from now, no matter how much she insists she won't let a little pulled muscle and sprained ankle keep her down.

I know she won't.

But she wouldn't have an awful day if she spent it with friends coming in to visit and rewatch *Only Murders in the Building* and *The Good Place* with her for the next week.

I'm not going straight home tonight.

Instead, I'm going to do something else that I may or may not regret later.

11

Goldie

DESPITE WHAT MIGHT APPEAR to be ulterior motives, guilt is my main guide to a condo building a few blocks from my apartment complex.

I wouldn't sweet-talk my way in to any other private building in the city, but at this one, I smile half-airheadedly at an older gentleman and tell him my boyfriend gave me the code to come check on his dog, but I moved and can't remember which numbers go with which codes to which buildings, so he lets me in.

Worked well the other night, too, when I took Fletcher left-overs after class was officially over.

Awkward is my favorite way of describing the rest of that evening after I went back to class, and I'd prefer to forget every bit of it.

Tonight, though, I take myself to the top floor and knock distinctly at condo number 1800.

There's only one other condo on this level. Fletcher definitely has at least a corner, if not most of the floor to himself. Views are probably amazing.

Unlike the US, European rugby players make sports car money. And that's where Fletcher's spent the past dozen or more years. But make no mistake—he didn't buy his sports car.

He got it for free with his endorsement deal.

He doesn't need an extra job to be able to afford swanky digs on the penthouse level of one of the most exclusive condo structures in Copper Valley's warehouse district.

Much like Silas doesn't need an extra job because he's living off of the substantial trust fund our grandparents left us.

I could live off of my half too, but I've been fortunate enough that my passion pays the bills.

I like supporting myself.

Fletcher doesn't answer.

I knock again.

Still no answer, though I hear Sweet Pea bark inside, and I hear a gruff, low voice answer her.

I don't see any obvious cameras in the hallway, there's not a doorbell or a doorbell camera, and I'm angling out of view of the peephole.

He's there.

He doesn't want to see me.

Or possibly anyone, but I'm intentionally hiding so he can't see who I am if he wants to know who's knocking.

I can tell my conscience I did my part in coming to check on him...*or* I can get creative.

See if I can get him to open the door because I'm charming and funny and want to check on someone who feels weirdly like a friend.

I knock one more time and, with my voice as low as I can make it, I call, "Fire marshal. Gas leak check."

Sweet Pea barks with joy inside.

The only other door on this level is all the way down the hall, so I don't think I'm disturbing them. But I still hope Sweet Pea isn't the kind of dog neighbor that causes problems.

She's too cute.

And I get the feeling Fletcher would probably rather piss off his neighbors so they move and he can have the whole floor for peace instead of worrying about irritating his neighbors.

And the door still doesn't open.

Fine.

Fine.

He doesn't want to see me.

I shove away from the wall and head toward the elevator as the distinct sound of a lock turning clicks through the hallway.

And a moment later, I'm staring at a very irritated Fletcher Huxley.

I think.

He doesn't...look...exactly like Fletcher.

His eyes are the same.

Nose the same.

Jaw the same.

But the complete and utter lack of a mustache in that area between his upper lip and nose is making his face sit differently.

I make a noise somewhere between a gasp and a pig squeal, and *I don't know why.*

Okay, fine. I know why.

I know exactly why.

He's *hot.*

Like, fresh lava had a torrid love affair with molten steel that resulted in a magical new kind of clay that a Greek god slapped on a pottery wheel to sculpt Fletcher Huxley while angels played Marvin Gaye's "Let's Get It On" on flutes and harps and an electric guitar.

"Put it back," I finally say.

He rolls his eyes, grabs my arm, and hauls me into his condo. "What do you want?"

I shield my eyes. "To see if you're okay."

"I'm bloody brilliant. Why are you—what the fuck's wrong with you? Quit hiding your eyes."

"You need the mustache back."

Silence is my only reply.

There's a lot of silence going around when I'm with Fletcher since his 'stache died a premature death.

I part two fingers and risk a glance at his face.

Holy fucking *hellhounds.*

Did his dark hair always have that hint of curl? Was his forehead always sloped that way over his brow? Were his eyes always that exact emerald shade of green?

Why did taking off the 'stache make him so hot?

He glares at me before leaving me in the foyer to stroll deeper into the condo. "First you hate it, then you want it back. Make up your fucking mind."

"Do you know that if you walked out your door like that right now, six women in a four-block radius would spontaneously ovulate off-cycle because you're unfortunately that attractive?"

"Yes."

Yes.

The absolute *ego* in that one word actually cracks me up.

"Why the fuck do you think I wear it?" he adds on a grumble.

"It never would've crossed my mind that it was your shield against women throwing their panties at you. Never. Wow. This is —this is crazy."

"Are you done?"

"No."

"Have you had dinner?"

"I ate at the wine bar with my besties. Are you okay? Honestly? I thought maybe some of it could be shaved—saved. *Saved.*"

His condo is nice. Gray tones in the carpet. White furniture that looks large and fluffy enough to support his tall, solid frame. Colorful abstract original paintings beneath spotlights, plus one of Sweet Pea in sunglasses and a pearl necklace that I can't stare at too long or I'll start giggling. Kitchen tucked around a corner with black steel appliances, white marble countertops, and black cabinets. Open to the living room and its wall of windows overlooking the city, and equally accessible to the dining room with its modern chandelier over the shiny black dining table. Out the floor-to-ceiling windows, daylight is fading. I still spot Reynolds Park and Duggan Field, where the Fireballs play, off in the distance, and the Blue Ridge Mountains farther beyond.

There's snow all around the city from yesterday's weather too.

It's lovely.

Also, I could fit three of my apartments in his kitchen, living room, and dining room, which also overlooks the city.

He slides his phone onto the countertop, open to a picture, and I belatedly realize I've been staring so much at his face that I missed that he's carrying Sweet Pea in the sling again.

At home.

He carries his dog in her sling at home.

She's sniffing at me, but she's also rolling her eyes back in utter bliss every time he scratches her head.

I glance down at the picture on his phone, and I shriek again.

Then apologize. "Sorry. That was—"

"The same noise I made."

Fletcher with a mustache is noteworthy.

Fletcher clean-shaven is a gloriously gorgeous threat to people trying to safely cross streets. Good thing he wasn't clean-shaven when everyone was handling knives at cooking class the other night.

I swipe right a few pictures and stifle more gasps and shrieks.

Fletcher with anything between the full-on overgrown witch's broom 'stache and no facial hair at all is terrifying.

I swallow the *you should not do the pencil 'stache or the Charlie Chaplin 'stache or the I-don't-even-know-what-that-other-one-was 'stache*, and I just look at him.

"I couldn't make it even," he says. "So it had to go."

I swallow one more time and wish I'd had another glass of wine before coming here. "I truly am sorry. I know it was a—a part of who you are."

"It'll grow back."

"Have you thought about the full beard?"

"Bad idea."

Because it itches? Because it makes him look like a scary recluse who's come in from six months solo in the mountains outside of the city for his biannual snack of small children and city rats?

Or because he's even hotter with the full beard?

I don't want to ask so instead slide onto one of the round black stools at the high counter between his kitchen and the dining room as he plops a mason jar of water in front of me. "I heard you skipped optional conditioning today."

"Pissed."

"Mad-pissed or drunk-pissed?"

"Drunk."

"Awesome." Now that he mentions it, he does smell a little unfortunate. "I was…surprised…that you posted the video the other night."

"Being a whiny-ass baby doesn't sell tickets."

"Worked well."

"Of course it did."

He unstraps Sweet Pea and sets her on the kitchen floor, then refills her food dish on the tile near the fridge.

UNTIL IT WAS LOVE

Her little tail wags a thousand miles a minute while she digs into her dinner. It is *so* cute.

I've always wanted a dog, but I've always wanted to travel the world more. And I can't yet afford a private jet where my dog could travel in style with me, and I probably wouldn't get a private jet even if I *could* afford it, so...no dog.

Maybe after I finish my tour of North America and decide where I want to settle.

If I want to settle.

Maybe I'm meant to roam the world for the rest of my days.

"I'm glad something good came out of the other night," I tell Fletcher.

He eyes me.

Disappears into the fridge.

Comes back out with a carton of hummus and a package of snack-size Gouda slices, which he tosses onto the counter in front of me.

He tears open a bag of pita chips and drops them on the counter too.

Probably smashed half of them.

I don't much care.

There's Gouda.

I'm in for Gouda all by itself. It's not gourmet Gouda, but *it's Gouda*, so who cares? And this is Fletcher, so I don't worry about being polite as I stuff my face with three slices at once.

"I'm sorry I was an ass," he mutters.

I blink with a mouthful of cheese, and a dribble of drool slips out between my lips as I realize I'm gawking. "Wha are *oo* owwy fo?" I ask.

He pinches his lips together briefly, but I see the softening of his eyes that suggests he's trying not to smile.

Thank fuck.

I need Fletcher to *not* smile at me while his face is in this temporary hot stage.

Especially since I might be here to offer him an opportunity that would be a favor to me.

"Never mind. Not sorry," he says. "You ruined my life. The cheese is poisoned."

I gulp it down. "We all have to go sometime. Wait. You mean *I'll be chained to my toilet* poisoned, or *call my niece and tell her I love her one last time* poisoned? Both definitions of *go* fit there."

"How are you so funny and your brother is such an ass?"

"I didn't leave any funny genes for him. I was in that womb like, *funny gene! It's all mine! Screw any future siblings! Oooh, another funny gene! Grab that one too!* You know. The normal way."

Fletcher Huxley *apologized* to me. That's unexpected.

And nice.

He digs into the hummus with his finger, and I think he's once again trying to stifle a smile.

I take another slice of cheese. Only one this time in case he says something else unexpected, such as *your brother and I have called a truce*. "How long have you had Sweet Pea?" I ask him.

Safe topic to ease him into what I need to ask next.

Probably.

"Three years."

"Did she find you, or did you find her?"

"She found me."

"Aww."

He rolls his eyes.

"She's my favorite thing about you."

"Same."

"If you ever need a dog sitter, let me know. A friend of a friend's husband's cousin dog-sat all through college here, and she still does on occasion for extra cash. Very discreet. You wouldn't be her first pro athlete client."

UNTIL IT WAS LOVE

He nods and takes another swipe of hummus with his finger.

Such a bachelor. I wonder if he'd be eating cucumbers or carrots with it too if I weren't here. Gnawing right off the end of the vegetable without cutting it.

Probably not, I decide.

Mostly because I think he'd do that with me here if he were going to do it.

"So, why rugby?" I'm here. I'm curious. I love people's stories. Wouldn't be good at my job if I didn't.

And yes, I'm still warming him up.

He eyes me while he licks his finger, which does something it's not supposed to do to my lady regions and simultaneously makes me glad I'm leaving the country in barely over two weeks.

"I'm good at it," he answers.

"How old were you when you started playing?"

"Six."

"That's young. Mom and Dad had to practically create a rugby league for Silas to play in when he said he was interested. Where were you?"

"Australia."

I tilt my head.

Every now and again, I get a hint of a foreign accent, and then there are the Britishisms he sprinkles into his speech, but I assumed he picked that up after playing in the UK for the past decade-plus. Otherwise, he sounds as American as I do.

"You're Australian?"

"Old man was stationed there with the military. Which is clearly spelled out for anyone who reads my bio."

I make a face. "Silas's bio says he was born on the pitch with a rugby ball in hand. I don't put a lot of stock in bios."

"That work out for you?"

"Not reading bios?"

"No. Using me to piss off your brother."

I grin. "Oh, that. To be determined. He hasn't talked to me since I pulled a mom move on him after I got back to Rosalia's the other night and actually made him feel guilty."

"You two often give each other the silent treatment?"

"Looking for hints on how to handle him in the locker room?"

"Don't want to handle him. Want him gone."

"His kid's here and going exactly nowhere else. He'll push right up to the line, but he won't do anything to get traded or kicked out of the league. He actually gave up the opportunity to play in France when he found out Brittany was pregnant."

He stares at me as if he's debating if he wants to make a comment about my brother polluting the gene pool, or if he wants to ask management if he can get traded somewhere else instead.

Or possibly he wants to talk about how my brother does occasionally play dirty. I've seen some of his tackles and they're not always legal.

Fletcher isn't the first teammate who hasn't appreciated my brother.

And he wouldn't be the first to question if Hallie is the real reason why Silas isn't playing in France today.

There's reasonable doubt as to if Silas could've made it long-term there.

I crunch loudly into a pita chip.

Plain salt. My favorite. "So, rugby from childhood. Why Copper Valley? You could've made a deal with any team in the league."

He took a massive pay cut coming here. He also has more meetings with the team brass than Silas thinks is appropriate. And while I don't *know*-know Fletcher, there's something about him that tells me Copper Valley is a stepping stone for him, even with there only being a dozen or so teams in the whole league right now.

Which is fascinating, since I *have* read his bio and a few articles about him—though I clearly missed the part about him first learning rugby in Australia and being a military brat—and his game isn't what it once was.

He's in his mid-thirties, which isn't ancient for the sport by any means, but he's not getting any younger either.

"Freshest crowd," is all he'll give me.

Makes sense. Our hockey team is pretty stellar. Won the championship a couple times in the past ten years and haven't missed the playoffs in all that time either. Our baseball team went from the worst in their league to champions under new ownership a few years ago too. And our women's soccer team—well.

They're good.

That's all I generally say about that.

"You planning to go into coaching when you retire?" I ask.

"Not retiring."

"Oo-kay."

He gives me half a glare that causes half a hot flash in my chest.

And that means it's either time to go or to ask what I'm still debating if I want to ask.

I've verified he's alive.

I've verified he's not a danger to himself or to his dog.

"You ever want to talk about what happens to your life when your body gives out and robs you of the sport you love, I'm your girl. Got some experience there." I take three more pieces of cheese while I silently tell myself this isn't a *favor*. It's an opportunity. "Random question that means absolutely nothing—how much longer are you planning on hiding in here?"

He strokes his freshly shaved upper lip, his eyes tracking me as I slide a piece of cheese into my mouth like he's been suspicious that I had ulterior motives for coming here and has been vindicated. "Should be grown back enough when the preseason starts next week."

I lift a brow. "Past the pencil and world dictator 'stache point?"

"Might do the full beard. Sell more tickets."

Now I'm stifling a smile.

Fletcher's annoying. His ego is also weirdly charming in its own way.

Which I will *not* be telling him.

Although he'll probably guess it anyway when I blurt out what's coming next. "You know the best way to tap into the sports market here is to make friends with the other athletes around town?"

"My PR guru is still teaching me not to grunt my name when I introduce myself at parties."

"I'm going to a party on Saturday that'll have a lot of professional sportsers at it."

He licks another scoop of hummus off his finger, then folds his thick tatted arms over his thicker chest and stares at me.

I resist the urge to tug my shirt away from my chest and fan myself with it.

Freaking attractive face.

"You could possibly come with me and meet them. Maybe. I technically already have a date, but she might have to cancel."

"You mean you might ask one of your ancient friends to not go with you so that you can take me to a party that's not actually a *party* for some reason you're not telling me? Will your brother be there?"

"My *life-seasoned* friend who was going to go with me to the Scorned's head coach's daughter's wedding reception sprained her knee and should stay off of it."

"There are these things called wheelchairs…"

"You clearly haven't fully met Odette. There aren't enough straps in the world to keep her in a wheelchair when 'YMCA' and anything by Beyoncé comes on over the speakers at a wedding reception. And don't ask what would happen if they decided to do the hokey pokey."

Points to Fletcher. He is *once again* stifling a smile.

"She and Evelyn and Sheila will still be here when I leave for Europe," I add. "I'll bet they'd adopt you. You'd love them. They write fake obituaries that are totally *National Enquirer*-worthy for their ex-boyfriends."

"You're friends with the women's soccer coach?" he says.

I strangely love our conversations. Neither of us ever answers the other, and that says *so much* about us.

But it's time to level with him. "She was a massive supporter in helping me find my path when it became clear that soccer wasn't in my future. We've kept in touch. I call her sometimes when I hear about school-age teams in the area who could use a morale boost and visit from the pro team, and she calls me when one of her players or staff could use a little support with big life or career decisions."

"So this is a big wedding reception."

"Not the biggest Copper Valley's ever seen, but it'll be well-attended by coaches and athletes from all of the major teams here. Plus a few other local celebrities."

"And your brother will be there and you get the joy of watching him see us together again."

"My brother will not be there."

He stares, a silent question of who *will* be there.

I don't squirm.

I have a full-on hot flash again.

Fletcher definitely needs to regrow the 'stache.

Which he can't do before Saturday. Saturday, I'll probably get rugged mountain man stubble if he can truly grow back the entire 'stache before the preseason starts next week.

That would absolutely do.

He shifts and turns the stare into a glare.

I casually take a bite of cheese and stare back.

Sweet Pea looks at me and growls.

And that breaks me.

Not leveling with Fletcher? Whatever.

His dog feeling betrayed?

I absolutely crack. "My last serious ex-boyfriend will also be there," I say around the cheese, hoping he doesn't understand me.

"And there we have it," he mutters.

"I'm happy to go by myself," I say primly, which is something I'm still working on convincing myself is true, "but given who else will be there from the professional sports world, and the fact that I still feel bad about the flaming cheese thing, I thought I'd offer you the chance to meet some people who could more easily help you reach your goals. I'm very popular around here, even though I don't like to say it out loud. You'd get cred for being with me."

"Your ex. Details."

"We were together almost three years and he dumped me because I cared more about my career than I did about him." That's the sanitized version, but it's all I'm giving him.

He doesn't need anything else.

He's watching me as though he's waiting for the rest of the story of a three-year relationship that crashes and burns over a job.

"Fine," he finally says.

"Don't get too excited there, buckaroo."

"But I choose my own facial hair."

"I'm leaving the entire country in a little over two weeks. What you do will impact you far longer than it'll impact me." I slide off of my stool. "I'll message you the details, including some people who should be there that you'll want to meet."

He tracks me with a heavy gaze while I snag one last piece of cheese.

"Got what you wanted, so now you're taking off?" he says.

"Busy times. And this is *mutually beneficial.*"

"You can stay if you want."

"Can't, but thank you."

"Date with another geriatric hottie?" he asks.

"More like a breakup. Me and my pots and pans. Which *are* geriatric, honestly. We're deciding who stays and who goes." I squat and scratch Sweet Pea's head as she waddles her adorable little body over to my feet.

She rolls over and shows me her long belly, so I give that all the rubs too. "Who's the cutest widdle puppy ever? Is it Sweet Pea? Is it? Awww, you're so sweet."

Her tongue lolls out and she gazes at me like I personally invented Snausages.

"Good girl. Don't take any crap from this guy, okay?"

She barks once in agreement.

And I head home.

Fletcher's offer of *you can stay if you want* has too many shades of *I could use a friend*, and it's doing something worse than giving me hot flashes.

It's making me wonder how lonely he is.

How much he might need a friend. It's hard being the new guy, and while I don't make a habit of hanging out with Silas and his teammates, I picked up some vibes at cooking school.

Fletcher's not easily fitting in.

I'm leaving in two weeks. I can introduce him to some other potential friends—friends who are his age, with his level of experience—but I don't have time to *be* that friend.

Especially when he looks like *that* without his mustache.

12

Fletcher

I HATE SUITS.

Reminds me of my old man. Formal military dinners. Changes of command. Promotions. Funerals.

All of the bad things.

But more today?

I hate *itching*.

And I'm itching like a mofo who bathed in itch powder.

It's not the suit though. It's the bloody *rash*.

From the middle of my chest around to my ass, I have what any normal person would think was a poison ivy rash.

It's not.

It's worse.

It's what happens when I eat mango, and *I ate fucking mango*.

This is my own damn fault.

I didn't ask what was in the salsa at the flaming cheese mustache murder class.

And now I'm knocking on Goldie's apartment door thirty minutes before the wedding with my ass itching because I didn't bathe thoroughly enough in calamine lotion and I have the smell of calamine lotion stuck in my nose and the good anti-itch pills I got in Europe the last time I had an allergic reaction to mango aren't available over the counter here.

Fuck if I'm going to urgent care to have some doctor tell me I shouldn't roll around naked in the woods.

That was a bloody fun trip to the doctor on base with my old man when I was seventeen. *Sir, your son has poison ivy. On his penis. If you're not supplying condoms, I strongly recommend it.*

I'm part of a miniscule part of the population that experiences a two to three-day delay from allergen exposure to rash. So it took two more trips to the doctor for increasingly worse breakouts—which came with more lectures on keeping it in my pants and staying out of nature—before we figured out that I was sensitive to the mango my sister was obsessed with eating as often as possible.

Today, I have a patch of mango rash on my face too, but since I have facial hair that grows like I'm a Yeti, you can't see it.

Except that also means I can't *treat* it.

Deep breaths.

Deep breath in. Deep breath out.

Goldie flings open her apartment door. She's wearing a tight, deep-red, knee-length dress that would make her look like a bleeding mermaid if it went to her feet, with a shimmery gold shawl twisted around her shoulders. She stands there blocking my view of her apartment, dancing into her strappy heels, her dark hair mostly swept up in some fancy twist-knot thing, with lightly curled tendrils swinging around her face.

Her gaze lands on mine, and there it is again—that look that says *quit being so damn hot.*

But she recovers quickly and smiles what seems to be an honest smile. "Hey! Hi. You look nice. Which you undoubtedly know."

My dick goes hard as a rock and unfortunately pulls my pants tighter across my ass where the bloody rash is.

Last time I accidentally ate mango, I got the rash across my feet and up my left calf.

Time before, it was all over my arms and neck.

This time, it's right where every boner I'll pop for the next three to five days will make my pants rub my rash wrong.

"Fletcher?"

"I hate suits."

She grins, and *fuck me*.

Women shouldn't be allowed to wear makeup and do their hair fancy and wear dresses that highlight every last curve and accentuate them with shawl-wrap things that make their already golden eyes sparkle and shimmer even more.

I should've asked for details about her ex.

This is a revenge dress.

This is one hundred and eighty million percent a revenge dress.

And I'm supposed to walk around Copper Valley's botanical gardens with her, at a bloody wedding reception, for *hours*, as her *date*.

And likely end the night without any benefits.

"Well, you look absolutely fabulous in it," she says. "I spent an extra hour meditating to find my zen place in case you looked this good so I wouldn't make a fool of myself. Is it working?"

I could push her back into her apartment, peel that dress off her, and make her come in four-point-three minutes, except the minute I got naked, she'd shriek in horror at the sight of my rash.

Bloody hell.

I grunt in response to the question. It's all I've got.

"Let me grab my keys, and I'm ready." She leaves the door open as she retreats into her apartment, so I take the opportunity to let myself in.

Maybe I'll find she has awful artwork or pink shag carpets or a body in her freezer.

Those would all help with the boner situation.

Instead, I find wood floors, a modest living room with a single fluffy pink chair, three shelves overflowing with books, a small kitchen devoid of appliances or crocks full of cooking utensils or flour, and a glimpse into a bedroom where there's a mattress on the floor, neatly made with a homemade quilt, piles and piles of books like she's gotten rid of the bookshelves in there already, stacks of boxes, and cords on the floor for a computer and her phone.

She's moving.

And she's nearly ready.

She strides out of her bedroom, black peacoat in one hand, keys and her phone in the other. "Still up for this?"

I'm *up* all right. "Suffered worse."

"I promise to introduce you to every athlete or athlete-adjacent person I spot, even if I don't already know them. There are a lot who've been playing for at least ten years. I think you'll get along well with them."

I grunt once again.

She leads me out of her apartment and double-checks that it's locked behind us, then we head for the elevator.

And then she slides me a look that says *hello, Mr. Grumpy Pants.* "Have to ask. Is it the suit, the wedding reception, or going with me? I won't be offended by any answer."

It's not her.

She's unexpectedly enjoyable as a human being.

Even when she's playing me for her own reasons.

Possibly even more then.

And that says all there is to say about why I don't do relationships anymore.

"All of the above," I tell her.

She smiles again as the elevator doors close, and I get the feeling she knows I'm lying. "I *did* finally read your bio. The juicy one on Wikipedia."

"I read yours too. It was boring."

"Did you have big weddings when you got married?"

"Did you take a pill to give you big balls tonight?"

The woman's eyes are *dancing* in absolute merriment.

Ex-boyfriend must not have been that bad.

Either that, or she has some plans to use me for an even bigger revenge scheme than I'm aware of.

I look at the elevator doors. We're only three floors up, but the thing's slow as vegemite on an ice luge.

Which are two things that do not go together, in case you were wondering.

"First one was as big as we could afford. Second one was a booze-fest on a yacht she borrowed from some lady billionaire friend."

"Six months after your divorce," she muses.

We aren't discussing what I did when I was only old enough to legally drink because I'd moved to Europe. "I don't have to let you inside my car."

She slips her hand into my elbow and squeezes. "I would've done the same after Miller, but Silas found out I had a date and set my new boyfriend's shoes on fire. He broke up with me before I could propose. Probably for the best since the shoe thing happened about ten days after I met him and I was already ring shopping."

The elevator door dings, and we step out into the small lobby.

My car's at the curb, technically parked illegally, and I don't care. I'd care if it got towed, mostly for the inconvenience of it, but I care more that my chest is itching and I have to sit on my ass to drive us to the botanical gardens.

Where I will *not* be eating anything if it's not a solid slab of meat or a raw vegetable that is clearly not mango.

Goldie eyes my Bentley. "You know you could've bought an entire rugby team with what you paid for that thing?"

"Thought about it, but being carried to a wedding reception by an entire rugby team would've looked awkward."

She snort-laughs at that, but then freezes and looks at me while I open the car door for her. "Did you seriously buy this just for tonight?"

"No."

She blows out a breath. "I didn't think you did, but also..." She gestures to me as if to say *you're Fletcher Huxley and you do crazy weird over-the-top shit sometimes.*

"Thank you."

She stifles another smile and climbs into my ride.

It's sweet. It's fast. It's pompous. It purrs.

And I traded in my Ferrari for it this morning because appearances are everything.

Same reason I'm not giving in to the urge to scratch my ass.

Although, I'd get more visibility for getting caught scratching my ass than for getting into a luxury car.

Could've driven my Range Rover or my Maserati instead, but the Bentley makes a better statement for a wedding reception.

I get in the driver's seat, crank the engine, listen to that beautiful purr, and smile as I check my mirror before pulling out into traffic.

Goldie's stroking the seat. And the dash. And eyeballing the screen. And me. "Thank you. Again. For coming with me tonight."

Once more, the best I can do is grunt.

But this time, it's because there's something in her voice that says she's faking her confidence.

I slide a glance at her, but she has her smile plastered on again while she keeps stroking the buttery leather of the seat. "There are at least a dozen high-profile athletes and recently retired athletes coming who are still active with their old teams or around the community. It'll be good for you to meet them. And that's on top of probably a third of the Scorned. Coach Elizabeth invited half the city."

I grunt again.

She pauses stroking and mentally stripping my car to look at me. "Do you go to a lot of weddings?"

"No."

"Do you have an opinion on weddings?"

"Yep."

"Any chance you'd care to talk out those feelings before we get there?"

"My feelings are fine."

"What's the last wedding you went to?"

"We're only going to the reception."

"What's the last *wedding reception* you went to?"

"My sister's."

"You have a sister?"

I slide a glance at her as I slow for traffic.

She's grinning again.

Makes her eyes pop like gold nuggets hiding in a stream when they're hit just right with sunlight.

I knew she was pretty.

I know why I'm going tonight.

I know I've got this. All of it.

Except I don't.

Fucking around with taking an asshole teammate's sister on a date or two to make a point is one thing.

Liking her is something entirely different.

13

Goldie

IT'S BEEN WELL over a year since the last time I visited the botanical gardens. I'm struck with wondering why I haven't been here more often—especially on days I have no reason to have nerves eating my stomach—the minute we step inside.

The massive greenhouse is host to tropical plants and birds and waterfall structures, transporting us worlds away from Copper Valley's winter. I force a smile and point at my favorite trees and random brightly colored birds flying around as we wander through the main exhibit toward the banquet hall. Fletcher offers me his arm like his military father drilled manners into his head, and if it weren't for the reason I wanted a date tonight, this might be the most comfortable date I've been on in years.

Not that this is a date.

It's two unlikely sort-of-friends mutually benefitting from what could've been awkward if either of us had come alone.

Plus, *holy hell.*

Fletcher in a suit with four days' worth of stubble?

If I was going for a *fuck you, I can do better* date, I've nailed it.

We turn a corner, and I squeeze his arm as I spot someone familiar. "That's Luca Rossi," I whisper. "He's a veteran on the Fireballs baseball team. You might recognize him from Kangapoo shampoo commercials. His partner, Henri—that's her next to him —writes romance novels, and if you insult her, he'll work overtime to get you blacklisted in the sports community here. Actually, that probably applies to every athlete I introduce you to with a spouse or partner."

"So I shouldn't insult either of the brides tonight?"

"I seem to recall you have a way of sticking your foot in your mouth around women..."

"Only women with whiny-ass baby brothers."

I actually smile a real smile.

Didn't think that would be possible tonight.

I don't *have* nerves. Tonight, I *am* a nerve. A very agitated nerve.

Hot as Fletcher might be, which is exactly what you want in a *fuck you* date, Odette would be fun.

A massive distraction.

Also, she can put a person in their place with a smile and a phrase that doesn't hit you until you've moved on to talking to the next person, which is a good skill in a wingperson for a night like tonight.

Henri spots us and waves. I wave back. I met her before I met Luca—she was signing her vampire romance novels at my favorite local bookstore that's also hosted me for signing my two books.

And then Luca looks at us, tosses his glorious silky brown locks, and smiles too. "Huxley. Didn't realize you were coming tonight. How do you know Goldie, and do I have to make a call to my favorite people and tell them to bring their favorite shovels?"

"You know him?" I whisper to Fletcher.

He lifts a shoulder in answer, then shakes Luca's hand. "I passed out on her at a blood drive, so I'm paying my penance by being her date to things like this."

Henri's eyes go wide, and if you've known Henri for any longer than five minutes, you know she's equal parts horrified and intrigued.

"What's the vampire equivalent of giving blood?" I murmur to her while I hug her in greeting. It's been several months since I've seen her, but Henri is nothing if not a hugger.

She laughs. "Give me five minutes, and I'll have my next book planned. That's an epic meet-cute."

"Not the first time we met. He's on the Pounders with my brother."

"Oh!" She smiles at Luca. "*This* is the guy you were telling me about last week."

Last week?

I eye Fletcher again while Luca hugs me too.

Fletcher stares at—actually, he could be staring at anything in the tropical rainforest inside this greenhouse. What he's *not* doing is making eye contact with me.

And I realize this could've been my worst idea ever.

Is he playing me? Is this vengeance for the mustache? Is he the worst person I could've asked to be my date on the night I face not only Miller again, but also all of the friends he got in our breakup?

"How's packing?" Luca asks me.

I catch myself before I start gnawing on a fingernail, which is something I haven't done in years. "Nearly done except for the part where all that's left are the things that I should get rid of but *can't.*"

"Like what?" Henri asks.

"Mostly my books, but also, I have this shark blanket that's completely impractical but it basically swallows me whole. Your arms go into his lower jaw and his upper jaw is over your head, so when someone annoys you, you can pretend to chomp them."

I demonstrate.

Henri's eyes go wide with excitement. *"No."*

"Yep."

My favorite thing about all of the people I sometimes hang out with in Copper Valley?

They *also* think shark blankets are cool.

"I can hold on to it for you," Henri says. "And I'll write your name in it and wash it and give it back the next time you're here. Promise."

Luca's sneaking a look at his phone.

Probably looking to see if he can order Henri one of her own, along with matching ones for their cat and baby.

"It's likely going into my storage unit, but thank you," I say.

"Quit blocking the path, assholes," a male voice says behind us, followed quickly by a woman's *"Nicholas Murphy, you said you'd be nice."*

We all turn, and before I can say *Fletcher, meet Nick Murphy, retired goaltender for the Thrusters,* the two men are shaking hands.

They, too, have clearly already met.

I snap my jaw shut and remind myself to smile at Kami, Nick's wife. She's a veterinarian and always has the best stories.

Sometimes about her own pets, sometimes about clients' pets, and sometimes about Nick himself.

I met Nick through the Thrusters' retirement assistance program. I'm on the list of life coaches that they recommend to help aging athletes figure out what they want to do with their lives post-sports.

And I'm on that list because Coach Elizabeth recommended me.

While I can't say I played for ten or fifteen years like a lot of the men and women I do short-term coaching with around town, I can one hundred percent relate to feeling lost after having the one thing you've loved taken from you.

114

"You doing okay?" Kami whispers to me while we hug each other in greeting.

"With the move? Yep."

"With *being here*."

Nick fell on the *I'm going to retire and do nothing but dote on my wife with all of my free time* end of the big dreams and goals spectrum, but it turned out he needed a little more to fill his days.

Kami called me on his behalf, asked me to pretend to be a new friend and come over for dinner to see if I could help him find a way to keep hockey in his life, since caring for their chickens and cows wasn't quite as satisfying as he'd hoped it would be. And also because he has a mischievous streak that doesn't play well with too much free time.

We became real friends, I made a few suggestions and calls pro bono, and then ended up in Kami's office asking her if there were animal therapies she could do on me for a broken heart.

I'm pretty sure Nick doesn't know that.

If he did, my ex wouldn't be attending this wedding tonight.

See again, Nick doesn't do well with time on his hands.

But also—I haven't seen these two in a few months either.

"I'm *great*," I tell Kami, making myself concentrate on the parts of that statement that are true. "I'm off to live my dreams in London in two weeks, and I found some arm candy in the meantime."

She slides a look at Fletcher, Nick and Luca, who are all talking like old friends while Henri squats low in her dress to take a picture of one of the placards amidst the ground foliage. Research, most likely.

"Nick came home after one of his office days last week and told me he was investing in the rugby league," she murmurs. "It seems your date's been making the rounds to all of the teams looking to build fan support here, with a plan of how to do it across the entire league."

Fletcher knows these people.

He already knows these people.

And if he's already been to talk to active players and staff members for the Thrusters and the Fireballs, who else has he talked to?

He agreed to come when I dangled networking.

But if he already knows the first two people I've introduced him to, he probably knows more people across the Copper Valley sports industry than I do.

Which begs the question, is he here to see them again, or is he here for me?

Or is my blossoming suspicion that I'm about to pay for burning off his mustache something I should've thought about more thoroughly before I proposed this date thing?

"Goldie?" Kami says softly. "You okay?"

I shake my head, then smile. "Yes. Yes. Of course."

"I can't believe I'm about to say this," Henri announces as she rises, "but Nick was right. We should keep walking if we want good seats."

"It's not assigned seating?" Kami says.

"It probably is, and that means people will be switching, and I want to make sure we don't get stuck on the wrong side of a seat swap."

All of us—even Fletcher—grimace at that.

Luca takes Henri's hand and leads.

"Hope you're getting more than eye candy out of this," Kami whispers, then she links her hand in Nick's and they stroll down the path behind Henri and Luca.

I eye Fletcher. "Why are you here?"

"Networking." He flexes his left shoulder, and I swear he also squeezes his ass cheeks.

There's something about his posture that says *I'm squeezing my ass cheeks.*

116

"You already know everyone you want to know from the baseball and hockey teams."

"Doesn't hurt to see them again with a stamp of approval from their favorite life coach."

"How do you know *I* know them and wasn't blowing smoke?"

"Research." He offers me his arm again, rolling his shoulder and shifting his weight oddly once more. "Let's go before a bird shits on one of us."

14

Fletcher

WHY AM I HERE?

I shouldn't be here. I hate weddings. I hate networking. I hate wearing a suit. I hate wearing a suit more when my ass is getting itchier by the minute.

I hate it so much that I told Shade to take the night off instead of following me here for publicity shots.

I hate losing most though, so I'm here, at a wedding, networking in pursuit of my ultimate goal.

And being Goldie's shield if her knob of an ex tries anything.

Fine.

Fine.

I'm here because Goldie isn't the type of woman to ask for a date to a wedding so that she doesn't have to be alone if her ex sees her.

She built her own business. She handles Silas all the time. She's moving to London solo as the featured guest of a prominent organization.

If she wants a date to a wedding because her ex will be here, then that ex is the biggest shit pile in the history of dung.

If I weren't here, I would've sat at home with Sweet Pea all night wondering if Goldie was having a breakdown in a bathroom if her ex showed up with a new girlfriend. Or wife. Or wife and baby.

If she still loves him.

If she asked me only as a pawn to make a cock-up jealous. A cock-up who can't possibly deserve her if he's her ex.

Not that I mind being a pawn.

I'm a fucking good pawn and I know it.

"You want a drink?" I ask her when we've found our table and I've verified that her facial expression doesn't say *fuck me, my ex and his wife and their three kids and their rescue dog and cat that does tricks and emotional support parrot are also sitting with us.*

This is nothing like any banquet hall I've ever seen, likely because I tend to decline invitations to shit like this. Lush green plants are growing around the edges and vines hang from the ceiling. Tables line wider walkways between flower gardens. We're still in danger of bird shit from the tropical birds squawking and chirping overhead. The head table is in front of a man-made rock waterfall, and the dance floor—what I assume is the dance floor, based on the band setup—is a triangular section of the room carved out between more rock formations and flower beds.

The tables are draped in black linens and a different tropical plant is the centerpiece on each.

The baseball players are at one table. Hockey guys at another. I don't know all of the women's soccer team players yet, but there are enough of them that they're scattered around the room, slowly making their way to seats as more guests arrive from the main part of the indoor gardens.

And the sight of all of the plants and the knowledge that they produce pollen is making my ass itch even worse.

Which I am not scratching.

And not because I don't want to.

What I *want* to do is go swimming in a vat of baking soda or oatmeal water.

Instead, I'm here, offering to be the drink boy.

"A drink would be fabulous, thank you." Goldie smiles at me. "A rosé, please. And if you don't mind, I see someone that I—"

She cuts herself off as she's turning away, clearly already on her way to say hi to her friend, but she freezes as she makes eye contact with a woman walking past our table.

The woman freezes too, then smiles the most uncomfortable smile a human being can actually smile. "Oh. Hey, Goldie. I didn't expect to see you here."

Goldie's posture has gone stiffer than the fine I got once for fighting a wanker from Yorkham when he shoved my teammate. But just as fast, her shoulders go back to resting position, her hands unclench, and her ass relaxes under that tight dress too. She pastes on a smile as fake as the other woman's is uncomfortable and nods regally. "Stefanie. So good to see you. How's your off-season going?"

Number thirty-four.

That's number thirty-four from Goldie's college team. Plays for the Scorned now.

And she's looking a little scorned as she smiles with obvious embarrassment back at Goldie. "Good. It's good. Lots of training. A little vacation."

"That sounds lovely. I saw your last game last year. Tough loss, but you were brilliant."

"I wasn't, but thank you."

"Oh! Stefanie, this is Fletcher Huxley, my—my date. He left the UK Premiere Rugby League to add his support to kick-starting the sport here. Fletcher, have you met Stefanie Woolsley?"

I shake the woman's hand with my right hand while Goldie grabs onto my left hand and squeezes.

Hard.

I squeeze back.

Not hard. Just *I got you.*

"So you're teammates with Silas?" Stefanie asks me.

"Unfortunately," slips out of my mouth before I can stop it.

She laughs. Half winces like this is *I'm seeing the dentist when I haven't flossed in years* levels of unpleasant. Looks over her shoulder. Looks back at us with a smile so pained that if I passed her on the street, I'd suggest popping into the nearest drugstore for the good stuff.

"Nice to see you. We should catch up and have coffee soon."

Goldie fake-smiles right back. "I'll check my calendar."

Stefanie scurries off on the pretense of saying hi to a teammate, and I glance at Goldie again.

"So, rosé," she says. "That would be excellent."

I look back at Stefanie, then at Goldie again. "What happened?" I ask, ignoring every instinct in my body screaming for me to pick a plant—any plant—and hang out behind it for the rest of the evening.

Full truth—I *want* to be in a concrete box without anything that produces pollens or allergens. After swimming in baking soda or oatmeal water.

But I weirdly want to be here as Goldie's shield more.

She makes a face. "Nothing. It's fine. It's old history. We're two people whose lives went in different directions. Seriously, I see a friend I want to say hi to, and you would absolutely be miserable and they can do nothing for rugby, so if you'll go grab us drinks, I'll say hi, and I'll meet you back here in five minutes."

I stare at her.

"She's a gynecologist that I—"

"I'll get drinks."

Goldie smiles a *this was a dumb victory* smile which is none-theless a smile when I'm picking up vibes that say something is still off, and I head over to get us drinks.

The reception starts not long after. As soon as the brides enter and are seated, dinner is served. Our table companions are fine.

No one worth networking with, but Goldie could carry on a conversation with a brick wall and no one at our table is making her visibly uncomfortable, so it's pleasant enough.

If her ex is here, I haven't picked him out yet.

I see her occasionally glance over at her former teammate and watch her expression go tight every time though.

There's a story there.

I want to know what it is. And not for networking reasons.

I also want to know what the story is more than I want to scratch at my rash, which says something I don't want it to say too.

The bridal party finishes eating and makes their rounds saying hi to all of the guests while the rest of us eat. When they reach us, the bride in the white pantsuit hugs Goldie so tightly that I'm convinced they're long-lost sisters.

Might be, in a manner, since her mother, the head coach for the Scorned, hugs Goldie equally as tightly when she, too, makes her way over.

On a hunch, I take a subtle glance around.

We're being watched.

And we're being watched in that way that suggests the people watching don't want us to know we're being watched.

Subtle eye slides over champagne flutes. Darted glances from people who look as though they're carrying on a conversation with their tablemates, but you can tell they're not. One woman misses her mouth with her fork while trying to play it cool about looking our way while she's taking a bite of chicken.

After hugging the coach, Goldie introduces us, which is the one big benefit to being here tonight.

She was out of the office the three days I tried to drop in to meet her.

Or she didn't want to see me.

I'm aware that's a possibility.

"So you're planning to siphon off the women's audience for yet another men's team?" she asks me with a twinkle that has an edge to it.

Definitely didn't want to see me. "If these other teams in town aren't treating you right, I'll fix it."

"Silas must love him," she murmurs to Goldie without replying to me.

"Silas feels exactly the way he deserves to feel," Goldie replies, which earns a laugh from the coach.

After dinner, the band switches from instrumentals to party music, drowning out the birds. Wonder if they went off to another part of the botanical gardens.

I'd also wonder if Goldie's former teammate is her ex if I wasn't positive she'd said *ex-boyfriend*.

Maybe it was a Goldie ploy to throw me off the scent.

Or maybe we still haven't seen the ex she claims would be here.

"Wanna dance?" she asks me as everyone else starts to vacate our table.

"No."

She grins, and the grin turns into a snicker, which turns into a full-on body-rolling laugh.

I lounge back in my seat. "You knew I'd say no."

She doesn't answer.

She's giggling too hard.

Not that she knows *why* I'm saying no.

Dancing with her while I have the rash from hell?

Nope.

Not a fucking chance.

The bottles of wine on our table are empty. I grab her glass. "You want more?"

"Yes, please."

She doesn't tell me we can leave.

She doesn't tell me I have to dance.

She sits there smiling at me as I walk away, looking more relaxed than I've seen her all evening.

If I said I had a personal problem, we'd go. But so long as she's happy here, we'll stay.

I chat with a former boy band guy and his wife while I'm getting drinks. Neither of them are athletes, but the guy still has visibility because of a solo career, even if it's on hold for a few years while he puts his family first, so I give him my pitch for getting more attention for the Pounders.

He says he might come to a match.

I leave it at that.

There's a time to push and a time to shut up.

With my ass itching more by the minute, I'm nowhere close to my most charming.

By the time I get through the line and turn back to the table, Goldie's not there.

I scan the room and don't see her.

Bathroom?

Or—no.

There she is.

By the dance floor.

Rigid as the stick up her brother's ass, talking to a man who's crowding her too closely and backing her toward a wall.

I see red.

No, red's too good of a color. Too *tame*.

Whatever I see, it's the hellscape version of blood red. A burnt burgundy that I borrowed from the devil himself.

I don't know where Goldie's wine goes.

I don't know who I run over while charging to her side.

I just know that the smile she's giving the guy who's grabbing her arm is her *I don't want to be smiling but smiling is better than making a scene* smile, and *this is done.*

"Five minutes, Goldie," the fucker's saying a split second before I grab his wrist, twist, and shove it back against his chest.

"Keep your fucking hands off my girlfriend, you useless fucking cunt fuck."

He staggers back.

She's free.

Staring at me with eyes that have gone wide and surprised. "Fletcher—" she starts, but I grab her by the hand and tug her before I do something worse that'll ruin every bloody bit of networking I've done with every bloke here since my ass landed back in the States.

"Dance with me," I say roughly.

She blinks once.

Licks her lips.

And then nods. "I'd love to."

15

Goldie

THAT WAS UNEXPECTED.

And I don't mean Fletcher turning into a charging bison ready to ram his head into Miller's midsection and toss my ex-boyfriend halfway across the botanical gardens.

I've caught highlights of Fletcher playing. He's aggressive. He doesn't tolerate bullshit. He's possessive.

Makes sense that his on-pitch presence would translate to off-pitch relationships.

But my body's reaction to Fletcher's growled *get your hands off my girlfriend?*

That has me completely off-kilter.

There's some squishy-squishy action happening in my chest. A dash of weakness in my knees. Unexpected thrill in my belly. And some wetness in my panties that does *not* get better when Fletcher sweeps his bulky, solid arm around me, pulling me against his crisp white shirt and hard body as we hit the edge of the dance floor.

"I was handling him," I murmur as he pulls me tighter, our cheeks nearly touching. I can almost feel the edges of his short whiskers against my skin, and it's making me wonder what it would be like to kiss him.

"And I was making a point," he replies, low and gravelly right in my ear. "You're bloody welcome."

I barely suppress a shiver.

After growing up in sports, I've dated more Renaissance men than cavemen by choice, but *I like this.*

And it's not just the priceless look on Miller's face at being confronted by a guy whose forearm is bigger than Miller's neck.

It's also the scowl I glimpse on my ex's face as Fletcher and I turn a slow circle on the dance floor.

And the mildly panicked look on Stefanie's face beside him.

"Is that your ex, or is there another wankerella I need to deal with here?" Fletcher adds.

"That was my ex."

"How long's he been with your teammate?"

The man doesn't miss much. "Since about six months before we broke up."

He's holding my hand, tucked between us possessively, and his grip tightens, which shouldn't make my heart pitter-patter more, but it does.

I hate being here.

No, I *like* being here for Elizabeth and her daughter—they're truly good people, and I hope I've done half as much for them as they've done for me. I like seeing the Fireballs and Thrusters players I've met over the years, and their wives and partners.

But I strongly dislike that I can't come *here* without seeing Miller and Stefanie.

I'm faking it well, but it doesn't matter that it's been two years.

Seeing them together makes my stomach hurt and sends adrenaline coursing through my veins the same way it did when I walked in on them together in my bedroom.

Betrayal isn't something I handle well. Nor is having Miller think he has any right to voice any opinions on my life choices, which is exactly what he was trying to do.

And don't ask how it feels that at least three women who used to be part of my tight inner circle haven't said hi at all tonight.

Maybe they think I betrayed them in how everything went down.

Honestly, I probably did.

But I did it for the right reasons. Is a *hi* too much to ask for?

"The whole point of us being on this date tonight is for me to have all of the right information so that I'm justified when I break his nose," Fletcher mutters as he pulls me closer.

"No breaking noses at wedding receptions."

"It would be an accident. Those happen a lot when I'm around, as my face can attest."

I bury my head in his shoulder and stifle an honest laugh that settles some of the nerves in my stomach, getting a thicker waft of cedarwood and patchouli. It reminds me of my grandpa.

Some of my favorite wispy childhood memories are of sneaking into my grandpa's den at their country home where he kept a wooden puzzle box that I'd play with while he smoked a pipe. Long before I found soccer, long before my parents' divorce, long before my injury, long before Miller and Stefanie tore my entire world apart.

It's a safe space. "Thank you. I needed that."

"I can still break his nose."

"I prefer psychological revenge, but again, thank you for the very kind offer."

"Want me to break her nose?"

"*Fletcher.*"

I pull back enough to see a half smirk on his face, which makes me do one more thing that I wasn't sure I'd pull off tonight.

I laugh. *Again.* Honestly.

I've laughed more tonight than I thought I would.

I even forgot for a while that Miller and Stefanie and all of the baggage that accompanies thoughts of them were even here.

"You're a very good wingman," I tell him.

"He hurt you."

"I—yes."

"He hurt you enough that you didn't think you could be a badass here tonight on your own."

I sigh and let myself lean my cheek against his again. "I thought we'd get old together."

"That guy? He's fucking ugly."

I stifle another smile. Fletcher's pettiness is remarkably comforting. "He brought me flowers every Friday. If I had a bad day, he'd come home with cheese dip. About the same time he started sleeping with Stefanie, he sent me and three of my best friends on a spa vacation."

"Including her?"

"Including her."

"Did your other friends know?"

"Doesn't matter if they knew or not. They were her teammates. I was the one who didn't fit."

He stops dancing, rears back, and looks down at me.

"I'm fine, Fletcher," I say lightly, forcing a smile in case anyone's watching. I squeeze his waist, and we start moving again.

He tucks me even more possessively against his body. "If you were fine, you wouldn't have asked the hottest guy in town that you can't stand to be your date tonight."

"I can stand you. Most of the time."

"She knew you two were dating."

"This happened a *long* time ago, and I'm better off without him."

"She still hurt you. And your friends took *her* side?"

"They were her teammates. Not just friends. *Teammates*. On a professional women's team where performance matters even more than it does for you. The team started struggling on the field, and it was so obvious that no matter how professional they tried to be, the trust was gone from some of the people who were on my side. *I* was hurting the team. So I...I left them. I left my friends so they could do what they needed to on the field."

"Fuck, Goldie," he mutters.

He gets the teammate angle.

He has to figure out how to put aside hating my brother off the pitch to be his teammate *on* the pitch.

I can't solve that for them. Agreeing to a couple dates with Fletcher probably won't help their situation, but Silas will get over it. I'm leaving before the season starts. They'll probably have a fist-fight and then be over it because men are dumb.

But for the Scorned?

I wasn't all of the problem, but I was definitely part of it. And it was obvious that me removing myself from the situation would improve the team's morale.

So that's what I did.

It meant I didn't have to see Miller and Stefanie together either.

Elizabeth knew. She called me on it. She made sure I knew that she didn't give two fucks what happened between Stefanie and me, that she still cared and I could still call her anytime.

That's the only reason I'm here tonight.

Because Elizabeth personally asked me to come, and there's no telling the next time I'll see her.

But my former friends? Stefanie's teammates?

"That's why I hang out with Odette and Evelyn and Sheila," I whisper. "They were my friends when I had no friends left."

I had Brittany, but that situation was weird. And I knew not to make friends with Hallie's nannies because they inevitably left. Even when Hallie was only a year and a half old, Silas was already going through the nannies.

I wasn't one of the Scorned, but they were my family. They'd been my family since I came home after college and Elizabeth took me under her wing to help me find my footing despite professional soccer not being in my future.

So no, it's not simply that I don't want to see Miller tonight.

It's that I don't want to see Miller still with Stefanie, reaping the rewards of sleeping with my former best friend.

It's that I don't want him to talk to me like I was a problem then and that I'm a problem now.

It's that most of the women on the team who've been on the team for more than two years haven't said hi, even if their coach did. It's that this is a place where *I* don't fit. Where I don't belong. But where I wanted to have one last chance to celebrate something with a woman who's meant the world to me and her daughter before I leave Copper Valley and never come back.

"You said your job was the problem," he says.

"That was his excuse. That if I paid as much attention to him as I paid to my career, then we would've been okay."

"He's still dating a bloody soccer player that he was sleeping with while dating you and *your career* was a problem?"

Fletcher Huxley is a thousand times more perceptive than I gave him credit for. "He's in corporate coaching," I whisper.

Translation: he didn't like that I was more successful as a younger, self-employed life coach than he was.

He didn't have book deals. He didn't get speaking gigs. He didn't have a hundred thousand followers on social media.

And why does it still fucking *hurt*?

I'm better off without a man like that. But he was good to me while we were together in a way that I hadn't had before or since.

"Fuck," Fletcher mutters, but it's not a *fuck, you got the short end of the stick on friends* kind of *fuck*.

It's a *there's one solution to this and I don't like it* fuck.

"We should kiss," he says.

My belly drops to my toes and my head goes light as a feather. "That's a very kind offer, but completely unnecessary."

"You have the hottest date here. You're obviously enjoying yourself with me. He's plotting how to slash my tires. Let's give him more motivation."

"He doesn't care what I do."

"If he didn't care, he wouldn't be watching us."

"Maybe he's watching us because you're watching him."

"He can't tell I'm watching him. I'm *subtle*."

I laugh again.

The last thing I ever expected was for Fletcher Huxley to be this fun.

Especially at a wedding.

Especially at *this* wedding.

He's not wrong. I asked him because he's easily the hottest man here.

"Do you have a photographer hiding in the wings waiting to snap a picture of us kissing to send directly to Silas?" I ask.

"Yes."

I veer back and look around.

He cracks a grin and lets out a single *heh*.

"Why didn't men look like that when I was dating?" an older lady mutters as her date sweeps her past us.

Fletcher's grin turns back into a smirk.

"I cannot even imagine how you live with your own ego," I murmur as I let him pull me closer again, still smiling.

"I used to stare at my 'stache anytime I got too full of myself. Now there's nothing between me being hot and me knowing I'm hot."

This might be the best date I've ever had.

Low expectations. Zero pressure. And I get a glimpse of Miller and Stefanie, and yeah.

It's not so much that I'm taking joy in their discomfort as it is that they wouldn't be uncomfortable at all if they hadn't broken my heart and put me on a path to walking away from most of my best friends.

And I still don't think either of them honestly wish the best for me.

How hard is it to want someone who was once important in your life to be happy, even if you don't want to be the one to make them happy anymore?

"Okay," I say to Fletcher. "One kiss."

"We should play it by tongue. Ear. By ear."

I roll my eyes.

He grins at me.

Fletcher being broody and possessive and growly? Hot. Fletcher bound and determined to single-handedly increase the visibility of rugby in the States? Admirable. Fletcher full of mischief with that chiseled, scruffy face split in the ultimate *I'm so much trouble* smile?

It's like finding the hidden door to let you inside the secret garden in the middle of a foreboding old building where every other hallway will take you to a dungeon with a cranky old troll.

He has a playful side, and he trusts me enough to share it with me.

Or else he's a hornball and is only in this for the kiss.

But so what if he is?

I'm leaving in two weeks.

And my brother has made sure I haven't had *any* fun of my own since Miller and Stefanie split my world apart.

Silas has good intentions. *Devastated* barely touches where I was two years ago. Add in a splash of *completely alone*, some *lost*, a healthy dose of *loss of confidence and massive distrust*, and that's closer.

He doesn't want me to hurt like that again.

But it was important for me to get out and date again to prove to myself that one man being a total and complete bastard doesn't mean that my life has to stop.

Even if I haven't had the courage to find new friends my own age. And even if I haven't voluntarily looked at a dating app in a few months now either.

All under the excuse of *I'm leaving soon*.

"We start with one," I say, matching Fletcher's grin because it's *easy*. "And if neither of us is appalled and we're not causing a scene, we can try two. But three is the limit."

"Why?"

"More than three, and you upstage the happy couple. It's a wedding rule."

"You made that up."

"It feels legitimate. Nobody wants to watch someone else making out at their own wedding."

"I didn't mind."

"You—wait. Which wedding? First or second?"

His turn to roll his eyes. "Does it matter?"

"You tell me. I don't know anything about how much your weddings meant to you."

"Talking about weddings makes me less inclined to agree to letting you kiss me."

With the lights lowered over the dance floor and fairy lights twinkling in the trees and the right amount of wine in my system, coupled with that rigid brow and the quirk of his lips, I *want* to kiss him.

It's a challenge now.

It's a challenge that I intend to win.

He's gripping my hand between us while he holds me tight with his other arm, but I disentangle it and run my fingers through his hair.

Holy *shit*.

It's soft.

It's baby-blanket soft. "You're only threatening to not kiss me because you hope it'll make me initiate a kiss."

"You need this kiss more than I do."

"I didn't ask for it though. You suggested it. Which begs the question... How much do you *want* it, Fletcher?"

His pupils are dilating and his lids are lowering and he's staring at my mouth.

He wants to kiss me.

Our bodies are lined up tighter than would ever be allowed at a middle school dance. There's a hard ridge nestled against my belly that tells me he's turned on.

Because I turn him on?

Or because he's a hornball who gets turned on at the drop of a hat?

Is this a game?

Does he play kissing chicken?

Does he want a kiss to turn into something more?

Or is it simply an honest offer to kiss me to make my ex jealous, when neither my ex-boyfriend nor my ex-best friend should give a crap who I'm kissing?

"I like kissing," Fletcher says, still watching my lips, his erection still pushing against me. "Like it even more when it pisses someone off and comes without strings."

"You're a disaster, aren't you?"

"Every fucking day. Only way to live."

I was supposed to be here with Odette. Playing games over dinner like *which of these couples do you think will make it* and *should I hit on that guy or will that make him more likely to need an obituary sooner?*, which is Odette's favorite at social events, but only social events where Sheila won't overhear, since Sheila's kind heart isn't always as amused by darker humor. I should be doing the "YMCA." Slow-dancing to Ed Sheeran love songs. Being something of a nuisance for fun in a place where I didn't want to care what anyone thought of me since this would be the last time I'd see most of them for probably years.

Coming with Fletcher is different.

It doesn't say *I have such a good life that I'm living it up with my elderly neighbor lady without a care in the world.*

It says *this hot, hard, muscular hunk of testosterone pounds me every night* and *fuck you, Miller and Stefanie.*

Our mouths are drifting closer together as if one of us is a planet thrown off its orbit and put on a collision course with disaster. He swipes his tongue over his lower lip, and I get a pull deep, deep in my belly in a place I haven't been satisfied in longer than I'd care to acknowledge right now.

"I don't have camera people here," he says, his voice hoarse and strained.

"I wouldn't care if you did."

We're doing this.

We're doing this kiss.

Is he a start-soft-then-go-deep kisser? Is he a licker? Is he aggressive, or will he surprise me like his hair?

There's a thick sensation building between my thighs that doesn't care the answer.

I want to know what it is.

I want to know how Fletcher kisses.

How he'll kiss *me.*

His chest is rising and falling more rapidly, and our slow swaying to the music is getting slower and slower.

Millimeters.

That's how far apart our lips are now.

My eyes drift shut. My pussy clenches. I tighten my grip around his neck and in his hair. My nipples are so hard they're almost painful. His breath is warm against my cheek.

So close.

So close.

Any moment now, our lips will meet, and—

He trips.

Trips?

No.

He's *shoved*, right into me, throwing both of us off-kilter as his lips leave a wet streak along my cheek.

"Oops," Nick Murphy says. "Guess I wasn't watching where I was going."

Kami squeezes her eyes shut and sighs while she clearly takes charge of their dance and pushes him away from us.

Fletcher grips me tighter, rebalanced and making sure I am too, and gives Nick a flat stare. "Happens when you have a hot date."

Nick grins. "It does."

Kami sucks her lips into her mouth and buries her head into his chest, clearly hiding how amused she is that her husband cock-blocked Fletcher.

And me.

"We should get a room," Fletcher says to me. "You ready, Goldie?"

No.

No, I am *not* ready.

But I also know what it says if I leave this dance floor while he's staring at me like this and when I'm well aware that he's suffering from a massive hard-on, and you know what?

Yes.

Yes, I'm ready for the message that sends.

A satisfied smirk tilts one side of his mouth up without me saying a word, and he subtly reaches between us and adjusts himself, which should not be hot, but is.

"Good seeing you," he says to Nick, then nods to Kami. "Nice to meet you too, ma'am."

"Call me before you leave for London," Kami says to me. Her eyes are dancing as much as everyone around us now that the song has changed to an upbeat number.

I open my mouth to promise I will, but Fletcher grabs my hand and drags me off the floor before I can make my tongue work.

And then we're strolling—quickly—out of the reception as if we have somewhere we desperately need to be, where we'll be tearing each other's clothes off the minute we get there.

Will we?

Will we?

I would. I absolutely would.

We hustle through the gardens toward the exit, and I realize there's something wrong.

Fletcher keeps jerking his shoulder or shaking his hip about every third step.

I slow and look at him.

He tugs me along.

Then does a weird hip thrust that doesn't look sexual at all. I've seen guys cope with walking with erections, and this is *not* that walk.

This walk says there's something wrong with his pants.

"Why are you walking weird?" It's the first thing I've said since we left the dance floor surrounded by a haze of lust—on my part—and whatever the hell is going through his head and hormones, which I honestly can't quite guess now.

"I'm not walking weird." He takes three more steps, twisting at the torso and grimacing on the third step.

"You look like Jack Sparrow."

He doesn't *smell* drunk.

Quite the opposite, actually. He smells like he bathed in the forest of *all good man things* and finished it off with a spritz of *bonus, he's not the type to smack your ass just because.*

His facial muscles contort like he's having an internal battle with himself. Or possibly like he's regretting telling me we had to kiss and everything that came after and just can't freaking *say so.*

"I'm bloody brilliant. All fine."

I stop in the middle of the walkway beside a large red hibiscus plant and cross my arms. "If the game's over and you're done, say so. No need to get weird."

"I have a rash, okay?" he mutters.

Hello, left turn. "What kind of rash?"

"This is the best date conversation I've ever had."

"*Fletcher.*"

"I ate a food I'm allergic to and my skin is paying the price."

Oh my god. "Tonight?"

He squeezes his eyes shut, and I get the impression this is the last conversation he wants to have. "No."

"Are you—"

"Yes, I'm sure."

How can he be—*oh.* "Have you had a rash *all night?*" I whisper.

The plants might have ears.

Or there might be other guests lurking around the corner.

"The exit is this way, Goldie."

Right.

Right. Leave the wedding. Ask questions about his rash later.

Except if I've learned anything about Fletcher Huxley in the past two weeks, I know the answer to my own question.

Yes.

Yes, he's had a rash *all night*.

And he still came to be my shield from Miller and Stefanie.

I hustle to catch up and tuck my hand into his elbow again, squeezing his thick biceps. "You're a good man," I whisper.

He slides me a completely unreadable look. "Do yourself a favor and don't believe that."

16

Fletcher

"YOU FUCKING KISSED MY SISTER."

Here we go.

It's the first day of preseason training. I'm in the changing room to get ready for pictures and meetings and basically everything except training.

And Silas Collins is in my face.

I stare back at him. "You're welcome."

His nostrils quiver and his eyes go dark as he puts both of his hands on my chest and pushes me. Or tries to. "Keep your fucking hands off my fucking sister."

"Your sister is a grown-ass adult who can decide for herself what she wants to do with her hands." I want to pound this little shit into the ground so deep, he'll never see the light of day again. Instead, I add a smirk. "And her mouth."

Silas grabs a fistful of my shirt, but Holt, the team captain, shoves between us. "Save it for the pitch. *After* pictures and all the bullshit the PR team has for us today. Dumbasses."

"Us, or the PR team?" I ask.

And yes, I mean it. I want to know if he thinks the PR team is full of dumbasses.

Better not, or he'll need an attitude adjustment. PR team's half of what will fill our stadium this year, and I've had enough meetings with them to think they're probably excellent at their jobs.

Holt makes eye contact with me and doesn't blink. "You. You're the dumbasses."

"He's fucking playing my sister," Silas seethes.

"And he's right. She's an adult. Pretty smart one at that. Get your kit on." He uses his shoulder to shove Silas away.

I haven't so much as lifted a finger. Arms still at my sides. Shoulders relaxed.

Completely nonthreatening position.

But Holt still turns and glares at me too. I have him by an inch, two at most, but he feels every bit as big as me.

And then he lifts his phone and waves my own Instagram page in my face. "Quit. Baiting. Your. Fucking. Teammates."

I don't bait my teammates.

Only Silas.

"If they don't want to know what I do when I'm not on the pitch, they shouldn't look at my profile."

"Everyone follows you because *that's what fucking teammates do.* Might want to offer a few follow-backs. Comment. Do this *teambuilding* thing you're talking about."

"Fletch commented on my post of my hike yesterday," Porter says.

"Liked all of mine from my trip to the beach," Crew adds. "Stalker-level weird. Made me uncomfortable. But only a little."

I let my eyebrows shrug for me as I stare back at Holt.

"You're annoying as fuck," he mutters.

"Her ex-boyfriend was at the wedding and she didn't want to go alone," I tell the captain. "What would you have done for a teammate's sister in that situation?"

I know the answer.

I know all of the answers.

Take her to the wedding. Be a gentleman. Don't kiss her. And especially don't kiss her and then post a whole goddamn set of photos starting with you putting her into a brand-new Bentley and ending with you kissing her on the dance floor.

You know what sucks in this entire situation?

I didn't even fucking kiss her.

There was no touching of the lips. None. My whiskers didn't even get close enough to brush against her mouth.

Picture makes it appear that we did.

And I've had a massive case of blue balls on top of the healing rash on my ass ever since Saturday night.

Which I will not be telling anyone in this locker room.

The way Holt's staring at me, I think he wants to believe me but he's not entirely sure.

And that's bad if I want this team to succeed this year.

Pissing off the captain on day one is never a good start.

"You find her someone else to go with when it'll piss off your teammate," he says.

"No one else is as pretty as I am."

He growls.

"I'm a fucking team player," I tell him. "You want to make progress, find out why whiny-boy over there has his head up his ass about his sister being an adult and me being here."

"He says you're washed-up, full of yourself, and have no place ruining our season for us by treating us like morons who can't sell tickets to the matches on our own," Porter says.

I twist my neck and stare at him. He's tugging his Pounders training jersey down and staring right back.

He shrugs. "Rest of us are willing to give you the benefit of the doubt, but we've all heard what went down with Rafferty over in Nottingshire. Does feel like maybe you've played your best days already. But we have a great medical staff here. Maybe they can fix you in ways those English doctors couldn't. And he's wrong about the ticket thing. Sales are up since you came on. But what I don't like is thinking new fans are coming to watch us be a shitshow, since that's all your social media is lately. You passed out? You with your mustache on fire? It's a shitshow."

Heat spreads from my chest.

I take a glance around the locker room.

Silas is gone, but the rest of the guys—they're watching.

They want to know if I'm a broken has-been who's going to ruin their chances this year by being the weak link on the team and make a mockery of them to boot.

Six months ago, I was playing for one of the best teams in the whole damn world. Elite. Premiere. God status.

And today my new teammates in a run-down locker room with water stains on the drop ceiling and creaky benches and worn gear and threadbare carpeting think me and my social media presence will be the problem.

Challenge fucking accepted.

I turn in a slow circle, making eye contact with every one of them. "Remember this. Remember this, and then tell me how you feel when we win the whole bloody championship in front of a sold-out crowd who are all wearing our colors in someone else's stadium in June. Because that's what we can bloody well do if we all step up and play some fucking rugby like a team. And that's what I'm here for. To win. As a fucking team. Any questions?"

You can see it.

More, you can *feel* it.

You can feel the shift in the room at the idea of being *the team* in the league. The guys who build a massive fan base across the entire nation. The team that plays together so well that no one can beat us. The team that goes all the way. The team that proves playing rugby as a full-time job here is possible the same way football and baseball and hockey and soccer are full-time jobs.

Except I don't think I'm feeling it.

I think I *want* to feel it, and no one here believes me.

Not good enough, Fletcher. Work harder. Be better. You think you're number one, but you're number three, at best.

You'll never be good enough.

Try harder.

You're a disappointment.

Your grades suck.

You were rude to your teacher.

Even in rugby, you're a disappointment.

I finish looking around, feeling not the inspiration now, but the doubt.

Fuck.

"I'm a team player, and I won't fucking hold anyone back," I tell Holt.

"You ready to prove you've got what it takes?"

"Bring it."

"Even if it means stopping seeing Goldie?" Crew says.

"Shut up, dumbass. She's a grown-ass woman," Porter mutters to him.

Crew rolls his eyes. "Tell Silas that."

"I leave shit at home," I tell Crew. "He can learn to do the same."

Not holding my breath.

But I'm here to be a damn team player. And I'm in the exact right spot to prove it.

They'll see.

Come June, they'll *all* see.

Or else I'll well and truly be done.

With no fucking clue where I'll belong next.

17

Goldie

I CAN'T DECIDE which is more perplexing—being recognized by six people on the walk between my apartment and the wine bar, or being recognized because Fletcher posted a picture of us nearly kissing that got some unexpected attention that's resulted in half of Copper Valley apparently shipping us as a couple.

"Who puts a picture on the internets of you kissing without telling you he's going to do it, and then doesn't have the decency to message you at all for four days?" Evelyn says over wine as all of us stare at our phones.

Odette is still in her wheelchair. She's tucked in at the end of the table, shaking her head while she scrolls her phone. "*Oh-em-gee, they're so cute together,*" she reads.

"*Couple of the century,*" Sheila quotes.

"*If they don't get married, I'll die.*"

"*It's giving opposites attract in all the best ways.*"

"*I hope she comes to the games and cheers him on.*"

"I'm getting tickets because I want to see them together there. When he scores and she rushes to the bottom of the stands or whatever it is and he dashes over to her and picks her up and twirls her and kisses her? Swoon."

"How cute would their babies be? Heart-eye emoticon. Heart-eye emoticon. Heart-eye emoticon. Baby-face emoticon."

"It's *emoji*, hon," Evelyn says, patting Odette's hand.

"You're the one who called it *the internets*."

"I did it ironically. Since I'm old."

"Has he called you at all?" Sheila asks me.

I shake my head. Technically, he doesn't even have my phone number. All of our communication has been through social media.

"And he hasn't hit you up in your DMs?" Evelyn says with a sly look at Odette, who stifles a smile while she rolls her eyes.

"Nope."

"So he's using you," Evelyn declares. "We should obituary his mustache."

I wince. "It might be my fault."

"How?"

"I wouldn't let him walk me to my apartment when we got back because he needed to get home and treat his rash."

All three of my friends set their wine glasses and phones aside and lean into the table.

"What rash?" Odette demands.

"Apparently he ate something he was allergic to and broke out in a rash and didn't tell me until the end of the night, when it became *very* clear he was super uncomfortable."

"What's he allergic to?"

I wince harder. "Mango," I whisper. "We had mango salsa at our cooking class date."

He didn't tell me. I googled him and *food allergy,* and I found an old, old, *old* interview that he did where he talked about how long it took him to realize he was allergic to mango since his rashes didn't appear for three to four days after he ate it and the doctors always told him he had poison ivy.

"And you didn't offer to go help him treat it?" Odette says.

"Same question," Sheila says.

Evelyn nods. "All three of us have to know now."

Oh, for the love of wine. "*Hi, thanks for making the exact right scene as my wedding date when my ex decided he still has a say in any part of my life, sorry I gave you an allergy rash, I like you as a friend way more than I thought I would, how about you strip so I can rub itch cream all over your body?* That's what you wanted me to say?"

They share a look, then nod as one. Even Sheila. "Yes."

"I'm leaving the country soon."

"And he's twice-divorced and in a current long-term relationship with his sport that's lasted exponentially longer than both of his marriages combined," Evelyn says. "Go ride the pony, sweetie pie. Have your fun while you're still dating guys young enough to get it up without the assistance of a pill."

"You basically owe it to the entire country," Odette agrees. "Their discovery of a new sport to obsess over rests on you dating a man who left a very successful European career behind to come and build attention for the players here too. Including your brother."

Ah, my brother.

I pull up my text messages from him and hand my phone to Odette, who tilts her head to read it all through her bifocals. "*If that bastard gets within a hundred yards of you again, no one will ever find his body,*" she reads.

"Eye roll," Evelyn says.

"What did she say back? I can't read it from here," Sheila says. "I hope she tells him to be nice."

"Goldie: *Good plan. Orange is your color. How did your first day go? It must've been hard posing for a camera in that silver and black kit all day.*"

Evelyn snickers.

"Is there more?" Sheila asks.

I gesture to Odette to keep reading.

"Silas: *He's fucking with the entire vibe of the team. Half the guys hate him. You should too. Do you know what his second ex-wife says about him?*"

"Goldie: *That he has a big penis?*"

"Silas: *That he's emotionally incapable of loving anything that's not himself or a rugby ball. You should've told me about the wedding and fuck-face. I would've gone with you and no one would've found his body either.*"

"Goldie: *It's much healthier and more productive to put your energy toward liking people and letting other people live their own lives, right? Studies show that excess hate and excess interfering with your sister's love life leads to premature hair thinning, muscle mass loss, and impotence.*"

Evelyn cackles.

Sheila presses her lips together like she's trying not to.

I sip my wine while Odette hands my phone back to me.

"Funny how he didn't reply to that last one," she murmurs.

"He had to go look up *impotence*, and now he's stewing."

"Do you know what I think?" Evelyn says.

I shake my head.

"I think Fletcher's embarrassed and waiting for you to reach out."

My heart thumps once, hard, and then I get a whole-body shiver like a horde of chipmunks are racing across my skin with their tiny little feet. "Possibly," I agree. "But more likely, he has rugby and not me on his brain."

Lies.

Fletcher doesn't *only* think about rugby.

He thinks about how to best get attention on rugby. He's probably thrilled at the attention his post is getting and the suggestion that we, together as a couple, are inspiring ticket sales.

But he also pays attention to what's going on around him. He's very observant. Unexpectedly so. And while kind isn't a word I would've associated with him after what he said in that VIP suite my senior year of college, I've realized he is.

He's very kind.

In his own way.

When he decides it's warranted.

Also, don't tell me he wouldn't donate a kidney to his dog if she needed one. And while humans technically can't donate kidneys to dogs, *he still would.*

I bite my lip.

And then I pull up my Instagram app, go to Fletcher's page, steal one particular photo from the collection he posted, and start my own post.

You never know who life will put in your path. When you stay open to the possibilities, magic can happen. #laughter #coachgoldie #life-coaching

I credit the wedding photographer for the photo, but I don't hit *post.*

Not yet.

Do I want the world to see this photo of Fletcher half smiling at me over dinner while I laugh at something he said?

It sends a very clear message.

I found someone who makes my world better.

And in ten days, I'm leaving the country. I won't be a prop around here anymore. We'll need a breakup story. Or a *we were accidental friends* story. He told Miller I'm his girlfriend, and people have started whispering about that too.

We definitely will need a story.

"Messaging him is more direct," Evelyn says as she leans over my shoulders, peering through her reading glasses at my phone.

"My friendship with Fletcher is based on anything but directness," I reply.

And that does it.

Mind made up.

I post the picture with the caption, and then I set my phone down and grab my wine spritzer.

"Do you think he'll—" Evelyn starts, but before she can finish, my phone vibrates loudly on the table.

Odette lunges for it, tilts her head to read through her glasses, and cackles while my pulse inches toward *oh my god, he messaged me* levels like I'm a teenager with my first crush.

"What?" Sheila says. "*What?* Did he call? Or text? You young people, never calling anymore. Let me see too."

Evelyn snorts. "If he was sitting around waiting for Goldie to post a new picture and hoping it was him and now he's messaging her, I officially object to even the riding the pony portion of this plan. Don't ride the pony with men who wait for you to post pictures of them on the internets before they offer to show you what's in their pants."

Odette shoves my phone at me. "Open this, Goldie. I can't see what it says. I can only see that he sent you a message."

"Maybe they were thinking of each other at the same time and it has nothing to do with him seeing Goldie's post," Sheila says to Evelyn.

Evelyn replies with a raised eyebrow that telegraphs infinite doubt that Fletcher ever thinks of anyone but himself.

I take my phone and unlock it, then pull up my DMs on Insta.

Fletcher has, in fact, seen my post.

Was scrolling and this popped up. You realize that's telling the world we're dating.

Odette squeals.

Evelyn huffs.

Sheila pumps a fist. "The World Wide Web gods for the win! You can be a cute couple for ten more days."

I set my phone down again, and Odette shoves it at me. "Answer him!"

"I'm having dinner with my besties. He can wait."

"How are we going to find a fourth member of our club when you're gone?" Evelyn says.

"*Shush your trap,*" Sheila hisses, which is the most aggressive thing I've ever heard her say.

It makes me have to swallow hard to battle the heat in my sinuses and the burn in my eyes. "I'll video call you."

"You better," Evelyn says.

Dammit.

Holding back the tears is getting harder.

These ladies might've started as a substitute for the friends I lost when I walked into my apartment to find Stefanie sucking off Miller in my bed, but they truly are my ride-or-die besties now.

I rub my hands together. "Can we get back to business, please? Anyone have an ex-boyfriend croak recently?"

"Just Jimbo," Sheila says.

Evelyn gasps. "*Jimbo died?* When? How? *Why didn't you say so?*"

"Talking about Goldie's online love life is way more exciting than talking about a guy I had three dates with a decade ago."

"Wasn't Jimbo the one who choked on a crab shell at dinner and then couldn't stop clearing his throat on your second date?"

"That's him."

"Tell me it wasn't a crab leg that did him in."

"Hit his head when he fell down a flight of stairs and never woke up again."

There's a moment of silence at the table.

Doesn't help that Odette's in a wheelchair.

By the time I make it back to Copper Valley—nope.

Not finishing that thought.

These ladies live to the fullest and they've adopted me as one of their own and taught me so much in the past two years.

That is what I choose to focus on.

"It would've been so much more poetic if it was a crab leg," Evelyn says.

"Or something unexpected like mashed potatoes," Odette agrees.

They pull out their notebooks, and I settle deeper into the plush cushion with my wine in hand, watching each of their expressions as they get to work writing alternate versions of Jimbo's obituary.

Odette brandishes her pen with a flourish. Evelyn mouths the words as she writes them. Sheila writes, scribbles, writes, scribbles, and then smiles to herself as if she's found exactly the phrase she was looking for.

I want to remember every minute of this.

And ignore the way my palms are itching for me to grab my phone and reply to Fletcher.

He, too, is not in my future.

But he's making my present another level of fun.

18

From the Instagram direct messages of Goldie and Fletcher

CoachGoldie: That dating thing. You realize you called me your girlfriend in front of my ex the other night, right?

RugbyFletch: You're welcome.

CoachGoldie: My statement was more factual than gratitudinal.

RugbyFletch: Gratitudinal?

CoachGoldie: It's a word.

RugbyFletch: A bad word.

CoachGoldie: There are no good or bad words. Merely words that are sometimes more or less appropriate depending on the situation. For example, it was more on the inappropriate side for you to call me your girlfriend. Though I do appreciate the sentiment and the effect it had.

RugbyFletch: Your girl squad approved.

CoachGoldie: My girl squad?

RugbyFletch: *screenshot of Fletcher's DMs with Sheila wherein Sheila thanks Fletcher for taking good care of Goldie at that wedding*

CoachGoldie: Tell me that's doctored.

RugbyFletch: If it were doctored, she'd be offering to have my babies too.

CoachGoldie: Do you want babies?

RugbyFletch: Do you want to continue this conversation?

CoachGoldie: *laughing emoji*

RugbyFletch: Fine. One point to you.

CoachGoldie: Way more than one point for that one.

RugbyFletch: One point and one point only, which Sweet Pea can take away at will if she decides you're too much trouble.

CoachGoldie: I think Sweet Pea is smart enough to know that this charade benefits you far more than it benefits me. You sell tickets when you post sweet little messages about going on dates with the woman who saved your life. When I post a picture of us together, my clients message asking if I've hit my head and if I'll still be able to get on a plane with a concussion.

RugbyFletch: Did you take three hours to reply to my message because you were practicing all of those zingers in your head?

CoachGoldie: Nope. I'm naturally quick on my feet. I open an app, I see messages, I reply. I was at dinner and didn't get to your message until now. Also, I don't hold it against you that you're not so quick. I know you've taken a few actual hits to the head over the years.

RugbyFletch: I don't need to be quick on my feet. I have something better.

CoachGoldie: I shouldn't ask. I'm going to regret asking. This is me NOT asking what's better.

RugbyFletch: My killer looks.

CoachGoldie: I didn't ask.

RugbyFletch: But you wanted to know.

CoachGoldie: Nope. Didn't want to know.

RugbyFletch: These looks got me a new endorsement deal today. Don't worry. The commercial comes with a script.

CoachGoldie: Let me guess. Facial bandages? Mustache growth serum? Athlete's foot cream? No. That's too predictable. Something to do with a travel-in-more-comfort product like those neck pillows or footrests for airplanes?

RugbyFletch: Wine.

CoachGoldie: NO.

RugbyFletch: You don't think I'm sophisticated enough to drink wine?

CoachGoldie: Oh. Sorry. I get WHINE and WINE confused. I thought you meant you got picked up to sponsor whining.

RugbyFletch: I'm not your brother.

CoachGoldie: You two kiss and make up yet?

RugbyFletch: Am I an asshole?

CoachGoldie: I…feel like this conversation is taking a turn into a lane I should not be in.

RugbyFletch: Apparently the entire team thinks I think I'm better than they are.

CoachGoldie: I have heard that rumbling from people who also think they are better than other people.

RugbyFletch: Which ones?

CoachGoldie: What?

RugbyFletch: Which ones? Which ones of my teammates told you I'm a self-centered asshole?

CoachGoldie: There's this thing called "I will never tell you that information for the collective good of all of society."

RugbyFletch: I'm a team player.

CoachGoldie: So you've said.

RugbyFletch: I am. I'm a fucking team player.

CoachGoldie: With your own camera person and a questionable mid-season departure from your last team and endorsement deals for wine…

RugbyFletch: You want to add in "you're old" there too?

CoachGoldie: Everyone's bodies age at different rates depending on genetics and environmental factors.

RugbyFletch: The camera person is for the team. It's for the whole damn league.

CoachGoldie: I know.

RugbyFletch: It is.

CoachGoldie: I KNOW. I believe you. Your goals are not in question, and I understand your theory and your methodology. And it seems to be working, and it's benefitting the entire team. Sometimes at great personal discomfort to you.

RugbyFletch: Oh. Thank you.

CoachGoldie: So what happened with your last team?

RugbyFletch: Thanks for letting the world think you're my girlfriend. I'll issue a press release saying we've decided we're better off as friends.

CoachGoldie: Being honest with your teammates is the first step in building trust. It doesn't matter if I believe you when you say that you want to grow American rugby. It matters that your teammates believe you and know they can count on you out on the pitch.

RugbyFletch: Think I know a thing or two about being part of a team.

CoachGoldie: You wouldn't have had a career as long as you have if you didn't. But you've never started with a fresh team that knows it's a step down for you to play with them and that your availability happened under questionable circumstances that might not have been your own choice.

RugbyFletch: Have you been reading the news about me?

CoachGoldie: I sometimes talk to a couple of your teammates, remember?

RugbyFletch: I'm not discussing this in places that can have screenshots made.

CoachGoldie: Afraid you'll use them against yourself?

RugbyFletch: Yes.

CoachGoldie: LOL. At least you're honest.

RugbyFletch: I don't mind that people think we're dating.

CoachGoldie: I'm leaving the country in ten days.

RugbyFletch: I know. That's why I don't mind if people think we're dating. But if you want me to set the record straight, I will.

CoachGoldie: Enjoy the attention while it lasts. Time an announcement right so that you can get a whole stadium full of women hoping to catch your attention. And if you ever do want to talk about whatever it was that happened in England, I happen to know someone who's a good listener with a strong sense of morals about not divulging private information.

RugbyFletch: Is she hot?

CoachGoldie: He's eighty-three and has been the community theater's choice actor every time there's a play that requires a troll. He needs very little makeup to fit the role.

RugbyFletch: So she IS hot. And she likes me.

CoachGoldie: You have this weird knack for being a good friend in completely unexpected ways despite your naturally annoying personality. Some people might want to return the favor. That's all.

RugbyFletch: You don't owe me anything. You've already been far more helpful than I deserve.

CoachGoldie: Everyone deserves good things, Fletcher. Even stubborn rugby players who don't want to talk about their feelings.

RugbyFletch: I'll keep that in mind.

19

Fletcher

GOLDIE COLLINS HAS OFFICIALLY OVERTAKEN her brother as my least-favorite person on the planet.

How?

By making me like her.

I don't generally give two shits who I like and who I don't like.

But I don't like that I like Goldie.

I think about her when I fall asleep because I reread her messages right before bed, like a total fucking moron. I think about her when I wake up since I thought about her until I fell asleep. I think about her when I'm walking Sweet Pea and pass Goldie's flat or the wine bar or the restaurant where we had cooking class. I think about her when I see cheese.

I think about her when I see her brother, who's still a douche-wanker.

And I think about her when I stop into the bookstore in our

neighborhood after training the day after she posted that picture of us.

Do they have a massive display of Goldie's books in the window prompting me to think about her?

No.

That's near the back of the store.

And even if they didn't, I'd still think about her.

She's at the top of my brain while I scowl at the small sports section near the back of the main level. The shop is busy. No shortage of customers.

And *this* is the sports section.

Not even two full rows, every last book about hockey. No football. No baseball. No soccer. No rugby.

Just hockey.

What the *hell*?

I'm working up my charming face before I go hunt down the manager when a pint-sized human in a tiara and a knight costume sprints around a row of books and almost crashes into me.

I squat down to her level and hover a hand at her side while she catches her balance.

She looks like the pirate Goldie accused *me* of being at the wedding last weekend, weaving and steadying herself. And the last thing any of us need is for a kid to crack her head on a bookshelf.

"Okay there, Madame Knight Pipsqueak?" I say in my best British accent. Seems to fit.

She stares at me with big hazel eyes. Creepy-crawlies inch up my spine.

Have I met this kid?

"*Doggie!*" she squeals.

Sweet Pea shifts in her sling, wagging her tail as she pokes her little nose toward the kid, who pets her with a force that Sweet Pea tolerates like bangs on the head are the only affection she gets all day.

Little liar.

"You like dogs?" Duh, Huxley. Of course she likes dogs.

Who doesn't like dogs?

"Da doggie kiss me!" she squeals.

I glance around. Not that I can see much while I'm squatting between bookshelves and letting a preschooler attack my dog.

Where are this kid's parents?

"Looking for a sports book?" I ask her. "You're out of luck unless you like hockey. Somebody needs to talk to management about that. You want to take one for the team and pass that along?"

She giggles. "You funny."

"Thank you. Where's your mama?"

She grins. "I no wif my mama."

"Your daddy?"

She shakes her head again. "I no wif my daddy. It my *birfday!*"

"Technically your *honorary* birthday since I'll miss your real birthday, but you're turning four, so we'll go with that," Goldie herself says as she, too, turns the corner around the same row of shelves. "Hello, Fletcher. This is a surprise. Aw, Sweet Pea, you're so cute. Careful, Hallie. We have to remember we're a lot bigger than the doggie. Here. *Soft* pets. This way."

She smiles one of her kind smiles. It doesn't say *I'm forcing this,* but it also doesn't say *seeing you is the highlight of my day.* It merely says *you're a person I recognize so I'll be nice.*

Shit shit shit.

Did I shave?

Am I wearing my Pounders sweatpants?

Do I have *Pounders* written across my ass again?

Do I look like a total tool?

Will she think I'm a total ass?

Of course she will. I *am* a total ass.

But she's squatting next to me now too, smelling like vanilla cupcakes and leaning in while she takes the little girl's hand and demonstrates how to pet Sweet Pea nicely.

"What are you doing here?" she asks me as she helps her niece.

"Looking for reading lessons." *Fuuuuuuck.* Sarcasm is my best friend. Until it's not.

"I heard the owner's daughter is looking for a part-time job. You might be in the right place."

Another point for Goldie. The last time I simultaneously wanted to hug someone and flip them off, I ended up married.

And now I'm sweating.

She's bloody pretty today in black leggings and a thick bluish-gray sweater that makes her golden eyes pop.

I wonder if that's where she got her name. From her eyes.

Can't be her hair.

That's what I'm contemplating—how she got her name—when my dog—my best friend, my loyal companion, the one who's supposed to choose me above everyone else—gets so excited that she wiggles her way out of her sling while I'm staring at Goldie.

"Doggie get me!" the little girl shrieks.

She falls over laughing while Sweet Pea dances between her and Goldie, whole little long brown body wagging, petite tail wagging harder, tongue working overtime to lick both of them as much as she can.

"Aww, who's such a sweet puppy?" Goldie croons while she sets her coat aside and lets Sweet Pea crawl into her lap. "Sweet Pea is such a sweet puppy. Yes, she is."

"Puppy wick me too!" Hallie cries.

A familiar dark-haired woman peeks in on us from the end of the row, eyebrows raised.

The wedding.

She was at the wedding.

With the former boy band-turned-solo artist guy.

She owns the store.

And my dog is running rampant and attacking customers.

Shit.

I snag Sweet Pea and tuck her back into her sling while I try to remember her name. E-something. Eloise? Emma?

The dots didn't connect at the wedding when she said she owned a bookstore that she owned *my* bookstore.

My neighborhood bookstore.

Once Sweet Pea is tucked back in against my chest, I rise, my knees creaking and my thighs groaning. Training was brutal today.

Doesn't matter how much you prep for it, the first few days are brutal.

Team's doing that right at least.

"She doesn't pee inside," I say to the woman.

Goldie rises too, her grin getting bigger. "He'd clean it up if she did," she tells the woman.

"This store has seen way worse than small dogs," the woman replies. "Generally courtesy of my own children."

Goldie laughs. "The squirrel. I remember your pet squirrel. Ingrid, did you meet Fletcher at the wedding last week?"

Ingrid. I-something. Not E-something.

Light dawns in Ingrid's eyes. "*Fletcher.* Yes. I *do* remember you. Pounders, right?"

"My daddy pways at da Pounders!" Hallie says.

"Yep. Your daddy and Fletcher here work together," Goldie tells her.

I nod toward the sports section. "You should expand."

Not *hi.*

Not *nice to see you again.*

Just *me man, me want sport book.*

I've managed to network my way into becoming acquaintances with half the professional athletes in the city, and here I'm a complete and total wanker.

"Fletcher's trying to get more attention on rugby," Goldie inter-prets for me.

Ingrid's smile turns apologetic. "We don't have a large sports section here. Our customer base is mostly women."

I slide a glance at the hockey shelf again.

Ingrid opens her mouth, then closes it again. She doesn't even look where I'm looking, but when her smile turns sheepish, it's obvious she gets my point.

"My daughter is a huge hockey fan," she says. "She plays, actually."

"Girls can play rugby too."

"I pway wugby!" Hallie announces. "I scwum! *Grrrrr.*"

The only thing keeping this kid from being freaking adorable is the fact that she's Silas's kid.

Not her fault.

"Girls play soccer too. And lacrosse. And football..." Goldie's grin is turning mischievous, and I've never been so glad to be over a rash in my life. Or so desperately in need of thinking about Silas Collins getting it on with my grandmother.

That's what kept my dick in check all night at the wedding.

It's only half working today.

Fuck.

"And baseball," Goldie says. "Baseball is a great sport too. Don't you have baseball players in here all the time?"

"They buy the romance novels," Ingrid deadpans.

Except I'm not sure that's deadpan.

That sounds like complete truth in her statement.

Goldie looks at me and shrugs. "Romance novels can't hurt. You might learn a thing or two."

Ingrid chokes on a laugh.

She must've heard the rumor we're "dating."

"Did you find books for the birthday girl?" Ingrid asks.

Goldie grabs a small stack of kid books that I hadn't noticed her put on a nearby shelf. "Your children's zombie picture book section is a little lacking too, but we prevailed."

"Just can't keep them in stock," Ingrid says dryly, and then both women crack up. "Ready for me to ring you up?" she asks Goldie.

"Yes, please. The birthday girl and I have a date with a horse next."

"Oh, a horse. That's exciting. Know what else is exciting? Birthday girls get stickers when they come into my bookstore."

I've trailed them to the counter, and I don't know why. My whole goal was to talk to the owner about stocking rugby books if there weren't any in the sports section. Got that done. Time to go.

Instead, I'm lingering like Goldie has a magnetic pull on me.

And it's barely in the back of my brain that it would be weird if I walked away since Goldie and I are "dating."

At the register up front, Ingrid pulls out a case of stickers and sets them on the counter for the birthday girl. "Would you like to pick one?"

Hallie climbs up onto a stool that's already at the counter—Ingrid's clearly a pro—and stares in wonder at the stickers like they're cotton candy and birthday cake and a bounce house all rolled into one.

Or like they're my dog.

"I want four dickers," her niece says.

"How about two?" Goldie says.

"Four."

"We have to leave some stickers for the other birthday girls and boys."

"I da birfday girl."

"Honorarily since I'll miss your real birthday next month. And you share your birthday with approximately twenty million other people. So if you have two birthdays this year, does that mean you technically share it with forty million other people?"

Ah, that mulish look.

I recognize that mulish look.

The kid's father wears it all the bloody time.

"I want a doggie," Hallie says.

"I'll buy them," I say. I grab a random romance novel off the nearest shelf and step up next to Goldie. "This and ten stickers, please. Birthday girl's choice."

Heh.

That'll piss off Silas.

And Goldie's giving me a look that says she's aware of exactly where my brain is, and she agrees.

Look at that.

I'm smiling again.

"So are you two real, or is this a PR move?" Ingrid says while she tears a bunch of stickers off and passes them to the kid.

"I'm *leaving the country* in nine days," Goldie says.

I sling an arm around her while her niece tries to take advantage of being on the stool to reach up and pet Sweet Pea again. "To go to my adopted second country."

Ingrid's entire face appears to be battling a smile. "Silas must love this. Considering how much he adores you dating in general..."

"Best news he's had all year," Goldie replies perkily. "If he comes in, will you tell him you caught us making out in the storage closet and had to break us apart with one of your yodeling pickles or something?"

Ingrid stares at her, goes beet red, and then stutters out a quick, "Of course," before ringing up the zombie kid books that the birthday girl apparently picked out.

"I got this." I hip-check Goldie out of the way and open the credit card app on my phone. "Put my book and stickers on it too."

"I can pay for Hallie's birthday presents myself," Goldie says.

"I do a good deed a day. This is today's. Can't argue or you fu— screw up my karma."

I don't believe in karma.

Goldie knows it. You can tell by the look she's giving me.

"If he's buying..." Ingrid murmurs with a grin.

"I'm *moving* and I already need a second storage unit for all of my books. I don't need anything else, regardless of who's paying."

I grab three chocolate bars that are in a little display on the counter. "Add these. They're consumable. You like chocolate, Hallie?"

The child has a price at which she can be bought, and it's apparently a dog, ten stickers, and a chocolate bar. "You my new fwend," she tells me. "You pwetty. And nice. I wike your dog. We be fwends."

Bollocks and damnation.

Silas's kid should *not* want to be my friend. "That's a bad idea."

Her chin wobbles and her eyes go shiny.

"And I love bad ideas. And zombies," I hear myself say.

Goldie stifles a laugh with a fist to her mouth.

That mouth.

The fantasies I've had about that mouth.

"Thank you, Fletcher." Her golden-brown eyes are dancing. "That's very kind of you."

"Aunt Gow-die, he go ride horses wif us?" Hallie says. "I want fwends for my birfday."

This is a bad idea.

This is the *worst* idea.

"He might have to go do work things with your daddy," Goldie replies.

Yes.

Yes, that.

Hallie's chin wobbles harder and a tear slips down her cheek.

"Nope. Free for the rest of the day." Once again, my mouth has not asked my brain's permission to talk.

Also, it's not technically true.

I promised my old man I'd video call him later.

Keep pushing that off.

Pushing it off once more won't hurt. Not like either of us get anything out of the calls. I'm a disappointing obligation. Always have been.

"You don't need to go eat three chicken breasts, a half-pound of raw spinach, an herbal energy drink, and have a massage, a dunk in a cold bath, and then sleep for ten hours before heading into training again tomorrow?" Goldie says.

She's getting a desperate note in her voice. She, too, has to know exactly how bad of an idea it would be for me to crash Silas's kid's honorary birthday date with Aunt Goldie.

I tap my phone against the credit card reader to pay for all of the books, stickers, and chocolate bars. "Plenty of time."

Do I want to go home and do exactly what she suggested?

Honestly, yes.

Pretty good recovery for tired, sore muscles.

But Hallie's sniffling. "I wan' my fwend and da doggie to wide hoooooooowses and come to teeeeaaa wif us."

How the hell do you say no to that?

She's crying.

I might be an asshole, but I have a heart.

Also, did she say *tea*?

I'm not fluent in toddler—preschooler—whatever she is, but I swear she said *tea*.

I haven't had a good cup of tea in the two months since I left England.

I look at Goldie in complete *I am a worthless man whose only redeeming quality today might be stopping your niece from crying even though this is a terrible, awful, horrible idea, and also, when she says tea, what does she mean?*

She squeezes her eyes shut and blows out a breath. "Okay. Okay." And then she adds, very strictly, "But no pictures."

I swallow.

Stern librarian Goldie is fucking hot.

"Agreed."

"My fwend wide horses and come to tea wif us?" Hallie says again, tugging on Goldie's hand while she sniffles.

"He can come along, but he might be too big for the horses, and he might be too busy for tea."

She said tea.

She said tea.

"He not too big," Hallie says.

Goldie squats in front of her to get down on her level. "This is *your* birthday date, Hallie. Are you sure you want someone else with us?"

Ingrid hands Hallie a sticker, which the little girl takes and meticulously places on her knight costume right in the center of her stomach.

It's a dragon.

It's a freaking dragon sticker.

Kid's three, and she's starting her collection of badges for all the dragons she's slain. Sideways, but she's wearing it.

I like it.

"He come too," Hallie says. "And he wet me pet his dog and he buy ice keem."

"Before or after tea?" Goldie's completely straight-faced.

Fuck yes, *tea.*

"Bof."

"We might not have time."

Hallie stares at her.

Goldie stares back with arched brows. "It's your birthday, but even birthday girls can't control time."

"I can," Hallie replies petulantly. So very much like her father.

Ingrid snickers softly.

"And you're sure you want Fletcher to come along?" Goldie asks.

Hallie puffs out her chest, showing off the dragon sticker. "He my fwend."

"I hope you hold out for more than a couple stickers and candy bars by the time you're old enough for men to buy you."

Hallie's nose wrinkles.

Ingrid coughs and shoves the bag of books at me. "Excuse me. I need to finish stocking the shelves. Goldie, can you still stop by and sign the rest of my stock before you leave?"

"You're on my calendar for Tuesday."

"See you next week, then. Happy birthday, Hallie. Enjoy. You only turn four once. I mean, twice, but once."

"I turn four *all da time*," Hallie declares. She climbs off the stool and grabs my hand, then grabs Goldie's too. "Horsey time!"

I meet Goldie's eyes.

They're so expressive.

She hasn't opened her mouth, but she's said so very, very much.

Silas will be pissed. That normally makes me happy, but I don't know how I feel about it when his kid's involved. Also, we are not kissing. I like your beard. We are not kissing. This is a bad idea. But if you're going to insert yourself into my niece's birthday date, I will absolutely without hesitation push you to the limit of what you can tolerate with children so that you don't pull this again.

Despite every reason I should be as upset as she is over this turn of events, I grin.

This is gonna be fun.

Torture, but also fun.

20

Goldie

MY BROTHER IS GOING to kill me.

Not because Hallie now wants a dog.

Not because I bought her cotton candy at the carousel at the park or because I let her coat go unbuttoned in the chilly late afternoon.

Not because of *the horses*. The horses are carousel horses, and every year for her birthday, I take Hallie to ride the horses.

So even Hallie going home tonight talking about wanting a horse too won't be a thing.

Plus, Silas would buy her a carousel horse—just the horse—if she asks.

He's extra. See also, he had her birthday costume custom-made for today and if she has a growth spurt before her princesses and knights birthday party next month, he'll have the costume adjusted or made again.

He probably won't even be pissed that I had an accidental date to my Aunt-Goldie-and-Hallie-birthday-date.

Not comparatively, that is, even with how he feels about me dating at all.

And *comparatively* is how pissed he'd be that I had a date versus how pissed he'll be that Fletcher, his mortal enemy on his team, crashed his daughter's early birthday celebration.

He *rode the carousel* with us.

He could've stayed on the side. Slipped away. Let Hallie get distracted with the horses and the cotton candy and tea coming next, but instead, he rode the carousel with us, with Sweet Pea tucked into her sling at his chest, completely breaking my rule about pictures when Hallie demanded he take a selfie of all of us, which he informed us is called an *ussie* in the UK.

"Oh, what a precious family," an older woman gushes as we sit on a bench beside the carousel while Hallie munches on her blue cotton candy and tries to feed it to Sweet Pea.

Fletcher's ears go pink while I smile at her. "Thank you. We're having a few last minutes together before he has to report to prison for grand theft auto."

"Or to my own grave," he mutters while she stutters something incoherent and rapidly changes course to go the other direction in the park.

The one saving grace so far?

We don't appear to have been recognized by anyone on the *Fletcher and Goldie are the cutest couple in Copper Valley!* bandwagon.

Likely because it's on the chillier side tonight. We're lucky the carousel was open. Hours are sporadic in the winter, especially on weekdays.

"I'm taking her back to her mom's tonight," I say. "There's a chance he won't hear."

"Where's Ms. *This Will Make Him Mad And I'm Giddy About It now?*"

"There are lines. We haven't just crossed this line, we've trampled it into the ground, lit it on fire, and roasted moldy marshmallows over it. But it's fine. It is. We'll tell him she wanted to hang with Sweet Pea and you weren't involved."

"Fetcher want cotton candy?" Hallie shoves a fistful of crumbled, wet, blue candy into his face, catching him with his mouth open like he's about to reply to me, which means she gets her hand all up in his mouth.

His eyes cross and then squint. "Mm," he says.

"Fetcher get more!" she shrieks.

"Oh, look at the time!" I grab my bag and pull out a wet wipe, snagging her arm and starting to rub all of the blue off her hands and face. "We need to hop the bus if we're going to make it to tea. Can you tell Fletcher thank you for letting Sweet Pea play?"

Wrong thing to say.

Wrong wrong wrong.

Hallie's chin juts out and her eyes narrow and she gives me the three-year-old version of the *what the fuck is wrong with you, lady?* look. "Fetcher and Sweet Pea come to tea wif us."

"Our reservation is only for two, and they don't let dogs in."

Logic is not my friend when it comes to almost-four-year-olds. Nor is any chance that she'll forget she said she wanted him to come to tea.

I know this, and yet I continue to hold out hope.

Why I hold out hope when she's starting to get the same expression on her face that Silas wears every time he finds out I'm seeing a guy, I have no idea.

I'm that level of optimistic, I guess.

"But maybe we can make another reservation for them to join us another time?" I add quickly.

"Dey come *today*."

"Don't you want to have something to tell them about the next time we see them? It's good to spend time away from our friends."

"Dey come *TODAY.*"

"It's her birthday," Fletcher says. "She makes the rules."

I slide him a *what the fuck is wrong with you?* look of my own.

The jerk stifles a grin. "Sweet Pea needs to find a good place for a quick potty."

"I take her!" Hallie leaps off the bench and grabs the leash that Fletcher's clipping the mini dachshund into for her trip to potty.

"You do not have to come to tea with us too," I whisper to him while we follow the threenager as she tugs Sweet Pea toward a tree. "They probably won't even let you in the door. They book up *months* in advance, so there's zero chance I can add you *and a dog* to the reservation."

The more I talk, the more his eyes light up. "Do you know who I am?"

The *ego.* And yet I'm still stifling an amused smile because I don't think he takes himself that seriously. I truly don't. "Do *they?*"

"They will."

"Know who you sound like?"

His noble nose wrinkles for a split second before he hits me with another grin. "Fascinating."

"What?"

"You haven't once said *you* don't want me to come along."

There's an unfortunate reason for that. And it's not the reason I give him. "I'm being polite."

He smiles broader.

I put a hand to Hallie's shoulder and pull her to a stop so I can zip up her coat over her knight costume, which is probably unnecessary but still gives me something to do. There's maybe thirty minutes of daylight left. We could walk to the tea house, but Hallie loves riding the city buses, so I have bus passes for both of us ready.

Sweet Pea stretches the leash as far as it will go until she's in a little flower garden that's devoid of flowers this time of year, pees in it, then sniffs around for a minute before finding a spot to squat and drop a tiny load as well.

Fletcher cleans it up without flinching, sanitizes his hands, and gives her a treat. "Good pup."

She pants up at him with utter adoration in her eyes while he rubs her little body.

"Fetcher come to tea," Hallie says again. "*Pwease, Aunt Gowdie?*"

Oh god.

She pulled out the *pwease*.

And it suddenly hits me that I'm leaving and I won't see her for months. We'll do video calls, but I don't know the next time I'll be in Copper Valley. Silas says he'll bring her to visit me during the Pounders' bye week if I find a cool place for them to stay in the city, but that's wishful thinking.

For as relaxed as Brittany is about letting our family hang out with Hallie regularly, she gives off strong *you are not ever taking my baby more than twenty-five miles from me* vibes.

Not that you can blame her.

Silas adores Hallie, but he's not always the best at respecting boundaries.

Or sometimes being an adult.

Letting him get on a plane to another country with her? I doubt that's happening.

And I'm not coming back to Copper Valley for anything more than to grab my car and load it up when I get back from London.

So I truly have no clue about the next chance I'll have to hang out with my niece.

"*Pwetty pwetty pwease?*" Hallie says.

Dammit.

My eyes get hot.

She could be saying her *r*'s and her *l*'s clearly every time the next time I see her in person.

175

This could be the last time she *pwetty pwetty pweases* me.

"Is that truly what you want for your birthday?" I ask her.

She nods.

And I cave.

Honestly?

Were it not for Silas and Fletcher's relationship as teammates, I would've caved immediately.

I like Fletcher.

He's the most fun kind of egotistical annoying that I've hung out with in a long time.

And I won't see him either once I leave the country.

I suck in a massive breath, and I do something I already regret for how much it makes my heart flutter in the exact wrong way. "Fletcher, would you join us for tea?"

He stares at me a beat too long. Too intensely too. I'm positive he can feel my pulse accelerating and sense the heat building behind my nose as I face one more thing that I'm doing for possibly the last time for years. "Only if they make the tea right."

I blink once, and then I actually laugh. "Can *you* make it right?"

"On three different continents, even though one of those continents doesn't know what's right."

Is he serious?

"North America," he clarifies. "You people here have no idea how to make proper tea."

"Tea tea tea!" Hallie sings.

And a little while later, after sweet-talking his way in at the posh tea house that he is in *zero* way dressed for, Fletcher agrees to don a princess tiara while he sits at the elegantly set table with the dainty chairs and heavy spoons and delicate teacups and saucers and shows Hallie the proper way to pour tea and hold a cup.

Her tea is hot chocolate.

Mine is Darjeeling. Fletcher orders Lapsang souchong for himself.

He also pulls a face when he touches the two small teapots delivered for each of us.

I lift a brow.

"Not warm enough. You're supposed to warm the teapot."

He grabs my porcelain, single-serving teapot, spoons looseleaf tea into it, and then pours hot water from the metal carafe over the leaves. He repeats it for himself, then sets a timer on his watch.

Sweet Pea has snuggled in against his chest and is snoring softly.

"No pinkies," he tells Hallie. "Here. This is how they hold it in England."

He takes her flowered bone china teacup by the teeny tiny handle in his big hand and demonstrates how to hold the cup the proper British way. "Pinkies down. It's okay if you grab the whole teacup right now, because you're a small human still, but when your hands get older, you only hold it by the handle."

My heart ker-thumps at the sight of the giant rugby player huddled over tea with my niece.

If Silas could see this—no.

Nope nope nope.

Silas wouldn't give Fletcher a chance.

"My hands get owder when my body gets owder," Hallie says.

"Correct. I should've said when your hands get stronger."

"My hands stwong like *grrr*."

"Can you palm a rugby ball?"

She flashes both hands at him and waves them back and forth. "They too wittle, siwwy!"

"When your hands are big and strong enough to palm a rugby ball, you have to hold the teacup by the handle. Deal?"

"I dwink my tea now, pwease."

"Good enough." He passes her back the cup.

She puts both hands around it and sticks her whole face in, coming up with a whipped-cream-and-hot-chocolate mustache.

"Now *that's* how you wear a mustache," I murmur.

He slides a look at me and rolls his eyes, but his lips are tipped up at the corners.

"You're good with kids."

"I am a kid."

"Very few kids are so business-minded about their professional sports careers." And attentive to what's not being said in a room. Intuitive about what various situations need. Able to talk a hostess into seating him and his dog as the third and fourth wheels at a table set for two in a place that doesn't generally allow dogs.

We're near the rear door, close to the kitchen in the princess palace room. *In case you do need to make a hasty exit*, the hostess said as she sat us, telling us without telling us that she knew who we were. Very few other guests will wander by us here, and there are no windows.

Fletcher slipped her a fifty and asked her to make sure we had privacy. *We're with a kid. Leave her out of it*, he said.

He holds my gaze for a long, serious moment. The man doesn't like being called out on being a grown-up, and an intelligent one at that. But he's saved by a low beeping on his watch. "Tea's ready."

I reach for the dainty milk carafe, but he stops me.

"Tea first."

"I thought it was milk first."

"Are we doing this the proper British way or not?"

"They don't put the milk in first?"

He rolls his eyes. "The palace doesn't. Their teacups don't crack when you pour in the hot tea, so they don't need the milk to go in first."

"Fletcher Huxley, are you secretly an anglophile?" I whisper.

His ears go pink again. "In my younger years, I liked to fit in where I was at. Here's the sugar if you want it. *After* the tea goes in your cup."

"And now?"

"I don't take sugar in my tea."

That is *not* what I was asking, and he knows it. "Why don't you try to fit in?"

"We're in mixed company and can't discuss that." He pours my tea for me, then his for himself. When I pick up my spoon after adding a splash of milk and a lump of sugar, he covers my hand with his. "Don't clink it. Stir gently. Not in a circle—do it back and forth. This way."

A current of *he's touching me* buzzes up my arm. "You're very picky about tea."

"If you're gonna do something, do it right."

After he helps me with my tea, he makes his own. I watch him while he sips his tea. No slurping for Fletcher. But he's still a giant, over-muscled, tattooed man wearing a tiara to humor a birthday girl and sipping tea delicately from an elegant teacup that he could probably crush with his bare hand.

And I wonder what he's doing *right* in being here with us tonight. What role this event is serving for him.

Is this some power play against Silas, and will I hear about it for the rest of my natural life?

Or does he want to be here, with me and Hallie, because we're friends and he, too, is too much of an island sometimes?

I have a lot of friends around town, of all ages and back-grounds, but since I broke up with Miller, I haven't been *tight*-tight with anyone who's not approximately forty years older than I am. Hanging out with Fletcher is making me miss what I used to have.

Not that I'd trade my ladies for the world, but sometimes, I want what I gave up two years ago too.

"Sammiches!" Hallie exclaims as our server arrives with our individual, three-tiered trays and sets them in front of each of us. Hallie's hot chocolate mustache is epic enough to battle Fletcher's former mustache in the wrong kind of glory, and she'll have the sugar buzz to end all sugar buzzes when she gets home.

Brittany's probably glad I'm leaving the country.

But also, Hallie will crash hard if we can get her through a bath.

Our server points out which sandwiches are which, our jam flavors, and the sweets on the bottom, then asks if we have any questions.

"Is that real clotted cream?" Fletcher asks, pointing to a ramekin on the middle level.

Our server smiles at him. "Our chef is British. It's real clotted cream. But if you prefer whipped cream—"

"I'm gonna need a pint of clotted cream to go."

He's serious.

He's completely dead serious.

And it's utterly adorable.

"What else do you miss about England?" I ask him after the server's departed and Hallie is digging into her finger sandwiches.

He stares at his own tray long enough that I chalk up my question to one more that I won't get a straight answer to.

Considering it's half of what our friendship is based on, this doesn't surprise me.

Or bother me.

But then, I hear, very softly, "My team."

And it suddenly makes complete sense why, now that we've cleared the air about what happened in that VIP suite all those years ago, Fletcher fits in my life.

I might not know his whole story, but I'm positive he gets the heartbreak of losing the friends closest to you. He understands the unique kind of loneliness that comes with not knowing where you'll fit next. With needing to go somewhere else—anywhere else —to find what's suddenly missing in your life.

"I miss that about Copper Valley too," I say softly.

He holds my gaze longer than should be comfortable.

So your truth finally comes out, Coach Goldie. You fake fitting in too. You're as lost as the rest of us.

I sip my tea and reach for a finger sandwich, then pause to explain to Hallie which sandwiches are which again.

She listens, then dives for the brownie bite on the bottom rack. Apparently salmon spread doesn't have the same appeal as sugar for an almost-four-year-old. Who knew?

Fletcher's still watching me over his own tea cup. No milk or sugar for him.

But I don't feel judged.

I feel understood.

Right as I'm about to leave the country.

Figures.

21

Fletcher

I'M STARING at a stack of board games and wrapping paper in my living room, thinking about the pinball machines I have in storage that I've ignored since I moved here, when someone knocks at my door. Sweet Pea doesn't stir from her plush doggie bed. I almost ignore whoever's dropping by unexpectedly, but in the weeks since I moved in here, there's been exactly one person who's ever knocked at my door.

And even if I didn't want to see her, I'd want to see her.

I should go to bed and pretend I didn't hear. Got another long day of training ahead of me tomorrow.

Instead, I check the hall camera, verify it's Goldie, and order myself to stop smiling before I answer the door.

Today was weird.

Training was hard. I'm not making progress fitting in with the team. Realized very quickly that my motivational speech was viewed as my ego instead of my dedication, and it's weighing on me harder by the day.

Especially since I'm not the only former star from another country who's come to American rugby as a late-career step. There are guys from Ireland and New Zealand and Germany and South America all over the rest of the league.

Holt's Canadian. Played in the same league I did for a few years, but the guys don't think anything of that.

So it's eating at me.

As if I'm the problem.

Which I probably am.

It's been on my mind since I left training today only to run into Goldie at the bookstore.

Running into her gave me that unwelcome feeling in my chest when she smiled.

And then riding a carousel for the first time in—fuck, since right before my mom died—made me feel other things.

So did having tea and showing Goldie and Hallie how it's done.

And now she's standing on the other side of my door, fidgeting with something I can't clearly see through the camera.

I open the door, and my heart gives a lurch.

Fucking heart.

It's not supposed to do that.

"Hallie was *very* upset when she realized you left your tiara at tea, so she made me promise I'd bring it back to you." Goldie shoves a sparkly metal object at me. "You don't have to wear it, but I can now honestly tell my niece I kept my promise."

I pull the door open wider, silently inviting her in, unsure if I want her to accept or not.

She stares at me like she, too, isn't sure if she should come in or not, still twisting the tiara in her hands.

"Did you get dinner?" she asks.

183

I nod. Didn't eat much of my spread at tea because none of it fit my body-as-a-temple philosophy.

The scones and clotted cream, *fuck* yes. I'm going back.

The rest of it I gave to Hallie. Except for the one cookie that Goldie kept eyeing.

"Hallie couldn't stop talking about you once we got her home," she says, still hovering in the doorway. "Your lessons in high tea made an impression. And that was before she got to talking about Sweet Pea. I told Brittany—that's her mom—about how, erm, *complicated* it will be for Silas and his feelings, and she was—well, let's just say she knows exactly who Hallie's father is, and she's declared herself to be on Team Fletcher, despite my warnings that Team Fletcher is basically Silas of another flavor. Which I say with affection, I swear. And thank you. It was fun to have you along today."

"I'm a shitty team player here," I say.

She stares at me for a beat, bites her lower lip, inhales deeply enough to make her chest rise in ways that my dick notices, and then steps inside to join me. "Why do you think that?"

I let the door shut and walk back to my living room, letting her follow. "You're right. They all look at me like I'm the arrogant asshole who doesn't give them credit."

"You're also the newest player on the team."

"Rookies are newer."

"You're the newest *experienced* player on the team. You have a history. They know it."

The question dangles in the air. *Want to talk about what happened in Nottingshire?*

No.

No, I don't.

Doesn't mean I don't need to, but needing to and wanting to are not the same here.

I sit on one end of the couch and stare at the board games on my coffee table.

She takes a seat at the other end, deposits the tiara on my end table, and then makes a noise. *"Monopoly?* Of course you have Monopoly."

"Presents," I say.

"For who?"

"My niece."

She stares at me. "You told me you were an only child."

"I've mentioned my sister."

She stares harder. "You sounded like you were joking."

Once again, I'm smiling.

This is fun.

She's not wrong. I can tell you the truth and make you question it, and I use it to my advantage when I don't want to let people close.

"Her birthday?" Goldie asks.

"My family celebrates the holidays on February third."

Her entire face goes on a journey of *he did not just say that*, and then she cracks up.

"Laugh all you want. It's what we do."

"No, no, it's—*my* family celebrates all of the holidays on Thanksgiving. That's when we do Christmas gifts. *Did*. When we did Christmas gifts."

I stare at her.

She stares back, but she's still smiling like this is the best surprise ever.

"Why Thanksgiving?" I ask.

"Before my parents got divorced, they'd always take us to high-end all-inclusive resorts for the entirety of winter break, and they hated taking presents on the plane, so they made up a story about how Santa brought the *best* kids presents for Thanksgiving instead. Why February third for you?"

"Why not February third?"

"It has no particular significance?"

"That's why it's a good day."

She leans forward and slides Monopoly out of the pile. "You know this is the very worst game in the entire world, right?"

"It's my favorite."

"Couples have broken up over this game. Friend circles have imploded. Lifelong enemies have been made. And you're sending this to your niece?"

"She's seventeen. Cutthroat. Like her uncle."

"And by *uncle*, you mean you, and not another brother?"

"I don't answer questions for people who hate Monopoly."

"I didn't say I hate it. I said it's the worst game in the world."

I watch her again.

Watching her might be my new favorite hobby, which is a problem.

A very large problem.

She grins. "I make Silas cry every time we play this."

"Told you he was a whiny-ass baby."

"If you want to fit in with your new team..."

Of course she goes there.

Which is basically exactly what I want.

I want her advice.

But I don't like exposing myself in asking for help.

She shakes the box at me. "We should play this to see if we can be friends."

"Clothing instead of money."

"Honesty instead of money."

"You have a way of making a guy's balls sweat."

"It's a gift."

I move to the floor, stifling grunts from my sore muscles and creaky joints that say that a strip board game isn't in my body's

186

best interest, which is frustrating as hell. I clear the rest of the boxes off the coffee table and take Monopoly from her.

We're set up in under five minutes.

Sweet Pea is still sleeping, which says something about how much fun she had today. Or possibly about how much she likes bedtime.

I wish I slept half as well as my dog.

Goldie's rubbing her hands together, her eyes shining with utter glee. "You're going down, Huxley."

I'd go anywhere she told me to go if she ordered me around while she's lit up like that.

One more reason this is a bad idea.

But I don't know who else to talk to.

She grabs a die and hands me the other. "Roll to see who goes first."

"You can go first."

"There's no chivalry in Monopoly. Roll the die."

"If you're planning to make me cry before we're done with this game, you're about to find yourself sorely disappointed."

She smirks and rolls.

And gets a six.

A fucking *six*.

I roll and get a one.

If I wanted an auspicious sign, that was not it.

"I choose to let you go first," she says.

"This isn't a coin toss. You don't get to pick who goes first when you roll highest. You go first."

Her golden eyes dance with mischief. "If you're not brave enough, that's fine. I'll go first."

"I'm brave enough."

"If you say so."

"I'm also a fucking gentleman. Roll the damn dice. Also, I'm the car."

"I like being the Titanic, so that's fine." She's grinning as she rolls the dice, and *are you fucking kidding me?*

A seven.

She rolls a seven. Lands on *chance*. And gets a freaking *get out of jail free* card.

"Your turn."

She passes me the dice. Her fingers brush my skin as she deposits them in my palm, and a shiver races up my arm.

I roll a five.

Fuck yeah.

Railroad. I *live* for owning all four railroads in this game.

Goldie dives for the stack of property cards. "Who likes you on the team?" she asks.

"That's your question?"

"That's my question."

"For a *railroad?*"

"Mm-hmm."

My suspicions hit the roof. "What would you ask if I landed on Park Place?"

"You didn't. Irrelevant."

But I will. And I'm getting the other three railroads too. "Your loss."

She smiles.

Did I say suspicious?

I meant *this woman is wanted for murder.*

The murder of my peace of mind.

"Porter likes me," I tell her. "So does Holt, but he doesn't like that he likes me. A few others. Zander. He came over from the Premiere League too. One of the rookies is star-struck."

"Mm," is all she says before she takes the dice and rolls.

And lands on the next railroad.

Fuuuuuucccckkkk.

She did not.

188

"That's my railroad," I say.

"It's open, and I'm buying it. Ask me a question."

"No."

"In the event a player refuses to operate as the bank, the bank is taken over by the hostile mini dachshund corporation, who will eat the refusing player's underwear while the cooperating player is allowed to use Monopoly money to buy the property."

"That's the most daft, bullshit rule I've ever heard."

She lifts her brows. "Or you can't win without cheating."

"Did you honestly have no clue that your ex was sleeping with your friend before you walked in on them?"

Dick move, Fletcher. Dick. Move.

But Goldie doesn't blink as she looks me square in the eye. "*Should* I have noticed clues? Probably. But we were still having sex regularly. He was still taking me on dates and bringing home flowers and other little treats. I hadn't noticed any significant changes in his work hours, and if anyone else knew, they didn't drop any hints."

My brain short-circuits at *we were still having sex.*

I don't want to think about Goldie having sex with the fuck-wanker who doesn't deserve her and tried to corner her for fuck-all knows why at the wedding.

I'm glad she's leaving the whole bloody country to get away from him.

And then my heart does that thing it's not allowed to do again when I think about her not being around the corner to drop by.

Fuck.

I grab the dice and roll.

And I get a *two.*

Now I'm on the chance spot, and when I draw, I have to pay taxes.

Or, in this version of the game, answer a question.

Goldie giggles.

I sigh. "Go on. Hit me with it."

"Are you physically able to make it through the season based on how your body feels right now?"

"Yes."

"Mm."

"What does *mm* mean?"

"I acknowledge your answer."

"But you don't believe me."

"Should I not believe you?"

No.

She shouldn't.

I could get tied up in the technicalities of *cans* and *shoulds*, but it's not her turn to ask another question.

I grab the dice and hand them to her.

And she rolls a ten.

A fucking ten.

Which puts her on the next railroad. "How the bloody hell are you doing that?"

"Is that your question?"

This is torture.

I hate it.

And I'm having a better time than I've had since I went to a wedding with a rash all over my body to play the role of the hotter, sexier, better boyfriend that Goldie got herself after the nincomtwat now known as her ex screwed around on her.

I shake my head. "Not my question. This is my question: how old were you when your parents got divorced?"

She doesn't hesitate. It's like she's worked all of this shit out in therapy. "Fourteen. Silas was ten. It wasn't super pleasant. Accusations of cheating on both sides. Fights over the validity of the prenup. My father doubled down on making sure Silas and I had the best equipment and were signed up for all of the sports camps and had every opportunity in the world because he only knew how to show love through demanding we achieve in athletics. He was pretty high up in management for the football team here, so he could afford whatever he wanted. My mother had the trust fund and she'd made a name for herself as an artist, so she could afford whatever she wanted too. By the time my father was done with her, most of what she wanted to afford was gin and tonics with pool boys."

This isn't something I've ever read in her books.

And she says it like it's mere fact, but there's a waver in the way she looks away that says she still hurts for the teenage her who went through watching her family fall apart.

"That's how old I was when my mom died," I say quietly.

"I read that in your bio. And I'm sorry. Parents are supposed to be there for us until we can take care of ourselves." She tucks her knees up to her chest. "My parents are still alive, but I don't see them much. They're...not healthy for me. And I don't know if I'm healthy for them either. So it's just Silas and me for Thanksgiving presents."

"They don't call to tell you they're proud of you?"

"I ceased to exist as a useful part of my father's life when I broke my hip and left soccer. Silas sees him regularly, but Brittany doesn't let him have much to do with Hallie. Which is apparently fine with him since Hallie can't win at sports yet. And my mother —she's been on a journey to finding herself since Silas graduated high school. Last I heard, she was somewhere in South America working on a mural or something."

I know what she's doing.

I'll tell you something deep so you'll trust me to tell me something deep back.

And I still want to hit something, and then I want to pull her into my arms and hug her and tell her that her parents are dicks and she deserves better than what they gave her, better than a cheating ex-boyfriend, better than a team of friends who let her

191

walk away when she was the one who was wronged, better than a brother who doesn't see that she's strong enough to survive whatever shit men throw at her.

And I want to tell her she's not alone.

For someone who's incredibly popular around town, she doesn't have a lot of friends other than her old lady group that she seems to see with any regularity.

It's a defense mechanism I recognize well.

And not one I employed until I got here.

Fuck, I miss my team. They still text on occasion, but it's not the same.

I'm not there.

I'm here. Starting over in my mid-thirties with a body that often feels much, much older.

She hands the dice to me. "My grandma made sure to split her trust out so that Mom didn't use it all when the divorce happened and there was something left for Silas and me, but I don't—I don't touch mine unless I'm in an actual emergency situation and have no choice. It's more of an albatross than a safety net."

I close both of my hands around hers as I take the dice.

She lifts her eyes, and I see myself in the defiance. The *I dare you to tell me I'm wrong for not wanting free money*.

"You're fucking awesome," I say instead.

"I know."

Her smirk breaks the tension, and I huff out a laugh while I roll the dice.

And land on her freaking railroad.

"Oooh, rent!" she exclaims, rubbing her hands together. "This is my favorite part."

"How the fuck did you rig this? What did you do to the dice?"

"Not your turn to ask questions, bub. It's *my* turn. Or else I'll have to send you to jail for failing to pay rent."

She's cackling.

Legit cackling.

And it's glorious.

I could sit here and listen to her cackle at my bad luck in this stupid game for hours.

She has a bloodthirsty streak.

My bloodthirsty streak salutes hers.

My bloodthirsty streak appreciates hers.

"Go on then," I say. "Ask me something."

"Hmm… Do I go for super-personal, or do I go for the big professional elephant in the room?"

I haven't known her nearly long enough to instantly recognize that she's debating between asking me about my divorces and asking me for my version of why I left England mid-season, but I have zero doubt that's what her brain is waffling between.

The divorces don't embarrass me—I was exceptionally young and naïve for the first one, and young and stupid for the second—and it's not what I want to talk to her about anyway.

"My coach fired me," I tell the board.

"I'm not familiar with rugby contracts in the UK, but that doesn't seem like the full story."

I growl softly to myself.

She shifts closer to me. "I'm on your side here, Fletcher."

"I got a small tear in my rotator cuff two seasons ago, and I haven't been—I haven't been right since."

"Not a fun recovery."

"I rehabbed the fuck out of it."

"I believe you."

"It's not my shoulder. It's my—it's my brain. It won't—it can't get over it."

"Brains are such bitches sometimes."

"Rafferty—my coach—I played for him for a long time. My whole career, basically. He started coaching the year I signed on with the Leopards. He taught me how to pour tea. Helped me get through some personal shit early on. Believed in me. Treated me like family. His wife did too. She was the aunt I never had. His daughter was like a little sister until she left for university. They had me over for Christmas the years that I couldn't see my own sister. She's busy. Orthopedic surgeon in Seattle. Kids. Wife. Life. And four months ago, he benched me."

"What for?"

"Being too old. Coddling my shoulder. Getting in my own bloody way on the pitch with mental fuckaroni. My game turning to a steaming pile of elk shit."

"Was your game shit?"

I shake my head. "It wasn't—it wasn't my best. But it wasn't shit. I could've turned it around. I *was* turning it around. But he didn't see it. And then I made a stupid fucking mistake, cost us the match, yelled at one of my teammates, and that—that was it. He sat me down, told me I was done, that I could retire on my own and walk off the pitch with my head held high, or I could sit on the bench the rest of the season and wait for the team to trade me somewhere that needed an old fucker like me to inspire the next generation."

"Ouch."

"I'm not done playing rugby."

"I know."

"I'm *not.*"

"It would go a long way with the team here if you trusted your teammates enough to tell them that."

It would be so easy to flip her off, but that's what Neanderthal Fletcher wants to do.

Not what team-player Fletcher needs to do. "So I should tell them that they're right—I'm only here because I couldn't cut it in a better league anymore."

"No, you should tell them you still love the sport to the pit of your soul. That your coach was wrong, that he hurt you, and that you're not here to show him he made a massive mistake, but instead, that you're here because you believe in building something bigger than yourself and that you want to do it with them. With the Pounders."

I slide a look at her. "I *am* here to show him he's a fucking ass-wanker who made a mistake. Last thing I told him before I left his office was that the next time I set foot on English soil, it would be as a bigger success in America than I could've ever been in Britain."

She cracks up. "You know what? Tell them that too. Ask them to help you prove to a crusty old British wanker that he fucked up. That you still have it, and more, that you can be the critical part of that team that *you chose* instead of waiting around for the English league to pick for you."

I swallow back my retort of *the Premiere League.*

Already a big enough ass. Don't need to rub that in too.

"I wouldn't have wanted to hear some Australian fuck-off tell me that when I was younger," I mutter instead.

"Tell them that too. *I'm being a guy I would've despised when I was your age, but also, let's show the entire world what we can do.* When's the next World Cup? Can you imagine a team made of players here triumphing over your old coach and teammates?"

"Yes."

She laughs again. "Crossed your mind a time or two, hmm?"

I fantasize about it daily. "I don't want to coach. I don't want to go into scouting. I don't want to do all of this marketing bullshit, even if I'm good at it. I want to *play*. And I—never mind. Your turn. Roll the dice."

She doesn't take the dice.

Instead, she scooches her ass over until she's next to me, both of us trapped between the couch and the coffee table.

And then she does the worst thing she could possibly do.

She slips her hand into mine and squeezes. "You can still play today. And tomorrow. And probably through this whole season.

195

Someday, a new chapter of your life will start, and you might be ready for it, or you might not, but you, Fletcher Huxley, are nothing if not stubborn and driven and determined. You'll figure out where to go next when it's time. I believe in you."

And there it goes again.

Stupid muscle in my chest. It's beating harder, teetering at the edge of a cliff, looking down onto a rocky shoreline, not certain if the parachute will open if it jumps.

It wants the thrill despite knowing that we'll crash on the boulders.

It's what we do every fucking time.

And despite knowing this, I'm currently safe.

Feeling like it'll be okay when the day comes that I take off my boots and budgie smugglers and the rest of my kit for the last time.

Because Goldie has faith in me.

"You're a pain in the ass," I mutter.

Her smile says she's aware that I don't mean it, and she squeezes my hand harder. "You'll be okay," she says softly. "Not because I said so. But because you're you. You'll figure it out when you need to."

I shouldn't be squeezing her hand back like a lifeline.

I don't need a lifeline.

I need to get over myself, be real with the Pounders, earn their trust, and help them decimate every other team in the league this year.

But I don't want to let go of Goldie's hand. "Are you going to London to run away from your ex?"

She leans closer to me. "I actually had the opportunity to attend this program as a student a few years ago, and I wanted to, but he asked me not to. He didn't want me to be gone for the single month that each of the classes get."

"So it's still a fuck you to him."

"If he wants to look at it that way. I don't think about him

196

much at all anymore unless I know I'll be somewhere that he'll be as well. Doing this residency has been a dream since Elizabeth suggested I take my degrees and get into life coaching. I'll miss Hallie. I'll miss my friends. But I am *so* excited about the opportunity and the doors it'll open. And I—I'm looking forward to a fresh start somewhere without—without the baggage that my social life has here."

"Will you miss me?" I don't mean to ask, but the words leave my mouth all on their own.

Her smile goes soft. "I will."

"I'd miss me too. I'm fucking awesome."

"It's precious how you hide your insecurities behind your ego."

Shit. "I'll miss you too."

I don't look at her when I say it.

I can't.

It's too damn true. I don't want to look at her and see that she's merely being nice. I don't want to see the pity over the fact that I'll miss her more than she'll miss me. I don't want her to see how much I mean it, because that's basically flopping my heart out of my chest and offering the beating thing to her in my hands.

I don't do that anymore.

Not my lot in life to mess around with the love bullshit. All it does is break you when it ends.

And it always ends.

They always leave.

My mom.

My first wife.

Rafferty might not have left physically, but emotionally, the prick abandoned me too.

"I'm not gone yet," she whispers.

There's a hungry note in her voice that has me lifting my eyes to hers while my cock gets heavy.

Her chest is rising and falling faster than it should. Her pupils have dilated to the point that there's the barest golden ring around them. And she's mere inches from me.

With a pink stain on her cheeks and her tongue doing a slow swipe of her bottom lip.

This is a bad idea.

Lucky for both of us, I love bad ideas.

22

Goldie

I'M GOING to kiss Fletcher.

Not in public where someone can jostle us.

Not because I want to make a scene.

Not because I want to prove a point.

I'm going to kiss Fletcher because I want to kiss Fletcher.

He's watching me with a heavy-lidded gaze like he's daring me to be the one to initiate the kiss.

Like he doesn't think I'm brave enough. Bold enough. Like I don't want it enough.

I smile. It's impossible *not* to.

This man knows how to push my buttons, and I like it.

"Fuck me," he mutters, and then his hand is hooked around the back of my neck, he's twisting on the floor beside the coffee table, and his lips brush mine.

Fuck me.

Agreed, Fletcher.

Agreed.

His whiskers are at that perfect length to be soft-scratchy around my mouth, and much like his hair, his lips are deceptively soft.

Plump. Firm.

Hot.

He doesn't rush the kiss. There's no question he thinks he's in charge, but he doesn't rush it. Instead, he takes his time, playing my mouth and using his hands on the rest of me like he's planned every move of this for months.

He doesn't object when I start exploring his chest. Feeling my way up his shoulders and around his thick neck.

The man is all muscle. He has to be for his job, but right now, it's all for me.

My breasts are heavy. My nipples are tight, hard peaks. And my vagina is asking if we can please straddle this man.

If he's half as good at sex as he is at kissing, I could have my first man-made orgasm in—actually, I don't want to think about how long.

Not important.

What *is* important is that his fingers are twirling in my hair, pulling hard enough to send sparks of pleasure across my scalp. That his other hand is splayed across my upper back, his thumb rubbing the back of my neck and giving me goosebumps. That his tongue is brushing against mine, teasing me, daring me to be the one to take things further.

That he smells like a winter forest on a snowy morning and tastes like a rich red wine.

That his whiskers are teasing the sensitive skin around my mouth.

I want to know how they'd feel on my inner thighs.

And I don't know when I'll get another chance.

So I ignore the quiet whispers in the back of my head of *is this smart?* and *is this safe?* and *will I regret this?*, and I give in to the desperate need to swing one leg over his hips.

I bang my ankle on the table, but I hold on to the kiss, ignoring the pain as other sensations take over.

Specifically, the sensation of Fletcher's thick, hard penis nestled between my thighs with only his sweatpants and my leggings between us.

He makes a low rumble in the back of his throat, then wraps an arm behind my back, holding me against him while he tightens his grip on my hair and deepens the kiss.

Yessss.

This.

This is what my body has been craving.

I'm seizing every opportunity before I leave the country.

Tonight, that opportunity is Fletcher.

Fletcher and his hard body and his scratchy face and his soft hair and all the tender spots he's hiding in his heart that he pretends aren't there.

Fletcher, my friend.

He's the perfect final fling.

He wrenches out of the kiss, chest heaving, lids heavy, mouth parted. "I'm not thinking about your brother."

I'm so thick in the cloudy haze of horny desire that it takes a minute for his words to register.

"I'm not thinking about him either," I say.

My chest is rapidly lifting and lowering. I can't focus on anything beyond his face. And I want to kiss him again.

"Good," he pants.

"Good," I agree.

We stare at each other.

"I'm leaving—" I start at the same time he says, "I don't do relationships," and then we leap on each other again.

Not that there's room for leaping.

He's sitting with his back against the couch. I'm straddling him.

We're attached at the mouth, and I'm thrusting my hands under his shirt while he palms my breast and squeezes.

Oooh, yes.

I tug his shirt off.

He slides his hands under mine and unhooks my bra, then cradles both of my breasts, rolling my nipples between his thumbs and forefingers and channeling electric jolts of pleasure from my chest to my pussy.

I rock against his erection.

He grunts once, and then he's shifting, pushing me onto my back.

My elbow smacks the coffee table. There's a distant clattering. The game box has flipped and pieces are scattering on the wood floor around the rug. When he lays me on the rug, something sharp pokes me in my shoulder blade.

"Car," I gasp.

"We can do it in my car later. Any car. All of my cars." He lifts my shirt and presses his mouth to my sternum, and *oh my holy god*.

But also—"Game. Piece. Back. Stab."

He lifts that heavy-lidded gaze, lips plump and wet, blinks once, and then mutters a solid *fuck* as he pulls back.

He grunts once more. Rises a little. Something pops. His knee?

And then he's hauling me over his shoulder in a fireman's carry. "Fletcher?"

"I'm too old for this floor shit."

The world bounces. The rug disappears, replaced with gray wood floors. We go through a doorway.

Clothes litter the floor.

Oh, there's Sweet Pea! She's sleeping in a doggie bed.

Everything shifts and I'm once again on my back, but this time, I'm on satiny sheets on a bed.

My shirt and bra have disappeared.

Fletcher shucks his pants and crawls onto the bed too, his cock standing thick and hard and proud against dark curls.

My vagina clenches.

"I've been fantasizing about this for an eternity," he murmurs while I reach for his penis and stroke the hot, rigid length. His eyes cross, then drift shut. "Fuck, Goldie."

"We're going to have fun tonight."

"Yes, we are."

"Condoms?"

"Whole fucking box. Nightstand."

"I'm on top."

His cock pulses in my hand, and I smile.

So does he.

He also leans forward, pushing me back again, and kisses me.

Those lips.

His hand sliding into my pants to cup my ass.

His pelvis flexing against mine, teasing me with the feel of his erection against my clit.

I miss this.

I miss physical connection. Kissing. Touching. Intimacy.

And when Fletcher moves his mouth, taking his kisses to my jaw, my neck, my collarbone, to my breasts—*oh my god*, I miss sex.

I miss *wanting* sex.

He sucks one nipple into his mouth, and my hips leave the bed.

"Good?" he murmurs.

I grip his soft hair and push his face back to my breast. "More."

"I only worship breasts if the lady they're attached to is completely naked."

"Oh my god, you truly are an asshole."

He laughs against my chest, and honestly?

So do I.

I also wiggle my hips while I tug off my leggings.

He helps me, and then I'm naked except for my socks.

I haven't been naked with a man in two years.

And I need to *not* focus on that.

Not when Fletcher's sliding a condom into my hand as he licks the underside of my breast, all the way to the tip of my nipple. I'm panting as I watch him, his tongue swirling around my areola before he sucks my whole nipple into his mouth.

My hips buck again. I tighten my grip in his hair while my legs wrap around his hips.

The condom.

I need to get the condom on him.

Now.

Before—just *before.*

One little flex, and I could take him all the way inside of me.

And I want to.

Oh my god, I want him inside of me.

He sucks my other nipple into his mouth, hard, and it's such a hot, fast jolt of electricity through my belly to my clit that I almost come.

I'm wet. I'm heavy with need. My clit is begging for the attention my breasts are getting. He's teasing me with his shaft, rubbing it softly against my clit.

"Fletcher," I gasp.

He lifts his head from my breasts and smirks at me, then takes the condom back. He rips it open with his teeth, holding eye contact with me, then rolls to his side to suit himself up.

Still watching me watching him like his cock is a seven-course meal when I haven't eaten in a month.

I think I just licked my lips for the fourth time.

He's winning this round.

He is *so* winning this round.

"You still want on top?" His voice is husky, his hands taking over to play where his mouth was a moment ago, and I have to swallow twice before I can answer.

"I'm always on top."

"In control."

It's the only way I get off.

If I'm in control.

Why—*why*—is he watching me like he knows that's exactly what I'm thinking? That smirk says *I could get you off with a single look.*

And based on the way I'm already tight and heavy in my vagina —I don't think he's wrong.

But I still shove his shoulder and push him to his back. "Thank you for being a gentleman."

"There's nothing gentlemanly about what I want to do to you."

I swing my leg over his hips, my own hip catching just wrong and sending a familiar ghost pain across my pelvis.

He steadies me.

Doesn't ask a thing.

Just watches.

That's Fletcher's quiet superpower.

Watching.

Observing.

Connecting dots.

His hands caress my hips, sliding back to cup my ass.

As quickly as it came, the pain disappears. And I'm still a hormonal ball of lust, wet between my thighs, my nipples demanding more attention, my clit objecting to not getting her turn.

I lean forward and kiss him, watching his eyes close as he strokes a hand up my spine to cup my neck again.

I'm teasing his tongue with mine as I slide onto his erection. The feel of him inside me, stretching and filling me, makes me suck in a breath.

He does the same, and we break apart, staring at each other.

I sink all the way down onto his cock, taking my time, feeling every inch of him penetrating me, parting my slick walls, feeling *home*.

I lift myself and sink back onto him again.

His broad chest rises quickly, and his eyes drop half-closed again, but he's still watching me.

Still being Fletcher.

Still taking everything in.

Taking *me* in.

Like he's memorizing this. Memorizing me.

"Play with my nipples," I whisper.

"Kiss me," he whispers back.

My heart melts into a puddle of *someone should love this man*.

And I do.

Kiss him, I mean.

Clearly, I don't love him.

I barely know him. How could I love him?

Be his friend?

Yes.

Love him?

This—my hips pumping faster as I ride his cock, my mouth attacking him while he pinches my nipples and cradles my breasts and then reaches between us to circle his thumb around my clit while I bounce faster and faster, chasing that high of all of the coiling inside me coming loose at once—this isn't love.

This is a fling with a friend who knows what he's doing.

And *oh my god*.

He thrusts his hips to meet mine, teasing my clit and then taking his thumb away, his cock rock-solid, and *oh my god, there it is*.

There's the spot.

That's the spot.

He flicks my clit once more as he strokes his tongue into my mouth and his cock hits that spot inside me, and I shatter into a billion pieces.

Light flashes behind my eyelids.

My toes curl.

I grind down hard on his pelvis, soaking up the sensations as I realize he's groaning my name, his fingers biting into my hips while he holds me still, our bodies as connected as two bodies can be, my orgasm ripping through me and his cock pulsing in time inside me.

I can't breathe.

Can't think.

I can only *be*.

Just me, a flaming ball of satisfied nerves, connected to a man who's so much more than I would've given him credit for a month ago.

I sag against his chest as the last tremors of my orgasm leave me.

He's breathing hard, as if he doesn't run five miles a day on the rugby pitch.

And when I should say *this was great, thanks, maybe we should do it again before I leave*, instead, I bury my face into his neck.

And he flings an arm around me.

Holding me there.

Silently telling me that he doesn't want me to leave either.

23

Fletcher

GOLDIE STEPS out of my bathroom, still completely naked, and my tired, sore, overworked body whimpers.

I want more of that.

My dick's on board. I like seeing Goldie naked in the doorway to my bathroom. She looks right against the marble floor and the clawfoot tub.

She'd look better *in* the clawfoot tub, but that's not the most pressing issue.

"I should—" she starts, and my brain goes into overdrive.

"You haven't said hi to Sweet Pea."

She blinks at me.

Then at my dog, who's slept in her bed by the door through all of the noise we made.

Naturally.

I got Sweet Pea the coziest, comfiest dog bed on the market. *I* could sleep through anything if I was on a me-sized dog bed like that.

"She's sleeping," Goldie says.

Still totally naked.

Not attempting to cover any part of her.

I can feast my eyes on her breasts. Her pussy. Her long legs. Her collarbone. Her hips. That hummingbird tattoo that she's been hiding on her shoulder blade that I could see if she turned a bit to her left.

"She'll know you were here and she'll think you don't like her."

I'm lounging on the bed, propped up by pillows and my padded headboard. Also completely naked and shameless and basking in the afterglow of sex. Too hot for even a sheet right now. And it wouldn't take much for her to realize I'll be ready for another go in under five minutes.

Goldie smiles at me.

Not a placating smile. Not a *got you, I'm leaving anyway despite your lame attempts to get me to stay* smirk.

But a real smile.

She crosses the short distance from the bathroom to the bed and takes a seat at the edge of it, giving me the tiniest glimpse of her tattoo again. "I should go."

She's trying to convince herself.

You can hear it in the lack of conviction behind her words.

"You ever have sleepovers when you were a kid?" I ask her.

"Are you asking me to have a sleepover?"

"No, I'm asking if you ever did it. I didn't. Parents wouldn't let me."

She stares at me for a beat like she's debating if this is a stall tactic to keep her from leaving—of course it is—and then she pulls her knees to the side and angles further onto the bed.

Still totally naked.

Who in his right mind would want her to leave right now?

"I didn't either," she says. "Even for birthday parties. If it was a sleepover, my parents picked me up by ten. Even through high school."

"We missed out."

"Completely."

"Total shame."

"I need to go home, and you need to get your rest before another long day of training."

"You have meetings first thing tomorrow?"

"Not until almost noon, but I need to pack books for my storage unit."

My heart hiccups.

Swear the damn thing does.

And it pisses me off.

Goldie's my *friend*.

I can want my *friend* to stay longer since she's moving away in nine days.

Not a hiccup that time.

Something bigger.

Harder.

Unwelcome.

Also?

She said she needs to go, but she's not moving from her spot.

"How many books do you have?" I ask.

She flares her eyes and grimaces. "Close to a thousand."

"A *thousand*?"

"Maybe not quite that many, but close."

"A thousand fucking books."

"Only four are about fucking. The rest are a mix of nonfiction related to psychology and sociology and self-help, some biographies, some historical fiction, plus a couple hundred romance and fantasy novels."

I need to stop gaping. "Do you read them or just collect them?"

"Oh, I've read them all." She frowns. "If not all, then most of them. Occasionally I've found a book I couldn't get into the way I hoped I would."

"You've read a thousand books."

Her cheeks go pink. "I read fast. Always have. And I *like* to read."

"What's your favorite?"

"My favorite book?"

"No, your favorite kind of waffle. Yes, your favorite book." I'm gonna read it.

"Fiction or nonfiction?"

"Either. Your very favorite of all."

"There is zero chance I can pick a favorite book."

"What's the point in reading if you can't rank one as your top?"

"Do you have a favorite rugby ball?"

"Yes."

She laughs and settles deeper onto the bed. "Okay. Right. I asked for that."

"When do you read?"

"Between meetings. Before bed. When I'm brushing my teeth. On the bus. Regularly when Silas gets me tickets to his matches and insists I go. I'll hold my phone up like I'm recording the match or taking pictures and yell when everyone else does, but really, I'm reading."

She's not lying.

And that's the funniest shit I've heard all day.

"Bink—my sister—was a bookworm when we were kids, but she didn't like to people. You like to be around people."

"One can both enjoy reading and be an extrovert. It happens."

"What's the last book you read?"

"Nora Dawn's final book in her *Confucius* series."

"Philosophical book?"

"No, Nora Dawn is my friend Henri's pen name. Luca Rossi's

long-time girlfriend? Confucius is the hero in her vampire romances."

Mental note, read Luca Rossi's girlfriend's romance novels.

And hope it doesn't get weird the next time I see the dude.

Showing interest in people and what they do is good, right? Even if it involves reading a mate's girlfriend's romance novels?

Shit. I'm confusing myself now.

"How'd she get into that?" I ask.

Goldie grins. "Looking for your next career?"

"Everyone needs a backup plan that they never use."

She scoots fully onto the bed and reaches for the dark gray sheet at the foot of the bed.

My dick stands straight up.

She's staying.

She's having a sleepover with me.

"I'm still leaving," she says. "In a minute. But I'm cold."

Her nipples report that she's not lying.

I like her nipples.

They're fucking delicious.

I help her grab the comforter too and make a show of tucking her in.

Covering her up to her collarbone and everything. While she's also leaning against my headboard.

My dick might be showing off, but I can still be a gentleman.

For now.

"What's your backup plan?" I ask her.

"For getting home?"

"If your Coach Goldie gig ever fails."

"Trust fund," she quips without hesitation.

I watch her without blinking, and she sighs as the smile slides off her face. "I've had to reinvent myself before. I can do it again."

"You're missing a little *oomph* behind that phrase."

She lifts one bare shoulder, then readjusts the comforter to cover herself back up. "It sucks. The process, I mean. I know the other side of the work is good, but *god*, there aren't shortcuts."

I grunt in agreement.

"When your life falls apart, there's this moment of, *that's it. It's over.* You know?" she says quietly.

I nod.

Been there a time or two.

"But then there's the next moment, when you put one foot in front of the other, and you keep going. You don't know where you're going, but there's something ahead, and if you can get to it, even if it's not what you're supposed to get to, you made it far enough to look. You can stop. You can rest. You can get a bite to eat. And then you can keep going until you find what's right. Because it's out there. Whatever it is, it's still out there."

I shift to turn toward her. "You believe that."

"I do."

"Before we moved to Australia, I played hockey."

"Aww, you must've been the cutest."

"And terrible."

"Weren't you like, five?"

"That's no excuse for being terrible."

She laughs and settles deeper under the covers. "You're ridiculous and it's adorable."

"You said *studly sex god* wrong."

She shivers.

I recognize that shiver.

It's a good shiver.

She's thinking about my penis.

I smirk.

She laughs softly and sleepily, and it lights up my bedroom.

I don't usually give a lot of thought to my bedroom. It's where I sleep. It's dark. The mattress is fucking top-notch. I don't give a shit if I don't pick up my clothes since it's only me, and I pay a cleaning service to come in once a week and do all of the picking up and laundry for me.

If I'd known Goldie was coming over and we'd end up in here, I would've straightened up. At least gotten my clothes off the floor.

But not made the bed.

Definitely glad I didn't make the bed.

"Do you still like hockey?" she asks me.

"I like all sports. Except lacrosse."

"Lacrosse?"

"It's a wussy sport."

"Oh my god, Fletcher."

I smile at her latest bark of quiet laughter.

If she wasn't related to Silas, she'd be the perfect woman.

We both settle lower on the bed.

"I like hockey," I tell her.

"I want to see another game before I leave."

"I'll get tickets."

"You might not be free the same nights I'm free."

"So I'll get tickets for every home game for the next two weeks. Problem solved."

"Ridiculous and adorable," she repeats. Her eyes are getting droopy.

Mine might be too. "Studly sex god."

"I should go home."

"And miss a chance to sleep on the *Slumber Seven Thousand?*"

"Is that a broomstick?"

"It's my mattress."

"Your mattress has a name."

"I did a commercial for them two years ago in France. *Slumber Seven Thousand* is a rough translation."

"I like you entirely too much." Her lips curve up in a smile as her eyes drift shut.

I like you too much too. "Relatable. I like me too much too."

214

"I'm getting up."

"I see that."

"I am."

She's not moving except to possibly sink deeper into the bed.

"Clearly," I agree.

"This mattress is ridiculous."

"It cures insomnia, hypertension, fallen arches, and bad breath."

She giggles softly. "I believe it. I'm still leaving."

"Uh-huh." I climb off the bed long enough to kill the lights and shut the blinds, then I crawl under the covers next to her.

Not touching.

Simply next to her.

Watching her outline. Listening to her breathing even out and get deeper.

I don't let women stay the night at my house.

But I'm glad Goldie isn't leaving.

24

Goldie

I'M in the middle of my usual morning stretch-yawn-pry-open-my-eyelids-in-bed routine when I realize something's off.

It's me.

I'm off.

I'm off because I'm not in my own bed.

My eyes fly open, and I sit straight up, the mattress beneath me adapting to make even sitting as comfortable as breathing.

Gray walls. Soft sunlight. City view. Black leather padded headboard. Wooden floor covered with a thick Turkish rug.

Fletcher.

I'm in Fletcher's bedroom.

And he can come back and play, my sleepy vagina murmurs.

I smile to myself, try to tamp it down, fail, and then realize I'm alone.

Where is he? It's too early for training. Is he mad that I fell asleep here?

I didn't mean to. Truly. But he kept talking. And I like talking to him. So I—so I broke the rule, and I fell asleep here.

Hard, if I'm being honest. I have no clue what his mattress is made of, but it's so comfortable, it's probably illegal.

That's very Fletcher.

I'm still smiling as I slide out of the bed and head to the bathroom, where I realize I don't know where my clothes are.

I give half a thought to leaving the bedroom naked to hunt them down, but I can't stay here naked all day, so I shouldn't set the expectation that I can. Instead, I treat myself to a fresh T-shirt from Fletcher's walk-in closet, which is surprisingly neatly organized compared to the scattered clothing and gear all over his bedroom floor.

And then I order myself not to inhale too deeply.

The shirt smells like him. That earthy, woodsy, tobacco-in-winter scent.

And I like it.

Of course I like it. He's my friend, so I like things that remind me of him. And I like that I swim in the T-shirt too.

It's good to have friends who are large enough to loan you T-shirts that can swallow you whole. There's...comfort...or something...in that.

That's what I'm telling myself as I slip out of the bedroom on the hunt for my pants, which are not in the bedroom where I swear I left them, and it takes me an eternity too long to realize what I'm seeing.

Sweet Pea is awake. She's found my pants, and she's pulling them along behind her across the living room and toward the kitchen.

Where someone appears to be cooking eggs at the stove.

And that someone is not Fletcher.

He's older. Gray, receding hairline. Trim. Tall. Familiar jaw and nose.

But not Fletcher unless I'm living in some kind of alternate dimension where he's some sort of shapeshifting thing that only reveals his true form after sex.

Possibly I need to read less.

The man spots me about the same moment that I spot him, and he freezes and gawks right back at me.

So, not Fletcher in a shapeshifted form.

I make a noise, and Sweet Pea drops my pants and comes running, barking and turning her long little body in circles like she can't believe I'm here and she's so excited and this is the best day ever.

My heart melts a little, and I want to get down on the floor and love all over her and show her I'm as excited to see her as she is to see me, but that's not gonna happen.

Not while the older man fixing eggs is staring at me too.

Is this shirt covering my vagina?

Or am I flashing the beaver at him?

I do a subtle check, brushing the tips of my fingers against the bottom of the shirt, and verify that I am not, in fact, showing anything inappropriate.

Sweet Pea leaps onto my shins, barking out her utter joy.

"Hi, Sweet Pea," I murmur, holding absolutely still. "It's so good to see you too. Yes, it is. Who's such a good puppy? Who's the best puppy? Where's your daddy?"

She barks again.

The powder room door on the other side of the kitchen squeaks, and there he is.

Fletcher slides around the edge of the bar-height countertop between the kitchen and dining room, his eyes unexpectedly wide while he looks between me and the older man like he can't decide if he wants to laugh at me standing here in nothing more than one of his T-shirts or vault across the condo and hustle me either out of his apartment or back to his bedroom.

Either way, watching his reaction spurs me into action of my own.

"Hi," I say brightly as I step around the dog—*I am so sorry, Sweet Pea, but I absolutely cannot risk flashing anyone this early in the morning.* I head across the living room toward the kitchen and the bar counter. Fuck it. Why not? What do I have to lose here? I'm leaving next weekend. Eight days from now, to be exact.

"I'm Goldie."

The older man looks me up and down in a way that says he knows exactly what went on here last night.

That scattered Monopoly board tells a whole story when you add me to the mix. Also, my bra is on full display hanging over the back of the couch.

Awesome.

Even if Sweet Pea hadn't dragged my pants in here—oh, yeah, there's my red thong peeking out at the waistband too—it would be very obvious what went on here last night.

Fletcher's shoulders relax and his mouth settles into resting neutral face while he looks at the older man, then back at me. "Goldie, this is my father, Daniel, who didn't tell me he was coming for a visit. General, this is Goldie."

General.

That says even more than my scattered clothing does. I reach General Daniel and hold out a hand, pretending I'm not standing here in nothing but one of his son's T-shirts. A Pounders T-shirt, actually. That says *We Pound All Day.*

"Lovely to meet you," I say.

Sweet Pea is right on my heels.

If she barked in glee when this man got here, I slept through it.

"How'd you get a name like Goldie with black hair?" he says by way of greeting.

"Oh, my legal name is Jessica. Goldie's a nickname. But my family's called me Goldie since before I can remember. Apparently it was my eyes. And then I fell in love with the story. *Goldilocks and the Three Bears?*"

Shut. Up. Goldie. Shut up right now.

Both men gape at me long enough that it takes the smell of burnt egg to spur General Daniel back to the stovetop.

And this is weirdly more awkward than walking out here in nothing but an innuendo-laced T-shirt while I clearly ignore a dog I'd love to pet in the interest of not putting on a show.

"Fuck me," Fletcher mutters at the same time his father looks up from the eggs that he's moving to a plate now to say, "You still have a type."

Oh god.

Oh god.

His bio.

His first wife.

His first wife's name was Jessica. I didn't think anything of it since I don't identify as a Jessica, but—well.

What's more awkward than awkward?

That might be where we're headed.

"So I'll get my clothes and head out," I say to Fletcher. "Thanks for a lovely evening. Good luck with training today."

"You want breakfast?" he asks.

"Oh, no, I live on mortification and discomfort most mornings. I'm good."

His father snorts into a coffee mug.

Coffee.

"My coffee's better than my bed," Fletcher says quickly.

The motherfucking bastard is reading my mind and taking it to the next level without having to pause to analyze if he's reading my facial expression right.

Also, if his coffee is better than his bed, I absolutely cannot stay here and drink it. "Can I get some to go?"

"No."

"I give you clotted cream and a tiara, and this is the thanks I get?"

He smiles. "Yep. How do you take your eggs?"

"Spicy. Sort of like me in the mornings before coffee."

His father snorts into his coffee mug again while he carries a plate of over-easy eggs around the other side of the island and sits two stools down from me.

Fletcher's eyelid twitches while he grabs a treat and tosses it across the condo, sending Sweet Pea on a mission to chase it down. Her little feet slap against the wood floor until she reaches the rug in the living room.

And my brain catches up.

General.

Stay for breakfast.

The tension.

How did I not notice the tension?

Fletcher doesn't want to be alone with his father.

Fine.

Fine.

I can do one more little thing for him.

I slide onto the stool beside General Daniel and level Fletcher with a look that I hope tells him I know exactly what's going on, and if he wants any more Goldie in his bed before I leave, he owes me another story about his personal life.

We're gonna be a lot easier on him than that, my vagina and clit and ovaries chime in together.

Traitors.

"Salsa spicy or hot sauce spicy?" Fletcher asks.

"Whatever you can handle, I'm sure I can handle too."

His lips twist, and I'm pretty sure that's some *game on* amusement. But he's stifling it.

He's stifling it hardcore.

"So, General Daniel, do you live in Copper Valley?" I ask as

Fletcher gets to work in the kitchen and I try to repress the little squeal of joy that my accidental sleepover is ending with him making me breakfast.

This would be way better if we were alone.

I'd bend over and pet Sweet Pea and give him a show if we were alone.

General Daniel shakes his head. "Hadn't heard from Fletch in a while, so I flew in last night from Arizona."

Fletch.

Isn't that sweet?

Also, I notice he doesn't tell me not to call him *General Daniel*.

"How did you meet my son?" he adds.

"He passed out on me while giving blood a couple weeks ago, and I decided to keep him."

"You a nurse?"

"No, I'm a life coach."

"How old are you?"

Ah, the old *you're not old enough to be a life coach* question couched as mere curiosity. I live for this one. "Twenty-eight, but I was born into the soul of a seventy-five-year-old woman, and I've read basically every human behavior book that's ever been written. Plus, I've lived through a few things."

"Wars and famine, hmm?"

"Death, divorce, injury, illness, broken dreams, broken hearts." I shrug. "Maybe I haven't lived through it as many times as other people, but that doesn't mean I can't understand what makes people tick and how to put them on a path to achieving their goals. My favorite thing about life is that you can do anything you want to do, no matter who doubts you or tries to tear you down."

He flinches and looks away while Fletcher glances at me sharply.

Bull's-eye.

It's always some variation on this theme when it comes to men and their fathers, I swear.

"And how old are you?" I ask the general.

Fletcher makes a noise that he covers by aggressively beating four cracked eggs with a fork in a glass measuring cup.

"Sixty-one," his father says.

"Which branch?" I ask.

"Army. Retired."

"Recently?"

"Two years ago."

"You taking full advantage of retirement, or are you still finding your purpose in the next phase of your life?"

"Are you life-coaching me?"

He doesn't seem bothered by me peppering him with questions, and he isn't giving *you're too young to do this job you claim to be able to do* vibes.

So I smile at him like I don't suspect he was hard as nails on Fletcher when he was growing up. "I'm puzzling out where Fletcher came from and what retirement might look like for him."

"That'll take way more than one breakfast," Fletcher himself mutters.

"You his life coach?" General Daniel asks.

"Oh, no. My client roster is full."

He studies me.

Again, I'm not getting the *you're full of shit* vibes that I got the last time I told my own father about my job, so I'm willing to continue giving him the benefit of the doubt until I have reason not to.

Fletcher slides a cup of coffee across the countertop to me, and follows it with a small plate of cheese.

My heart thumps so loudly, I'm surprised it doesn't startle either of them.

"You want the cheese spicy too?" Fletcher asks me.

"No, I'm a cheese purist. But thank you."

He sets four bottles of hot sauce on the counter in front of me. "If you change your mind…"

There's a sizzle at the stove.

My eggs are cooking.

I smile at Fletcher, even though he's not looking at me, then take a sip of the coffee.

And nearly die of *oh my god, that's delicious.*

He glances back at me.

"Is this what they teach you in Europe? How to make orgasmic coffee and where to buy the best mattresses?"

"No."

"*Dammit.* My hopes are now dashed. What kind of beans are these?"

"Guatemalan. Present from my sister and her wife. Fresh-roasted yesterday."

"Who roasted them?"

"Me."

"You're hired. You can stow away in my luggage on the way to London and make me coffee every day."

He rolls his eyes and goes back to the eggs.

"London?" his dad repeats.

"Oh, that." I flap a hand. "I've been selected as the coach in residence for a quarter for the Worldwide Coaching Association's intensive training at the University of London. I start in a little over a week."

I sip my coffee again and stifle another moan.

Then I take a bite of cheese.

Room temperature.

Oh god.

Fletcher pulled my cheese out. He let it warm up.

It's so much more delicious when it's room temperature.

I'm absolutely dropping by later with scones and clotted cream from the tea shop for him. I don't care what favors I have to call in to pull off a to-go order.

Fletcher visibly bites the inside of his cheek like that's what it's taking to keep him from smiling at me as he flips the eggs onto two plates.

A moment later, I have eggs in front of me.

Fletcher doesn't sit.

He hovers across the high countertop.

I take the spiciest hot sauce and shake it on my eggs.

He takes the bottle from me, our fingers brushing and sending an electric current from my hands to my pussy, and shakes even more hot sauce on his eggs than I put on mine.

I meet his eyes.

Game on, they say. *You really like it spicy?*

If his father weren't here, spicy eggs would definitely lead us back to the bedroom.

I take a bite, and are you kidding me?

Drool slips out of my mouth. I slurp it back in and wipe my lips. "What did you put in these eggs?"

"Secret ingredient." He takes a bite of his own eggs, larger than mine, with more hot sauce, and stares at me without blinking while he chews and swallows.

"Are they actually the best eggs I've ever eaten, or am I just in a good mood?"

He smirks.

I take another bite, then decide I need more hot sauce.

He shakes more hot sauce onto his eggs too.

So I add a dollop more to mine as well.

We both stare at each other as we take giant bites.

Shew.

Spicy.

Shame, actually, since those eggs are freaking delicious with less spice, but I know what game Fletcher's playing here.

And he knows what game I'm playing.

And it's fun as hell.

Even if my mouth is starting to burn.

His cheeks take on a pink hue when he takes his next bite.

My ears are sweating before I'm done with my next bite.

Don't ask about my tongue.

And that's before he makes a thoughtful noise, turns to the cabinet next to his fridge, and pulls out a black bottle with a flaming asteroid on the label. "Still needs something hotter," he says.

He's not looking at his father.

I'm not looking at his father.

We're both looking at the bottle.

Salty Marvin's Fire In Your Hole And Yes We Mean That Hole Sauce.

Hot sauce always has the best names.

He pops the lid and shakes the thick red liquid onto his eggs.

I reach for the bottle too, but he covers my hand with his. "You sure, Goldie? There's no going back."

"Afraid I'll find out it's mislabeled and it's actually ketchup?"

He grins.

I grin back.

I love this.

I truly do.

I love messing around with Fletcher.

The fun's been missing in my life.

That's what he's given me back.

I love my friends. I love my job. I love my clients.

But I haven't had this much fun in ages.

I tug on the bottle.

"Your funeral," he mutters.

I'm smiling even broader when I shake the sauce onto my eggs.

Will I regret this?

Possibly.

But there's cheese right there if it's truly too spicy.

And coffee.

The coffee might help.

He forks up a bite, but doesn't eat it until I'm ready to eat my bite too.

And *holy fucking cheese balls.*

That's hot.

That's *hot* hot.

They bottled blue flames to make this hot sauce.

Fletcher's eyes bulge.

Mine are sweating.

I chew.

And swallow.

And feel the heat all the way down my throat.

Behind my heart.

Into my stomach.

"That's good," I rasp.

"The best," he agrees, equally raspy.

We both take another bite.

His father makes a noise and rises. "Definitely a type," he says as he heads toward the powder room.

Once the door shuts, Fletcher lowers his head to mine. He's sweating. He's sweating like he ran seventeen miles through a swamp in August. "I thought you were going to sleep for another hour with the way you were sawing logs."

Dear god, my tongue needs a fan. And ice. And a surgical procedure to reattach it from where it burned off inside my mouth. "I live to destroy the lives of men who don't kick me out of their beds and send me home at night."

He takes another bite of eggs.

Chokes.

Pretends he's not choking.

And I start laughing.

227

I shouldn't.

My mouth is on fire too. I can't feel my lips. My taste buds might be permanently burned off. I'm sweating like it's a hundred and ten with a heat index of one-forty even though Fletcher's condo can't be warmer than sixty-eight degrees.

And I'm having the best time ever.

Fletcher makes a noise that I recognize well.

It's a stifled laugh that's accompanied with a look at the bathroom.

He doesn't want his father to hear him enjoying himself with me.

And that's sad.

I impulsively reach across the counter and grab his hand. "I had fun last night. Thank you," I whisper.

He meets my gaze and doesn't reply.

He doesn't have to.

That look says it all. *I'm terrified to say it back to you.*

Which is fine.

It's fine. Seriously. All fine.

This?

This is fun. Short-term. Only fun.

The hot sauce is more serious than our relationship is.

And that's completely and totally fine.

It's so fine, I can't stop saying *fine*.

And I think that pretty much says it all.

25

Fletcher

My ass is on fire.

TMI, but it's the truth.

And it's a truth that everyone in the changing room is well aware of.

"Fucking hell, Huxley, what did you do in there?" Holt snaps as he comes out of the bathroom and into the changing room.

"My business," I reply.

I hope Goldie's not feeling this the same way I am. I don't care that she technically started it. I'd be a flaming asshole—and trust me, those are ugly—if I wished anything like this on her.

She's—just—fuck.

I like her.

And not because I *have a type*.

"Do your business at your own house." Holt waves a hand in front of his face. "Jesus. I thought my nose was dead, but apparently not. What the *fuck* did you eat?"

"Hot sauce."

"Don't fucking do it again."

"Thanks for making sure I'm okay. Appreciate it."

He stares at me like he's debating tackling me during training for shits and giggles.

Neither of which I would like to do again for the rest of today.

"You *fucker*," Silas snarls as he charges into the changing room. "Stay the *fuck* away from my daughter."

I pull off my shirt and glance at him while I grab my training kit.

Dude's livid.

Holt leaps to hold him back, but the captain's giving me a look.

I've clearly now earned two spots on his shit list.

"Brittany told Goldie it was okay," I say.

Calmly.

Like a rational fucking adult.

When I'd rather put my fist through his face and get this over with.

"And *stay the fuck away from my sister*."

"Your sister's doing me the favor of being seen in public with me as a publicity stunt to sell tickets so that I can prove to the wanker formerly known as my UK coach that he was fucking wrong when he told me I was done playing rugby."

Fuck.

All of that tastes worse in my mouth than my morning eggs did and feels worse than my eggs did coming out the other end.

Smells worse too.

But the *very, very, very* worst part?

The worst part is the utter silence falling in the changing room.

Not just the three of us.

Some of the younger guys are in.

Two other dudes are lingering in the doorway.

At least ten of my teammates heard me say that.

Might as well strip off my shorts and budgie smugglers too. Stand there letting it all hang out to go with what I've confessed because Goldie fucking told me to.

"Fuck your old coach, man," Crew says.

I jerk my head around to look at the tall Black man, who nods like he's repeating himself. *Fuck your old coach.*

"He still in your head?" Holt asks.

I scoff.

That means yes. Likely they know it.

"You need a good therapist," Porter says.

"I don't need a fucking therapist. I need to play. And sell out this fucking stadium and show him he's an ass-wanker."

"You think we don't want to sell out too?" Holt says quietly.

"Tired of working three jobs, bruh," Crew adds.

He's like me.

Caught the rugby bug when his military family was stationed overseas.

Unlike me, he seems to genuinely still like his family and not think he constantly needs to prove himself and live up to some abnormal level of perfectionist standards.

Bloody hell.

Maybe I do need a therapist.

Rather talk to Goldie though.

I'm doing my best not to growl as I look around the locker room. "You know why I picked this team?"

"Here goes the ego," Silas mutters.

"Because you have the fewest experienced foreign players and you can still fucking win."

"*You?*" Holt says.

"*You.* Fuck it. I'm old. I'm not as good as I used to be. But I'm still as fucking good as any of those other nut-buggies who came to play here after they got told *they* weren't good enough for the top leagues in the world anymore either. And I can still help you win. And I can teach you to make our ticket sales the envy of every other team in the league."

Silas is seething still. "By using my sister."

"She's leaving the country, asswipe. She knows what I'm doing, and she's using me to piss you off because you don't respect her ability to make her own choices." I'm probably overstepping.

I don't give a fuck.

At least, I'm trying not to. Having Goldie mad at me isn't top of my list of favorite things to do.

"That part's funny," Porter mutters.

"Goldie's fucking brilliant and funny," Crew agrees.

Pretty obvious based on the way Silas is curling his hands into fists and leaning like he's gonna try to get around Holt that Goldie's brother doesn't agree.

But what's he gonna do?

Punch me?

"Back off, Collins," Holt says. "I won't say this again—your sister's an adult. Besides, this can't be fun for her. Look at him. Now get ready for training, all of you. We've got a stadium to fill and matches to win."

"By playing by the rules," I say.

Oh, good.

More dead silence broken only by the squeak on the floor when Crew shifts his weight and looks at Silas.

Everyone else is looking at Silas without shifting their weight.

"You got something to say, fucker?" Silas growls.

Hell with it. Past time to get this out. "Knock it off with the high tackles and fucking *stand up all the way* before you grab a fumble."

The tension is getting thick enough that even the most clueless among us should pick up on it.

"Might want to worry about your own game, old man," Silas says.

"You might want to think about the fact that most of your teammates need three jobs in the offseason to make ends meet. Winning matters. Bonuses matter. This league fucking *matters*." I yank my training jersey over my head, then tug it down. "I'm gonna hit the pitch and do my job with my whole damn heart and soul because it's all I fucking know how to do. If you don't like it, that's your problem."

I shoulder past both Holt and Silas, ignoring the murmurs and mutters as I head down the tunnel toward the pitch.

The old man's coming to watch today.

Probably gonna watch me get my ass beat by the teammates who likely hate me more now than they did before.

And what difference does it make?

If it doesn't work with this team, I've got a few others to try.

Not like there'll be anything else in Copper Valley worth staying for in another week or so anyway.

26

Goldie

It's a chilly day to watch a bunch of grown men tackle each other on a rugby pitch, but when Fletcher messaged that he'd told the team about his former coach and did I want to come watch training today so some pictures could be leaked to the press, I decided I was in.

But only if I could bring friends.

"Why are they tossing the ball backwards over there?" Odette asks. "That's not how you move forward."

"Rugby rules," I answer.

We have hot chocolate in sassy insulated tumblers, coats, and blankets, and we're sitting in the first row at the halfway line of the pitch when I should be at home packing boxes before my client call at noon. I can't stay long, but when I asked my friends if they wanted to see a rugby training session, they all dropped everything and showed up.

"This is the strangest sport," Evelyn says.

"Only here." I sip my hot chocolate and track Fletcher on the pitch. He's a forward, part of the scrum pack, which is what he's practicing now. They're running one-on-one scrum drills, each player lined up against another to push against each other with their heads and shoulders while down on all fours.

But no knees on the ground.

Just feet and hands.

I'd be lying if I said it wasn't something of a turn-on to watch Fletcher clear an entire line of his teammates one by one. Especially knowing that he knows his body isn't what it once was.

I don't know if something's eating at him or if he's having a good day because the day after good sex is always a good day.

Or possibly this isn't a good day.

For him, I mean.

After all, his father's sitting three rows behind us.

I see ice baths and heating pads and lots of painkillers in his immediate future.

"I sent him my obituary for his mustache," Odette says.

Good thing I finished that last sip. "When?"

"Last night. Before I knew you were getting jiggy with him."

"Oh my god."

"You did, didn't you?" Evelyn nudges me, beaming behind her glasses. She has a pink knit hat with a brighter pink ribbon on it pulled over her short gray hair. "You have a glow."

I flex my shoulders back. "We played Monopoly."

"And you're still talking?" Odette shakes her head. She's on her last day in her wheelchair and pretty testy about still being stuck in it. "That game is the devil's game."

"I like it," Sheila says. "I like getting the purple properties. No one else ever wants them, but I always imagine I take them and plant flowers and fix up the grass and maybe add a garden gnome. I love the idea of doing a great job of raising their property values."

Odette and Evelyn both stare at her for a brief moment, then look back at me.

"The only thing that game's good for is a psychological test of your enemies," Evelyn says.

"Agreed." I clink my hot chocolate tumbler to hers. Mine says *classy as fuck* on it, and hers has the outline of a sexy lady's face over the words *I'm silently judging you.*

"And what's your official assessment of his personality after this game?" Odette asks.

I smile. "He's a very good...player."

All three of them shriek in utter glee, earning a look from two of the coaches standing not too far from us on the pitch.

"Did you finish the game, or did you just get naked?" Evelyn wants to know.

"His father's sitting three rows behind us," I murmur.

And the three of them do what you do when you have no fucks left to give in the world, and they all turn and stare.

I should've anticipated that.

I blame the mellowing effect of my high-end hot chocolate.

And the complete and utter satisfaction still relaxing my body.

"You're Fletcher's dad?" Odette says to the general.

I'm still breathing to build up my own courage to turn around when he answers a quiet but authoritative, "Yes."

"We like Fletcher," Evelyn says. "He bought us wine one night."

"And his dog is the sweetest," Sheila adds.

"And he's been *such* a gentleman about wooing Goldie," Odette continues.

"Such a gentleman," Evelyn and Sheila agree.

Wooing. I'm still stuck on the *wooing.* And it makes me gulp my hot chocolate too fast, which nearly singes the tip of my tongue.

"Are you single?" Evelyn adds.

And it's time for me to get over myself. I turn at that and smile

236

at him as if I didn't have breakfast with him without my underwear on this morning. "Morning again, General Daniel. Good to see you."

He holds my gaze for a long moment, then nods and says, "Goldie," in a way that makes me wonder if he was contemplating calling me *Jessica*.

"This take you back to Fletcher's early years in rugby?" I ask.

Something flickers over his face as he lifts his gaze to the pitch, but he returns his attention to me quickly. "My wife did the taxi-driving for the kids. I didn't attend most practices."

My brain leaps to conclusions that I don't question.

The general worked a lot. Of course he did. You don't get promoted to general in the military if you don't.

He probably had high standards for his kids. Fletcher's work ethic is undeniable. And he said that his sister is an orthopedic surgeon. They probably had a regimented childhood with a lot of expectations.

Or maybe I'm projecting after watching what my own father expected of Silas and me in order to earn his love.

"It's nice that you can be here now," I say, since I'm honestly out of my element at this point.

I don't help clients heal relationships with their parents. I help them find the path they want for themselves.

The parent thing is a job for therapy.

Or at least for a coach who doesn't have her own parental baggage.

I turn around to face forward and find Fletcher watching me from the pitch while he and about half the team stand around one of the coaches, probably getting instruction on their next drills.

A full-body shiver races across my skin.

The man does nothing half-assed, and that includes looking at me when he's supposed to be practicing.

But this is Fletcher.

I'd bet the last of my stash of gourmet chocolate bars that he's listening to every word his coach says while still making me tingle in the lady bits.

"Lord have mercy," Sheila whispers.

"I haven't had a hot flash in twenty years, but I'm sweating right now," Evelyn murmurs.

"Is he picturing you naked?" Odette asks.

"What kind of question is that?" Evelyn retorts. "Of course he is. Look at the man."

I bite my lip, because honestly?

Him looking at me like that is making me picture *him* naked.

And Fletcher Huxley naked should be classified as one of the greatest world wonders.

I shift in my seat, pressing my thighs tighter together.

And then I blow him a kiss.

He freezes for half a second, then licks his lips, and then looks back at his coach.

Another man makes a noise from somewhere on the other side of the pitch, and I realize we have an audience.

Specifically, my brother.

I locate him on the grass and blow him a kiss too. Where Fletcher is a forward, Silas is a back. He's made a name for himself as a pretty physical defender. Right now, he's in the middle of a passing drill.

No, check that.

Right now, he's flipping me off.

"Eyes on the ball, Collins," the head coach yells. "You drop it, we lose. And I shouldn't have to tell you that."

I don't cackle.

Out loud.

But I definitely cackle in my head, and my smile can absolutely be classified as a smirk.

There's movement on Evelyn's other side, and I realize Fletcher's dad has decided to join us.

"Trying to make up for a lifetime of not being what he needed?" Odette murmurs to him.

He looks at her, then at the ground. "You have a way with words, ma'am."

"You can't be a parent and not fuck it up."

"I'd prefer to be a parent who can fix it."

My heart squeezes.

I know a little bit about parents not understanding what I need, and I know a lot more about feeling like they don't care.

Seeing Fletcher's dad trying?

It's more than my own father would do.

Unless it's merely lip service.

I don't think it is—my father certainly wouldn't fly across the country because he hadn't heard from me in a while—but clearly, I'm not an expert here.

"If you want my advice," Evelyn says, "don't start yelling that he's doing it all wrong out there."

General Daniel's eyebrows lift. "He can recite more about this sport in his sleep than I could awake after studying it for a week. And last I was aware, he didn't talk in his sleep."

"Doesn't mean you wouldn't yell at him anyway," Evelyn murmurs.

"Those days are over."

All of us fall silent and look back at the players on the pitch.

"But I don't know how to prove it to him," he says on a sigh.

Yep.

Heart officially hurts. And this one is not my business.

I glance at my watch. "Oh, look at the time. Have to run. Meetings. Enjoy training, ladies. I'll see if I can find anyone to give you a full stadium tour. General Daniel, lovely to see you again."

Yes, yes, my chicken side is showing.

But Fletcher's relationship with his dad is *not my business*.

My three besties can handle this in a way I'll never be able to.

And I'm completely fine with that.

27

Fletcher

AFTER AN AWKWARD DINNER with my father where he tells me Goldie and her friends are nice, I tell him I have to get to bed early before training tomorrow.

I do head home, but I don't stay there. Instead, I scoop Sweet Pea up into her puppy sling—getting close to her bedtime, and you do *not* want to mess with this dog when she's tired—and we head out for a little late evening shopping.

The neighborhood stores are more crowded than I've seen them before, but I'm not out often at this time of day.

Maybe this is normal.

What's not normal?

How much I want to go see Goldie.

I shouldn't.

I should go home again.

I should definitely not go see Goldie.

You don't show up at a woman's place the night after you slept together unless you want to send a clear message, and the message I'm sending in showing up here is *I'm obsessed with you.*

I want to screw around with you again.

I want to be your friend.

Friend.

Yeah, that's a word.

Fuck it. She's leaving. We're letting the world think we're dating. Even if all I do is walk into her building and Shade takes a picture and leaks it online, then I'm here for something other than being obsessed with a woman I don't need in my life.

No matter how much I like her.

But I can't show up at her flat empty-handed when I have information in my back pocket that says she likes the stupid-expensive gourmet cookies from one very specific local place.

And I can't walk into her building while carrying her favorite local cookies without heading up to her flat.

She'll see the post talking about me taking her cookies and think it's weird that I never showed up. Plus, after tea yesterday and all of last week's food, I can't eat it myself. Nor can I feed it to my dog. It'd make Sweet Pea sick.

And I can't loiter in the hallway without knocking on Goldie's door.

That would be weird too.

So I stand there in the ivory-walled hallway and knock at the navy blue door with the gold lion head knocker on it, same as I did when I picked her up for the wedding.

I doubt she's home. She's trying to pack as much as possible into her last days here. But I wait long enough to assume she's not here before I pull open my phone to check my Instagram messages and see if her friend who wrote my mustache an obituary would deliver a cookie for me.

She's in one of the other flats in this building. If I can track her down, I can give her Goldie's cookie.

And that's when the door opens beside me. "If you're looking for a rematch with the Monopoly queen, unfortunately, my games are already in storage."

I glance back, and there she is.

Goldie.

Leaning in her doorway in purple pajama pants decorated with cartoon hummingbirds, an oversize Copper Valley Thrusters Pride T-shirt, fluffy yellow slippers, and a smile that doesn't quite reach her eyes despite the teasing note in her voice.

Her face is scrubbed clean and her hair is down, falling over her shoulders in silky dark waves. She looks like she's three friends and six pillows short of an epic pillow fight night, and that image has my overactive dick doing his thing again.

Sweet Pea notices.

Swear she does.

She half growls and glares at me like she's ordering me to keep it in my pants.

"Just wanted to say thanks. For coming. To training." Stutter much, Huxley? Jesus. I'm a thirteen-year-old boy again.

I could've DM'ed her that. "And Sweet Pea wanted to say sorry for dragging your pants through my apartment when I had another visitor this morning."

Goldie eyes the shimmery gold cookie box in my hand, then smiles at my dog, leaning in to scratch her ears and get within licking distance.

Of the dog, I mean.

Technically I could lick her too. She's *this close*. And she smells like cupcakes and temptation, both of which I enjoy licking.

"Did you bring me something good, Sweet Pea?" she says. "Did you? Who's such a kind, thoughtful puppy?"

"It was all Sweet Pea," I assure Goldie. "I wouldn't have been this thoughtful on my own."

Her smile broadens. "That looks suspiciously like a Freckle Cookies box."

"You have a good eye for cookie boxes."

She's still scratching my dog's ears while she studies me again. I think she's looking for my hidden agenda.

As though it's not obvious that I like her and want to spend time with her and the pictures are all an excuse.

Bonus that my dog is getting extra pets from someone she adores.

Whatever Goldie finds after her silent inspection, she apparently decides she's okay with it. "Would you two like to come in for a drink?" she asks. "I have the most delicious tap water. And three more servings of hot chocolate that I need to drink in the next few days, but I'm guessing that'll be a *no* from both of you."

Unfortunately, she's correct. "Water's great. Thanks."

"And cookies sound delicious. Thank you too." She pushes away from the door, winces, and when she steps into her apartment, she's limping.

Every protective instinct I've ever had in my life goes on alert and I leap through the doorway too fast, getting too close. "What happened? Are you okay? Who hurt you? Shit. Did I do that? Or was it the hot sauce? Tell me it wasn't the hot sauce."

Her lips tip up again despite the wince. "It was not the hot sauce."

"So you didn't have any...unwanted side effects?"

She pauses at that, and her smile gets bigger. "Not at all. You?"

"Hot sauce doesn't bother me."

She makes a noise that tells me she knows I'm lying.

Bloody hell.

If Silas told her about my issue in the bathroom at training this morning, I'll fucking kill him.

She takes another step, clearly favoring her left side, and my heart lurches again. "What happened? Why are you limping?"

"Snowstorm's coming. I'll be fine tomorrow. Or the day after."

"Forecast is clear for the next two weeks."

"Okay, Mr. Trust The Forecast."

Sweet Pea barks and grins.

She has a keen appreciation for sarcasm. Especially when it's directed at me.

We follow Goldie the rest of the way into her apartment. There's a single pink floral chair in the living area that wasn't here the last time, draped with a lumpy blue fleece blanket. Piles of empty boxes. A half-full trash bag. The bookshelves are still heavy with paperbacks and hardback books, plus a few trinkets. A wooden hummingbird, a bobblehead of the Scorned's mascot, a framed picture of Goldie with Hallie on the same carousel horses we rode yesterday.

I moved enough as a kid that I recognize the boxes both assembled and flat on her floor. They're heavy-duty. Smaller.

She needs to pack her books.

And she's grimacing again as she limps into the efficient kitchen, opens a white cabinet, and pulls out a plain white bowl, plus the solitary pint glass still inside.

It's a Copper Valley Scorned pint glass.

Wonder if she's leaving them behind.

I follow her into the small kitchen and set the cookie on the counter. "You usually feel it like this when the forecast is clear?"

"I called a snowstorm ahead of the meteorologist once four years ago, and I called it again two winters ago when I hadn't checked the weather in a few days. Only time I've felt it this intense since I got hurt."

"How many inches?"

She sticks the glass under the faucet and fills it with water. "At least a foot."

I was halfway expecting her to make a joke back about *my* inches.

Then, because I'm that guy, I pull out my phone and check my weather app.

Nothing—oh.

No, wait.

The forecast is refreshing.

And she's right.

Sometime in the past few hours, we've gotten a winter storm watch starting tomorrow afternoon.

With a likelihood of a foot to a foot and a half of snow across the metropolitan area before noon Sunday.

She leaves my glass on the counter in front of me and grabs the bowl to fill it with water too.

"Go sit." I reach around her and take the bowl. "I've got this."

"Too many boxes to pack to sit."

"Sit. My dog needs a warm lap. She hates snow. Plus, you have a cookie that shouldn't be neglected. You're morally obligated now."

Goldie leans back against the counter and crosses her arms, looking at me like I'm missing something incredibly obvious.

Oh. Right. Duh. "I'll pack your boxes. You need any groceries? Want me to go fight the masses to get you bread and milk that you won't be able to finish before you move? Is it actually a snowstorm if you don't participate in the emptying of the egg section?"

She laughs at that, her eyes twinkling merrily, and there goes my heart again.

Flopping around like a fish on a bank in desperate need of finding a puddle of murky water to hide in.

"Between my stash of Biscoff cookies, chocolate bars that *someone* bought me at the bookstore last week, now a cookie the size of my head, and my emergency stash of muscle relaxers, I should be fine," she says as she shoves away from the counter and limps into the living room. "Thank you. But if you need to get your own blizzard survival food—"

"Got enough chicken to last me a week."

She's still smiling, but she's clearly in pain as she walks. "Enough kibble for Sweet Pea too?"

"She eats more chicken than I do. *Sit.* Let a guy be useful. Unless there are books here you don't want me to know you own."

"You got me. I don't want you to figure out which of my books is a secret lever to open my even-more secret laboratory."

"Evil genius intentionally trying to destroy the world kind of lab, or diabolical life coach working on a secret serum that'll trick your clients into doing the work they say they're going to do and then don't kind of lab?"

"If I told you, I'd have to make you the first victim of my serum." She squats, winces so hard she gasps, then goes all the way down to her knees on the floor in front of the left bookshelf.

Stubborn woman.

I'm at her side in an instant, squatting despite my own knees and quads groaning while I reach for her arm. "Get your ass out of the way and let me pack your boxes."

Stop fucking feeling like you're sucking in on yourself, heart.

"Sitting hurts."

"Clearly, so does standing. And squatting. And kneeling. And walking."

"I was going to lie down for half an hour on an ice pack and *then* tackle the boxes," she mutters. "But now I want to earn a cookie."

"Congratulations. You're breathing. You've earned a cookie."

I unstrap Sweet Pea and set her on the floor. Her paws are barely touching the wood before she's darting to Goldie, trying to climb up onto her thighs.

And when Goldie winces one more time, I growl.

"Okay. Okay." She throws her hands up. "You win."

I eyeball her.

She's watching me right back with an expression that's somehow both mulish and resigned, which I interpret to mean she's thinking she'd rather challenge me to see who can pack boxes of books faster.

Don't ask me what my feelings are doing right now.

Finding a woman who thinks it's fun to challenge me?

And knowing that this exact challenge will help her leave?

Just *fuck*.

"There's an ice pack in the freezer, and I would be incredibly grateful if you could get it for me," she finally says as she lowers herself all the way to the floor.

"Would it be better if I wait for the snow to start, collect it, and make you a homemade ice pack with it?"

Sweet Pea looks at me and growls again.

But Goldie—Goldie smiles through the other faces she's making while she scoots herself around so she's lying on the floor. And not any smile.

This is a glowing, unabashedly amused smile.

Which she turns on my dog. "You are *such* a good dog, Sweet Pea."

Sweet Pea pants at her adoringly.

"She says you are too," I interpret.

And then I open Goldie's freezer.

And realize I'm an absolute dumbass.

It's full.

It's fucking *full*.

But does it have the frozen turkey from last year's Thanksgiving turkey sale that my father always insisted we get two of, even though Mom would only cook one and the other would get frostbite before she cooked it, too, the next October to make room for the new year's turkeys? Does it have backup ice trays to the ice maker? Does it have freezer meals of undetermined origin frosted over on the edges of the packages?

No.

No, it's got over a dozen large baggies with half-eaten cookies.

From Freckle Cookies.

"Don't look in my freezer," Goldie says from the floor.

"I have to get your ice pack out of the freezer."

"Don't *judge* my freezer."

She's flung an arm over her face like she doesn't want to watch my face have reactions to her cookie hoarding, but she twists and *ack!*s when Sweet Pea licks her armpit, and then grimaces again in pain.

Watching her hurting is breaking my soul.

But I stuff down the worry and say something far more expected than *I will do anything to make you feel better.* "You're lying to your old lady friends."

"What do my friends have to do with anything?"

"They said you love these cookies. Specifically the peanut butter cookies."

"When did they tell you that?"

"When they DM'ed me an obituary for my mustache."

She lifts her arm and peers at me. "*No.*"

I locate the ice pack, shut the freezer, and cross back to Goldie on the floor. "They think you love cookies so they keep giving you cookies."

"That is *not* what's going on here."

"Then what is?"

"You show me the obituary, I'll tell you my cookie confession."

"Not sure a cookie confession is worth what's in this obituary. Where's your tape and your Sharpie?"

She lifts her hips, settles onto the ice pack, and almost immediately sighs in relief.

My own anxiety ratchets down.

She'll be okay.

"Bedroom," she says. "I'll give you twenty dollars to read me that obituary."

That's hilarious. "Don't need your twenty bucks." I stride into her bedroom, locate the tape and a thick Sharpie, and accidentally spot another ice pack on her bed. It's warm. She must've used it earlier and forgotten to refreeze it.

"I'll tell you where you can go to get real Cadbury chocolate," she calls.

I abruptly halt on my path back to the kitchen to refreeze this ice pack for her. "*Real* Cadbury chocolate? The kind they won't import here? And the candy bar flavors you couldn't get even if they did?"

"The real stuff. Pick your candy bar variety, and it can happen."

Shit.

I'm drooling. "I don't eat that crap anymore."

"Season only lasts so long."

"I don't do chocolate after the season. I go to Bruges and get Liège waffles and eat them until I puke instead."

She laughs, and Sweet Pea crawls up onto her belly, making her laugh more.

"Well worth it," I add.

Also, I do the chocolate binge *after* I do the waffle binge.

Bruges is also a good place to start for that, though it won't be nearly as close this year as it has been at the end of every other rugby season.

"You should take a few weekends to visit Europe while you're in London," I tell her, ignoring that fucking bumping in my chest again that gets worse as Sweet Pea turns in a circle on Goldie's stomach, then plops down like Goldie's her bed. "Can't beat it for food and history. I can tell you the best places. But only if you tell me why you have thirty-eight bags of half-eaten cookies in your freezer."

"Nine. Not thirty-eight. *Nine.* And I'd rather have the mustache obituary."

"Where do you get the real Cadbury bars?"

"Evelyn's neighbor has a grandkid currently at university in

Ireland who ships cartons of them home a couple times a month. She'll sell them to you at a twenty percent mark-up unless you agree to receive one of the cartons, in which case she'll charge you regular price."

My father would choke on his own tongue at the idea of me getting involved with a senior citizen chocolate-smuggling ring. "No freebies for the inconvenience?"

"She has enough people accepting deliveries that she can take her pick in who she works with. The discount is all you get."

"And your friends are involved with this."

"No, my friends occasionally make purchases from their dealer, but they're never involved with the deliveries. The Old Man Bikers Club found out and threatened to report them to the police. That's what started their war."

"This is fucking nuts."

"If you can keep a secret, I can hook you up. Or, I suppose for the next few months, *I* could mail you some chocolate. You could build up your supply before the season's over. And all I ask in exchange is to see the obituary."

She has her eyes closed and she's petting my dog, who looks as if she's in absolute heaven getting Goldie love.

And I cave.

Like I wasn't going to anyway.

I grunt and groan too while I lower myself to the floor by her head, pull out my phone, and open up my Instagram.

"In early January, the facial hair catastrophe of Fletcher Huxley died a premature death despite also lasting too long in this world," I read.

Goldie giggles, making Sweet Pea jiggle on top of her.

"If you can't be dignified in the face of death, I'm not going to read this to you," I say, which makes her laugh harder.

But laughing harder makes her wince and grab her hip.

Dammit.

"Massage ever help?" I ask her.

"Not as much as I wish it did. Keep reading? Please?"

I don't want to read her this obituary. I want to rub her hip and help her stretch and make her feel better.

But instead, I do as she asked. "The death of the 'stache was seen around the world, though its graphic demise was censored in pockets of the world that worship mustaches. Fire was a fitting end to a facial feature that had clearly seen things in its day. Some good. Some bad. Some dirty. It was rumored to still be hiding half an airplane meal from three years ago in its depths."

Goldie gets a full cackle out of that one.

"During its time on earth, it spawned many imitators, much to the chagrin of three-quarters of the population of the world's women. But despite the near-universal hatred of the 'stache from hell, it found its supporters in various pockets of society. Memorials have appeared on places such a *Rate That 'Stache dot com*, an Instagram account dedicated to the weirdest wonders of the world, and on a billboard in a random town in Kansas. The dearly departed mustache is also reported to be inspiration for Guy Knightly's newest installation at New York's Museum of Modern Art, a sculpture that some say resembles a dying chicken, which he entitled *Death of Huxley's Third Mustache Hair from the Right*."

Even I have to pause and clear my throat after that one.

As far as burns go, that was solid.

And Goldie's laughing so hard now that a little piggy snort escapes her nose.

Fucking. Delightful.

"You might have to stop," she gasps. "This hurts."

"There's only one more paragraph, you wimp," I say.

That cracks her up even more.

But she sobers as another wince of pain crosses her features.

"Okay, I'm done," I say.

"No, please finish. I don't know when I'll get another chance to hear you read it."

Motherfucker.

I can't say no to that.

And again with the *knock it the hell off, heart.*

I clear my throat and look back at my phone. "Fletcher's mustache is survived by the man himself, whom we can't entirely blame for choosing to decorate his face with such a monstrosity when his clothing, cars, and former uniform choice all suggest he was born lacking the genes required for good fashion taste. He compensates for his deficiency with a razor by occasionally being an incredibly good friend to a woman who deserves it more than she knows."

Goldie blinks at me as I put my phone down. "Does it really say that?"

"I can't make up things that nice."

"I'm sorry we mocked your mustache," she whispers. "That wasn't nice of us."

"Been through a lot worse than being mocked for having the most epic mustache to ever live."

She peers at me, her face an open question. *Tell me all of the bad things. You can trust me. You're safe here.*

I don't dislike it as much as I should. "My mom would've thought this obituary was hilarious. She had a great sense of humor."

Goldie smiles softly. "Everyone needs someone with a good sense of humor in their life."

"I grew it in the first place because my second ex-wife told me I didn't have the face for it."

"Before or after your divorce?"

"During. She was cheating. I didn't care, and that made her mad, and her being mad made me petty."

"Why didn't you care?"

"Married her for revenge."

"On?"

"First wife."

If ever there was a more pointed *do go on* eyebrow arch, I haven't seen it.

And I ignore it and head for the bookshelf. "You have an order you want these to go in? Any special labeling on the box?"

"No. I like being surprised by finding my favorite books in every box I open."

"None you want put in specific boxes so you can find them again easily on the other side?"

"I'll buy another copy if I'm desperate. Or get it in audio or ebook."

"You still haven't told me why you have eighty-six cookies in your freezer."

"Nine. And it's because I love these cookies, but they are *ridiculously* huge. I can only eat half at a time, so I put the other half in the freezer to make it last longer, and then I get a fresh cookie when I want another because they're better fresh."

She's completely serious. And that's fucking delightful too. "What are you going to do with your freezer?"

"I don't know," she whispers. "And that's probably the worst part of this whole move."

She's so forlorn.

But she's wrong.

Sacrificing frozen cookies isn't the worst part of her move.

The worst part is that she's leaving.

28

Goldie

I DON'T REALIZE I've fallen asleep on the floor in my living room until I jolt awake.

My hip still aches, but less than before. Sweet Pea is a warm lump snoring on my belly. Two-thirds of my bookshelves are empty, the barren spaces a stark reminder that I'm leaving this apartment and the country very soon.

But what has my heart drawing an unplanned shuddery breath over that isn't the thought of leaving my apartment. Or Copper Valley. Or my friends.

No, the unexpected pull in my chest region is one hundred percent a response to Fletcher standing in the middle of all of the boxes that he packed for me.

If he's shaved at all since the flaming cheese incident, you can't tell. His facial hair is hovering on that line between thick scruff and full short beard. He's wearing jeans that hug his powerful ass and thighs and he's shed his jacket, leaving him in a gray Pounders

T-shirt that's stretched as tight as it can go across his chest and tattooed biceps. I let my gaze linger on his forearms, even though I shouldn't.

I'm such a sucker for well-defined forearms. The kind with the thick veins that go all the way down a man's hands to his long, strong—I mentally clear my throat.

Last night was a *one-time* hookup between friends. He's not here for me to drool over him.

Especially with the way he's holding the hummingbird figurine that's been on display somewhere in every place I've lived since I was seven.

Not simply holding it though.

He's staring at it as though it holds the answer to a question that's weighed on him for decades, but he can't find the key to unlock its puzzle.

He jerks his head in my direction like he's suddenly aware that I'm awake and didn't want to be caught studying my figurine.

"My grandpa gave it to me when I was seven. He always said I flitted like a hummingbird." My voice is groggy, and my body feels heavy.

It's late.

He has training tomorrow.

He's probably exhausted, and that was likely true before he started packing my books for me.

But it feels imperative to tell him about the hummingbird. No judgment. Just *that's what it is.*

His eyes drift back to it. "My mom loved hummingbirds. Can't see one without thinking of her. That's why I remembered who you were. I heard your nickname, and it was like my mom—like I was supposed to know who you were."

"What was she like?"

He pauses before he answers, carefully positioning the hummingbird back on the empty shelf like he wants to make sure its best side is showing before it's packed away too. "Infinitely patient. She loved to laugh. Stunk like hell anytime she ate broccoli. Let me win in Monopoly. And she went out of her way to show up to all of my matches and made sure I didn't miss any training when she was hiding how sick she was. The opposite of my old man in every way."

My heart squeezes again.

He misses her.

You can hear it.

And I'm not at all surprised when he abruptly changes the subject. "How's your hip?"

"Stiff, but okay."

"Would stretching help?"

I don't move. Not with Sweet Pea still snoring softly on my belly. "Probably. You didn't have to pack all of my books."

He squints one eyeball at me, a clear *shut up, yes, I did*. "I ran out of boxes before I found the secret lever to your even-more secret lair."

That shouldn't make my heart squeeze more, but it does. He's fun.

I will honestly and unexpectedly miss him when I leave.

Which, clearly, I should not tell him right now. Instead, I settle on a soft, "Thank you."

He moves closer to me while we talk, squatting with a *pop* in one of his joints and a grimace on his face that says he's feeling every bit of today's training. "You say *thank you*, but you have no idea how many books I hid in my pants while you were sleeping."

"Ooh, which ones?"

"That's classified."

"Did you hear that a lot when you were growing up too?"

"Every single day. It's fascinating to me that you stored books on the history of eggs next to historical pirate porn."

"If you call my romance novels *porn* again, I'll spread the rumor among the athletes in town that you think their partners are ugly."

He smirks as he drops to kneel on the floor beside me. "They won't believe you."

"Yes, they will."

"You couldn't lie effectively about that."

"Wanna bet?"

His smirk has turned into a full-on grin that makes my heart do a little pitter-patter the same way it sometimes does when I'm watching the best part of a rom-com film. Fletcher Huxley grinning with that beard and those eyes and that jawline—yes.

Yes, please.

"I salute your competitive streak, but you'd lose this one," he tells me.

I involuntarily twist on the floor as a tight flare of pain shoots across my pelvis, making Sweet Pea *hmph* and lift half a sleepy eyelid. Poor pup. She's gonna have to move, because I need to move. I gave my rug away last week, so there's hard wood beneath me. My neck is getting stiff and achy, but not for the same reason as the throbbing in my hip.

Fletcher gently pulls her off of me, the back of his hand sliding across my stomach and making it drop like I'm on a roller coaster. "Sorry, pup. Your bed has needs. I'll buy you a steak later to make up for it."

She yawns loudly, but when he grabs my shark blanket from the chair Odette loaned me for the next week and makes a nest with it on the floor, Sweet Pea happily settles into the soft fleece and goes back to sleep.

"She doesn't go crazy if she wakes up in the middle of the night?" I ask.

He grins. "Don't fuck with my dog's sleep schedule. She'll cut a bitch."

And then he wraps his massive hand around my shin as I pull my knee toward my chest. "Need help?"

He's snuck into my brain a time or two in the years since that incident at the college showcase. I don't remember everything he was wearing that day, but I remember the jacket. It was loud and flashy, neon green and ripped with some designer's logo printed on it so large, the entire word didn't fit. One of those fashion pieces that most of the world would call ugly—*neon green? Really?*—but those in the industry would probably call a *breathtaking statement piece* that cost more than some people's annual rent. Any time I'd think about him, I'd tell myself he was all arrogant swagger and no substance.

But this Fletcher?

The one who's quietly adding the smallest amount of extra stretch to my hip that I couldn't reach on my own? Who brought me a cookie and packed my boxes? Who's watching me with an alertness that he has no right to have this late at night after a long, grueling day of his own?

This Fletcher is all substance.

He's still swagger. But it's a different kind of swagger. It's inherent rather than flashy. Earned. Natural.

Sometimes hilarious, like when he uses it while attempting to beat me in Monopoly.

"More?" I say quietly.

He slowly adds pressure to my shin, putting enough extra pull in my glute that it hurts. I close my eyes and breathe into the pain.

"Goldie?"

"Has to hurt before it feels better."

He grunts.

He knows.

Far more than me at this point, I'm sure.

He rubs my calf with his thumb while he keeps the pressure on my shin. Not hard. More *I'm here. I've got you.*

And I breathe until the pain fades to a dull ache. My jaw unclenches. My eyelids relax. My shoulders settle back on the floor.

He taps my other knee. "Balance it."

"Bossy."

"Prefer this side of the trainer's table."

I smile, eyes still closed while he helps me straighten my aching left side and moves on to stretching my right leg too.

He keeps one hand on my left thigh the whole time.

No pressure.

It's all presence. *Still here if you need me.*

He helps me through three more stretches—two I'm familiar with, one that he says his trainers make him do every day—and when we're done, there's still a dull ache in my left hip, but it's bearable.

No shooting pain down my leg. No feeling of flaming metal spikes crushing my hip.

Merely a vague reminder that weather's coming.

While we've ended up lying next to each other on the floor, our faces inches from each other again. "Thank you," I whisper.

He brushes a thumb over my cheek, eyes searching mine like I'm a bigger mystery than my hummingbird.

I wish he'd say something.

Anything.

Because the way he's staring at me is making my belly flutter and my nipples tingle and my clit ache.

But sleeping with him again would be a bad idea.

Once is once.

Period.

Twice is an implication that there will be a third time, and a fourth, and *I'm leaving.*

Yes, yes, we could say we're having a temporary friends-with-benefits arrangement, but the problem is—

I think I like him.

No, I *know* I like him.

If we'd met two years from now, after my time in the UK and touring the US, I'd consider dating him.

Not that I have any idea if he'd consider dating me. If he dates at all. What he wants in relationships.

But when he's watching me with questions lingering in his gaze like he's thinking the same things, like whatever he's thinking is too vulnerable to share, *I know him.*

Like I *am* him.

Leaving behind the things that have caused me pain and made me afraid to get close to anyone again. Looking for a fresh start in a place that I can be truly open again. Where I can believe no one has an ulterior motive. Where no one knows my personal history.

Except I know a little about his.

And he knows a little about mine.

"You didn't want your cookie." His voice is husky and raw and I want to close my eyes and live in it.

"I always want cookies, but I couldn't enjoy it when I was hurting."

"Feel better now?"

"So much better."

"Can I watch you eat your cookie?"

I smile while every nerve in my body does a happy dance, which I wouldn't have thought possible three hours ago. "Would that make you happy?"

"If you ate it naked."

29

Fletcher

I AM SUCH AN ASSHOLE.

To myself.

I am an asshole to myself.

Is there any other explanation for me *requesting* that Goldie, *who will always fucking rise to a challenge*, eat a cookie naked in front of me?

Because that's exactly what she's doing.

She's standing in her kitchen, bare-ass naked, pulling the large cookie out of its box while I stare at her smooth ass and the hint of side boob and her long arms and that hummingbird tattoo on her shoulder.

While I'm sitting on the floor of her living room, sweating.

My dick is an iron rod. My balls are so tight they're cramping. My heart is racing like I'm chasing an Olympic sprinter the entire length of the pitch. My hands are itching to stroke her skin and my mouth—my mouth wants to feast on her entire body.

"Oh, *peanut butter*, my favorite," she says, her voice breathy in a way that makes me imagine her saying *Oh, Fletcher's cock, my favorite*, the same way.

Not helping the situation in the nuts.

Nor does her turning to give me a full view of her lush, round breasts and rosy nipples. Her smooth, taut skin. The curve of her waist dipping down to those hips. The dark curls hiding her pussy.

My mustache's obituary won't be the only one her friend writes about me this year.

And that's before Goldie breaks off a bite of the soft cookie and uses her fingers to put it into her mouth, slides her eyes closed, and sighs one of those *I just came* sighs that makes her shoulders fall back while her head tilts. I watch the motion in her long neck as she swallows, and every last ounce of blood in my body channels straight to my dick.

I'm never walking again.

There's zero chance my legs will ever get blood flow back.

"Please tell me there are cookies this amazing in London too," she says.

I force out an incoherent sound that is definitely not an answer.

I've seen naked women before.

I've slept with naked women before.

Fuck, I slept with Goldie—naked—just last night.

But I cannot remember the last time I wanted someone so badly and felt so very damn incapable of saying so.

It wasn't last night.

It was this morning.

Her walking out of my bedroom in nothing but my T-shirt, sitting down, and having breakfast with my father and me like none of us were thinking about the fact that she wasn't wearing underwear. The hot sauce challenge. Showing up for my training.

Blowing me a kiss.

The hummingbirds.

The fact that she has a copy of *Dungeon Crawler Carl* on her bookshelves.

Dungeon Crawler Carl. The entire goddamn series.

That series is fucking awesome and it's nothing I expected to find here, but I could talk about *Dungeon Crawler Carl* with her and —fuck.

If I were the type of guy who thought I could fall in love ever again, *Dungeon Crawler Carl* on her bookshelves would be my tipping point.

I hope she rereads the whole series when she unpacks her boxes and finds the note I left her inside of the first book.

And the other note I left her at the beginning of chapter sixteen in the fourth book.

So wanting Goldie now?

Yeah.

This is different.

And I should leave.

She strides into the living room without an ounce of modesty or bashfulness, breaks off another bite of cookie, slides it into her mouth, then licks her fingers as she pulls them out.

"My god, I'm going to miss this."

Miss me. I want you to miss me.

Also, *fucking work, tongue.* "If you send me good enough Cadbury, I'll use my secret skills to get you the best cookies."

Don't contact me when you leave.

Don't fucking do it.

It'll hurt too damn bad.

She kneels in front of me, not wincing at all. "Want a bite?"

Yes. Yes, I want a bite.

Of her collarbone. Of her nipple. Of her ear. Of that birthmark next to her belly button. Of her clit. Her pussy.

I want a bite of *all* of her.

I shake my head at the cookie piece she's offering me with her fingers. It's peanut butter, but it has melted chocolate chips in it too. It was fresh enough when I bought it that the chocolate is barely starting to congeal, and it looks bloody delicious.

She stares me dead in the eye while she eats it herself. She chews, swallows, licks her lips, and drops her voice as she says, "Want to know how it tastes now?"

Fuck me.

Fuck me inside out and upside down and in all the ways a man can be fucked.

Yes.

Yes, I want to know how it tastes now.

I have zero self-control as I wrap a hand around her neck and pull her in close to sample her mouth. Her lips. Her tongue. The cookie flavor lingering with her inherent taste.

Is there such a thing as too much blood flow to a man's dick?

Mine's had enough.

But I can't get enough of Goldie.

She wraps an arm around my neck. Something plops to the floor, and then her other arm is looped under my armpit and around my back, her mouth open to me, her tongue dancing with mine.

I don't know where her breath ends and mine begins.

All I know is that I need to kiss her more than I need air. More than I need food. More than I need chocolate and cookies and hot sauce.

More than I need rugby.

She makes it okay for me to be me in a way that rugby, that my father, that fans and ex-wives and coaches never have.

She sees me, she accepts me, and she *likes* me.

It's insanity.

It'll pass.

Maybe.

She pulls me down to the floor, her kisses as desperate and sloppy as mine. I settle between her thighs, kneading her neck and one ass cheek, still fully dressed.

Trapped inside my fucking jeans.

Do I have a condom?

I don't know if I have a condom in my wallet.

Shit.

Fuck.

I don't. *I fucking don't.*

Goldie makes a desperate noise and pulls back. "We should not—"

"Agreed."

"It's—"

"A bad idea."

She stares at me, lips plump and glistening, pupils dilated, breath coming fast, eyelids heavy.

I stare back, probably looking as desperate and wild and hungry as my heart feels.

And then we're kissing again.

I can't kiss her deep enough. Hard enough. Close enough.

And I need to not want to so badly.

But it's Goldie.

How can anyone *not* want Goldie?

"Tell me to stop," I say against her lips.

"You tell me to stop," she gasps back.

"I'm stopping."

"Okay."

I'm not stopping.

I'm sliding down her body, licking her neck, biting her collarbone, sucking on her nipples while she gasps and grips my hair tight and clenches one leg around my hips.

"We shouldn't do this," she wheezes.

"I know."

"But it's—we're just—we're good at this."

"You're fucking good at this."

"You're—*oh my god, Fletcher.*"

Mental note: she likes it when I lick her belly button.

And the skin beneath her belly button.

And the noise she makes when I work my way lower, gently pushing her legs farther apart, biting her inner thigh, scratching my beard over the delicate skin there, repeating on the other side, and then giving in to my desperate need to feast on her pretty pussy—

Yeah.

Yeah, we both like this.

She's fucking delicious. And she's not holding back her reactions, gasping my name, grabbing me by the hair and moving my head where she wants it, her hips pumping against my mouth while I lick and suck and tease her clit, her thighs quivering as she gets closer and closer and closer to—

"*Oh god, yes yes yes, Fletcher, YES.*"

Fuck me.

I'm coming in my pants while I taste her orgasm.

Of bloody course I am.

She's fucking hot, and I was already primed.

Her fingers relax in my hair, and her thighs collapse to the side.

I look up at her, and fuck me once again.

Her long hair is a crazy mess beneath her head, her chest rising and falling while she rubs one breast like she doesn't even realize she's doing it. Her chin is tipped back, her cheeks tinted pink, her lips tipped up like she doesn't realize she's smiling either. Her belly moves in time with her chest, and she looks completely and undeniably happy.

Not only relaxed.

Not satisfied.

Happy.

I want to make her happy every damn day.

"Fletcher?" she whispers, her eyes drifting closed while I shift to watch her more closely.

"Yeah?"

"I think I'm lying on my cookie."

I stare at her for a beat, and then I crack up.

She does too. "I can feel it under my shoulder," she says through giggles.

Yeah.

This.

This is what's been missing from every relationship I've ever had.

The Goldie factor.

And she's leaving.

Just *fuck*.

30

Goldie

THIS IS IT.

Seven days.

Seven.

And right now, my final goodbyes begin.

With the snowstorm coming in later today, my Little Kickers soccer practice is inside the dome at Reynolds Park. I half expect a bunch of my team to miss while their parents get ready to be snowed in for a few days, but every last one of them arrives.

The cool thing about three- and four-year-olds is that they don't always understand what *this is the last time you'll see Coach Goldie* means.

But I do.

And so do the parents.

Two parents in particular.

"I'm so pissed at you," Brittany says as she hugs me. She's here before Silas and Hallie, who are on their way. The rugby boys got a recovery day in their training, so he's bringing her. "I'm going to have to learn to coach soccer now."

I hug my niece's mom back tightly. "I'll call an old friend and see if she can find a replacement for me."

"I don't want any of those bitches who didn't stand up for you."

"Not their fault, B."

"Bullshit. And you've been lonely, no matter how much you say your old lady friends make up for everything. I hope—god, Goldie. Find what you're looking for in London, okay? Make it worthwhile that you're leaving."

Dammit.

Is it raining inside this dome? Directly into my eyes?

"Aunt Gow-die!" a little voice shrieks.

Brittany lets me go and wipes her own eyes, which is not an auspicious start to this last event of the season.

We're playing Coach Beck's team in a mock game today, and we have big plans to win.

But we can't do that if all of the coaches and parents are on the sidelines crying.

I squat and take a full-force Hallie hug, which sends a ripple of pain from my hip down my femur.

But I don't cringe.

I hope.

This won't be fully better until the storm starts moving through.

"You ready to be a soccer star?" I ask my niece.

"Uh-huh. And den I get a big twophy for my twophy woom."

I squint up at my brother. "A trophy room? She's *three*."

"I *four*, Aunt Gow-die. I five soon too."

Silas lifts a shoulder while he smirks at me. He's in training pants and a Pounders hoodie, and his brown hair is overdue for a haircut.

"She's a Collins. She'll need three trophy rooms before she's done."

Brittany rolls her eyes.

And then the very worst-best-worst thing that could possibly happen happens.

Hallie's eyes go wide.

A smile blossoms that stretches her lips almost from ear to ear.

And then she puts her head down and charges away from me, away from Brittany and Silas, and away from the indoor field, howling, *"Feeeeettttcccchhhhhhhhheerrrrrr!"*

Silas jerks his head toward the dome entrance.

Brittany makes a noise.

Half a dozen other parents turn and look at us.

And I—honestly, I don't know what I do.

I stare.

I definitely stare.

Fletcher has zero business showing up for my Little Kickers soccer clinic finale, but there he is, striding in like he owns the place, long legs taking confident strides in his jeans, his T-shirt hidden behind Sweet Pea's sling, and a plain black jacket covering his arms.

I recognize that jacket.

It has *Pounders* in massive letters on the back.

Much better than his Pounders sweatpants.

He drops to one knee and takes a hug from Hallie, one of his massive arms briefly looping around her back.

"Don't you *dare*," I hear myself say.

I'm talking to Silas, but I'm also silently sending a *what the fuck are you thinking?* to Fletcher.

Last night was—okay, I'm not going to finish that, because if I think about last night, I'm going to get hot and bothered and here on the soccer field with my kids is not the place.

Compartmentalize, Goldie.

Compartmentalize.

"Is that the guy who was bothering you, Coach Goldie?" Coach Beck says beside me.

"Yes. No. I mean, he bothers me, but not in the bad way."

More parents look at me.

Usually they're looking at Beck, which is completely and totally understandable. Especially since the former internationally known underwear model is also wearing a sling today. But unlike Fletcher, Beck's sling has an actual baby in it.

How often do you get to stand in the same breathing space as one of the world's objectively most attractive men while he holds a baby and coaches another daughter's soccer practice?

He should be the main event, and I say that with all the love and respect for his wife, who is also a fabulous—and very patient and understanding—human being. And also with complete acknowledgement that I'd pick watching Fletcher over watching Beck for personal reasons.

But no one's staring at Beck.

They're watching me confess to being *bothered* by Fletcher, and yes, they're appropriately reading between those lines.

Or so say their knowing smirks and grins.

Silas moves, and I shake myself out of my stupor. "Do not—I repeat, *do not* do something that'll get you plastered all over the news."

"What the fu—"

I pinch his elbow. "Language. Other people's kids are around."

"I told him—"

"Let it go, Silas," Brittany interrupts.

"It's good to play nice with your teammates," I agree.

He glowers at me.

"And Fletcher's not wrong," I continue. "You play dirty, and that does your game a disservice. Not only *your* game either. The entire sport."

Hello, sore spot.

That's a glower I don't get from my brother every day.

I'm right—and Fletcher's right—and he knows it as well as I know that Fletcher called him on it in the changing room the other day.

I've excused it for years because I know why Silas plays rough. He's looking for approval from our father. And if you think our father gives a damn about the gentlemen's agreements to play a dignified match on the rugby pitch...unfortunately, you'll have to think again.

"You want Hallie growing up the way we did?" I add, softer.

"Fuck you."

There's no heat to it, though he does get a few looks from some of the other parents.

Fletcher's letting Hallie pet Sweet Pea, but he says something to her that sends her running back to us. "Aunt Gow-die, I ready to pway!" she says. "Put me in, coach!"

"When my sister started dating my best friend, I was happy for her," Beck says to Silas. "Made my life a lot easier."

"You set your sister up with your best friend," Sarah, his wife, reminds him. She's holding their middle daughter, who's still in the cutie-patootie toddler stage, while their oldest clings to Beck's leg.

"Also made my life easier."

"He's not my friend," Silas says.

"He could be." I leave it at that and head the same direction Hallie came from to meet Fletcher halfway to our group.

And then I have to restrain myself to keep from hugging him. And possibly kissing him. *Dammit, dammit, dammit.* "What are you doing here?"

"We were walking by. Heard an old lady scream and came to investigate."

I briefly squeeze my eyes closed while I try to not smile. "Fletcher."

He grins.

And not a little grin either.

This is a full-force, *I saved all of my grinning muscles for an entire week so I could grin at you like this* grin behind that ever-thickening dark beard and accompanied by the most mischievous twinkle in his bright green eyes. "Goldie. You know I'm not here to fuck spiders."

I am completely unable to resist the smile blossoming on my own face in response, and not only because I recognize the phrase that one of my Australian clients uses regularly. "You shouldn't be here."

"You'd come to cheer me on for my last match of the season. Why shouldn't I be here to cheer you on for yours?"

"*Fletcher.*" I'm positive he knows *exactly* why.

"It's what friends do. Frankly, I'm disappointed in your lady friends that they're not here too."

I like this man.

I like him entirely too much.

He's absolutely irresistible.

And I think I'd say that even if he were sporting that horrid mustache.

Oh god.

I would.

I'd think he was handsome in his mustache.

I try to give him my stern *you need to leave* look. "I have to go coach. All the old ladies are safe here. You should continue on your way."

"We're curious now. This seems fun."

"It's a bunch of little kids awkwardly chasing a soccer ball and falling all over each other and the ball for twenty minutes so their parents can take photos and videos. That's it."

"Sweet Pea didn't want me to tell you this—she's shy about these things—but she asked to come. She likes balls. And little kids. Even if they pick the wrong balls. But she's shy, so she made me make up the story about hearing an old lady scream so you wouldn't be suspicious."

"You're not leaving, are you?"

"It's a great opportunity for me to play nice with your brother and compliment his daughter's skills."

I pinch my eyes shut briefly again. "I swear on Monopoly, Fletcher, if I have to break up a fight between you two—"

"You won't."

I cross my arms and stare at him.

He stares back for a millisecond before he cracks and smiles again.

"One of you ending a fight by knocking the other out doesn't count," I say.

I'm well aware that his smile means he knows exactly why I'm glaring at him, but I still need to say it out loud to make sure that he knows I know he knows, and to make sure that he knows I won't tolerate him breaking my ground rules on what he'd call a technicality.

"People show up for drama, Goldie," he says. "He'd be doing the whole club a solid if he let me knock him out."

"All while Shade records it for posting to your socials?"

He winces. "Ah, no. Shade quit this morning."

There's something in his expression that says he's telling the truth on this one. "Why?"

"Job offer in LA." He slides a look around us and lowers his voice. "Might've been a *blow job* offer too. Wasn't getting that from me."

I should not giggle at that.

I shouldn't. "I'm going to go coach my kids now."

"Make sure you tell them they're doing a good job. Athletes respond well to positive affirmations."

He's in a *mood*. The good kind of mood.

The kind of mood you'd expect if he'd gotten off instead of only him getting *me* off last night.

His eyes are crinkling and his smile's popping out far more often than I ever would've thought possible from the scowly faced man who passed out on me at a blood drive a few weeks ago.

I scratch Sweet Pea behind the ears. "Thank you for coming to cheer me on, Sweet Pea. If you're my good luck charm, I'll have to treat you to a reward."

She barks and grins at me.

Beck and I get the littles organized and the game underway. His kids are in yellow shirts, and mine are wearing blue. The pint-sized field has chalk boxes drawn on it to show each player the position they're supposed to stay in, with one child from each team in each box, and they are freaking adorable.

After the first ten-minute half, where we stop every two to three minutes to rotate positions, we huddle up for a water break and a pep talk.

And that's when I realize things are going sideways with the parents behind me.

But it's not Fletcher and Silas.

They're standing shoulder-to-shoulder, blocking Campbell's dad from our huddle.

"He's not moving fast enough and the coach sucks," he says.

"Say that about my sister again—" Silas starts, but Fletcher interrupts him. "Your kid's four. Let him be a kid."

"Who had so much fun this half?" I say loudly to my team, shifting around the circle to keep a better eye on the grown-ups while distracting the kids from watching.

And also while ignoring the pain radiating in my hip again.

Freaking weather.

276

And I have to finish packing my books and drive all of the boxes to my storage unit when I'm done coaching today.

Dammit.

Hallie's hand shoots up.

So do most of the rest of the players' hands.

"I had fun!" Hallie shrieks.

"I pway goawie!" Archie flexes his arm. "I pway so good!"

But not Campbell. He stares at me forlornly, "I missed a ball."

"Grown-up soccer players miss the ball sometimes too," I tell him. "What counts is how much fun you're having out there."

He eyes me like he's forty instead of four, and my heart cracks a little.

"I like your shirt," Sienna says to him.

"I wanna blow bubbles," Archie announces.

"Coach Goldie, you tie my shoes?" Wilma Jane asks.

I pat the ground, beckoning her closer so I can tie her shoe while I look at all of the kids. "Are you all up for your very important jobs this next half?"

"I have to win," Campbell says.

My heart fully cracks in two.

I know this kid.

I have been this kid.

Silas still is. I think Fletcher might be too.

And there's nothing that I can say as his coach that will erase what he'll hear at home.

So I say the best thing I can think of. "Do you know what it means to win?" I ask the whole team.

Some of them shake their heads. Some nod. Some stare at me like I asked why the sun rises from the south in the sea-green sky every morning.

"Winning isn't about the score. It's about supporting your teammates and trying your best and having fun. If you play by the rules and you cheer for your teammates and give it

277

your all and you have fun in every part of that, you're winning."

"Aunt Gow-die, I don't know da wules," Hallie says.

"That's what I'm here for." I sneak a glance at Fletcher and Silas, who are both subtly shifting their stances and continuing to push Campbell's dad farther back down the field and out of earshot while Campbell's mom huddles closer to the rest of the moms. They're divorced and they've been trying family counseling. And I hope for Campbell's sake that it works. "You all know that when I tell you that you need to remember a rule, you didn't do anything wrong in forgetting it because you're still learning and it's okay to make mistakes, right?"

That gets more head bobs.

We've been over that lesson since week one, and for some of the kids on my team, this is their third or fourth month-long session now.

"One more drink of water for all of you," I tell them. "It's about time to get back on the field. Who's ready for fun?"

"Me!" most of them chorus.

I hold my hand to my ear. "What's that? I didn't hear you. Who's ready for fun?"

"*Me!*" they all shout.

"And who are we?" I ask.

"*The Fishies!*" they shriek.

I freaking love the names kids give their teams. "Go, Fishies!" I cry.

"*GO, FISHIES!*" they yell back.

"Let's go play some soccer!"

They all run onto the field in complete disarray.

It's so damn cute.

Especially with Beck corralling his kids too. They're the Elbows.

I'm actively not asking why.

It's three- and four-year-olds. There's not always a logical why.

Campbell scores a goal in the second half, and all of the kids dogpile him. Beck's kids score a goal too, and we end the game all tied up at three.

Which is fine with us.

And where I'd normally take my team to the concession stand for snow cones, instead, the parents produce a going away cake for me.

It takes everything inside of me not to cry.

Fletcher's gone.

So is Campbell's dad.

Silas refuses to reply to my silent questions, even though I know he knows what I'm asking every time I look at him.

But once all of my kids and their parents have said their final goodbyes, he does the last thing I expect.

He hooks an arm around my shoulder and says, "I'll be by in an hour with a bunch of the guys from the team to get your books into storage."

I stare at him.

He scowls back briefly, then turns to Hallie. "Let's go get lunch, short stuff. Who's ready for a steak?"

Hell's freezing over.

I take two steps to follow him, a piercing ache shoots down my leg on my bad side again, and I sigh.

Copper Valley isn't hell. It's so far from it.

But it's freezing over tonight, and I couldn't be more grateful for my brother's help with packing.

279

31

Fletcher

My old man's waiting with his luggage at the entrance to his hotel when I pull up in the Bentley. His eyebrows lift a little, but he doesn't comment on the car.

Nor on Sweet Pea's doggie car seat in the back.

I pop the boot—the trunk, I mean—and help him get his bags in back, then return to the driver's seat. He takes the passenger seat.

I put the car in gear, and we head to the airport.

In silence.

My shoulders are tight. I'm clenching my ass, and I don't know why.

Okay, fine.

I know why.

I don't like why.

"I spent ten minutes this morning explaining to a dad at a peewee soccer game that he needed to lighten up on his kid or his kid wouldn't talk to him when he grows up," I say in the silence.

My ass isn't just clenching now.

My ass muscles are vibrating.

Anger? Rage? Hurt? Regrets? Shame?

Probably all of the above.

My mom would be horrified that I avoid my old man at all costs. She always told me he was *a good man doing his best.* Her dying request was *look out for your sister and your dad.*

But nothing I ever did was good enough for him.

And sometime in the past two years, he started calling more.

He texts.

He drops by whenever the fuck he wants like he belongs here.

Like seeing him doesn't make me feel inadequate.

Never good enough.

There's silence again.

Silence and another stoplight. Fucking downtown. So many stoplights.

Fucking clouds overtaking the blue sky.

Fucking atmosphere so heavy inside this car that I'm gonna have to trade it in too.

Sweet Pea whines in the backseat.

And after a bloody eternity that's not even a full stoplight's cycle, my father clears his throat. "You're right. I was too hard on you. That—that wasn't fair. To you or your sister. I'm sorry."

I'm so startled, my foot leaves the brake and I almost roll into the SUV in front of me.

I correct in time, my thighs taut as a new spring, my stomach clenching.

"I thought I was doing the right thing. Making you tough to face a tough world. And instead, I accidentally taught you that you had to earn affection."

I glance at the climate controls as the light turns green.

Still set at sixty-six. Nobody turned up the heater.

But I'm sweating like I'm in a sauna.

"I'm in therapy," he continues. "I know you don't have to accept any of my apologies. I understand if you don't want to. This is my fault. I was the parent. You were the kid. It wasn't your fault I was hard on you. In a lot of ways, it wasn't entirely my fault that I didn't understand what I was doing, but I take responsibility for how it affected you. Full responsibility. I understand if it's too late, but if it's not, I want to do better."

Full-on sauna.

I hit the button and roll my window down to get fresh air.

Sweet Pea whines in the back seat.

Pretty sure it's not the forty-degree temps suddenly blasting in.

Not entirely, anyway.

She's a good dog. Knows when I need a hug.

I fucking love my dog.

We make it out of downtown and onto the highway without him saying anything else.

I don't say anything either.

What the fuck am I supposed to say?

Oh, okay. Got it. All's good now. Let's hug.

Not my style.

Get the fuck out of my car.

Nope. For the past twenty years, I've sworn I'd be the bigger man. That I wouldn't bend and crack under his scrutiny. That I wouldn't let him see how much he hurt me.

You're the reason I don't feel like I deserve to be loved. Mom loved me, and she left. Jessica loved me, and she left too. Bink loves me but lives far away and has her own life. There's no one who loves me because you never loved me.

Goddamn fucking heat in my eyeballs now.

The twenty minutes on the highway to the airport exit are the longest fucking twenty minutes of my life. But finally—*finally*—we reach the terminal.

I find a spot at the curb and get out to take care of his luggage.

When I set it on the pavement, I make myself look at him. "Thanks for coming."

I don't mean it.

The way he winces tells me he knows it.

He takes half a step like he wants to hug me, but switches his posture and grabs his bag instead. "I don't know how to be here for you now. But I'd like to be. So you tell me what you want. Whenever you're ready. I won't drop by without an invitation again. If I don't text, it doesn't mean I'm not thinking of you. It means I'm letting you drive."

I nod.

What else am I supposed to do?

"I love you, son," he says, and then the bastard turns and walks into the airport.

I make it two exits down the highway before I pull off and head up toward the Blue Ridge Mountains.

And the first place I find that's a little secluded, I pull over.

Climb into the back seat with my dog.

Hug her as tight as I can without hurting her.

And force myself to not grab my phone and message Goldie.

She'd get it. She'd listen. She'd understand.

And she's fucking leaving too.

32

From the Instagram direct messages of Goldie and Fletcher

CoachGoldie: Did you tell my brother I can't pack myself and order him to get half the Pounders to come finish putting my boxes in storage?

RugbyFletch: Good afternoon, Coach Goldie. How's the rest of your smushed cookie today?

CoachGoldie: Dodging the question as always, I see.

RugbyFletch: I dropped into your friend's DMs and told her you were sad she didn't come to your game today. Friends should be there for friends. You're welcome.

CoachGoldie: And more dodging the topic. She couldn't make it because she was on a date with your dad, btw.

RugbyFletch: *GIF of a crown spinning and sparkling* Fuck. I think you dropped this.

CoachGoldie: Thank you. Also, it was lovely to see you and Silas bonding today.

RugbyFletch: *side-eye emoji*

CoachGoldie: I got a text from Campbell's mom. Whatever the two

284

of you said to his dad made an impression. He apparently apologized profusely, told Campbell he played very well even before the goal, and took Campbell out to lunch at his favorite macaroni and cheese place.

RugbyFletch: It was all Sweet Pea.

CoachGoldie: Make sure Sweet Pea knows she made a major difference in a little boy's life today. I hope she understands what a massive gift that was to him and how it'll likely impact father and son for the rest of their lives.

RugbyFletch: Has anyone ever told you you're an asshole?

CoachGoldie: Apologies to Sweet Pea if I made her cry.

RugbyFletch: She accepts your apology.

CoachGoldie: You okay?

RugbyFletch: On top of the whole goddamn world.

CoachGoldie: This world, or an imaginary world where you don't think about how you wish someone had stepped in and done for you and your father what you did for another kid and his dad today?

RugbyFletch: You know what's most annoying about you?

CoachGoldie: My irresistible charm and innate attractiveness?

RugbyFletch: No, I like that part.

CoachGoldie: *suspicious emoji*

RugbyFletch: You say the same things my ex tried to say, but you say them better.

CoachGoldie: Or maybe you're older and wiser and see the world through a different perspective now than you did the last time you had an ex?

RugbyFletch: No. It's you. You're the difference.

CoachGoldie: I can see where that's annoying.

RugbyFletch: So annoying.

CoachGoldie: Wanna know what's annoying about you?

RugbyFletch: You've already made your feelings on my mustache very clear.

CoachGoldie: It's annoying to me that you're not the judgmental asshole I thought you were six years ago.

RugbyFletch: I'm a massive judgmental asshole.

CoachGoldie: Judgmental assholes are rarely self-aware enough to call themselves judgmental assholes.

RugbyFletch: Always knew I was one in a billion.

CoachGoldie: Can confirm. You are definitely one in a billion. Are you and your dad having a snowstorm party?

RugbyFletch: Dropped him at the airport a couple hours ago.

CoachGoldie: That's why you left the game.

RugbyFletch: That's why I left the game.

CoachGoldie: All okay there?

RugbyFletch: Know my way around Copper Valley pretty well now. Wasn't hard to leave Reynolds Park, get to his hotel, and get to the airport.

CoachGoldie: I revise my earlier statement. Your intentional dodging of questions is definitely the most annoying thing about you.

RugbyFletch: He said some shit. I said some shit. We might punch each other and hug later.

CoachGoldie: If you want to talk about it, I can introduce you to some seasoned ladies who give excellent relationship advice.

RugbyFletch: Did they get enough milk and eggs and bread to survive three days without getting to the store?

CoachGoldie: Pffffttt. They cleared out the local cupcake shop and the liquor store.

RugbyFletch: I just laughed out loud and scared my dog.

CoachGoldie: If you laughed more often, it wouldn't be so traumatic for her.

RugbyFletch: Guess you're hanging with them then?

CoachGoldie: They're pregaming for a slew of new obituaries they'll need to write. This kind of weather is hard on their ex-boyfriends.

RugbyFletch: So that's a yes.

CoachGoldie: That's definitely a yes. If you don't want to be snowed in solo, I'm sure they wouldn't mind if you joined us.

RugbyFletch: Huh.

CoachGoldie: They're going to need a new young person to guide when I'm gone. You seem like an excellent candidate.

RugbyFletch: *silence*

33

Goldie

I'M LYING on a heating pad and stretching my still-aching hips on Odette's thick rug in her apartment while the snowfall picks up outside when Sheila suddenly shrieks and immediately follows it with, "Oh, he brought the puppy!"

I peel one eyelid open and look up. There's Odette's floral couch. Her wall of family photos. The glass-doored cabinet full of her grandmother's china. The light fixtures that need to be cleaned.

Evelyn sits at the dining room table, gaping toward the short hallway to the door with a deck of cards paused mid-shuffle in her hands.

"And he better behave himself as well as the puppy does," Odette's saying.

Her apartment is bigger than mine—she has three bedrooms so she can host her kids and grandkids anytime they're visiting—

which means I have to twist my neck to fully see what's happening in the entryway.

And what's happening is that Odette and Sheila are leading Fletcher and Sweet Pea into the apartment, Odette leaning on a cane since she graduated from her wheelchair yesterday.

My heart hiccups and then leaps.

He's here.

He took my invitation, and *he's here.*

I start to smile, and then I fully take in the expression on his face.

He's not scowling, nor is he smiling. There's no cocky *you're welcome for gracing you with my presence* that I've seen him pull off either.

And I do mean *pull off.* I think it's mostly an act.

But tonight, there's a gravity about him that feels too real and too deep.

His gaze finds mine, and my heart hiccups and leaps again. I smile. Can't help myself. "You came. I didn't think you'd take me seriously."

He sweeps his eyes over my entire body. "Hip hurt still?"

"We gave her the good painkillers," Sheila says. "Extra-strength Motrin. She'll be up and on her feet again in no time."

"Lingering aches," I tell him. "I'll be better in a few hours. I'm barely limping."

All three of my lady friends snort or *hmph* at that.

"Hope you're good at bridge," I add. "I forgot to mention. It's a prerequisite that you play bridge when you're snowed in with us."

"Playing for cash?"

"It's strip bridge," Evelyn says.

All three of them look from Fletcher's handsome face to his solid body.

"My, my," Odette murmurs.

"This seems unfair, but also, I'm getting a little excited," Sheila whispers.

That finally gets a smirk out of Fletcher.

I finish my stretch and pull myself up to sitting. With the front moving through, I *am* feeling better. Better still for not having to do all of the manual labor to get my books into storage.

All Silas said was *next time, tell me yourself when you're hurting and need a hand.*

Something changed between those two men today.

Whether they're willing to acknowledge it or not.

Fletcher studies me for a second, then looks at Evelyn. "I don't lose. Thought you should know before you deal me in."

Ooooh, shit.

That made Evelyn smile her *you're so cute* smile.

Odette's stifling a cackle.

Sheila bites her lip, her eyes getting worried. "Do you truly want to sit around with a bunch of naked old ladies?"

"He can't play bridge. He's bluffing," I tell them.

Self-assured green eyes settle on me. "My ex's grandmother played competitively."

"Which ex?" Odette asks.

"First wife."

"Haven't you been divorced from her for fifteen years?"

"Never met a game I couldn't remember how to dominate at."

"Bridge is a partner game and there are five of us," I say.

Yes. I'm backtracking. I'm backtracking hardcore because I forgot rule number one with Fletcher: he will win at all costs.

"You're sitting out," Evelyn tells me.

"Everyone has their line, and I am not watching the four of you play strip bridge. Especially considering the shape some of you are already in. I'm not taking you to the ER for a strip bridge injury."

"Spoilsport," Odette says with a sniff, knowing full well I'm talking about her trying to shimmy out of her pants too fast on her knee.

Evelyn shakes her head. "I agree with Goldie. I'll do a lot of things in my old age, but shaking my saggy titties at a man who looks like that isn't one of them."

Fletcher doesn't say a word.

Probably knows there's no right answer.

"Fine," Odette says. "We'll do this the old-fashioned way and play for blackmail material instead."

"Dominoes," Sheila says. "So we can all play."

"Do you know how to play dominoes?" Evelyn asks Fletcher.

Something heavy flickers over his expression again. "My mom taught me."

All three of my friends study him closer. They, too, seem to recognize that something's a little off.

"Hope you do her proud," Odette finally says.

"No other way," he replies.

She leans on her cane while she heads to her china cabinet, where her games are stored in the lower drawers, while Evelyn and Sheila clear the table.

Fletcher turns to me again. "Gonna make it?"

"Of course." I hold out a hand, a silent request for help up. He obliges, and soon I'm standing.

Though he doesn't let go of my hand.

Sweet Pea sticks her head out of the sling and grins at me.

"You okay?" I ask him quietly.

His eyes say no, but he nods. "Never better."

Sweet Pea growls.

"That's what I thought too," I tell her. "But you can't make a man talk about his feelings. You can only hope he opens up before you're tired of how annoying he is."

To my absolute complete surprise, he pulls me into a hug, squishing Sweet Pea between us and resting his chin on my head.

I wrap my arms around his waist without conscious thought.

And then he sucks in a massive, uneven, rattling breath.

Just one.

He blows it out a lot slower, and his next inhale is steady, but it's absolutely clear that something definitely happened today.

And he doesn't want to talk about it.

Why would he?

He doesn't know my friends well, and I'm leaving in a week.

I wouldn't want to invest more time and effort in letting me closer right now if I were him.

I shouldn't want to know more about him either.

This is temporary.

For fun.

Not deep. Not a real relationship.

Liar, my heart whispers.

Like I let it have any say in my life right now.

I've recovered from Miller. I think. But I have too many other things coming in my life to have time for a relationship too.

Fletcher lets go and steps back, glancing down as if he doesn't want to acknowledge that he hugged me as though I was a lifeline. When he looks back again, the old Fletcher mask is firmly in place.

Cocky. Confident. A hint of a smirk lingering on his lips. I wonder if he's about to tell my three friends that they're all going to owe him every embarrassing story from their entire lives before he's done mopping the domino board with them.

"You can let your dog down," Odette tells him. "But you're in charge of any messes."

Clearly she's talking about Sweet Pea's messes.

But I can't help but wonder how many other messes we'll uncover before the night's over.

34

Fletcher

I GET IT NOW.

I get why Goldie hangs out with three old ladies instead of any of her acquaintances closer to her own age.

They're fucking hilarious sages of wisdom.

During dominoes, I learn that Sheila married the love of her life five days after she met him, was widowed young, dates the least of the three older women, and is a recent breast cancer survivor, which I'd already half guessed based on her hair.

I've decided she's my new grandma, but I keep that to myself.

Evelyn hits on me at every opportunity to the point that I start to worry she's serious until Odette assures me that they only date men likely to kick the bucket before they do, and I'm unfortunately too healthy-looking for my age.

I also find out that she has more ex-husbands than I have ex-wives, will drop anything on a moment's notice to reach her kids and grandkids for any reason, and she spent forty years working

her way up to a board of directors position at the largest environmental engineering firm in Copper Valley.

Odette is a former teacher who was also widowed relatively
young, but unlike Sheila, she remarried.

But only once.

And never again.

She says the divorce was more pleasant than the marriage itself.

She hired Goldie not long after her divorce, when a fourth
member of their group passed unexpectedly from a massive heart
attack. *Gonna make the most of what time I have left*, she says. And
when Goldie had her own heartbreak, Odette pulled her into the
friend group as the start of the next generation of their *Outlive Our
Ex-Boyfriends Club*.

Goldie wasn't kidding about the cupcakes and liquor either.

The three older ladies go through a bottle and a half before
we're done with dominoes, and I count at least eight cupcake
wrappers as I'm putting the dominoes back in their box.

Sweet Pea has decided Odette is her new favorite person, and
since the dog must be obeyed and is demanding a lap to sit in, they
pull up *Pride and Prejudice* on the TV that's almost as large as mine.

"Is this the point when you bail?" Goldie asks me. She's been
nursing the same glass of wine all evening so far.

I assume because of the pain meds.

"Which version are they watching?" I ask with a nod at the TV.

"There is no other version except the Colin Firth version,"
Evelyn calls.

"And that's one more test your friends have passed," I say to Goldie.

She studies me, waiting for a punchline. "You've watched this
before?"

"Yep."

"Lately?"

"Couple years ago."

"By yourself or on a date?"

"With my sister."

"Your idea or hers?"

"Don't remember." It was my idea.

Bink came to visit me in the UK. Left her family at home, and she got a call that her oldest had come down with the flu. Knowing that her wife was handling it solo and her baby was sick made for a shitty day that I couldn't fix for her, but I knew watching one of her favorite shows would make her feel better.

Plus, we've seen it enough that it was easy to pause when she wanted to call home and check in on things.

Goldie's watching me like she can see straight through to my brain.

But she doesn't call me on it.

Instead, she nods to the kitchen. "There's hummus and veggies in the fridge, along with a cheese tray if you're hungry and don't want cupcakes."

I shouldn't have come here tonight.

She's making me feel like I fit in her life. Like she wanted to be prepared to make me comfortable too in the event that I showed up, when we both know I shouldn't be here.

She's leaving.

But the idea of being alone with my own thoughts tonight was even worse than knowing it'll hurt like hell to get closer and then watch her leave.

You can still call her keeps echoing in my head.

But that would mean acknowledging I like her enough to want to have a real relationship.

And I don't do real relationships.

Pretty fucking sucky at them even in person, to be honest.

That's not fair to her.

"Can I—" I start, but she grins and cuts me off.

"You can only serve yourself with your finger once it's on your own plate."

"Takes all the fun out of it."

"If you get hungry enough, you can find your manners."

Whispers from the living room make both of us look toward the three older ladies.

Sheila immediately bends over and starts fluffing pillows on the couch.

Odette smirks and looks back at the TV, pointing the remote to start the movie. "*Pride and Prejudice* doesn't wait for stragglers."

Evelyn's smirking too as she takes one of the easy chairs next to the couch.

The opening sequence flashes on the TV. Goldie grabs the mason jar I've been drinking out of and refills it with water, barely limping as she moves around the kitchen.

"You hungry?" she asks me.

Always. Especially once training starts.

I don't answer, but she pulls out a plate and dives into the fridge anyway.

And five minutes later, I'm sitting next to her on the couch.

She's in the middle with Odette on her other side, my dog curled up in Odette's lap.

Evelyn and Sheila keep sneaking glances at me like they think they'll catch me making a move on Goldie.

Or maybe they're checking to see if I'm reacting appropriately to the movie.

Of fucking course I am.

I might be a Neanderthal in a lot of ways, and I might still be holding out hope for a *Dungeon Crawler Carl* movie, but there are rules when it comes to reacting to *Pride and Prejudice*.

I don't make them, but I do respect them.

As we're getting to the first dance scene, Odette pauses the movie. "Potty break, ladies."

"Oh, thank goodness," Sheila says. "I've had way too much wine and I need to make room for more."

Goldie goes with me to take Sweet Pea out into the snowy night.

Definitely not my dog's favorite activity. Poor little paws. Need to get her some booties before this happens again.

The street's empty. Snow falling thick enough that when we step out from beneath the overhang at the entrance to the building, I can't see Goldie clearly.

"You shouldn't be out here with your hip," I tell her while Sweet Pea picks a corner to do her business in.

"I didn't think you'd be here at all," she replies.

I glance at her, then back at my dog, and then I sigh. "Bad day."

She doesn't push.

And that makes it easier to keep talking. "My dad—he was hard on us growing up. Demanded perfection. I couldn't meet his standards in school, but rugby—I knew I was good on the pitch. So that's where I put all of my energy."

"Looking for validation," she says softly.

"Still wasn't good enough in school, and I picked fights with Bink too much, and he didn't even make it to half of my matches, but *I* knew. I knew I was good."

She slips her bare hand into mine and squeezes.

"He apologized today." The words taste like ash.

"And you feel like shit because you can't say *it's okay*, because it's not," she says quietly.

For the first time since I left that damn dome this morning, I let every last molecule of air leave my lungs. "Yes."

She squeezes tighter. "It's okay to make him prove to you that he means it, and it's okay if you're not in a place where you want to see him right now."

"Fucker said that to me too."

"And now you feel like you don't have a right to be angry

anymore because he said the right things that you never thought you'd hear him say."

"*Yes.*"

Leave it to Goldie to put it into words for me.

Fuck, I'm gonna miss her.

She huddles closer to me while Sweet Pea finishes up. "Life's a complicated bowl of crap sometimes."

I snort. "That's exactly what Jessica said when she told me she wanted a divorce."

"You loved her."

"Fucking worshipped everything about her."

"Why'd she leave?"

"Too young. Graduated high school, got married, moved to Britain so I could play for Nottingshire. She hated living so far from family. Got one too many bottles of sparkling water when she was expecting still. Struggled to make friends. I was gone half the time with the team. And then she was late and thought she was pregnant, and she wasn't, but it shook her up. I wasn't leaving Europe, and she didn't want to raise kids so far from family. So that was it. She left."

I haven't talked about this in fifteen years.

Haven't *wanted* to talk about it in fifteen years.

But letting it go into the swirling snow feels good.

Maybe I've reached a point where I can forgive myself for all the things I did wrong.

I hurt her. Can't deny it.

And that was as hard to face as her leaving.

"And your heart broke," Goldie says softly.

"Everyone's does sometime."

"*It happens to everyone* doesn't mean it doesn't hurt when it happens to you. And you're allowed to hurt when your heart breaks."

I swallow and look up at the swirling snow. "Coach did for me what Odette did for you. Picked me up. Supported me through it. Became more of my family than my own family had ever been."

"The same coach who fired you?" she whispers.

"Same coach."

"Ouch."

"One word for it."

"What you're doing here with the Pounders—it's personal."

It's so much more than just *personal*. "Yep."

She goes quiet for a moment, then— "Is she happy now? Your ex-wife?"

"Went to college, got a degree in fashion management, fell in love with her boss's son, got married, had two kids, and now works as a buyer for one of the last big department stores. Is she happy? More than she was with me, I'm sure."

"You miss her?"

I shake my head.

Goldie doesn't press.

But she does shiver.

I pick Sweet Pea up, tell her she's a good girl and let her lick my face, then steer both of them back inside. Snowflakes cling to Goldie's dark hair, melting as we make our way to the lift.

Upstairs, they've restarted the movie without us. "Only so many hours until they all pass out," Goldie whispers to me while we make our way back to the couch.

She lets me loop an arm around her while we watch the next hour of the movie.

And when the older ladies start to fall asleep with the movie still playing, she takes my hand, pulls me up, and leads me to her flat.

Like she's not leaving.

Like this could be real.

Even though we both know better.

35

Goldie

Is this man for freaking real? *"Cheater."*

Fletcher grins at me over his egg white omelet at the Palace of Pancakes three blocks down from his condo. "I'm not cheating. I'm using my resources wisely."

"Bribing Sheila with a gift from your dog to find out my favorite breakfast place is cheating."

"You wanted me to use my psychic powers instead?"

"I wanted you to tell me where *you* wanted to go for breakfast instead of waiting until we're almost done to confess that *you cheated* and did this for me."

It's pretty early in the day, three days since the snowstorm. We've spent the last two nights together at his condo after he slept over at my place the night before. He wakes up each morning and goes to training. I leave his place to see my clients and continue the last-minute move preparations.

And we're acting like this is a friends-with-benefits situation that won't bother either of us when I move in four days and leave it all behind.

"I'm still finding my favorite places," he says. "You're leaving. So we go where you like today."

I don't flinch.

He doesn't flinch.

But I want to, and I think he does too.

"That omelet looks disgusting," I tell him.

"Tastes pretty bad too. How's your waffle?"

"Transcendent."

It's easy being with Fletcher because this has an end date. My heart doesn't have to get involved.

It's torture being with Fletcher because my heart didn't get that memo and has very much gotten involved.

How can it not?

He's a big, tough athlete hiding a heart of marshmallow behind the stone walls he's built for it after being let down by everyone who's ever been important to him in his life. And he's spent the past several weeks learning my favorite breakfast place, noticing when I'm hurt or when I'm surrounded by people who have hurt me, helping my Little Kickers team, and giving me orgasms.

He is most definitely not the asshole I once thought he was.

He has struggles with his parent. He feels abandoned by the team that was his family. He knows how it feels to have your heart broken so thoroughly that you don't think you can ever love again.

I don't think Fletcher only cares about rugby.

I think he puts all of his energy into rugby because he's always believed it wouldn't hurt him.

Except it has.

It's hurting him the same way soccer hurt me.

A sport can't help but hurt you when it's inevitable that one day, your body won't be able to do it anymore.

"You know what would be a great way to get attention on the Pounders and sell more tickets?" I say.

"Hit me. I'm all ears."

"Random raffle for a date with a player of their choice for all season ticket holders."

He chokes on his energy drink.

"Porter is charming as hell. Holt has that look like he's a total dom in the bedroom. Crew is complete heartbreaker material. And you and Silas aren't bad."

"Do not hit me. I am not all ears. In fact, I'd prefer you stop talking."

"You're not raffling off an engagement ring. This isn't *Pounders: Bachelor Edition*. And you can have it be a hang-out sesh and let dudes enter too."

"I'm paying for your breakfast and we're leaving and never talking about this again."

"It's a good idea."

"For someone who's never been bought by a woman old enough to be her mother who wanted to talk about spankings during that *hang-out sesh*."

Oh. Huh.

Okay then.

So that's why he's not throwing a more off-the-wall idea right back at me and making it bigger.

Sore spot.

Poor Fletcher.

I take pity on him and drop my idea. We spend the rest of breakfast chatting about the Pounders.

Training. Locker room pranks. How Silas is putting in extra effort, and Fletcher thinks he'll play cleaner when the season starts.

The two of them not arguing about me anymore.

Silas even texted that he won't fly to London to kick anyone's ass if I decide to date while I'm there.

I told him I won't have time to date.

And the full truth of why I won't be dating is a lot more complicated than that.

It involves the man who pays for my breakfast and accompanies me on the walk back from breakfast to my apartment.

While I'm bundled up in snow boots and a thick winter coat, he's in a light jacket—Pounders, of course—and work boots. We're both wearing jeans, but I doubt he put long underwear on under his.

It's not that cold out.

I'm cold today.

Much as I love how pretty the snow is, the white stuff on the ground telegraphs *freezing cold! Stay inside!* and always has. My hip isn't aching anymore, but I still could go for a hot chocolate and a roaring fire.

That's what I'm thinking as we're quietly walking side-by-side through a small park to my apartment building when I'm suddenly slapped straight-on in the face.

My body jolts.

I gasp and fling my arms up, bracing myself against another hit.

I try to see who's attacking, but there are white dots dripping off my eyelashes and into my eyes.

And then I feel the sting.

The cold.

And Fletcher shoving me behind him. "Who did that?" he growls to the world. "Show yourself. Now."

All is silent for a moment.

And then—

"I didn't mean to," a little voice says.

A snowball.

I just took a snowball straight to the face.

I scrub it off with my gloved hands, blink a few times to clear my vision, and glance around Fletcher.

A young girl, maybe eight, maybe ten, with brown skin and big brown eyes, all wrapped up in a pink coat and matching snow pants, is hovering behind an evergreen bush beside the sidewalk.

"She has bad aim," a boy not much older says on the other side of the sidewalk. He has the same eyes and an identical coat-snow pants suit, except his is black. "She was trying to hit me."

They're both bundled up in matching stocking hats too, their breaths little puffs in the morning air.

"Shouldn't you be in school?" I blurt.

"We're homeschooled," the kid answers. He points to one of the apartment buildings across from the park. "We don't start yet."

"I didn't mean to," the girl whispers again.

Fletcher's rigid body relaxes. He glances back at me, then turns to the girl. "You need help learning to aim? My sister was awful at it too."

Gone is Mr. *I Will Destroy You*, and instead, there's a quiet, patient man slowly approaching the young girl.

She eyes him warily, then looks at the older boy, whom I assume is her brother.

"I keep trying to show her, and it doesn't work," he says.

Fletcher squats to the ground about an arm and a half's length from her, packs a snowball, and stretches to hand it to her. "Look where you're throwing. Take your arm straight back—no, like this —there you go—and wait until your hand is right here to throw it. But keep it straight. Don't twist your wrist. Make sense?"

She looks at her brother again.

He nods.

She nods.

And then she throws a snowball, aiming for the other kid, and instead sends it flying sideways in the opposite direction from where her last throw landed.

"Don't go for force yet," Fletcher says. "Accuracy first. Speed after you have accuracy. Here. Toss this one like it only has to go a meter. Foot. Only has to go a foot. Arm straight. Don't twist your wrist. There you go. Nice."

The snow is melting off my face, but something bigger, deeper, and far more terrifying is melting in my heart.

Fletcher helps the girl for a few more minutes while her brother covertly makes a pile of snowballs on his side of the sidewalk. Under normal circumstances, I'd scoot over to his side and help plan an all-out assault for once his sister has her throw down, but I can't move.

Not with the thoughts racing through my head.

He's a good man.

He's so much more than he lets anyone see.

I want so badly to hug him right now.

How did I ever think he was ugly?

Did his dad do this with him?

Will he be okay?

I love him.

Can he love me back?

My eyes get hot, and my throat goes thick like it has an icicle stuck inside it.

And that's exactly when he glances at me. "Okay, Goldie?"

No.

No, I'm not okay.

I'm leaving in four days. I'm in love with the last man on earth I ever could've imagined giving the time of day a month ago. And I don't know if he can consciously love me back.

"Wind got in my eyes," I lie. "And I realized I need to go or I'll be late for my meeting. And you're going to be late for training too."

He studies me, seeing right through me.

I smile like nothing's wrong.

Like everything's fine.

Knowing that tonight, I'm going to a Thrusters game with him, and then likely back to his place afterward for more casual sex that won't feel casual at all.

Not to me.

But there's zero chance I'd miss tonight for the world.

Seize the day, right?

Even when the more you seize it, the more it'll hurt when it's over.

"Keep practicing that throw," he says to the girl. He pulls out his wallet, removes a business card, and hands that to her. "Here. You ever want tickets to a rugby match, have your parents text this number. And you—give her half your snowballs. Don't be a dick. Got it?"

The girl giggles.

The boy makes a face, then he giggles too.

"And let the lady through before you throw again," he adds as I start down the sidewalk.

He falls into step with me, glances at me once, tucks his hands into his pockets, and walks me the rest of the way back to my apartment in silence.

"Still on for tonight?" he says when we reach my door.

"I love hockey. I'd go to a game with my worst enemy." I don't have enough cheek behind it, and I think he notices.

"Give good advice today," he says instead of calling me on anything.

He kisses the top of my head, and then he strides away.

And yes—I absolutely stare at his ass.

Then I shove all of my feelings into a box.

I have client meetings. Another preparatory call with the center in London. And I'm having lunch with Hallie and Brittany today.

My pre-broken heart can wait.

Or you can find your courage, a voice that sounds annoyingly like me on social media whispers in my head.

I'll deal with that later too.

Possibly much later.

After I'm on an airplane.

36

Fletcher

GOLDIE AT A HOCKEY game is a cutthroat competitive banshee.

It's fucking gorgeous.

"Where's the penalty, ref?" she yells midway through the second period while boos erupt around us. "My grandmother saw that high-sticking from halfway around the country and she has cataracts."

I stifle a grin and take a swig from my water bottle.

She glares at me. "Why aren't you outraged too?"

"Don't know the rules."

The glare turns to a stern librarian frown. "Yes, you do."

God, I love this woman.

Fuck.

Fuck.

I didn't think that.

I didn't mean it like that.

I meant it like *she's funny.*

Like *who wouldn't appreciate someone who cares about a sports team this way?*

Yeah. That's the word. It's *appreciation.*

It's not *love.*

My balls aren't sweating.

My heart isn't racing.

My whole world isn't flipping upside down while *danger, danger* alarms blare in my head.

And I'm a bloody liar.

"It's more fun to pretend I don't know the rules," I say.

My voice is hoarse. I don't even believe myself right now.

And it's not *fun* to *pretend* that I *don't know the rules.*

It's a coping mechanism to believe that I don't have to acknowledge the thoughts in my own damn head.

She stares at me, curiosity overtaking the sexy stern librarian eyebrow tilt.

I stare back like I don't want to shed my jacket and my T-shirt in search of some cooler air.

Here.

In a hockey arena.

Where it's climate-controlled to a nice chilly temperature for the ice.

Everyone around us shoots to their feet yelling, and both of us leap up too.

I have no idea what we're cheering for until a buzzer blasts through the arena. It takes me too long to focus on the padded-up players on the ice gathering into a group hug.

Goal.

Thrusters scored a goal.

"That's what happens when you make bad calls, ref!" Goldie yells.

The entire arena bursts into a victory chant—something about *thrust this*—led by a rocket-powered bratwurst beating a drum on the jumbotron over center ice.

And it's not until we're all seated again with play resumed that it occurs to me that the Pounders need a victory chant.

We need our fans yelling something every time we score a try or a drop goal.

And that should've been the first thing I thought of.

The Thrusters are up two-nothing at the end of the second period. We're at the end of a row in the lower bowl behind the penalty boxes with access to a private lounge. When we get up to stretch and get more drinks during the break, there's a seven-foot-tall rocket-powered bratwurst mascot hanging out and taking pictures with fans.

Goldie drags me over and makes me stand in line, and I hold her hand too tightly the whole time we're waiting.

Four days.

She's leaving in four days. Three months in London, then at least a year on the road.

I saw the map on her phone last night. She's been playing with routes. Looking up vacation rental houses. Making notes about what she wants to ask people for her book.

My chest is getting tighter and tighter. Sweat drips down my spine.

My heart hasn't been this attached in fifteen years.

I don't like it.

Goldie chats with the people around us. Apparently one of the Thrusters' long-time big stars is retiring this year. There's chatter about draft picks and head office turnover. How much longer the team's ventriloquist will stay on staff, which, yes, I did hear right. Some celebrity is in attendance and people are hoping for pictures with them too.

And none of it matters.

Not when I'm trapped in a steel box wanting something I've

sworn I would never want again.

Especially from someone who's leaving.

I smile for pictures on Goldie's phone when it's our turn to pose with the bratwurst mascot. I buy her an ice cream and get myself another water. She introduces me to someone who's apparently important in the Copper Valley sports world, but it doesn't penetrate why that matters.

"Are you okay?" she whispers while we're heading back to our seats after she's eaten her ice cream.

No.

No, I'm not okay.

"Tired," I lie.

She studies me that way she does, like she's looking for all of the things I'm not saying behind that single five-letter word.

And then she says the magic phrase. "We can blow off the rest of the game."

I swallow and make myself sound as normal as I can when I ask, "Wanna come over?"

She slips her hand in mine, squeezes, and whispers, "I'd love to."

I don't remember the drive home.

I don't know if I take Sweet Pea out for one last potty when I get there.

Doesn't matter. I'm finally alone with Goldie.

Pushing her seventy-five layers of shirts and undershirts off. Helping her shove my shirt over my head.

Dropping my pants and tripping on them while I try to kick off my shoes at the same time.

Goldie's jeans join mine in the hallway from the living room to my bedroom.

She's in a red lace bra and a matching thong, and once again, I have no idea how I'm going to survive the hard-on straining thick and heavy at the very sight of her.

She's fucking gorgeous.

Plump breasts. Curvy hips. Long legs. Pink stain on her porcelain cheeks. A ring of gold around her dilated pupils. Breath coming fast. Arms reaching for me. Lips parted.

I want this every night.

I want *her* every night.

I don't know if she kisses me or if I kiss her. If she jumps up into my arms or if I pull her up. How I'm moving with her legs wrapped around my hips and her honeypot rubbing against my cock, the lace of her thong adding an element of sensation against my bare stick that makes me almost come on the spot.

But I make it to the bedroom still vertical.

I've been picking up my clothes since she's started staying over, so it's a straight shot to the bed without tripping over anything. I toss her onto the mattress, slide down her body, strip her of her thong, and feast on her pussy until she's screaming my name with her hands gripping my ears.

And then I suit up with a condom, and I slide into her.

This.

Home.

"Oh my god, Fletcher, more," she gasps like she didn't just come all over my face.

Like she's not on bottom when she keeps insisting on being on top.

Like she's not leaving me in four days.

I slam into her, my body as tight as a string, desperate for more.

More Goldie.

More of her pussy.

More of her laughter.

More of her hand squeezes.

More of her kisses.

More of all of her.

I can't get deep enough. I can't show her hard enough how much she means to me.

How much I don't want her to go.

How much I need her to stay.

If I can make her feel good enough, maybe she won't leave.

If I can promise her endless orgasms, maybe she'll stay.

If I'm just *fucking enough*, maybe she could love me.

Or like me enough to pretend to love me.

Forever.

Her breath hitches, and her channel squeezes hard once, then spasms around my cock.

"*Too much*," she gasps.

I freeze, my balls so hard and tight that one wrong move could shatter them, my cock aching with the desperate need for release.

"Don't stop," she orders. "Like—it. Too much—like it."

"You sure?"

She wiggles her hips, arches her neck, and moans as her pussy clenches around me again.

I pump once, twice, and then I'm coming too.

Physically.

Emotionally, I can't let it out.

I can't say it.

I can't ask her for more.

I shouldn't *want* more.

But she's my Goldie.

She's been a bright spot in my world when I thought leaving England would mean the rest of my life spent in darkness.

I've lived in fear and uncertainty since I tore my rotator cuff.

But Goldie makes me feel free.

She brings me joy.

She brings me peace.

She makes it okay for me to be *me*.

The good and bad parts. The easy and the hard parts.

I collapse on top of her, her breast my pillow, panting and choked up and completely out of my element.

I love you.

I want to tell her.

But I can't.

I can't.

If she doesn't love me back, I will be absolutely crushed, and nothing will matter anymore.

Not rugby. Not my father. Not my dog.

Not me.

She loops shaky arms around my shoulders, panting for breath. "You are seriously good at this," she says, wheezing between her words.

I should chuckle.

Laugh.

Smirk.

Tell her *I know.*

Reach deep for that obnoxious cocky charm.

But one word slips out of my mouth instead. *"Stay."*

37

Goldie

My limbs are rubber. My vagina is floating on a cloud of ecstasy. I can't quite catch my breath.

And my entire heart has gone completely still.

Stay?

What does he mean, *stay?*

"I'm not going anywhere," I say, then cringe.

You think I can walk like this? would've been more on-brand for our relationship. Or *and miss round two?*

Fletcher tightens his grip around my ribs and buries his face in my breasts. "Don't leave me."

No more still heart.

Now it's cramping.

"Fletcher—"

"Don't go to London."

My rubbery arms start to tingle.

And not in a *we just woke up* kind of way, but in a *fight or flight* kind of way.

I draw in as deep of a breath as I can manage with his head weighing down my chest. "What did you say?"

"Don't go. Don't go to London. Stay. Stay right here." He lifts his head and looks at me, and *oh*.

Just *oh*.

The defiance.

The anger.

The *dare*.

That look?

That look says *prove to me I matter more to you than your job does*.

And I don't like it.

For the first time in weeks, I am absolutely not comfortable with Fletcher right now.

"You can have the whole closet," he says, his voice doing a dark thing I've never heard before. "I have a spare bedroom for an office. Just—*stay*."

My head is full of helium, and my pulse is rapidly picking up momentum, headed for lift-off.

This isn't *I love you*.

This isn't even *I could love you*.

Nor is it *we can make a relationship work*.

It's exactly what Miller did.

Sacrifice your professional opportunities for me.

I try to shake myself out of it, to tell myself that there's more going on here, that this isn't what he's asking, but that wounded part of me that apparently *isn't* over what Miller did is howling in pain.

"You want me," I say, my voice wavering despite my best efforts to control it, "to give up my dream residency, to cancel the commitments I've made, and stay here."

No.

No.

This isn't happening.

Not again.

Not *one more man* asking me to put my dreams on hold for promises of *a closet?*

While glaring at me like *I'm* in the wrong for making plans before I met him? Like the *only* solution to our relationship is for me to give up the opportunity of a lifetime that's *temporary?*

His jaw flexes while he unfurls himself from around me and pushes up on his elbows. "There's nothing in London you can't get here."

"Except for *a competitive residency* that I already essentially gave up *for a man* once before." The words fly out of my mouth before I can stop them.

A sheet.

I need a sheet.

Better yet, I need my clothes.

Something ignites in his eyes. "I'm not your fucking ex."

"And what are you? What is *this?*"

His jaw flexes again behind all of that thick stubble that's nearly a full beard now. "I don't know. What *is* this?"

What *is* this?

It's me desperately wishing that he'd say anything other than *stay.*

It's me not understanding how someone who sees *so much* could think *stay* and *I'll give you a closet* is the only answer. "I thought it was a lot of fun with someone who's been one of the best friends I've had in a very, very long time."

It's honest.

But it's not everything.

Do I want to go?

No.

Yes.

Dammit.

"Right," he mutters. "And you don't walk away from your job for *fun,* do you?"

"It's *three months.*"

"It's you *walking fucking away.*"

Oh god.

That's what this is.

It's not about him thinking he's more important than I am. It's not about him demanding that I give up my life for him.

It's about him being more afraid than I am and completely unable to communicate it any other way.

"Fletcher—"

He climbs off the bed and heads to the bathroom. "Forget it. Don't stay. Go to London. Go take your road trip. Go live your life. Have all the fun. Fuck all the fancy Englishmen. Piss your brother off."

I desperately want my clothes back.

But more, I want to get on the other side of that door that just shut into the bathroom.

I leap up and cross the room to knock on it. "Fletcher. I'm not leaving you."

"I didn't say you were."

"*Fletcher. Yes, you did.*"

"It's been fun, but you have things to do. Places to go. Friends to make if you're fucking brave enough."

"*I'm not fucking leaving you,*" I repeat.

"Are you going to London?"

I've wanted nothing more than I've wanted this residency since I turned down the opportunity to go as a student for Miller.

Do I want to leave Fletcher right now?

No.

No, I don't.

But can I look myself in the mirror for the next fifty years of

318

my life and say I did what I knew was right if I bail on going to London for a guy I've been sleeping with for a week?

And what happens when we break up?

What happens if I give up my dream, *again*, for a man, *again*, and he pulls *this exact shit that he's pulling now?*

If he can't tell me what's going on right now, what are the chances we could survive a long-distance relationship?

What are the chances that this won't happen again?

What are the chances that he'll do the work necessary to truly, openly, willingly love me without all of the fear that *I cannot fix for him?*

It doesn't matter how much I can see what this is.

It matters that *he* sees it.

It matters that *he* wants to fix it.

Am I going to London?

I take a deep breath. "Yes. I'm going to London."

He doesn't answer, but I hear the shower turn on.

I test the handle.

Locked.

"Fletcher, let me in."

"I don't need to be *Coach Goldie*-ed. Doing fine. You know where the door is."

I suck in an unsteady breath. "So that's it?" I say to the door. "Do you have any idea what you've meant to me the past month? How nice it's been to have a friend my age again that I trust? To laugh with you and fight with you and have sex with you? You've been so much more than a friend, Fletcher. So. Much. More."

My heart hurts.

My head hurts.

My eyes are on fire from holding back tears and there's an iceberg in my throat.

He doesn't answer.

I lean into the door and squeeze my eyes shut. "I'm not leaving you," I repeat.

"Wish you would," he replies.

I wish I could say it's self-respect that makes me push myself away from the bathroom door and go in search of my clothes, but it's not.

It's the aching pain of rejection.

There's nothing I can say that will make him see me leaving for London, for this trip I've been anticipating for *years*, as anything more than me abandoning him.

There are fucking *phones*.

It's *three months*.

This isn't about me going to London. It's not about me being a digital nomad and traveling the States to gather research for my next book when I get back.

It's about him not being willing to have enough faith in me for us to work out how to have a real relationship.

And that's what hurts most.

I'm not worth the risk to him.

I'm not enough.

And it wouldn't matter if I was leaving for London or not.

No matter what I could've done, no matter how much I could've tried, I was never going to be enough.

38

Fletcher

I DID THE RIGHT THING.

That's what I keep telling myself while I toss and turn all night.

I did the right thing.

I'm not relationship material. It was dumb to ask her to stay.

She needed to go.

It was end shitty now, or end shitty later.

Might as well be now.

But that doesn't stop me from wanting to roar when I find the note she left in the kitchen.

Thank you for being the friend that I needed exactly when I needed you. Here's my phone number in case I can ever return the favor.

I should throw it away.

Sweet Pea growls at me for thinking it, so instead, I shove the note behind the stash of Cadbury chocolate bars that I don't acknowledge I have ninety-nine percent of the time.

"Happy now?" I ask my dog.

She stares at me with mournful eyes, then turns her back on me, trots to the living room, and curls up in her extra doggie bed.

And then I pretend everything's fine and I head to the stadium for training.

Where I park right next to Silas as he's getting out of his Ferrari.

Fuck.

Since we both jumped on that parent who was demanding perfection from his four-year-old last weekend, there's been this unspoken truce between us.

He didn't ask me for help with the asshat.

I didn't ask him either.

We both turned and told him to knock it off at the same time—both of us, in unison like we planned it, "Knock it off," and that was that.

But he's giving me one of his old mulish fuck-wanker looks while he waits for me to get out of my Range Rover.

Left the Bentley in the parking garage at my building.

Probably gonna sell it.

For obvious reasons.

"Why did my sister show up at my house this morning and threaten to disembowel me if I'm not nice to you?" he says.

Fucking Goldie.

Fucking Goldie.

Any other woman would've gone to her brother and told him to end me.

Goldie?

She goes to her brother and *tells him to be nice.*

"Why the fuck should I know?" I say as evenly as I can.

"You break up with her?"

We weren't dating. I don't do relationships.

Why?

Because they always end like this.

Because I'm shit at this. I get attached and they leave.

Every damn time.

She was already leaving, my bloody conscience interjects. *It was never about you.*

I still wasn't enough for her to want to stay, I fire back.

My conscience rolls its eyes at me.

I jerk my chin at Silas in acknowledgement. "You're fucking welcome."

He doesn't have the consideration to start a fistfight at my response. Instead, the wanker has the audacity to look me straight in the eye, shake his head, and say, "You're an idiot."

Silas Collins.

Calling *me* an idiot.

Worse?

He's not bloody wrong.

Fuck.

Tires squeal on the parking garage pavement.

A Jeep.

Holt's here.

Probably ready to hop out of his car and break us up.

But Silas isn't throwing punches or even insults.

Instead, he's turning his back on me, flinging his gear bag over his shoulder, and heading toward the stadium.

I pop open my boot—my *trunk*—look inside, and realize I left my own gear bag in my other car.

If I say *fuck* in my head one more time, it's gonna fucking explode.

"What's this about?" Holt appears at my side and gestures to me. "You eat bad oysters? Or did Collins put you in your place?"

"Trying something new."

"You broke up with Goldie."

It takes every ounce of control in my body to not shove him.

Did she fucking tell everybody? "Wasn't seeing her."

He snorts. "Keep telling yourself that."

I'm late to training because of running back to my flat to get my gear. When I hit the pitch, everyone else is already running laps.

"You're late," Coach says.

"Shitty day."

"Leave it outside."

"Already left it."

Whole point of training is to get stronger. Get faster. Get ready.

Instead, I hit a tackle bag wrong and tweak my shoulder.

By the time training's over, the only thing I want to do is go home, hug my dog, and drink myself into oblivion until it's time to do this all over again tomorrow.

Instead, half the damn team follows me home.

The ones who don't make it into my private parking garage show up outside my door.

"What the fuck do I have a door code for?" I mutter to myself while I wade through them to unlock my flat.

Condo.

Fucking American words.

"We're irresistibly charming when we need to be," Porter says.

"And this is Pounders tradition," Crew adds like he's been on the team longer than me, which he hasn't.

"Breakups require *The Fast and the Furious* marathons and steak dinners," Tatum says.

Are they fucking kidding? I drop my head to my door. "I didn't have a breakup."

Holt joins the group, along with a few other guys who got off the elevator. "You're mopey, you're unfocused, you kept looking at the stands during training, and Goldie's leaving for London in three days. If you didn't break up, you're getting ready to. And if you don't let us love-bomb you, we'll tell Coach and get you traded."

I stare at him.

He stares right back like he didn't say *let us love-bomb you*.

I've never been on a team that *love-bombs* its players.

"Chef's on the way," Holt adds. "We requested Yorkshire puddings to go with the steak."

And then the fucking worst thing happens.

Silas.

Silas.

He strolls out of the stairwell door, not even fucking winded—bet he rode the lift to the floor beneath mine and only did one set of stairs—holding a brown paper bag.

"None of us are drinking," I say with a scowl.

"It's from the chocolate smuggling ring, asshole," he replies, shoving the bag at me.

Goddammit.

These fuckers are making my eyes hot.

Not even the Leopards back in Nottingshire would've done this.

"I heard you have a pinball collection," Porter says.

I stare at him. Where the *fuck* did he hear that? "It's in storage."

"Here? In this building? Or somewhere else?"

And that's how my teammates end up shoving their way into my place, rearranging the furniture that I paid a designer to put together before I moved in, when I was so pissed about being fired that I forgot to tell her to leave room for any of my pinball machines, and give me something back in my life that I didn't even know I was missing.

They give me something I did know I was missing too.

A team.

Friends.

Comfort.

Belonging.

Belief, for the first time in months, that I'll be okay.

On the team, anyway.

39

Goldie

Apparently London is hell.

It's really not. My first week here has been spectacular, but I should've said no when the faculty asked if they could take me out for Friday night fun.

Their version of fun?

A rugby match.

In person.

In Nottingshire, a town so close to the outskirts of London that it's basically still in the city, where the Leopards are playing Yorkham's team.

Nottingshire.

Fletcher's team.

"In rugby, love, they can only pass the ball backwards," Judith, my boss in this coach in residence adventure, says to me. Aside from this *surprise* tonight, she's been a delightful part of my time here so far. "It's very different from what Americans call *football.*"

"My brother plays," I say absently.

Am I staring at the Leopards' head coach on the sidelines of the pitch? Wondering what on *earth* he could've been thinking with the way he let Fletcher go?

Yes.

Yes, I am.

Fletcher hasn't called. He hasn't texted. He hasn't slid into my DMs.

He just...let me go.

Maybe I truly was nothing to him, and asking me to stay was the afterglow of sex talking and he didn't mean to say it at all.

Maybe that's why he got mad.

"Pity they released Huxley," Gareth, my office's administrative assistant says on my other side. He looks at me like he needs to explain, and I smile patiently while my bruised and beaten heart begs him silently to stop talking. "Fixture on the team for years. Good bloke. He was getting on in years, but he still had it. Been hard to watch the team struggle since he left."

The players on the pitch are gathering for a scrum after a loose ball.

Fletcher was number four. He would've been in there.

Are those the friends he had when he lived in London?

How close were they?

He plays things so close to the vest, it's a wonder that I even knew he missed his old teammates.

The match is absolute torture.

The Leopards lose.

"Happening a lot this year," Gareth says on a sigh as he straightens his tweed flat cap while we prepare to leave the stadium. "Might be time for a change in leadership."

"Hush, hush," Judith tells him. "You know Rafferty has had a rough year. Not that way, Goldie. One more surprise! Gareth, we'll see you on Monday."

No.

No more surprises.

Please, no more surprises.

But I smile happily and follow Judith to a stairwell. She flashes something on her phone at the security guard, and several minutes later, we're being hustled into a cramped office in the stadium's underbelly.

"Several years back, I was at a mixer with athletic coaches in addition to life coaches," she tells me on the way. "Similar to what you've done in the States, our organization helps retiring athletes, and oftentimes, we become friends with the staff of the local teams. When I told Oliver we had the youngest coach in residence in history arriving, and about your history with your own sport, he gave me tickets and insisted I bring you down for a meet and greet. His daughter has had some...struggles...in the past few months, and I suggested you might be able to help her."

"Struggles?" I concentrate on what I can help with rather than the knot growing in my stomach.

This is the stadium Fletcher called home for years. *Years*. He walked these halls. He trained here. He was injured here. Healed here. Had teammates here.

Teammates that I can hear quietly talking in a room further down the tunnel.

My heart aches. It just *aches*.

"Terrible break-up just weeks before her wedding," Judith says. "No one saw it coming. He claims she cheated on him, she claims she simply realized she loved someone else but never acted on it, and she's been isolating ever since."

That doesn't help my heartache.

"This might be bigger than what I can do."

"She needs a stepping stone." Judith winks at me. "And I'm apparently *too old* to understand."

"Kids these days," I murmur.

"Indeed."

She smiles.

I force one back.

We enter a deeper room inside the coaching complex while the tingling on my neck gets heavy enough that I want to scratch at it.

A gray-haired man sporting a look of utter frustration pulls away from a private conversation with one of the associate coaches, a smile briefly passing over his face as he spots Judith.

And then he spots me.

His brown eyes meet mine and a series of emotions flit across his face in rapid succession.

It would be comical if my heart wasn't creeping toward anxiety territory.

This is the man who cut Fletcher from the team.

The coach who jerked the rug from beneath a man who thought he'd be able to rely on rugby forever.

"Oliver!" Judith steps smartly into the room, arms outstretched. "Pity about the match. You'll get them next week. I wanted to introduce you to—"

"Goldie Collins," says Oliver Rafferty, head coach of the Nottingshire Leopards rugby club.

It's the first time all week that I haven't made myself smile while meeting someone.

Not anyone else's fault for the rest of them—bruised-heart Goldie is not easy-smiling Goldie.

"You've met?" Judith says.

Rafferty doesn't immediately answer her, so I make a leap in assuming why he's staring at me the way he is.

"We have a mutual acquaintance," I tell my boss.

Judith peers at me.

Rafferty doesn't correct me.

"Goldie's been a lovely addition to our staff this term," Judith says. "I think she's perfect for your situation too."

330

He doesn't look at me as he answers her. "Don't bloody well think that's a good idea."

I haven't known my boss long, but I suspect flabbergasted isn't a look she wears often. "I—but Oliver—Goldie would be a lovely bit of support for Annalise. She's been through her own relationship struggles, and she's of an age to connect—"

"I said no."

Unease slithers through me. I know what Fletcher thinks of Rafferty after the way they parted.

The feeling must be mutual if I'm being denied an opportunity to help his daughter merely for the connection.

Am I reading this wrong? Is there another reason this coach wouldn't like me on sight?

Judith frowns at him. "Or perhaps *you* should have a session or two with someone who could discuss your personal and professional goals."

"Lovely to see you, Judith. Please excuse me. I have a meeting to attend to."

Something raw and ugly ignites inside of me. This man is being rude. He hurt Fletcher, and now he's being rude to Judith. "Does this have anything to do with Fletcher?" I ask.

Judith squeaks and covers it with a cough.

It would be amusing that she doesn't personally follow me on Instagram if it wasn't so awkward right now.

Rafferty's cheeks go ruddy. "How is he?"

Were we talking about anyone else, I'd be politely honest. *He could use an apology for what you did to him, but I'm sure you had your reasons. There are always two sides to every breakup story, aren't there?*

And then he wouldn't tell me his side. I might have his friend's stamp of approval, but I'm still a complete stranger whom he clearly doesn't want talking to his daughter. Plus, he's the head coach for a top rugby club in a country where people watch rugby.

But we're talking about Fletcher.

And I don't want to talk about Fletcher. "I don't know anything about managing a rugby team, but it's a sign of a massive leadership failure when a longtime star player and team leader departs mid-season under questionable circumstances and you keep getting your ass handed to you on the pitch now that he's gone."

Judith makes another strangled noise.

She's not simply peering at me anymore.

She's staring at me with her eyes almost as wide open as her mouth.

Probably thinking I shouldn't be repeating things Gareth said during the game.

But it's true.

They haven't played well since Fletcher left.

And he doesn't want you, I remind myself. *Let it go. This isn't your battle.*

"Pardon me, Judith," I say quietly. "I don't think I'm myself tonight. Jet lag must be catching up with me. I'd like to head home, if it's all right with you."

"O-of course," she stammers. "I'll call for the car. Oliver, I'll— we'll have tea next week."

"Annalise broke her engagement because she fancied herself in love with him," Rafferty says.

It's my turn for my eyes to bug out.

And for me to choke on air.

He was dating his coach's daughter and didn't tell me?

"He didn't know," Rafferty adds quietly. "He never knew how she felt. She was thirteen when he started for the team. Always treated her like a little sister. But she—she needed him to go."

"She needed him to go?" I repeat. What does that mean?

"You dated him yourself. You know how it ends. How it *always* ends."

The reminder is a lovely kick in the teeth, but I blow out a small breath and ignore the pain to focus instead on something that just doesn't feel right.

You know how it ends.

She needed him to go.

You can't talk to my daughter.

Terrible break-up. She's been isolating.

"How does it always end?" I ask.

"Look, he's a nice kid. Good player. But he has no business fucking around in relationships. Especially with my daughter."

I'm not a seeing-red person.

Competitive? Yes.

Driven? Also yes.

Prone to creative revenge? When needed.

But *angry*?

That's not generally me.

Until *right now*, as all of these little bits and pieces click together in an implication that I absolutely do not want to believe.

The Leopards' losing streak since Fletcher left. His insistence that he's not done. Feeling abandoned by this man who was like a father to him.

And this man is standing here saying Fletcher *had to go* because *he has no business fucking around with my daughter.*

"Are you telling me," I say, not even recognizing my own voice, "that you let Fletcher believe he was fired for *his performance* because of an injury that *you knew he was sensitive about,* when it was all about you thinking he wasn't good enough for your daughter?"

"He didn't have more than another season in him anyway."

"That's clearly helping you win this year."

He clears his throat and starts to move around us. "I'm due upstairs. Judith, tea sounds lovely."

Oh, no.

He is *not* dismissing us like this.

He's not dismissing *me* like this.

I don't care if Fletcher Huxley never speaks to me again, but I do care that this man knows what an absolute prick he is. "You were *his family*. He trusted you. He confided in you. He would have done *anything* for you. Do you have any idea how much damage you've done to his sense of self-worth? To his belief in himself? You have forty-eight hours to tell him, or I will. Judith, again, please forgive me. I sincerely need to go now."

It's odd having a boss.

It's even odder making a complete and total fool of myself in front of her.

But she sniffs in Oliver Rafferty's direction, then slips an arm around my shoulders and marches out with me.

"Are you sure you need rest," she asks, "or would a hit off a bottle of vodka be more in line?"

My eyes sting.

Rest won't fix what's wrong.

Vodka won't fix what's wrong.

The only thing that will fix what's wrong is far, far outside of my hands.

40

Fletcher

IT'S BEEN three weeks since I last saw Goldie, and I have reached the stage of grief known as *binge eating expensive as fuck cookies*.

Not great for my game, but fuck it.

I'm not the guy on the team leading the charges to our two victories so far. Since the Pounders invaded my space to help me set up my favorite pinball machine and feed me and commiserate on how much it sucks when women dump us, things have changed.

We all acknowledge I'm a bloody old fucker who's better for presence than plays.

And for ticket sales.

Doesn't matter how I play, so I'm eating whatever the hell I want.

"Oh, he's going for the lemon, Odette," a familiar voice whispers behind me in the line at Freckle Cookies. "Lemon is a particular stage of heartbreak, isn't it?"

My shoulders twitch.

Clearly my face does too because the teenager working behind the counter blanches. "I—I can get you a different one. This one isn't perfectly round. Do you want one that's more perfectly round?"

"That one's fine," I mutter. "Add in one of those caramel apple ones. I don't give a shi—I don't care how round it is."

The caramel apple cookies are responsible for a little love handle I found on my left hip this morning.

No regrets.

It's part of my process.

And who cares if I get a little love handle?

Rugby doesn't. Women don't. Sweet Pea doesn't.

Even if she's giving me the same exasperated eye roll she's given me every day for the past three weeks.

Unblock Goldie from Instagram, dumbass.

That's what that eye roll says.

I scowl at her.

She growls back at me.

"I didn't take him for a caramel apple kind," Odette says.

My shoulders twitch again.

"Maybe it's for a new lady friend," Evelyn says.

Awesome.

All three of them.

And the teenager behind the counter is looking at me like she pities any lady friend stupid enough to get involved with me.

"It's not for a new lady friend," Odette says. "Look at him. He's still regretting all of his life decisions. If it *is* a new lady friend, it's not serious."

"Should we write an obituary for his love life?" Evelyn murmurs.

I look over my shoulder. "I can fucking hear you."

The three senior citizens smile at me.

"We know, honey," Evelyn says. "That was the point."

"How are you doing?" Sheila asks. "It's always hard to go through a breakup."

"We weren't dating," I said.

Odette's a short Black woman who wears clothes that make it seem like she wishes she was still in a classroom. Sheila's a pleasantly plump white woman with downy hair that finally lays flat, who has an obsession with house dresses. And Evelyn is another white woman going into her seventies with hair dye, stylish clothes, and more sass than a dozen of my dog put together.

But they all snort an identical snort at my announcement.

I rub my eyes, then gesture them to the counter. "Add whatever they want," I tell the teenager.

The relief on her face is palpable.

But it's not as big as my sudden need to ask how Goldie's doing.

Like I have any right.

I freaked the fuck out at opening myself up to the possibility that she didn't feel the same about me as I felt about her, and that's that.

I don't deserve to know how she's doing.

And it's undoubtedly great.

She's Goldie.

There's no chance she's not doing great.

"I'll have a chocolate chip cookie with a side of *why did Fletcher block Goldie on Instagram?*" Odette says to the teenager.

"That was my order," Evelyn says. "Now what question will I ask with my cookie? And do I still want chocolate chip?"

"I want a sugar cookie and to know if Fletcher's doing okay," Sheila says.

"Peanut butter," Evelyn declares. "Peanut butter, in honor of Goldie, and I thought of my question. It's *why in the hell did he think growing that mustache back was a good idea?*"

Why don't I carry cash?

If I carried cash, I could toss a couple hundred dollars at the kid behind the counter and walk away.

Instead, I'm the wanker who said I'd pay for these three nutjobs and have to wait for the kid to ring it up.

Nice to see Odette moving around without her cane though.

And Sheila's hair getting longer.

I wonder if Goldie did something drastic with her own hair. Women do that shit. *Change my life, change my hair.*

"He's not answering any of our questions," Sheila whispers.

"We probably need to pay for *his* cookies if we're going to get anywhere with him," Evelyn whispers back.

"You missed the blood drive today," Odette says directly to me. "No one passed out. It was unexciting and boring as far as blood drives go."

Fuck, I miss Goldie. "How is she?"

Bloody hell.

Betrayed by my own mouth.

"Beating off suitors with a stick," Evelyn says.

Odette pokes her. "Don't torture the man. We still need to know why he blocked her on Instagram before we decide if he's worthy of our intel."

The teenager behind the counter gives me the look of *your bill is ready but your mustache scares me so I'm going to hope you come over here and give me money on your own,* so I tap my phone to pay, add a stupid tip, hand out the cookie boxes, and debate leaving.

Fuck it.

I paid for cookies.

They're warm right now.

I'm eating my damn cookie at one of the damn tables.

The three seasoned citizens join me.

Uninvited.

Sweet Pea pants in happy glee. Especially when Sheila gets too close and scratches behind her ears. "Such a good puppy."

"She's three," I mutter.

"She'll always be a puppy to me. Probably to you too."

"Do you want to talk about the mustache or Instagram first?" Evelyn asks.

I eye her. I'm being a dick and I don't care. "Maybe we talk about how I'm doing."

"I don't need to know that anymore," Sheila says. "Now that I got a closer look, I can tell you're miserable."

"And using the mustache to try to hide it," Evelyn agrees.

They're not bloody wrong.

I shove a bite of cookie into my mouth, warm lemon exploding on my taste buds while I remember Goldie feeding herself her peanut butter cookie that night I packed her books for her, and my dick rolls over and plays dead because we're never seeing Goldie again.

She told me herself she picked the timing on this residency so she'd have an excuse to not go to Silas's matches.

"So we're back to the question of why you blocked Goldie on Instagram," Odette says.

"She tell you that?" I ask.

"Yep."

"For a good reason," Sheila adds.

"Which we're not telling you until you explain yourself," Evelyn says.

Odette's using a fork to eat her cookie, and she pauses between bites to point it at me. "We don't care what your reason is. We just want to know you had one before we tell you our secret."

I look down at Sweet Pea.

She's glaring at me.

Happening a lot the past few weeks.

We had happiness and love and dog treats and you threw it all away because you were scared.

That's what my tiny-ass dog keeps saying to me.

She packs a lot of attitude into every pound.

Or possibly my conscience is projecting.

"She left," I mutter, the same guilt seeping into my pores that I've felt every time I've thought about Goldie leaving and every time I've thought about me asking her to stay.

I had no right to do that.

She'd given it all up before for a guy who wasn't what she deserved.

I'm not what she deserves either.

I don't look at my three companions, but I sense them watching me.

I suck in the biggest breath I can take without bothering my bruised and battered heart. And for the record, yes, I'm the sole reason it's bruised and battered.

It's all my fault. And— "She deserves better than me."

There.

I did it.

I finally said it out loud.

She left, I took it personally, then I took it out on her, and I don't deserve her.

The three ladies sigh in unison.

"Is that the best you've got?" Odette says.

"Boring," Evelyn chimes in with a yawn.

"I think you can dig deeper," Sheila adds. "I believe in you. But you won't fix what's wrong if you don't face all of it. And you have to live with you for the rest of your life."

I shoot a look at her. "I thought you were the nice one."

"I'm *kind*," she replies. "And that was very kind. Nice would be smiling and nodding. Kind is telling you the truth."

"Mm-hmm," Odette agrees.

"My word, this cookie's better than my last boyfriend, and he could still get it up without a pill," Evelyn says.

Sweet Pea barks.

Her equivalent of a *you go, girl*.

And screw it.

What more do I have to lose? "Everyone. Fucking. Leaves. Me."

I look up to gauge their reactions, expecting them to *oh, honey, that's not true* me, but instead, all three of them rise from their chairs like they've planned this.

Odette and Sheila are closest.

They get to me first, wrapping their arms around me in a tight hug.

Evelyn joins them after making her way around the table. She squeezes my hand. "Speaking as a woman with three ex-husbands, I can assure you that divorce isn't always about leaving. While I've never met either of your ex-wives, I can promise you that they likely wish you well. They've both probably lived with a lot of regrets that they let you down too."

I suck in a hard breath.

My exes' regrets aren't something I've ever thought about.

"Not the second one," I manage to force out.

Fuck if that doesn't make the three of them squeeze me tighter.

Sheila tightest of all. "And you can take this from me, as a mother and a breast cancer survivor, that your mother did not leave you because she wanted to."

My eyes hurt.

So do my sinuses.

Even Sweet Pea's getting in on the action, twisting in her sling like she, too, wants to get closer.

And then the little devil licks my T-shirt right over my heart.

"Goldie met your old coach a couple weeks ago," Odette says, "and he told her why he really fired you, and it had absolutely nothing to do with you, or your performance, or your value to the team. He fucked you over, and she read him the riot act."

My heart thumps once, loudly and painfully. "What?"

"She tried to tell you, but you blocked her, so she can't," Evelyn adds.

"Such a horrible situation." Sheila's rubbing my back. "The man had the audacity to fire you because his daughter thought she was in love with you."

"*Annalise?*" What the ever-loving *fuck*? She's still a teenager in my brain. The last time I sent her a holiday present, it was a goddamn *doll*. The last time I saw her at the stadium, I gave her a fist bump and called her *kid*.

I think.

That's what I usually did.

I don't actually remember the last time I saw her at the stadium. Not specifically.

Again, *what the ever-loving fuck?*

"Is that her name?" Evelyn asks.

This doesn't make sense.

"She's engaged," I mutter.

Odette tsks. "Broke it off and told her father she was in love with you. According to him."

They're all three still smothering me.

My heart's pounding. I can't suck enough air into my lungs. My thighs are shaking.

"And according to some of your old teammates," Sheila whispers, "Goldie tracked them down and Goldie-ed them and got them to talk. They said you were oblivious."

She *Goldie-ed* them.

And not a single one of the wankers reached out to tell me they'd seen her.

Why would they?

I never told any of them I was seeing anyone, much less went into specifics. And if any of them still track my socials, which I don't expect them to do, they'd know we had a thing and they'd know it's over.

They're not my teammates anymore. Not the way the Pounders are. They have other shit to do besides hold my hand when I break up with a casual fling.

But they could've bloody well told me it wasn't my fault I was fired.

If they thought I'd listen.

"I wasn't fired because of my game," I say out loud, the words crashing across my heart and leaving a flaming path of destruction in their wake.

He lied.

He made me feel broken. Inept. Done.

He hit me where he knew it would hurt the most to make me leave.

And it was never about me at all.

Sweet Pea whimpers and licks my chest again. I scratch behind her ears, then shake the three ladies off of me.

I need to go.

I need air.

I need—

I need to make an enormous wrong right again.

41

Goldie

I'VE BEEN in London a little less than a month, and I've decided *bloody* is my favorite new word.

It fits when I say I'm *bloody tired* after a long day of coaching sessions and classes and private calls with my other clients that I'm still seeing.

It fits when I say I'm *bloody chuffed* anytime I see one of the students in the intensive get excited over a new concept to try with their own clients.

It fits when I say I'm *bloody pissed*, which is what I was last night after entirely too many glasses of wine with Judith to celebrate Friday night.

But unfortunately, right now, I'm bloody wrecked as I'm wrapping up the question-and-answer session of my Saturday morning motivational talk for the students.

Hangovers and I don't get along well.

Also, I miss Odette and Sheila and Evelyn, even though we've texted nearly every day and had a group phone call while they were at the wine bar last weekend.

And every day, I swear my heart hurts a little more for Fletcher.

I shouldn't have tracked down any of his teammates on my Sundays off the past two weekends. I shouldn't have stuck my nose in it.

But I did, and if I'm being honest, that's why I'm *bloody tired* and willing to get *bloody pissed.*

I should let it go.

The man blocked me on socials.

If that's not a sign, I don't know what is.

But *I miss him.*

It's been a month, and I still miss him.

"Your best will never be the same from one day to the next," I'm saying into a microphone in a small auditorium on the university campus in response to the last question of the day. It's an answer I've given in coaching so many times the past five years that it's ingrained in my head and I don't have to think. "You catch a cold or you eat something that doesn't agree with you or you have an argument with a loved one, and your best won't be the same as it was on a day when everything is going right. And that's okay. Also, sometimes our clients need to see that *we* are human too. There's power in demonstrating that we have bad days too. Does that help?"

With the stage lights as they are, I can't see the student's features clearly, but I can see that he's nodding from his spot in the aisle to my left. There are microphones set up in both aisles so that everyone can hear the questions without me having to repeat them.

"Yes, thank you," he says.

I open my mouth to thank everyone for coming, but before I can get a sound out, Judith interrupts me from the edge of the stage with her own microphone.

"Ladies and gentlemen, it appears we have time for one last question. Go ahead, young man."

Everyone in the auditorium shifts to look at the aisle on my right.

I do too, inwardly groaning because I want to go home and take a nap. Once again, the lighting prevents me from seeing the questioner clearly.

That doesn't stop a full-body shiver from racing from my scalp to my toes at his outline though.

And when he speaks—*oh my god.*

"What advice would you give a mate who let the best thing that's ever happened to him walk away because he was too afraid to tell her that he loves her?"

Fletcher.

Fletcher.

He's here. Standing in the aisle. At my Saturday morning motivational talk.

Asking what I'd tell him to do.

I don't know what my face is doing, but I know what my body's doing.

It's completely frozen in place in absolute shock.

It's Saturday.

He has a match.

He has a match. In the States. Thousands of miles away.

"It's not her fault," he continues. "She did everything right. She made me feel like I deserved to be loved for the first time in a long, long time, but all of my own insecurities kept me from believing that she could ever be the one who would love me. Because I'm a fucked-up mess, but I can do better. I can be better. If there's anyone in this world who can make me believe in me, it's you."

"Oh my word, is that Fletcher Huxley?" someone says in the front row.

346

"Come back to Nottingshire!" someone else calls with far less restraint.

"Shut your trap and let the man propose," someone hisses back.

My feet suddenly remember how to move again. I drop my microphone, sending a deafening *thud* throughout the auditorium while I stride quickly toward the stairs off the stage.

Fletcher.

My heart.

"I quit rugby," he says into the microphone while class participants start to lift their phones and aim them at him. "I'm done. I don't want to play. I want to be here, with you. I want to be by your side no matter where you go next. I want to prove to you that I can be everything you deserve and more. If you—if you'll still have me."

His voice cracks as I race up the aisle.

"If I've fucked this up too much, just—just tell me, and I'll go, but I—"

I grab his mic and shove it to the floor, drowning out whatever else he was saying with another deafening *thump*.

And then I do the only sensible, logical, rational thing that a woman can do when the man she's missed desperately shows up in the most unexpected of places to tell her that he loves her, to *show* her that he loves her, and I throw myself at him.

He catches me while gasps and cheers go up around us, but the ragged breath that he sucks in as he pulls me closer and closer and tighter and tighter makes my heart swell with the desperate need to assure him that he's worthy. That he's lovable. That he's *mine*.

"I'll do anything, Goldie," he whispers to me. "I'm sorry. I'm so sorry."

"Oh my god, you crazy man, I love you too," I whisper back.

This is real.

He's here.

Squeezing me tighter while his breath whooshes out of him.

"You don't have to say it just because I did. You don't have to love me back. But I had to tell you. You deserve to know."

My heart nearly bursts.

Of all the tossing and turning I've done at night this past month, telling myself not to drift into fantasies of him coming to tell me he loves me, never—*never*—did those dreams I wished I didn't have include him telling me I didn't have to love him back.

That he loved me no matter how I felt about him.

I pepper his face with kisses. "Fletcher. I love your heart and I love your determination and I love the way you love your dog and I love the way you see things when no one thinks you're watching, and *I love you*. I love *you*."

"I don't deserve you."

"Yes, you do."

"No, I—"

This *man*.

He's making me be highly unprofessional.

But when a man's being a *man*, there's only one thing to do.

And that's kiss him the way I've wanted to kiss him for weeks.

And shudder in absolute relief that he's *here*, that he would come all this way to apologize, that he's kissing me back and holding me like nothing else in the world will ever matter to him the way that I do.

I don't need to be someone's world to live a happy life.

But the utter joy that's blossoming in my soul at Fletcher being here is undeniable.

I don't *need* this. But I will absolutely bask in it.

"I brought you a dozen cookies," he says between kisses.

"You didn't have to bring me anything but you."

"Have we met?"

I laugh and kiss him again.

Fletcher's here. *My* Fletcher. Smart-ass Fletcher. Vulnerable Fletcher. Determined Fletcher.

He came all the way here for me.

For *us*.

And it's not until the auditorium has somehow emptied itself and we're alone that I realize what I've missed.

The 'stache is back.

And even with that monstrosity on his upper lip, he's never been more attractive than he is right now.

42

Fletcher

I AM NEVER LEAVING Goldie's bed.

Ever.

Until she has to move back to the States, and then I'm booking us a private jet so that we can have a bed the whole way, and I'm taking her straight to my place where she'll never leave my bed again.

I approve of this plan.

And I tell her as much, which makes her laugh until she piggy-snorts, which is so fucking perfect that my heart swells big enough to make my eyes hot.

All because loving Goldie is so right and so easy and exactly what I was put on this earth to do.

It's early Sunday, her day off, and we're lounging in bed having cookies for breakfast. Even I can't be a twenty-four seven sex god for my woman if I don't feed myself.

Eventually I'll need protein again. A vegetable or something.

Right now, I'm riding the high of being with Goldie.

Protein can probably wait a few weeks.

Or maybe for a few hours.

I don't want my dog to worry or think I'm not taking good care of myself when we call Sheila later to see how Sweet Pea is doing. Pup doesn't like international flights, and Sheila promised to take good care of her as long as we need.

And to call so we can talk until I'm back in the States.

"I have to tell you something," Goldie says as she finishes a cookie. "And you have to promise to let me finish before you tell me no."

"I don't tell you no."

She makes a noise that says *you will be telling me no*.

I make a noise back that says *bet*.

We both grin, and *fuck*.

She's everything I never knew I wanted and now cannot live without. I know loving her won't always be easy, but it's so damn right.

So damn worth it.

She shifts in the bed until she's straddling me, which is my favorite. Right along with cradling her breasts. Licking her neck. Rubbing my cock against her clit.

If it's Goldie, it's my favorite.

Her eyes roll back in her head as I tilt my hips, but she shakes her head and scoots back down my thighs so I can't rub her with my cock. "No, this first."

"Sounds serious."

"You need to go home and finish the season."

I jerk backward, but she grabs me by the cheeks and kisses me hard until I relax again.

And then she pulls back and freaking says it again, those golden eyes searching mine and picking up on every bit of every reaction that I know she knows I'm tamping down.

"You need to go back to Copper Valley and finish the season. Ah-ah-ah. No talking until I'm done. I'm not done. I love you, Fletcher. I love you and I will love you if you're here or if you're there. What you're doing for the Pounders matters. What you're doing for the entire league matters. And not for them. For *you*. I'll be done here in about two months. We can text. We can talk. We can have phone sex, which I suspect you'll be *excellent* at, and when my commitment here is over, I'll move home to Copper Valley to be with you."

"Your book—" I start, but she puts a finger to my mouth and shakes her head.

"I'll handle arrangements to deliver something else. Or I turn it into a shorter road trip and you can come with me after your season is over."

I'm gripping her hips too tightly.

I don't want to have phone sex.

I want to have sex-sex. I want to take her out to dinner at all of my favorite places in London. I want to give her a proper British tea at the palace gardens. I want to tour all the tourist traps I never went to while I lived here because I always said I'd get to them next year, and I want to do them with her.

Yes, fine, that requires leaving her bed.

Shut up.

"I quit the team," I say quietly. "There was no question that I quit the team."

"I happen to know a guy who tells me that the coach hasn't accepted your resignation because your team wouldn't let him. They know you're here. They know why. And they're keeping your spot for you."

I let go of her hips to press my palms into my eye sockets.

She rubs her hands over my chest. "They want you there, Fletcher. It's two months, and then I'm home. We can do this."

"I don't want to be away from you."

She snuggles into me. "I don't want to be away from you either, but I know how much rugby means to you. How much it's *always* meant to you. You still have some years left if you want them. I couldn't live with myself if I didn't support you finishing out your dreams the same way you're supporting mine."

I swallow.

Swallow again and wrap my arms around her bare back. "How many days?"

"Until I'm home?"

"Until I can't—until I can't go back."

She squeezes me tight. "I wasn't given a number, but I'm sure they'd understand if you needed a few days to fully deal with your personal family emergency. And Sweet Pea would miss you terribly if you were gone for a full two months."

My heart hiccups. "That's low."

"I'm bloodthirsty when I'm right."

"Will you—will you think less of me if I don't go back? If I stay with you instead?"

"Fletcher. No. Absolutely not." She straightens and presses a kiss to my cheek. "But I want you to be sure that you're done—no question, no doubts, no regrets when you look back in ten years— if you stay. You are absolutely everything that's been missing in my life, and your happiness matters more to me than nearly anything else ever could. Whatever you decide, whatever you do—I'm behind you. Okay?"

I tug her closer again and nod into her hair. "Okay."

"And you can take a couple days to think about it," she adds.

"Can we stay naked while I think?"

She laughs. "Yes."

She's humoring me.

She has work to do that requires her getting out of bed and putting on clothes, and I won't keep her from it. That's why she's here.

I love that other people recognize how amazing she is.

But there's my answer, isn't it?

She's here making a difference, and she can't be with me twenty-four seven. She has commitments.

She's right.

I need to go back.

I need to finish this season.

I need to see if I have another season—or three, or five, or more —in me.

"Promise you'll come home when you're done?" I whisper.

"There is no place else that I could imagine going except for home to you."

EPILOGUE

Fletcher

My MIND IS on the match. I swear it is.

But there's been a whisper of *two days, two days, two days* in my head all day.

Goldie's home in *two days*.

It's so close now that I can't compartmentalize it out.

We're up by twenty in Minneapolis with a few minutes of play remaining until halftime. We're organizing for a scrum after a knock-on when I hear something from the sidelines that makes me glance over at Coach.

But I don't see Coach.

I see the stands.

Specifically, a dark-haired woman bundled up in a puffy pink vest over a long-sleeve black shirt, pink Pounders cap covering her head, familiar sunglasses shielding her eyes, standing in the front row waving a silver and black streamer thing.

Goldie.

355

What the hell?

She's not supposed to be back for two more days.

And she's sure as hell not supposed to be coming to an away match.

"Huxley," Holt barks.

Goldie's here.

Goldie's *here*.

Watching me play for the first time.

I grin at the captain. "Here."

He gives me a funny look, but we move into position, and for the next three and a half minutes of match play, I bust my ass like I'm ten years younger.

Get two tackles.

Force a turnover.

And am instrumental in the Pounders scoring a try.

My lady's watching.

Fuck right I'm on fire.

When the whistle blows for halftime, we're supposed to run back into the changing room.

That's how this goes.

That's how this always goes.

But today?

Fuck that.

Today, I run off the pitch as if I'm heading into the changing rooms, but I veer at the last minute and head to the stands.

Right to Goldie.

She tucks her sunglasses on top of her head and leans over the barrier as I reach her. "What are you doing?" she says on a laugh.

I don't stop.

Don't think.

I act.

And acting means flinging her over my shoulder and lifting her out of the stands in a fireman's carry.

Security comes running from above.

Security on the pitch stares at me open-mouthed for a second before they, too, come running.

But my team—my goddamn amazing fucking team—all have my back.

They've followed me and they're surrounding us.

"What the hell, Fletch?" is the only comment I get from Holt.

Once again, I grin at him. "Back off. I need my emotional support girlfriend."

"I'm gonna puke," Silas mutters.

"What are you doing here?" I ask Goldie while the team shields me and we run to the tunnel.

"Got packed—early—*oof*—so—came home—see you," she grunts from my back.

"Aww, that's the best," Crew says beside me.

We have to funnel down into a single file line, but by the time we're heading into the changing room, security has given up on us.

I'm probably facing a fine.

Don't care.

Worth it.

Especially when I drop Goldie to her feet and wrap her in a hug, breathing in that cupcake scent mixed with hints of pending snow. "You're here."

"We consolidated my schedule so I could leave a couple days early."

"*You're here.*"

"I'm here."

She's here.

She's *home*.

"Huxley, you can hug your emotional support girlfriend later," Coach says. "Huddle up. Focus. No distractions. If we blow a nearly thirty-point lead because you're thinking with your dick—"

"You'll sell out your next home match for everyone wanting to see what crazy thing he'll do next," Goldie interrupts. "Oops. Sorry, Coach. Your changing room. Apologies. I'm not here."

"We need Fletch's emotional support girlfriend in every half-time meeting," Porter says.

Silas hip-checks me and goes in to hug his sister. "She was my emotional support sister first," he grumbles.

"It's so gross watching you play," she says to him.

"It's so sad that you don't have anything better to do than show up for my matches," he replies.

They stare at each other for a second, then both crack up.

One of the assistant coaches appears with a badge for Goldie that'll keep security from booting her off the pitch or out of the changing room.

Holt grabs me.

Porter grabs Silas.

And we have a shortened discussion of strategy for the second half of the match.

Not that we need it.

We're on fucking *fire* in the second half.

When we head to the airport after the match, we're leading the league in the standings.

Ticket sales for our next home match have indeed nearly sold out.

Goldie's flying with us, as family often does.

I can't stop staring at her and I can't stop touching her. Her face. Her hair. Her arms. Her hands. Her knees.

Soon, every part of her.

She's *here*.

After two months of nothing but texts, video calls, and phone sex, she's *here*. She's *home*.

And for the first time in my entire memory, I am finally whole.

"I love you," I whisper to her when she lays her head on my shoulder and closes her eyes.

"I love you more," she whispers back.

I start to smile.

She giggles softly.

"So this is how it's gonna be?" I ask.

"Was there ever any other way?"

Never.

And I can't wait to win this argument with her every single day for the rest of my life.

BONUS EPILOGUE

Sweet Pea, aka a dog who's the center of her humans' world

THERE'S something wrong with my humans.

My daddy human keeps saying the same thing over and over and over. And he's holding one of my mummy human's favorite glasses that he almost never drinks out of, but he's acting like he does.

At least we're somewhere pretty. I like being in the mountains. There are chipmunks! And grass to roll in! And sunshine without buildings in the way! And so many people here who think I'm awesome.

My mummy human is petting me and giggling while she watches my daddy human get told by a big human in a strange hat to *try it again, but this time, I want your eyes to make love to the wine in that glass*, whatever that means.

It definitely makes my mummy human laugh harder.

Especially when my daddy human looks at the big guy and says back, "This is a commercial for *Sarcasm Cellars*. Doesn't exactly scream *wine you want to make love to*, does it?"

Aww.

My mummy human snorted like a little piggy.

That's my favorite.

It's my daddy human's favorite too. He says so every time he makes her laugh this hard.

"You wanna do this?" my daddy human says to her, smiling. How can you not smile when mummy human laughs like that?

"She can't be any worse," the big guy says.

He doesn't sound nice.

"I did commercials all over Europe fine." Uh-oh. That's my daddy human's *you're getting on my nerves* voice.

I know that one.

He uses it on my mummy human's brother a lot.

"That's because they thought your American accent was hilarious," the big guy says. "Here, you have to do more than look like a fool."

"You might want to rephrase that," my mummy human calls to him. "Baiting a guy with that many muscles in the name of getting a good take probably won't end well for you. Or the wine glass in his hand."

"And I'm not the one sporting a ridiculous mustache," my daddy human adds, which sends my mummy human into a fit of laughter that makes her snort again.

Probably because my daddy human only shaved his own mustache a couple days ago.

Honestly, I think it's pretty funny too.

I don't care if my daddy human wears a mustache or not. He saved me from a scary place with people who didn't like dogs, and I will love him until the end of time no matter what his face looks like.

"Here, let me try. If nothing else, it'll give you a break. And make you look fantastic in comparison so maybe we can head over to Shipwreck and get some donuts before we go home." My mummy human tells me to stay—like I can go too far when she has my leash clipped to a bench, but at least I look fabulous in my new collar—and then she gets up and goes to help my daddy human.

She'll come back.

So will he.

They live to love me.

"Psst. Hey, kid," someone says nearby.

I jump in a circle—jumping's more fun when you're in the grass —and look for who's talking.

It takes me two circles before I spot him, and I smell him before I spot him.

He needs a bath.

Also, he's definitely a dog.

Like me!

"Are you talking to me?" I ask him.

"Yeah. Your humans give you treats?"

"Duh. That's what they exist for."

"Can I have one?"

The fur on the back of my neck stands up. "Why do you want one of my treats? Where are your humans? Don't they get you treats?"

"Psh. Like I need humans."

Oh, wow.

Oh, wow wow wow.

I've heard of this at the dog park, but I didn't believe it. There are *dogs without humans*.

"You don't have humans?" I whisper.

I don't want to offend him if my little doggie brain isn't following the right train track, so I say it quietly.

"Humans are for the weak."

"But you still want the treats they buy."

"So it's gonna be like that?" he says.

My daddy human is confusing sometimes too. When that happens, my mummy human whispers to me that it's a man thing, and that he makes up for it in all the other ways.

Whatever that means.

Okay, okay, I know what it means, but I pretend I don't when it comes to meaning *that*, if you get what I'm throwing out here.

"Where'd you come from?" I ask my new dog friend.

He's bigger than me, but not by a lot. Definitely a mutt with the way his brown and black and white fur is all mixed like that and the way his body doesn't quite fit any standard for any dog I've ever met.

And I meet a lot of dogs now that it's warm enough to go to the dog park all the time.

Maybe he has some beagle in him? Maybe some terrier? I'm getting a whiff of poodle in there too. Possibly a dash of chihuahua.

"Wherever," is all he'll tell me about where he came from. "Are you gonna share treats or not?"

I sigh.

My mummy human would say his posturing is a defense mechanism.

I love sitting in her office while she's talking to people on her computer. I learn so much.

She talks a lot about kindness too.

And if this guy's hungry, even if he's taking advantage of me, it's just treats.

My humans will get more.

It takes a few jumps for me to get my teeth on the strap of my mummy human's bag and pull it down.

She and my daddy human are laughing hard at something while the big guy points a camera at them, so they don't notice at all.

"How long have you been around here?" I ask my new friend.

And yes, I know we're not *really* friends.

Again, I'm simply being nice.

"A while," he says while he creeps out of the bushes behind the bench.

His fur says it's been a long while. It's all matted and tangled, especially on his tail.

That can't feel good.

He needs a spa day.

Or a bunch of spa days.

"What do you usually eat?" I ask him.

"Whatever." He attacks the bag of treats, putting it in his mouth and shaking his head hard like that's the way to open it.

It does work.

Eventually.

But not before he's panting hard with the effort.

"Do you need water?" I ask him. "I have water. My humans always make sure I have water."

"I have a *stream*, thank you very much," he replies around a mouthful of treats.

Whoa.

He's eating *all* of the treats.

He must really be hungry.

I nose into my mummy human's bag. Usually it would be my daddy human's bag, but he was nervous about this today, so she took care of me.

And she brought a small baggie of my food in case we decided to not go back to the city.

Yay!

More food to share with my friend.

I carry it over to him, and when I get close, he shies away.

But as soon as I drop the baggie of food, he pounces on that too.

I settle in the grass—I love the way it tickles my belly—and watch him.

Poor guy.

"Oh, what do we have here?" my mummy human suddenly says above me.

She doesn't yell at me for getting into the treats or the food.

Instead, she squats next to me and looks at my new friend.

He glares at her.

"She brought that food," I tell him. "She's a good one."

"Sweet Pea, did you make a friend?" my mummy human says.

I bark once in affirmation, then, after the briefest hesitation, I add, "He's homeless! He needs food and the spa!"

"Don't tell them that!" my friend says to me.

"But you do," I insist.

My humans don't always understand me, but I can tell by the way my mummy human is looking at my new friend that she gets it.

I crawl three little steps closer to him. "It's okay. They're the good kind of people. They're helpers."

I was super little when my daddy human saved me. I don't remember a lot about it, but I remember that things were bad before with people who don't like dogs, and after, I was safe and happy and loved.

"What's your name?" my mummy human says softly to him. "And where did you come from?"

He stares at her like he can't trust her.

"She's a good one," I insist. "She gives belly rubs and she doesn't yell when I drag her underwear all over the house."

She strokes me gently while she keeps talking to my new friend. "You look like you could use a bath. Do you have a collar?"

"He doesn't," I report. Then I look at him. "Are you microchipped?"

He stares at me like I'm speaking a foreign language.

Understandable.

My accent gets people all the time. Comes from being born in Britain.

"What's going on here?" my daddy human says above us too.

"Sweet Pea made a friend," my mummy human reports.

My daddy human doesn't say anything for a long minute.

"Fletcher. *Look* at him. Just look at him. Isn't that face begging to be loved?"

"That face says he doesn't trust you."

"But he could. Look. He already likes Sweet Pea."

I grin at my new friend. "Do you really not have humans?"

He stares back at me with the same stubborn look my daddy human sometimes gets. And then he sighs. "No."

"Do you want humans? Because these are the *best* humans. And they'll get you a doggy bed and they'll let you sit on the couch and if you're good, they'll carry you in a baby sling."

He scoffs. "I'm not a baby."

"It's warm and cozy, and it makes you look like royalty to have to be carried everywhere."

"We need to at least find out if he belongs to someone," my mummy human says to my daddy human. "Look at his fur. If he has a home, he hasn't been there in quite a while."

My daddy human looks at my mummy human.

I know that look.

I love it when he gives her that look!

It always means he knows she's right and he wants her to be happy.

I wag my tail and pant happily. "You're gonna love these humans. They're *the best*. But you have to get your own doggy bed. I don't share."

"It's fate," my mummy human says to my daddy human. "We were talking about it anyway, and look. Here he is."

"I can't even shoot a commercial without you causing trouble, can I?" my daddy human says to her, but he's joking.

That's his fun voice.

He squats next to us too and looks at my new friend. "Hey, little fella. You wanna come on out and let us take you somewhere to get checked out and get more food?"

My new friend looks at me.

Then at them.

And then he does the same thing I couldn't resist doing a few years ago, and he slowly crawls to my daddy human.

My mummy human is the best, but my daddy human is the *best* best.

And my new friend knows it.

I wag my tail even harder and pant even happier.

I get to take home a new friend.

This is the best day ever.

PIPPA GRANT BOOK LIST

The Girl Band Series (Complete)

Mister McHottie

Stud in the Stacks

Rockaway Bride

The Hero and the Hacktivist

The Thrusters Hockey Series

The Pilot and the Puck-Up

Royally Pucked

Beauty and the Beefcake

Charming as Puck

I Pucking Love You

The Bro Code Series

Flirting with the Frenemy

America's Geekheart

Liar, Liar, Hearts on Fire

The Hot Mess and the Heartthrob

Copper Valley Fireballs Series (Complete)

Jock Blocked

Real Fake Love

The Grumpy Player Next Door

Irresistible Trouble

Pippa Grant writing as Jamie Farrell:

The Misfit Brides Series (Complete)

Blissed

Matched

Smittened

Sugared

Married

Spiced

Unhitched

The Officers' Ex-Wives Club Series (Complete)

Her Rebel Heart

Southern Fried Blues

ABOUT THE AUTHOR

Pippa Grant wanted to write books, so she did.

Before she became a *USA Today* and #1 Amazon bestselling romantic comedy author, she was a young military spouse who got into writing as self-therapy. That happened around the time she discovered reading romance novels, and the two eventually merged into a career. Today, she has more than 30 knee-slapping Pippa Grant titles and nine published under the name Jamie Farrell.

When she's not writing romantic comedies, she's fumbling through being a mom, wife, and mountain woman, and sometimes tries to find hobbies. Her crowning achievement? Having impeccable timing for telling stories that will make people snort beverages out of their noses. Consider yourself warned.

Find Pippa at...
www.pippagrant.com
pippa@pippagrant.com